WOLF TECH 3

WOLF TECH 3

ADAM WEBSTER

CONTENTS

Dedication — vi
Author Notes — vii

Prologue (Previously...) — 1

1 New Bonds — 7

2 Chapter 2 – Birthdays — 21

3 Chapter 3 – Lost Wolves — 38

4 Chapter 4 – First Elder Meeting — 52

5 Chapter 5 – First Shovels of Dirt — 67

6 Chapter 6 - Arrival — 82

7 Chapter 7 – Cousin Wolves — 98

8 Chapter 8 – Punishments — 114

9 Chapter 9 – Returning Heirs — 129

10 Chapter 10 – Hunter Captured — 144

11 Chapter 11 – Unexpected Visitors — 158

12 Chapter 12 - Rescue — 172

13 Chapter 13 – Talks — 186

14 Chapter 14 - Trials — 200

15 Chapter 15 – Surprises — 214

16 Chapter 16 – Meetings and a Turnings   230

17 Chapter 17 – Finally Married!   244

18 Chapter 18 – Cat!   263

19 Chapter 19 - Preparing   283

20 Chapter 20 – Pack Tour   306

21 Chapter 21 – WereNet Starts to Take Off...   325

22 Chapter 22 – Adam Talks   346

23 Chapter 23 – The Fight   367

24 Chapter 24 – Wolf Lunch   382

25 Chapter 25 - Firepit   395

26 Chapter 26 – Changing Rules   412

27 Chapter 27 – Rogue Issues   430

28 Chapter 28—Pups Relax   450

29 Chapter 29 – Patrols   465

30 Chapter 30 – Recovery   484

31 Chapter 31 – Start of the Next Chapter of Life   499

Epilogue   516

Letter from the Author   521

Reviews   523

I am dedicating this book to all my readers, those who were along for the first draft write, but have since disappeared, and may not ever know about this final version now existing, to those who I know love my stories so much they have read it many times, and to the new readers, to whom this is their first time reading it, and maybe even werewolf stories in general.
Thanks!

Author Notes

This is a work of fiction. All resemblance to any actual place or person living or dead is either a coincident or used fictitiously.

There are several scenes which have violence in them, do keep it in perspective they are not human, so human moral values are not in effect.

Linked Stories:
The characters Ethan, Josh, and the Fossil Valley Pack had his story start in what had the working title of 'A Pregnancy Story' by Brian Clark. It will have a different title when published.

The character Zane, his team, Beta Mike, and the Mac Tire' Dona Pack's story starts in Why Us by Brian Clark. It then continues in Why Us 2, with this book's Chapter 18 through 29 overlapping and shared with this story as they were co-authored by Brian and myself. Why Us 2 continues after the part in this story. He does return in Wolf Tech 4 for more fun.

Happily, I recently have been able to finalize the transfer of the copyright of the stories from Brian's estate, so they can be published posthumously. When they are published, I will be making announcements of it in the Wolf Tech Facebook group, on both account's pages on Wattpad, and on my website.

Wolf Dogs:
While many people enjoy having wolfdogs or other wolf hybrids as pets, as they can be very affectionate, playful, loyal, and smart, not all are suitable as pets. Their traits and behaviour, not just their looks, vary dramatically between individual animals, not always just from how much wolf is in them. Some of the negative traits include fearfulness of humans, high prey drive, high energy, territorial, destructive, extremely independent, and being escape artists. If you are considering them, make sure to check out the resources available, including Wolfdog and Wolf Sanctuaries, as the staff at those places likely can give you more details, other local resources, and any restrictions for your area.

As with any plans for bringing a new animal into your home, research needs to be done before doing so, as they are a living being, and don't understand why you must leave them or why you abandon them to a shelter, where often they are not able to be placed with others. Committing to any sort of animal should be a life-long commitment, and never just for the status of having the animal as a possession.

Prologue
(Previously...)

Brook had smelled something good. As she tried to find it, she realised it was her mate! One problem was a loose shale slope between them, and another potential problem was him being human. Humans generally had one of three responses to learning of their werewolf mate: not caring about the difference about it, happy about it, or being one of the few who would outright reject her for it.

It ended up taking being rescued by her mate to meet up, after triggering a rockslide. Once they met, her human mate, Adam, was quite happy to accept a werewolf mate, and help her any way he could. He could feel a welcome right from the start, so he immediately joined the pack, and moved in.

For Adam's protection, he was given a very special dog named Charlie as a companion. In the beginning, Adam wasn't told just how special Charlie was, just he was very smart.

As soon as he could, Adam took his chances and got Turned to become a werewolf; the turning had him out for a while, but still was much shorter than he was told he would be.

Discussing it with his sister and mother was interesting, as both were stunned, but supportive. Seemingly from the beginning, Adam's wolf was well-disciplined, and quite willing to help his human half settle in. Almost as if the wolf had a separate agenda, one which required a well-adjusted human-side. His wolf helped turn Adam as soon as possible, so he could feel the awesome power of being a wolf. Christmas was fun, as some of his human relatives had some 'old fashioned' human ideas, which riled up the wolves, and even Adam's mother!

Helping another pack, allowed them to made friends and for closer ties between the two packs, when they stayed there. After that, they could settle down for a bit, and Adam could get used to living with a large pack.

Since not having a good internet service was making it hard for them to blend in, it was decided Adam would help the pack move into the 21st century. Some of the pack needed to be brought in kicking and screaming, but most just embraced the changes. Plans were started for making a secure network between the two packs before expanding out more, to bring more packs in with a secure connection so they would protect them all by allowing them to share ideas without the humans able to connect.

Learning to hunt was eventful. The first time all he did was groom a bunny's tail with his teeth! Eventually, he got better and even lead hunts.

His wolf was not done with the surprises. He kept pushing new skills to his human which let him advance in his fighting skills he needed almost faster than they could teach him! It startled most of his trainers, when he would go from starting with them, to surpassing their skills in the time it usually took to master one move.

Having an attack on a wolf who they had under their care was bad, and the fact the wolf escaped was very bad. It also was Adam's first failure at doing something, but it brought him and his new wolf together more. It did cause those who were reluctant to allow passive sensors and cameras to detect when they had intruders to make installing them a priority, instead of just relying on patrols, which had been shown was insufficient.

Over time, Adam and Brook adopted four pups. Robin and Toby were dumped on him by Toby's mother, since he was willing to give them more options than she was , as she grieved for a lost mate and was unable to handle changes. Finding out the pair who took care of the cleaning and laundry for them were orphans, they adopted Jess and Joshua. Other pups seemed to be drawn to them, and they took care of them as well as they could. Brook put her foot down, as she didn't want to have him adopting basically all the pups from their parents, just because they came for comfort.

More and more hints were found, showing Adam's wolf was more than just a normal wolf, but kept showing leadership skills. He advanced by leaps and bounds. Brook had trouble keeping up, even with her wolf seeming to be learning the skills fast and agreeing with the advancements in rank they received.

When the current Seconds told the Alphas they were stepping down, Adam and Brook started to take on those duties, dealing with them as if they had been doing the job for years, but bringing a fresh view to the duties.

Their first major job was to take down the Shadowed River Pack, which they did nearly flawlessly, and without loosing any packmates. They did find out there were a large number of non-combatants, which MacLaren pack took in and helped most to join several other packs, as they could not handle them all. They also captured a few key players either in the fight or at the pack house.

Adam, Brook, and their four pups travelled with the group going to Longview Pack, as they had some family business nearby. While leading the group moving to Longview Pack, Adam had to deal with a young wolf who decided to go against the pack's decision to have the group join them. It caused major issues with the young wolf, as how he expressed his protest of the decision broke major laws could have altered his life permanently, but when Adam found out the circumstances around the young wolf's promotion to team leader and how young he was, Adam decided to be lenient with him. After a good rousing wolf-fight with a lecture, he basically got a decade of probation.

Following his family gathering for his mother's birthday, there was a party to welcome the new members of the Longview Pack, and Ryan realised Adam's sister was his mate! It was quickly arranged for her to meet him.

When they got back to the MacLaren Pack, Duncan fought the wolf who caused him and his mate to be forced to flee for their lives. Following the fight, the pack which was doing the cleanout of the Shadowed River's Pack house finally found the Wolfsbane, and there was much more than they expected.

Others decided to try to get the wolfsbane but weren't able to get it before Adam and Brook arrived and secured it. This attempt revealed some betrayals within the cleanup pack, and another pack working their way into the territory. They did some work to find out why individuals were forced to help the aggressor pack trying to get the Wolfsbane, and of the root cause was fear of something. When given a way out, they instantly took it, preferring the chance to live without fear.

Due to this, the leader of the wolves who were clearing the pack house got a major demotion, as their pack laws were results-based and didn't look into circumstances. Because Adam and Brook didn't think the demotion was fair, they recommended he be accepted into the MacLaren pack along with several others who had been part of the attack.

There were some surprises about the white wolf Adam kept encountering, but they didn't change the final decision of his fate of Trial by Claw. During the trial fight, Adam did take some injuries and was on the injured list for the week before the next full moon.

At the Full Moon howl, Adam and Brook were able to finally adopt Jess and Joshua formally and gave the Oath of Seconds before the gathered pack. In celebration, they had also been given the honour of leading the Pack Hunt.

When dealing with bully-pups, Adam gave unique punishments, tailored to each offence and the offender. It seemed to get the pups to behave how he wanted, and rarely did he have to deal with the offender twice. Including a lecture on what problems it could cause for the pack if left unchecked, let the pups know why the rule exists, and with most of the pups being good at heart, the thoughts of what could have happened made them much more aware of how they need to act.

Adam, Brook, and Alpha Gareth decided to use the territory of the pack they had just taken down to help relieve their population issue by starting plans to split the pack, since the pack has been successful and has grown nearly to the limits of what their territory could support. Adam and Brook's wolves did some soft pushing and made comments about them becoming the Alphas of the new pack. Initial plans for the split implemented, but many decisions would not be made until the summer. In fact, some of the changes planned to take decades to fully implement.

After all the security checks between the two packs passed, Adam got to talk to his sister to test out the video link. They caught up with the changes in both their lives. Tara had Mated but hadn't decided if she wanted to be Turned. Most mates eventually decided to be turned, although some took decades to make the choice. Ultimately, it was her decision to make. He just hoped she would be eventually able to join them on four feet.

They finalised the plans for the pack house and all the outbuildings, with the thought of building them over two to three years. They would be doing the ground-breaking as soon as the ground was thawed enough, and they had the equipment there.

When the wind did a momentary change, a patrol smelled those preparing to do a surprise attack and sounded the alert. When they realised it was less than half of the attack force, they started searching for another attack group. They found it, and as Adam and Brook were already on their way to the first one, the Alphas headed to the second.

Realising the Alpha was at the site where Adam and Brook were startling, but Alpha Gareth felt they could handle him and told them they could have the challenge. Coordinating the two forces to launch their counter surprise attack, they were able capture many of the attacking pack before they were aware MacLaren had become aware of them. More were taken out before they could respond.

Adam defeated the Alpha without killing him, but the Alpha used his own weapon to kill himself, rather than submitting to Adam . To Adam's surprise, the pack followed an old law of the one who killed the Alpha became the new Alpha. Adam tried to protest, but his wolf refused to have him turn away from those who would be leaderless otherwise, as the pack lacked anyone able to lead the pack.

After a discussion with Brook, they had decided to call their new pack 'Wild Valley' instead of retaining the name Night Depths or Shadowed River. They wanted to have a fresh start. Many of those who heard it liked the new pack name.

Alpha Gareth took them aside when they return to the MacLaren pack to discuss a few key things about being Alphas, including a few secrets which only Alphas knew. He told them they could only be away from the pack for a month at most without the bonds snapping, which would hurt the entire pack.

They arranged for the MacLaren loft to contain all the new pack, until the new pack house could be built for them. Since plans had already been made to split the MacLaren pack, many of the plans for the pack house were adjusted and pushed forward, as they now needed a place to house the new pack as soon as possible.

Going to pick up the non-combatants, they were shot at as they got off the bus. They found out one she wolf was very much opposed to them taking over, and one reason was their age. Adam ended up using his new powers and give her a painful death as an example for clear disrespect.

Once back at the MacLaren pack house, there were a few tearful reunions. Following the evening for the memorials, they spent the day working on the creating laws for the new pack, so they knew what they were getting into before they formally bonded to their new Alpha.

That evening, they had a combined hunt, but due to almost four hundred wolves now staying at MacLaren, from the influx of two pack taken down and their own happy wolves having plenty of pups, the Alphas Gareth and Maria had Adam and Brook take one hunting group while they took the other. The hunt was successful, and the wolves piled together to sleep that night on the snow.

Adam and Brook had a big set of pawprints to fill; their journey as Alphas was just beginning...

CHAPTER 1

New Bonds

Waking up slowly, Adam smiled. His wolf was feeling more relaxed than he had ever felt him.

****Why not? Our pack is content around us.**** Wolf-Adam commented while sprawled on his back in his mind.

Snuggling Brook in his arms, he dozed off; the content feeling of his wolf lulled him back to sleep as he waited for the others to start moving.

If we want to get them all bonded, we're going to need to get up soon, Brook commented softly, waking Adam up. **As much as I want to just stay here and revel in the content pack, we need them properly and fully bonded to us.**

Sighing, Adam opened his eyes and gave his mate a soft kiss before stretching and moving. Brook followed, as they got some nice shorts and t-shirts on, before moving to grab a quick bite to eat; they would be quite busy all day. While they were not going to be doing physical work, the mental energy to form the bonds was going to need the fuel.

Tapping Jess and Joshua on the shoulder as they got up, Brook motioned for them to follow, as they headed to the office on one side. Closing the door behind them, Adam held up a hand, "Before you say anything, we will need your help with organising the pack, so we can get everyone bonded. First, we want to transfer your bonds to us."

Gareth stood up from the couch he was lounging on, unnoticed, "You cannot belong to two packs, but as Adam and Brook as still members of MacLaren, it makes the transfer both easier and harder. Easier, in you don't have to break your pack bonds with me, and harder, because it takes not only Brook or Adam, but me or Maria as well."

Both Jess and Joshua nodded, before Jess answered for them both, "We realised we would need to do it and want to stay with our parents."

Gareth placed his hand on Adam's shoulder and nodded.

"Since you are just about of age, Gareth agreed we can do your formal oath here as well, so we worked out a slightly modified oath." Adam advised them.

Both smiled at them, "We are honoured." Joshua answered.

"Jess, do you wish to transfer your allegiance to the new pack?" Adam asked, feeling a gathering of energy, as he intoned formally and clearly and held her by her shoulders. Gareth's hand felt warm on his own shoulder.

Jess stood tall, "Yes, I do," she answered.

"Will you uphold the Pack Laws?" Adam asked. They had been involved with the pack laws. They had a copy beside them, for if there were any issues, or they wanted to make sure they were following was the changed version.

"Yes, I will."

"Will you protect all those who are weaker than you, even if it means laying down your life for them?" Adam asked. He really hoped they would not have to die for the pack.

"Yes, I will."

"Will you guard the pack secrets which are entrusted to you with your life?"

"Yes, I will."

"Will you obey those in the pack who are senior to you to the best of your abilities?"

"Yes, I will."

"Will you help your packmates to the best of your ability, whenever possible?"

"Yes, I will."

Adam smiled, "Then welcome to the Wild Valley Pack, Jess," he told her, before touching his head to hers. He felt a rush of energy flow from Gareth's hand through his head and into Jess. Pulling back slowly, both he and Jess would have staggered, if Brook wasn't there to catch his arm and for Joshua to catch his sister.

"I can still feel the MacLaren Pack" Jess exclaimed as Joshua sat her down on a couch, expecting to have lost it and confused to feel two pack bonds.

"Your bond to MacLaren will seem to fade over the next few days, as if you are outside the pack territory. As long as Adam or Brook are considered and consider themselves part of my pack, it will still be there, although it will just be through them. Your own direct bond to me will fade completely." Gareth told Jess.

Turning to Adam, "That was very well done. I fell down and was out of it for a half hour after my first bond. Don't rush it. If it takes two or even three days to do them all, it is fine. Once we have your four pups, I will leave you to your pack. We can do the transfers of those who have already requested to join you, including Sam and Lea, and their parents, Lupita, and Chris, among others later."

Adam grinned, still feeling shaky, "I'll let Brook do the next one." He said as he stood up.

Joshua nodded and stood in front of Brook with Gareth having a hand on her shoulder. Adam stood to her side.

"Joshua, do you wish to transfer your allegiance to the new pack?" Brook asked, starting his oath. Welcoming him to the new pack was a totally new feeling for her too, and she would have collapsed if Adam hadn't wrapped an arm around her waist in time. He guided her to a chair, where she sat blinking. Joshua staggered but didn't fall.

Joshua shook his head, "That is a weird feeling; having two pack bonds."

Gareth handed Brook then Adam a cup of tea from a large teapot. "You will need to keep drinking this; it helps with the effects from the bondings, so you can continue." Looking at Jess and Joshua, "This is an Alpha Secret, but I'm letting you in so you can care for them." Both looked away and nodded when he met their eyes. "If you are doing one or two, you generally don't need it, but if you are doing many, you will need it. It keeps the bonds from overwhelming you and from giving you a splitting headache."

Adam and Brook choked down the small cup of very bitter brew, before putting the cups down. Both felt better as soon as it hit their stomach.

"What was in it?" Adam asked.

Gareth shook his head as he shuddered, "You don't want to know; I wish I didn't." Turning to Jess and Joshua again, "Talk to Lupita, as she knows how to make it. Have her teach you."

Jess nodded, mostly recovered. "I'll go get Toby and Robin." She said, before skipping out of the room. Some of the others were starting to wake up and ask where the Alphas were. "They are getting their pups transferred, then will be starting to get the formal bonds with you. My brother and I will come get you as you finish eating. Brook said not to worry about any order, so we will get whoever is free, and they will continue doing it till everyone is done." She paused, "It may take a few days to get everyone."

It satisfied most, but a few, wanting to be first, immediately got up and headed to eat, so they would be ready to go early.

Bending down, Jess shook the two awake, from where they had curled up with their girlfriends and the other pups around Charlie. *Time to change your pack membership.* She told them silently. Both nodded and looked eager. Stepping lightly, they moved past the still sleeping wolves, out of the room.

Adam and Brook had both recovered. They gave them a hug before moving to the reason why they were there.

"Toby, do you wish to transfer your allegiance to the new pack?" Brook asked, as Gareth put his hand on her shoulder.

"Yes, I do."

Since he was much too young for doing the oath, that part was skipped. He was over ten, so needed to be asked about the transfer. Under that age, a guardian would have to stand in for them; since they were their own pups, they didn't need to worry about it. They would give their formal oath on their twentieth birthday.

"Welcome to Wild Valley Pack, Toby." She said cheerfully, before touching foreheads. This time, since she was expecting the energy drain, she only stumbled a little.

"Almost had it," she complained under her breath.

Jess guided Toby to the couch, as Adam brought in Robin. He too stumbled just a little. Taking the cup of tea, he forced down another mouthful.

"I think you will need to round up some help." Adam commented as Joshua helped Robin to sit down. "It will be a greater shock to the others. Maybe couches just outside the room for them to recover on?"

Jess nodded, "I'll go see about that. Those who help will be the first to get bonded, too." She said with a smirk. She liked Adam's idea of rewarding those who worked hard, not just punishing the rule breakers. She had seen how it made for wolves who were eager to help, as they got something for doing so.

Adam smiled, "Go," was all he said, before the two headed out. They were quickly back, "I have two couches now, and three more will be here shortly."

Shooing the two younger ones out, now that they had recovered. Gareth followed them out as well, since his job was done for now.

Working steadily but slowly through the morning, they needed to take a break about every hour. Jess and Joshua and several of the former omegas were keeping them supplied with tea and finger foods.

When lunch came around, both needed a sit-down meal and talking with their helpers, they had one. Looking through the records they had been passed from the pack house, they worked out the facts of the stories for those labelled as omega, and none of them they felt deserved to be an omega. They had it completely removed from their records and returned them their dignity. Right now, they were not dealing with ranks, as the Spring Trials were just over a month away and would let them start off with ranks which made sense, rather than just what the Alpha had decided. While it might not be enough time for some to qualify at the right rank, they could give them a tentative promotion and let them try again over the next few years, while they performed the duties of the rank.

By the end of the lunch, Adam and Brook knew they had the undying loyalty of all of those who had been given the dishonour of being omega, first by giving them a new chance, then by believing in them. As they filed out of the room, they started to organise those who were giving their oaths that afternoon. Adam asked for volunteers to deal with their former alpha and the fake-mate's bodies. All put up their hands, so they picked six to deal with them. Both were being buried deep in unmarked graves. Nobody would be told where they had been buried, and they would be quickly forgotten.

The first up was one of the females who was friends with the bimbo, "I have a couple questions before I give the oath." She started, hesitantly.

Brook nodded, "Go ahead, Kelsey. What you say here is private and will not be shared with anyone."

"Alpha Night had told us since we had to do what he said, he could do what he wanted to us." She said before hesitating to go farther.

Adam snarled, "He raped you?" Living with humans, he connected the dots much faster. Most wolves would shift and take out the offender, so it was much less prevalent with wolves.

When Brook heard that, she started growling too. If the body hadn't already been dealt with, she would have separated it and left it for the scavengers; an indignity they rarely did.

Kelsey just hung her head and barely nodded. Adam pulled out the laws and flipped through them to the page. *All persons on the pack territory are entitled to the protection of their body from assault, including rape. The Alpha is not above this law, nor can he set it aside with the Law of the Alpha. Penalty is immediate death of the offender and burial.*

It went onto the part about attempted rape. Brook had demanded the penalty be the removal of their sexual parts. If they attempted to force themselves on someone, they didn't deserve to pass on their genes. With how open and promiscuous a pack was, if someone asked, usually they could find another for some fun, even if it was just scratching the itch, and nothing more than that. Most had friends they shared the closeness with to be able to ask.

Kelsey blinked and read it a few times before sighing, tears in her eyes, "I missed that when we had the meeting. With that protection I will feel safe. I am willing to give my oath." Mostly, she had missed the part where it couldn't be set aside by the Alpha's law, and how even the Alphas were subject to it.

The rest of the afternoon went fine, and at dinner, they had Kelsey join them. A couple others of the group who they realised had the same feeling were asked to join them. They all had a different feel to them, and they were no longer wearing what Adam thought of as hooker outfits, but general training clothes. They had been getting some self defence training after an off-hand comment as Kelsey left following her oath and bonding. They smiled and seemed to enjoy themselves.

Letting the past be the past, *I wonder how many other 'damaged' wolves we will find in this pack?* Adam wondered to Brook, as they joined the pack for an evening of relaxing. They had got just over half the pack done, and since they were exhausted, they were going to wait for the next day. They watched the pups play with his Charlie, Chris's Mika, and several other of the dogs who had made their way up to the floor. They chatted with the others about light topics. Those who had been bonded could feel they were tired. Both curled up on the pile of mattresses when the pups were put to bed and were asleep fast enough, they didn't notice the pups move to curl up around them.

*****

Just before supper the next day, Jess came in, "Just did a check and asked around, nobody seemed to know of anyone who had been missed in the oath and bonds. They are all done." The pups had been brought in with their parents for the most part but finding two were being cared for by the rest of the pups but had lost both parents—in both cases, one parent had been gone for a while, they confirmed the parent of their friend who was caring for them as their guardians, which they recognised formally.

Adam flopped on the couch, "Finally! I really feel for the Alphas who accepted part of Sh— the Nameless Pack." Not only was he exhausted, but the headache was also strong enough he didn't want to do much.

Brook pulled her mate back up, "Well, we should eat with our pack and give them the news."

Adam nodded, but held out his arms, "It isn't quite dinner time. Come here, and we'll think of what's next for us."

Brook smiled and sat in his lap and cuddled in, "Well, Chris and the others need to be transferred, Chis needs to be Turned, which means a week or two, then all the pack stuff."

Adam smiled, "Add in the WereNet to that, as well."

Brook shook her head, "That is a long-term project; it's not something which needs to be done anytime soon. I suspect it will be done for many years to get it ready, and I think we will be supporting it for many, many more." As they headed out to the dining area.

Walking in, there was a pause in the conversations before they went back to what they were doing. Giving a short howl, everyone was silent.

"We believe everyone has been bonded. Is there any who were missed?" Adam asked. Silence was his only response. "In that case, if any don't have bonds, they will be considered Lone Wolves and be treated as such. Starting tomorrow, you all can go down to the Security and get your IDs updated. You have been passed out the details on the training which needs to be done for the ranking. We will be combining the trials with MacLaren. They start May first; it gives you a bit over a month to prepare. If you don't get the rank which you feel you deserve, you can try again each year to get it."

Taking a breath, at the sly look of some, he gave a warning, "Do not attempt to cheat. As I really don't like the omega rank, and the lifetime stigma of it, I will have cheaters ranked as just above Omega and will be doing bathroom and garbage cleanup until we feel better about them and be stuck there for a decade after that." Those who looked sly now looked very disappointed. He hoped he didn't have to discipline anyone, as it would probably be years to feel better. He would also have a heavy course-load of retraining on top of the work, to make an example of them. "If I feel *really* bad about the attempt to cheat, I might even consider the Omega rank; it is how much I hate cheaters. I consider it a form of lying, as you didn't actually complete the testing for the rank as it is done."

"Also," Adam started, "Starting tomorrow, you will be expected to eat with MacLaren Pack in the dining room. I want the two packs to mingle and get to know everyone. I will be using some of the pack to work on preparing for building the pack house, others will have duties here. What we need at first, is some for patrols, cleaning, and for the kitchen. Those who want to do it, instead of being scheduled to do other tasks which will be coming, come see us after dinner."

"Last item before we get down to dinner," Adam told his pack, "I will be bringing the completed plans for the property here. If you see issues or see something which could be done better, please let us know. This pack house is the source concept. It is over a hundred years old already. I am building for ours to last at least five centuries. The two packs will be doing the majority of the work to build it, so many of you will be leaving a legacy for the pack. We have a couple of other legacy items which will be surprises when we move in. Let's eat!"

The pack howled and headed off to the buffet tables to get their food, or to start eating, for those who had got their food already. Already those who had pushed had stopped and were being considerate of the rest of the pack. It seemed many were much smarter than he had thought, and since they gave them an incentive to act how he wanted them, they were.

Chowing down on the food Adam and Brook chatted about some short-term plans. They had plenty of items which they needed to deal with. They had been sitting at different tables, and chatting with different wolves, to learn about their pack.

I still can't believe we are totally responsible for these wolves. Adam commented to his mate. The feeling of being over his head was felt by his mate.

I know what you mean, Brook replied, *I totally feel over my head too, and I was born a wolf. You probably feel more out of place than me, since half a year ago, you didn't even know we existed!*

Both felt their wolves nuzzle them and offer them reassurances. **We are here to help you.** They told their human halves, **We will support you, you just need to ask us,**

Have we been doing the right thing? Brook asked her wolf in a small voice.

So far, yes. You want to listen to the Alphas and Elders, Wolf-Brook replied, as both halves of Adam listened in, meaning Alphas Gareth and Maria and the Elders in their own pack, **They have been around for long enough to have some good experiences. If you need some help, they will at least help you weigh the options, but the decision has to be made by us.**

Their human-halves traded a smile, happy to have those reassurances.

Toby flopped into a seat beside them, with his plate. He had been working to get the information on their pack registered, so they could make their permanent IDs. *I had some free time, and looked in the history, the last time there was Alphas as young as you two. It was four hundred years ago. A pack war had decimated the pack, leaving the Alpha's son and his mate to run the half of the pack which was left. That pack took nearly two hundred years to recover.*

Adam mock-glared at his son, *Thanks for the reassuring thoughts.* He replied, sarcastically. *Do you have any good news?*

The sensors and parts for our pack's territory is all in. You can start scheduling parties to start getting the lines and sensors installed. Chris has the layout of them mapped. Came the reply.

Adam mentally groaned, *That's another thing to add to our list of things to do!* he complained to his mate, before thinking of one thing. *Have Chris and the security who is transferring to see us tomorrow morning, after breakfast. We'll get them transferred then immediately put to work.* With them having done MacLaren, they had many who would know how to do it, and what issues to watch out for. The plans Chris and the other had already worked out for the network layout to support the sensors was already approved, and they were working on what they could. Parts close to the pack house was waiting for the construction to be started in some areas and finished in others. They weren't going to put fibre lines under where construction vehicles were going to be driving.

Having a thought, Adam got a slow feral grin as he looked at Toby, deciding to share the headache of the work he brought, *I am tasking you with setting up a schedule for our pack to get the sensors installed. Pair our pack with those from MacLaren who got them installed before, so they can learn.* He got a grumble but acceptance of it.

Robin bounced in and dropped a tube of the plans for the pack house, before heading off to get his own food. There had been some network changes, which they did during the dinner time for the pack, to minimize the impact to the pack. As he was learning the job of being the tech lead from Erin, he had to be there. Erin had brought in some special meal, but he wanted to eat with the pack, so left the food for those who had done the work. He had used the plotter to make a fresh copy of the latest changes to the plans, sending the job to the plotter before the network was taken offline, and the plotter just churned through it once the print server had downloaded the job to it.

Brook gathered their dishes, and took them off, as Adam co-opted the others from the table to help wipe it down then dry it, so they could lay them out when they were all done eating. Most of the pack came over to see how the pack would be laid out as they finished eating. Most came away grinning as they really liked the plans. Off to one side, he had put some paper for those who wanted the Patrol or Kitchen duties, instead of just having various ones assigned. A third sheet was there to have them put their preferences for any other duties. As much as they could, they would have them do what they liked doing.

"What's the 'Display Space' that is along the balconies around the common room?" One asked.

Adam grinned and shook his head, "It is one of the legacy surprises. It will represent every single member. It will be announced when we move into the building." Nobody could get him to say anything more. Those who knew about the paw-print plan were few but had been Alpha Ordered to not talk about it, even with hints. Several looked disappointed, but many speculated, and both Adam and Brook ignored the speculation, not giving any hints or even commenting if they were close or not.

Most of the pack were very interested and liked how it was going to be done. Many commented on the size and features of the gym and how well it blended into the natural environment.

Many stuck around all evening discussing it excitedly. Others came to give Brook and Adam hugs and thanks for a fresh start.

Just before they were heading off to bed down with the pack together for the last night, Elder Elise came up, "Well, it looks like Ralph's ideal design updated for current construction abilities and location." She looked younger than she had when they had first met her; the fact of the pack not being stressed, and all feeling safe and well fed did wonders. She barely needed the cane she had needed before.

Both were startled. "You knew Alpha Ralph?" Brook asked.

"I knew him when he was younger. Before the relations between the two packs really were strained and broken. That was the original MacLaren pack house, this one, and now the one you are planning, the three show a clear progression of the same ideas. Each with the same idea of blending in as best possible, and supporting the pack with comfort, but while also being as kind as possible to the environment. It looks to be a beautiful building." The elder told them, sounding a little wistful, "I wish I could have made it for the memorial when he died, but we were nearly at war then."

Brook nodded, "Night Depths was the last pack in this area to refuse to sign the Inter-Pack Treaty. Officially, we will be having an Alpha Conference this summer and be signing it then. As the laws are already in the pack laws, basically it is just a formality to ratify our membership. Alpha Gareth has let us know the Arctic Shadow and Longview Packs already acknowledge our pack and have agreed to treat us as provisionally signed on to the treaty." There were other packs who had sent messages of welcome and if not outright stated it, both read between the lines that they would support them if attacked, so there were even more already supporting them.

Elise cackled, "Probably for the Arctic Shadow, they fear you. The accepting you on the treaty means they have protections and safeguards against you ever attacking. Rufus was always like that."

Adam was surprised, but his wolf was very much liking this Elder. A thought was shared with Brook, and she confirmed it. While she had opinions and wasn't shy of sharing them, she was willing to listen to them, and think about it, before making her thoughts known.

"We want to set up a weekly meeting with the Elders on Tuesday mornings, to start after breakfast, and last no longer than lunch." Adam asked, rather than ordered.

Elise had a smile light up her face, "So you want to meet with us oldies?" She seemed to be needling them, to see how they reacted.

Adam grinned in reply and decided to not take offence, and just take it as her way of teasing them and was glad she was sure enough of them to tease, "You 'Oldies' have a unique view, and have been through much. The fact I have you is an honour. I would be negligent to not at least hear your views and ask for your advice. I can't say we will follow it, as Brook and I are the Alphas, and we make the decisions for the pack, and we feel the way the local packs have been living will make them discovered, as it is majorly out of step with the way humans are, for the most part."

Elise continued smiling, "With that sort of attitude, you may survive to become an Elder and be respected the way Ralph was known by the Norse meaning of his name, 'Council Wolf'. Most of the packs went to him for advice, well, other than the last three Alphas for Night Depths. Those didn't last even a century each." Stopping for a moment, "You seem to have a similar presence he did when I first met him, just weaker, probably because you are so new to your power. We will be there for the meeting. I know I will be honoured to be consulted, unlike the last two Night Depths Alphas. Where is this meeting?"

"We have arranged for the conference room in the Alpha's wing." Brook told her; she had asked Maria where to meet, and that room had been offered. She was finding some nice side benefits of the change in status; in it seemed Gareth and Maria were willing to let them use their private meeting room.

Exchanging goodnight, they smiled and curled up with the rest of the pack. It seems less who needed it, as more were moving the mattresses. Through the bonds, their wolves were teaching them to sense the pack's emotions, and they were settling down, and becoming more relaxed. The fear and stress they had felt when they first bonded to them was already draining away, being dissolved in the content feeling, hope for the future, and even happiness.

They were looking forward to their own bed the next night, as it had been a rocky time for their pack. Again, Adam's wolf had to swamp his mind with sleep, as he kept thinking about too much to rest.

Once his human was asleep, Wolf-Adam prowled forward, and sniffing softly, smiled and relaxed. Their pack was here and was theirs to protect and nurture. If the old Night Depths Alpha was here, he'd kill them again, after shredding his body, as they had abused the trust given to them by the pack. Relaxing, he let their body rest; their human needed the strength to deal with the issues tomorrow.

Chapter 2 – Birthdays

Adam woke up the next morning and grinned, thinking back to the end of February and Brook's birthday. She almost got out the surprise from him, but he had her friends, and their pups handle it. It had been after dinner, and they made it back to their suite before Adam and Brook and surprised her with the small gathering. Even both Alphas had dropped in.

He remembered her thanks the best, and even now it brought a smile to his lips. *Brook turned to Adam, "Here I thought everyone had forgotten about my birthday! This was a great surprise, and I forgive you for keeping it from me." She told him before pulling him in for a heated kiss, not aware of the noise made by the others.*

He smiled, as it was Jess and Joshua's twentieth today. He had passed it to a few of the new pack, and they were going to be doing some good for them.

Coming into the main dining hall, it was full to overflowing, with nearly the entirety pack there.

Jess and Joshua had been placed in the Alpha's table, which was raised up a step, so all could see and be seen by them; it was their coming-of-age birthday, after all.

As the parents, they got the honour of giving the first gifts. Adam placed down a sheathed sword in front of each of them. Both were awed along with those close to them. "You two have earned the respect of your sword teacher, when I asked if you should get them, he not only said yes, but also helped me pick them out. Wear them with pride and honour." He gave both a hug. Those swords would have been worth a fortune, if they had been made for them. The trainer had told him they were sitting collecting dust for the right bearer was surprising. The sheaths he and Brook had worked at making, as the original ones were falling apart.

Brook passed them a bow which fit each of them, for their strength and style. They smiled at it. The Bow and Sword were still the pack's main weapons, as they could be dealt without much human oversight. Both knew some packs had switched to using guns, mostly down in the US, where they had next to no oversight, while in Canada there was much less access to firearms and ammo. Them giving the weapons showed they were trusted to know how to use them and could be relied upon to help defend the pack.

Toby and Robin brought up a quiver full of arrows they had made over the last few months for them, they smiled and hugged them as well; they had been in on the surprises.

The MacLaren Alphas gave each of them a dagger, before the rest of their friend descended and gave them other small practical gifts. The chefs had made the normal food but had made some treats and even a cake. Many stayed and chatted, those who didn't have duties they couldn't get out of. Some had to run after the breakfast party, but when it broke up, several helped the two take their gifts back to their room. Adam had some work he needed to check on, so slipped out fairly soon after the cake was distributed.

Since they had already given the oaths, they didn't need to give them again, but when one complained, the two stood and recited their oaths from memory, just to satisfy those calling for it, which just had them moving onto something else to complain about.

*****

Dante was handling the main phone line for the pack, and since he wasn't too close to Adam or his pups, wasn't too concerned about missing the birthday party. He did get brought some of the treats, including the cake, though.

It was still early so getting a call wasn't too surprising. The number was flagged as a known number from another pack but wasn't a pack name he knew, but was not a secured line, "MacLaren Pack, how may I direct the call?"

"Good morning, this is Beta Joshua Calahan of the Fossil Valley pack in Oregon. I need to talk to… Alpha Gareth I believe. It is in reference to a Night Depths pack."

He blinked for a moment and looked at the time, "Alpha Gareth is currently in a meeting with the Elders. Would a Second be acceptable?"

Josh wasn't familiar with the term Second, but he was guessing it was similar to a Beta, "Yes, that would be fine."

"Just a minute then," Dante replied, putting the call on hold and transferring to one of the wireless handsets. Grabbing the handset from the charger, he raced out to the dining hall and catching Adam just as he was just heading out.

"Alpha Adam, I have a Beta Joshua from the Fossil Valley pack in Oregon. They asked to talk to Alpha Gareth about Night Depths pack, but he just went into a meeting with the Elders. They are fine with a Second; could you take it?" He held out the Wi-Fi handset. "The line is not fully secured."

Adam was startled, "I'm definitely the one to talk to then. Thanks." He told him, as he took the handset.

"This is Acting-Second Adam of the MacLaren Pack. I understand you want details on the Night Depths Pack? Can you secure the line at your end, the details are fairly sensitive." Adam spoke, as he walked back to his room.

Another voice piped up "What encryption method do you use? We have a Cisco VoIP encryption system. I can make adjustments as needed to secure the line."

Adam was confused too; that system was compatible with theirs; it should show as encrypted. "One second while I check this end. I just had the network set up here, and it *should* have showed as secured." After getting an agreement, he put the call on hold and made a beeline for his computer. Checking the servers, he found the issue being it rejected the unknown source. Changing a setting to just flag as unknown, but still connect securely, instead of only connect regularly, it now switched to secure, and the handset beeped to notify the change.

"Sorry, the issue was here; it didn't recognise your connection so didn't bother trying to connect securely. I have fixed it, and it's now fully secured." Adam advised.

Once both were sure, Josh started speaking again, "I am calling in reference to a young man by the name of Ethan Fortune from a Night Shade, no, I meant Night Depths pack. He indicates he has been ruled a rogue for asking the wrong question. I need to talk to someone who can give me information about this pack."

Brook, can you see if you can find Ethan Fortune in the Night Depths pack records? He seems to have been picked up by a pack down in Oregon Adam asked and got a startled reply, but she would do it.

"I am probably the best person to give you details. As of four days ago, that pack ceased to exist: I killed their Alpha when they attacked us. They had eighteen lost in the fight, and the survivors declared me as the Alpha, currently being housed here at MacLaren. I am more correctly Alpha, but for now, I am also an acting-second within MacLaren."

Josh had to blink at the surprising information provided. When he spoke his first comment was, "Huh?" He frowned at the term Second or Acting-Second as well, "Just to make sure we are singing the same song; by Acting Second, you are a Beta? And you are an Alpha? Interesting. So, the pack doesn't exist anymore? I hope when they attacked your pack you didn't lose to many. Would you be able to find out if Ethan Fortune should be classified as a rogue? He was picked up with a group of other rogues which attacked some of our pack. The moment we retaliated he gave up and surrendered."

"We use the rank Second for the person or pair who assists the Alphas and reports only to the Alphas. Betas are below them. The Betas are in charge of specific areas, like security or maintenance." Alpha Adam advised, "I take it you rank differently?"

Josh scratched his head, "We do. I would say we use a more traditional set of titles. Alpha and Luna run the pack. Below them are the Betas. We do have two ranks of Betas; I am the senior Beta as well as the future Alpha. The junior Betas manage sections of the pack as you said yours do. Below Beta are the Deltas and Gammas. Below those we have junior wolves. At the very bottom are the Thetas who are being punished for something." Now he had some information on the ranks they had, it was easier to deal with.

Alpha Adam nodded, even if the other didn't see it, "In small packs, that is how they do it, but when you have well over two hundred, more formalizing of the upper ranks are done." He advised. He didn't bother adding 'Next-Alpha' was also a rank they used, which depended on the abilities of the wolves ranked above, equal to, or just below Second in the pack's seniority.

Adam sighed, "We lost two in the fight. The old alpha was dealing in a liquefied Wolfsbane and hollow bullet delivery with another pack. Both hadn't realised we had just covered the territory with passive sensors, so their ambush was ambushed. We lost three in the first attack."

Josh let out a low howl in sympathy, "I am sorry to hear that, you have our sympathy." At the mention of wolfsbane a low growl broke out, "Glad you took him out. What about the other pack involved? Passive sensors? What type do you use? We use... Ah, never mind. It isn't the issue right now"

Adam suppressed a laugh, as he suspected Josh oversaw their tech as well. Brook walked in and handed him the file, "My mate just walked in with the file, one second while I glance over it."

Adam quickly skimmed the record, and saw nothing to warrant even a disciplinary action, looking at Brook, she shook her head, who had read it over his shoulder. "My opinion, and of my mate, is he should have had no action over the last infraction. It is listed as back-talking to a superior. There were several of those reported in there. Unfortunately, the one who filed it as a complaint is one who was killed. I would consider him a Lone Wolf, as we have just finished reforming as Wild Valley Pack. If you wish, I could forward you the entire record?"

Adam could hear the rattle of fingernails on a hard surface as Josh decided. "Please do. Once I review them and talk to my father, how would you like to handle this? If you have reformed the pack as a new one, do you want me to give the young wolf an option to come up there?"

Throwing the file in the feeder of the scanner, Adam entered in Josh's e-mail, already having set them up as being secured. He was glad they had the multi-page scanner and didn't need to feed each page manually, or worse: a flat-bed scanner. "It should be on your e-mail shortly. You can give him the option to come back up; he will be treated as a Lone Wolf, or you can keep him, if he wishes to stay. I'll give you my direct contact information, and you can contact me directly for more details."

"If he wants to come back, will he have an option of pleading his case and possibly joining the new pack? Before I talk to him, I want all the possible outcomes discussed." Josh asked, "I know the feeling about hoping things quiet down. We have our own rogue issue right now."

I only took Adam a moment to think about it, "Yes. We would be willing to accept him to the pack, provided he hasn't killed anyone which wasn't in self-defence. Be glad you didn't have to deal with having a pack declared Rogue and then dissolving it. It has been fairly eventful up here as well. Mostly I have been working on getting the packs up here upgraded on their tech, and a secured network established between them. When things are a little quieter, contact me so we can talk tech. Before I started showing flashes of Alpha skills, I was the head of the tech, and had to start with analog phones, and barely any internet or computers—They still had CRT monitors, but that's another talk. The other pack which was trying to use the wolfsbane was dissolved, and the innocent redistributed. We are in the process of breaking down the wolfsbane under extreme security, but due to how they made it, it is a slow process."

Josh was impressed, "Wow, that is a hell of an undertaking. I feel for you. I run the security and tech company the pack owns. We provide security for several businesses in the region. That does include other pack businesses as well."

"Once I am done talking to my father what I can do is bring him into my office, set up a secure link and let you talk to him. We have a full Video Conference suite which is heavily encrypted as well. I am going to let you go since I have some other things I need to deal with." Josh confirmed.

"Send me an e-mail with the connection details, and I will get the security link enabled at this end so all communications travel through the secure link." Adam replied, "I have full video conferencing set up here as well. It is refreshing to deal with a pack which is already good with the technology, unlike many up here. If your Alpha wishes to discuss it or the other issues, we have had up here, I can make myself available. I will be doing some membership transfers today, as we are working to split the pack as it is getting too big."

"Once I get the e-mail from you, I will reply to it with my contact information. I will include the connection requirements for the video conference. Not sure who all will be in here, my father might be as well. Chances are this will be tomorrow or the next day. It isn't urgent now that we have a better idea of what is going on. I am going to let you go since I have some other work to do as well. Thank you for your time, Adam." Josh replied.

"Nice to meet you and hope the rest of the day goes well for you." Alpha Adam commented, before ending the call.

He wrote up a quick report for Gareth, passing the phone to Jess as she led the first of the transfers, Sam and her parents, along with Alpha Maria. It didn't take too long to move them over, and he let them get back to work. Next, he had Lea and her parents, which also went smoothly.

Taking a break to have some of the nasty bond-tea, and a snack, and let Maria know about the call, giving her the details, and passing her the report, for her and Gareth to review. It also noted a link to the log of the phone call which he had recorded, since it dealt with inter-pack issues.

"Well, it sounds like that wolf had been kicked out before they even started doing the Wolfsbane, so it would not be something which could have involved him. It sounds like he should be given another chance, but it is up to you, as it's your pack. If he doesn't fit well with your pack, we could see about another around here or help him migrate to another area." Maria commented, "Even just being relabeled as a Lone Wolf would give him much more freedom to move, and to approach other packs on his own." None of them thought to see if he still had any living family.

Lupita was next, with Chris being the last of this batch. They discussed arranging having him turned in a week or so, honouring the request, even though it kept being pushed off.

*****

After a quiet weekend and e-mailing back and forth with Josh, instead of their normal meeting they were going to have the video chat. When he had found out Elder Elise had known him before he had been kicked out, when he had a discussion with the elders about it and had asked her to sit in on the meeting. From what they had found out, it sounded like he'd be a good fit with the new pack.

Alpha Adam accepted the video conference call in the Alpha's boardroom. Once it was connected Josh started, "Morning, I am Beta Josh, this is my father Alpha Calahan, my assistant Beta Adam and Delta Maxon. Finally, this is Ethan from the Night Shade—" He covered his eyes, "Don't know why I keep doing that, Night Depths pack." He waited for the others to introduce themselves.

Alpha Adam smiled in greeting, "Morning everyone, I'm Alpha Adam, beside me is my mate, Alpha Brook and beside her is Elder Elise. We are from the new Wild Valley Pack. Elder Elise was a member of Night Depths. The other two are Alpha Gareth and Alpha Maria from MacLaren pack. Do you have a problem with us recording this meeting?"

Alpha Calahan gave each a nod as they were introduced, "Not a problem and I am sure Beta Josh is recording as well. I know I prefer to have meetings like this recorded. It helps keep misunderstandings down the road kept to a minimum." Or at least kept both sides from trying to tilt the truth.

Alpha Adam smiled, "Now, down to business. I am going to give you an overview of what has happened in the last while, to get you up to speed." At the nod, "Last winter two wolves fled false accusations and broke their Pack Bonds which would have had them tossed out of the pack as rogues. They were able to seek asylum with MacLaren Pack before the false report of them being dangerous rogues arrived. As the report was completely different than what the Alphas saw, they gave them a chance but were watched. Mid-January a scout found them, and as I had not been able to get permission to install the sensor network yet, they not only penetrated the territory but right into the rooms of the two who had fled them, in the pack house." Alpha Adam had to stop for a moment to calm his wolf, as he was growling audibly.

Taking a breath, he continued, "I was not able to catch the scout, but was able to chase him right from the territory. That got me an instant approval, and we got the sensor network done in under two weeks, with much of the pack helping." He smiled in pride as several of the other pack started in surprise at how fast they worked. He didn't bother stating out loud his thought of 'Many hands make light work.' As with many of the pack working on it, they had got them done almost as fast as the sensors could be delivered, "We kept heightened watch out, knowing they would be back, which they were. They decided to get their guns with hollow bullets filled with a liquefied wolfsbane ready at the edge of what we had claimed as our territory and was covered in sensors. We ambushed them before they were ready, and as such were able to take them down with the loss on our side of only three members."

Josh looked startled when Adam was talking about the networking and getting the sensors approved, "You didn't have them before earlier this year? We have had them for a good ten or so years. Several of the nearby packs finally broke down and asked us to do the installs for them. That was after we had a few attacks by rogues beaten off by using the sensors." At the mention of the pack jumping up to help Josh had grinned slightly, "We informed the pack if they wanted the network drops in their rooms they had to help or pay." They would have gotten them anyways but this way much of the costs of the individual drops had been offset.

Alpha Adam grinned in reply, "They didn't think they needed anything more than actual patrols, as nothing had gotten through them to the pack house before. This really shook those who refused to go for it, saying it was privacy issues." At the comment about networking, "It was fairly cheap to network the pack house and was easier to start from scratch. The pack house had been made to allow easy upgrades."

Changing the topic a little, "All the packs, other than Night Depths, in our area had signed an Inter-Pack Treaty, which has specific laws which govern inter-pack communications, movement, and a very few other common rules, which are required to be added into the member packs' laws. This has made most of the region very stable, and in my opinion complacent about security. One part outright banned the use of Wolfsbane. Another is on how to deal with rule breakers and the penalties. If there are three major offences which can be confirmed, and consensus can be made with a Triad of packs, a member pack could be declared Rogue and dissolved. That pack was the Shadowed River Pack, which is now nameless."

As they continued with the overview of the last few months, they mostly kept their expressions neutral. When the subject of the hollow bullets came up all of them reacted even though they had known about the Wolfsbane. "I assume the Wolfsbane has been destroyed or rendered neutral?" Alpha Calahan had to know, since it was going to need to be reported to the nearby alphas and to the council.

Even Ethan had looked up and stared, though as soon as he realised it, he quickly lowered his head again, so he was looking back down at the table. He hadn't liked his pack since the Alpha had been a bastard. Even look at him the wrong way and he would beat you—or more often have another beat you. Most of the females, pups, and junior males tended to avoid him as much as possible. One thing he was wondering about, but didn't ask, was why all the stuff about the Shadowed River pack. He had been from Night Depths, not there. He had thought this was about ensuring he wasn't an actual rogue.

Turning to the next part, Alpha Adam continued, "During the takedown and cleanup of the nameless pack's territory which was being done by MacLaren and another pack, Arctic Shadow, an entire beer barrel was found of the Wolfsbane. There were some traitors found, and others who infiltrated from Night Depths Pack. At the same time as we did a secure transport of the Wolfsbane for disposal—due to the amount being estimated about fifty Litres, or twelve gallons," He had looked up the conversion, since most in the US refuse to use metric units. He had to pause for the angry growl from those on the other side and continued once they had quieted, "We are still working at breaking it down and rendering it inert. Night Depths knew we had it, and gave an ultimatum to return it, which we never even bothered replying. What we still have is under extreme security and is being destroyed as fast as we can safely." The Enforcers who were guarding it had orders to not let it fall into enemy hands, at any cost, with the only ones authorized entry was the medical lab leader and the Alphas. Even then, any which was removed then was escorted by an armed Enforcer pair, and the medical lab had more Enforcers guarding there with similar orders, until it was all gone. Both areas, if anyone tried to enter, who wasn't authorized, they would be detained, and Alpha Gareth would deal with them.

"Before Night Depths attacked MacLaren, we had captured several of their scouts, and when offered asylum, jumped on it. They had been told those from the packs around them would kill on sight, which was not true. When their attack was detected, Brook and I were ready, and headed out almost instantly. Before the rest, led by Alphas Gareth and Maria, were ready to go, it was realized they had a second force trying to flank the pack. They went after that one." Adam smiled, "The one myself and my mate were dealing with contained the Alpha. I was able to defeat him, but instead of submitting, he killed himself."

Taking another breath, as the next part was hard, "I was told by the survivors of the fight I was now their Alpha, as I had defeated their Alpha. Both Brook and I have been working to learn the skills for being Alpha, but were going to be Acting Alphas, with the rank of Seconds, Senior Beta in your rankings, for a satellite pack for a century, to gain experience, while still under the oversight of Alphas Gareth and Maria. As it is, both packs are currently at MacLaren's pack house, while we build a new one, as both pack houses from the two taken down are considered uninhabitable by our standards and are being demolished. We have taken those who were not responsible for the issues in, and started the forming of Wild Valley Pack, which will be taking the territory which had been the nameless pack's territory. We are still using it as population relief for the MacLaren Pack, which after absorbing parts of the nameless pack, is nearly too big to stay hidden." Stopping there, he asked, "Questions?"

Alpha Calahan quirked an eyebrow at the mention of Adam becoming Alpha by the old laws. "Congratulations on becoming Alpha. It is a weighty responsibility, but it sounds like you are taking the long approach." The young Alpha had his respect, as he was clearly showing his leadership in how he was providing this information to them, giving the overview but without wandering into trying to relive it, as many wolves would do, thinking it would show their skills, when all it did was usually bore the others. Nor were they hiding the fact they had a security breach, which some could take as a failure. They also were not giving away details which could be pack secrets. They clearly had the respect of those who followed them already.

Alpha Adam bowed his head in respect, "Thank you. My mate and I are just starting to see the amount of work an Alpha must do to care for their pack."

Alpha Adam had been keeping a close eye on Ethan's reaction, and he was looking fairly satisfied. "Ethan, I had talked to Elder Elise, who does remember you, although didn't know what happened to get you kicked out as a rogue. The story put out was you refused to do an order, but from what I have heard from others, other times you were punished, you were just asking for details. From Josh, I have gotten the details on what you have done since then, and, you have tried to act with honour but got caught up with the group of actual rogues." Catching his mate's thought, he gave her a mental nod, "My mate and I were wondering if you would like to come back, and join us in building an entire new pack?" Holding up a hand to stop him from a hasty answer, "Josh has a binder of the new pack laws for you to read before you answer. You would have to agree to follow them. One thing I do not tolerate is bullying of any sort."

Ethan figured the Alpha was expecting him to speak at this point, so he looked up and met Adam's eyes before submitting, "I tried my best, Alpha. It was hard, but I knew I wasn't a rogue though being reported as one I also knew it was a death sentence. I was mostly a lone wolf until the pack I was found with captured me. They gave me the choice of join them or die. I figured since I already had a death sentence, I should. I didn't join in any of the stuff they did, if possible. When they were attacked on this pack territory, I surrendered since I figured I might as well try and hopefully get an honourable death among other wolves."

Alpha Adam smiled as he could see the binder slid over. It also included a copy of their training requirements, and ranking details. They had made sure it didn't have any pack secrets, as he knew it would make the rounds of at least a few packs down there, or even to their council. There hadn't been time for the tentative friendliness to turn into friendship and trust between the packs, yet. Hopefully, all would see he was just trying to protect his wolves and to allow them to be happy.

When the binder was slid over Ethan carefully read through the rules. He wasn't going to just jump at rejoining any pack until he knew what the rules were. There was no way he was going to end up in a pack like the one he had been kicked out of. Being a lone wolf was better than that by miles. He had already read the rules since Josh had given them to him earlier, but he just had to check. He would like to go back because he did have some family. He looked up, "Can you tell me what might have happened with my sister Sarabeth and my mom Rene?"

Alpha Adam closed his eyes for a moment, and pulled up the pack bonds to them, "They are both safe, but right now are busy helping clear part of the site for the new pack house. It is a four-hour run as a wolf from here. Right now, there is no network connection there, otherwise I would bring them into the call. I am not expecting an answer right now but will leave the offer for you. If you wish, you can come as a Guest, and see how the new pack is running, before deciding if you want to join. If not, I have contacts in three other packs, and can get others, to see if those packs are a better fit." He was mentally kicking himself for not thinking to see if he had living relatives and have them there.

Ethan struggled to keep his expression neutral, but he had been so worried. His sister was getting close to maturity, and he knew one of the senior wolves was considering her. There wouldn't have been anything he could have done to protect her other than to take her and his mother and run. It wasn't something he had felt he could do since they had all been told the other packs would kill them. It left him in a hard spot. When he was kicked out of the pack it had almost destroyed him since he knew there wasn't going to be anyone to protect his sister. His fists were clenched in his lap as he worked to keep from breaking down.

Eventually he was able to look up, "I would like to at least visit then and see a few of my friends. I wish I could say I would jump to join the pack but..." He just didn't feel safe accepting without having ever seen what he might be getting into, "I would like to come up and visit and see what it is like when possible."

Alpha Calahan scratched his chin as he was thinking before lightly tugging on his goatee, "How do you want to get him to you? I am not sure how he made it here, probably as a wolf crossing the border. Do you want to have him brought to the border and met by some wolves? It would avoid the whole visa or passport problem. If it is what you would like to do it will take some time to arrange safe passage through the other pack territories. I will leave the details to Adam and Josh to work out if it is acceptable?"

Alpha Adam looked to Gareth, who nodded, "That probably would be for the best." Gareth told them, "We are Northeast of Cranbrook, right against the Alberta border. I have many contacts, so could secure safe passage from this side of the border. Adam and Josh could work out the specific routes and what packs to contact for the passage."

Alpha Calahan nodded, "That works, and we need to get to work. Thank you for helping us deal with this. Josh will keep me updated and we will take care of Ethan while we are organizing this."

Once the connection ended, a message popped up on the screen of "Saved" with the path for a minute, before it cleared to appear to be a large window, showing the view of a webcam on the outside wall which Adam had installed for that purpose. Tapping a few keys on the keyboard, he restricted the video to Alpha-only level. The details were sensitive enough they didn't want the pack knowing about it.

They spun to face the table, "Well, I think that went well." Adam commented.

Gareth let out a belly laugh, "Well? That went excellent! They were willing to deal with you as an Alpha, even as inexperienced as you are. It allowed us to just sit back and listen. It will be some work to arrange for the passage rights to get him here. The fact we have gotten rid of the Rogue designation and reassigned him Lone Wolf will help immeasurably. It will take two to four weeks for him to get it all arranged and for him to get here. Let me know if you have any issues."

Adam smiled, "I'm glad you're amused. I will pass on to Josh to have it passed on about the Spring Trials, as he should be here just as they start. I think it would be good for him to be involved. I think Josh had just as a hard of time not devolving into a tech-talk as I did. I am thinking about investigating them as a second hub site, as from what I have learned, the US has councils which the packs report to, instead of being independent. It both makes it harder, but also easier to set up the network." He had discussed it with the Elders, and partly the councils came from how the packs needed structure to hide better, with the much higher population, but the councils had also come from some wanting power over the packs, and a couple of Alphas who had wanted more power than a single pack used the idea of councils to get power over more than their own packs. Now, they were too entrenched into how the US packs ran, as there wasn't any way to challenge a council's right to control the packs in the area.

The councils hadn't gotten their claws into those which were in Canada, nor in Alaska, as there were too many packs and each were larger, and they refused to accept their dominance over them. In several cases, they had gone even to almost wars over it, and unlike the US Human governments, the councils couldn't try to suppress the history which wasn't to their taste, and learned to leave the packs alone, and didn't try again, and they tried to not antagonise the packs either. Elise had the opinion where if they did antagonize the packs, they could move against the councils and force them to give up their power over the packs and would support the packs to keep them independent instead of just staying neutral.

Gareth shook his head, "You're an Alpha now, you don't need my approval or permission to do anything. For the tech, as long as it doesn't impact this pack's own network, I don't want to hear about it; you go for it."

Adam turned to Elise, "Elder? Your take on Ethan?"

Elise looked thoughtful for a few minutes, "He looks hurt from what I remember of him. The fact his sister and mother are safe and happy meant a big deal to him, even though he tried to hide it, and I think it is his biggest draw to coming back. I think he's hopeful you are truthful, but still has been hurt badly enough by the old alpha, and how while that pack had different rules written from those which were used, he fully doesn't trust you and will sort of be expecting the same here as he was kicked out from."

"That's what I thought too," Brook commented. She had mostly just watched Ethan, ignoring the other pack. "He did perk up a little when he was reading the pack laws, especially since we built in laws that even the alphas can't get around to protect the vulnerable."

Turning to pull out a notepad, Gareth said "There a couple of things we need to discuss. First, I have had the treasurer separate the accounts and put them in your pack's name. You will need to pick a treasurer or two, so they can handle your money. Second, Wednesday they will be doing the sod turning for the new pack house. You will want as many as can make it to be there." He reminded.

"Give us Elders a vehicle ride, we can't run fast as wolves, anymore." Elise piped up. The start of a new pack house, at the start of a new pack wasn't something she would miss.

Adam nodded, "I think we'll need all the buses for the pups and the Elders, and the lowest, who don't feel up to a run. I think MacLaren Pack should be there too, for the fact without them it would not have been possible.

A grin spread across both older Alpha's faces, "Well done, you are learning well to think of others. With that, meeting adjourned! We have been sitting long enough." Gareth announced, heading for the door.

Chapter 3 – Lost Wolves

Adam and Brook chuckled as they headed back to their room, even though it was only mid-morning. "That went better than I thought it could. I like the sound of Ethan from the little we have chatted." Adam commented, moving to the computer, making sure the video log was linked to the report he was making on Ethan, which was attached to the digitized records. They had co-opted four of the pups who were digitizing the MacLaren records and were in Wild Valley now, since they were into the historical documents now, to do those from Shadowed River and Night Depths for those who were members and for those who were in other packs now first. Those for the wolves who had gone to other packs, a digital copy was going to be forwarded to their Alpha, and he could do what he wanted with it, with the paper copies destroyed a week later unless they wanted the original too, at which point they would send them with the next wolf-courier through. When they were done, they would have to physically review all the records, starting with those who had been declared Omega. Then it seemed, they were going to have to review those who were ejected as Rogue.

"I wonder how many others were dealt the same fate as Ethan. That pack seemed to have a fair amount of turnover on the members. Several have come to thank me for having good solid rules." Brook stated thoughtfully.

Adam glanced at her, "I have been wondering too." Pulling up his e-mail, he quickly composed a message to the other Alphas around both of the now dead packs – he was glad now he had digitized Alpha Gareth's rolodex of contacts into the e-mail address book – and as an after-thought added Alpha Calahan of Fossil Valley.

Alphas,

I know I am very green at being an Alpha, but it has come to my attention that the former Alpha of Night Depths, who I am the successor of, had kicked out and made Rogues of a wolf who just asked for details on their orders, and their superior took the question as a challenge of their position.

I will be looking through the records to see if there is any more. I will send you names, as we find them. So far, the one we know of, made his way all the way down to Fossil Valley Pack in Oregon. I have already had him re-designated a Lone wolf, and if he wishes, will accept him into the Wild Valley Pack in clear standing.

If any of you come across any who had been kicked out under similar conditions, please treat them as Lone Wolves, not as Rogues. If they would like to return to their friends and family, please let me or my mate know, and we will arrange for them to travel and cover all expenses.

If you have already dealt with any, and know their names, please pass them on to us with their fate, so we can complete the records, as we will try to find the fate of all the lost wolves and give closure to their friends and family.

Sincerely,

Alpha Adam

Wild Valley Pack

Adam could feel Brook leaning on the back of his chair, "What do you think?" he asked, wanting to know if he was missing anything.

"It's simple, to the point, humble but assertive. It's not putting blame anywhere on the other Alphas if they have already dealt with them as rogues. It'll do." She confirmed.

Before hitting send, he added in a CC for Alpha Gareth, since they were still in his pack, they didn't want him to be blindsided, as it was just asking for trouble. One thing he had checked for in the tech class, was how e-mail worked and how to send messages. The 'To' field was for who messages were addressed to, and typically would be the one responding. The 'CC' or Carbon Copy — the name was a hold-over from typewriter days, when a sheet of carbon was used between multiple sheets of paper, to make copies while typing — is used for sending someone a copy of the message, when they weren't actually addressed to, and no response is expected. 'Bcc' or Blind Carbon Copy is the same as CC, except all the recipients can see who was in the CC list, they couldn't see those in the Bcc, and even if they were, they would only see themselves, not anyone else. Sometimes, Bcc was used for sending to themselves, or to another so they know about the message while the recipient cannot see it. Another common use for Bcc, is to send out a mailing list, to respect the recipients' privacy, so all the recipients don't get everyone else's addresses.

They also covered how a 'reply-to' could be used to change where the responses would be delivered to. Also, what the differences between Reply, Reply All, Forward, and Forward as Attachment, and when to use each; Reply was to reply to the sender only, while Reply All would send a reply to everyone in the To field, and CC everyone in that list, which generally was not a good response, unless everyone needed to be told. Forward was to send the message on to someone it hadn't been sent to otherwise, and worked like reply, but left the To field blank. Forward as Attachment attached the message along with any headers, or any hidden details, and was best if they needed to send it to a tech to investigate an issue with the message. Another he made sure of was how to recall a message, and how some clients didn't respect it, and how rarely did it get rid of all those it was sent to. There was a whole day where they dealt with security, and what should and should not be sent over email, and especially what to not send over the unsecured Internet.

Turning to the other work, he emailed Josh, asking to arrange for a video chat the next afternoon for Ethan, so he can chat with his sister and mother; it was the least he could do to show he was much more compassionate than the old alpha. For his side, he set it up for them to be back before lunch from the Wild Valley Pack territory, so they would have all afternoon to chat. It had been several years since he had been kicked out.

Finishing up the documentation he had worked with Hank on, to set up another network connection, he forwarded them to the local packs, to see if they could set up more packs. He had included the 're-quired', 'recommended', and 'preferred' items. It didn't even go into anything for networking their pack in any way. As a note, from the fact he had learned Fossil Valley was basically the tech support for the sur-rounding packs, and thought it could be a possible revenue stream, he put a comment about possibly negotiating tech support or to set up their internal network or doing automated sensor networks on the ter-ritories.

Getting through his e-mail was easier, as most of his old addresses from his human life were fairly silent. He was happy about it, as it let him go on with his wolf-life. He was down to a single e-mail address which he monitored; all his others forwarded to that one. He was just starting to get e-mails from other packs now; mostly contacts he had made. Those came in on the new addresses he had.

Adam sent a pitch to Josh about linking the two networks with a major network tunnel, and included his long-term vision of a global WereNet, linking all Were together, and have a free flow of communica-tion. He had asked that since he had already got a network going for the local packs, if he was interested in being the second node site. Knowing he'd have to discuss it within the pack, he just left it there.

Finishing up from the five-day backlog of messages, his stomach growled.

Brook laughed, "I think your stomach is telling you it's lunchtime."

Looking at the time, it was almost lunchtime, "I guess you're right, lets go!" He said, locking his computer, before grabbing her hand and pulling her out the door. Charlie scampered to follow them.

Smiling they walked into the dining area, sharing smiles, nods, and the occasional hug with others in greetings. Adam did what had become normal for him, placing a bowl of food down for Charlie to eat, before filling his own plate with food.

Sitting down at their usual table, they got some ribbing and more hugs. They had barely seen their friends in the last week.

"So, are any of you going to transfer and join us?" Brook asked. She was curious if any of her close friends would join them.

Evan had an arm around his mate. "We are considering it, but right now, Kuri is still very much missing Ali." He said with a sigh, pulling her close. She in turn was mostly moving food around on her plate, not eating it. Everyone could smell her depression over the loss.

Brook reached out a hand across the table and gave Kuri's arm a squeeze, "If you need a cuddle, you can come find us." She told her friend. Kuri just nodded, not bothering to look up. Mostly she ate when her wolf took over and made her eat.

Erin and Aurora both shook their heads. "We talked about it," Erin said, speaking for both of them, "We need to stay here, as the tech-leads." Giving a half grin, "Who knows, I may get promoted." Erin joked, getting the laugh she was wanting.

"I hope you are working hard to qualify for it." Adam told her when the laugher subsided.

Erin nodded, "I have unofficially been confirmed at the trainer levels I need, and talked with Gareth, and Disciplinary Action is my only item left to do, but it can be done after I gain the rank."

Adam smiled, "Good for you!" he praised, feeling agreement from Brook, "You have our blessing. I will start moving the remaining tech management duties to you."

Shana looked down, "I just got my promotion this year." She looked up at Adam and Brook, "I had wanted to move with you, but there is nobody to fill my position."

Brook gave a side hug, as she was beside her, "We will put you on the list of wanting to come." She told her, writing a quick note in a notebook she kept with her now. "We will work with Rein to free you up. It may take a bit of time." Rein, she was sure, had others who could do the job, even if not fully qualified. Since they knew she wanted to move, Rein could even open it up to anyone in the pack, who might want to move to a totally different job.

Adam leaned forward a bit to see her around his mate, "Would you want a similar job of managing the warehouse?" It was a fairly public job, as they were the one who dealt with many humans. They were also the main person who tended to receive those who walked in, and needed to deal with the pack, as there wasn't enough to need a dedicated receptionist.

Shana nodded, "I'm enjoying myself. I would enjoy doing this for a while. Ask me in a few decades."

Most at their table laughed at her joke. Spending a century in one industry was nearly unheard of, as even with wolves, they got bored, so there was a fair amount of movement and changing jobs. It was one reason the packs covered the costs of training for all members in good standing, or even with the Alpha's approval to study full-time and take a break from working to learn something completely different. During the time they were learning, if needed, they would suspend any payments needing to go to the pack and help with any of the expenses they had. With almost all the pack having a good amount of savings, often nothing needed to be done beyond having the time to do the learning.

Moving onto other topics, they discussed the minor gossip which flowed within the pack. Martin pulled Adam and Brook aside as they left the hall at the end of lunch. Both had eaten lightly, as they were heading to do some running as humans. "I hear you are collecting a list of those you are accepting to your pack."

Brook smiled, "We are, but you are on the list of those who we can't have, sorry."

Martin shook his head, "Alpha Maria told me that. It wasn't for me, but for Rachel and her son Jake. She is basically not there when she works, she goes through the motions, but the only thing which gets her out of her funk was Jake, or one day I had her do something new." He sighed sadly, "Her and James were one of my best pairs. I think having her do the same job is bringing back memories. She has been doing a little better on areas where she had never patrolled before, but she is still not all there." He really didn't want to have to remove her as an issue, or do any sort of suspension, but with her being less than fully attentive, it made her not the best Enforcer.

Adam nodded as his wolf whined in sympathy for Rachel.

Martin looked at the clock, "She should be just about done her patrol and will be here soon for food." He told them, before walking out. It was their decision, he just brought it up to them.

Brook looked upset too, "I think a total change for her is needed." At Adam's agreeing nod, *Alpha,* She called Maria while sharing it with her mate, *I think we need to have Rachel, and her son transferred; Martin just came to us about the fact she is not doing well continuing in her current position. I think a total new pack, where there are others who can understand her pain and different duties would be best.*

They didn't have to wait more than a breath, *Give her the choice, don't make it for her. If she wants, I am free right now to do the transfer.* Came the reply, mostly approving of their idea.

Adam stepped out of the meeting room, and quickly returned. Rachel looked what he would call burned out; hunched shoulders and looking at the ground and shuffling a bit. Others as they went past could feel it and would move towards her to give a quick shoulder or back touch trying to comfort her. "We won't keep you from your lunch long. Martin let us know you are not doing well. He suggested a change of scenery and duties." She just numbly stared at her hands as she sat in one of the chairs, and gave a slight nod, to which Adam continued, "We would like to invite you to our pack, and get you some different duties, so you and Jake could heal."

She stared at him in surprise, before looking down again, "You want me? I'm just a broken wolf." She could understand inviting her Jake when he was older, as they seemed to have formed a bond, even though they refused to take guardianship of him, so she could join her mate. She didn't know why she survived, and he didn't. He had been right at her side, all the way to the end.

Adam pulled her out of the chair and into his lap. She started to pull away, but Adam wrapped his arms around her, "You are not a broken wolf. You are an injured one. You need to heal, and you can do it with support. I know of several wolves who have had similar losses in the pack. Some need to get back to their old routine to heal, but you are not doing well. You want a change?"

She started crying silently on his shoulder, realised they had somewhat guessed her issue, "Every patrol I do, it brings back memories of my James doing patrols with me. I had hoped they would stop after a bit, but they are getting worse." After a bit, she quietly commented, "Yes I want something new." She said, so quietly they nearly missed it, even with their wolf-hearing.

Brook rubbed her back, "Did you want to do it right now? Maria is available if you wanted."

She nodded, against his chest, "Yes."

Moments later, Brook opened the door at a knock, and Jake and Alpha Maria walked in.

Brook knelt in front of Jake, "We are going to transfer you and your mother to our pack, do you have any questions?"

Jake looked excited, as his mother tried to look neutral, and not look like she had cried. "Does it mean we get to move?"

Adam laughed, "Well, we are still building the pack house, so eventually, yes, we will move. Just not right away."

Jake smiled, "I like that!"

Adam stood and put his hands on Rachel's shoulders, as Maria moved to put one on his and Rachel held Jake's hand, "Rachel, do you wish to transfer your allegiance, and that of your pup, Jake, to the Wild Valley Pack?"

"I do" Rachel stated clearly.

"Do you affirm your pack oath and be there to teach your pup it, and what it means?" Adam asked, adjusting it for the fact Jake couldn't give an oath yet himself.

"I do"

Adam smiled, "Then I welcome both of you to the Wild Valley Pack." He said warmly, before touching his forehead to Rachel, then when he felt the bond, to Jake.

As they stood there blinking, a slight relieved smile on Rachel's face, "The bonds to MacLaren will fade over the next few days, but as we are still linked, you will still have a slight bond, as if you are outside the pack territory. It will stay as long as we are linked to them." Adam informed them.

Leading them out, "I'm hungry!" Jake declared, making all three Alphas laugh.

"Thanks." Whispered Brook to Maria, as Adam led the two to a couple of wolves who had also come late to the lunch.

"This is Piers and Eleonora. Piers and Eleonora, this is Rachel and her pup Jake. They have just been transferred into our pack. You three have something in common; Rachel recently lost her mate in the fight with the Nameless Pack." The other two both gave a sharp intake of breath, and their expression changed from polite interest to concern and even a little bit of pain, as they wrapped both in hugs, and made room for them to sit. Another at the table quietly left and got them plates of food.

*You are off duty this afternoon, Rachel, and I am going to have you help care for the pups for the next few months, so you and Jake can be together, and you can do something different. Right now, the pups seem to be staying up in the loft. Feel free to have them mingle with the MacLaren *ones. I want lifelong bonds between the two packs** Adam told Rachel, as he headed off. Having a wolf who was trained and ranked as an Enforcer moving to help the pups was something which brought all the parents an extra sense of reassurance, as they had someone who knew how to fight being an extra layer of protection.

Yes, Alpha. Thank you. Was her response before starting to get to know her two new friends. She could already feel they could understand her pain in a way nobody else could.

Adam smiled and nodded in thanks as he headed out. Brook was waiting in their room, as she changed to some clothes for a run. Adam stripped and changed into the blue turtleneck leotard and black leggings with matching blue accents she had picked out for him; it would be warm enough while they were running. She was wearing a matching outfit. "I introduced her to a couple who had lost their mates too. I hope having others with similar story will help her heal."

Brook pulled him over for a heated kiss, "That is one reason why I love you, my Alpha Mate. You care about all those who look to you." Pushing him towards the door, "Now we need to get going before I get bothered enough to not want to start."

Grabbing the stopwatch and water bottles as they headed out, he started it as they hit the start line for the 50 km trail. "Three hours?" Adam asked as they jogged it. It was the pace which Deltas had to run it. Their four pups, Lea, and Sam joined them. All six of their pups groaned, knowing it would push them, but knew they could do it. After seeing the clothes Brook and Adam wore, all had asked for stuff similar. Adam grinned, as all were wearing leggings and tight shirt; he couldn't tell if it was a leotard or not, but he suspected it was, as both Robin and Toby had asked for them specifically. For a joke, he had got Sam, Toby, Lea, and Robin matching outfits, as Brook seemed to have gotten a second copy of her outfits, so they could match. After the first time wearing it, they had agreed it was very comfy. He wondered if he was setting a fashion trend for the pack.

"Yes, it would be a good training pace. *We* must do it in *two* for the trials." Brook told them, reminding how much faster they had to be.

*****

Relaxing in the hot pool in the greenhouse with the others after they made it back, Jess and Joshua were nearly asleep as they rested in the shallow end, exhausted with maintaining the pace, but he was proud they had done so. The other four were chatting excitedly. They had kept up on the run and were only a little bit tired; they could have gone faster.

Adam watched them and speculated some thoughts.

Not till they are of age can we do anything, let them be pups, and don't put too much more responsibility on them. Brook chastised her mate. *Let them be happy pups till then.*

I guess you're right. It's not like we need a Next Alpha yet. Adam sighed the thought. He had learned there was that role, of the best to lead the pack, as basically the Heir. Right now, MacLaren didn't officially have one, but Gareth and Maria's twin pups were set to come home soon. They had been in training for the last two years at The Academy, a special training program, which was more of a boot camp. Since they had a pack now, and were bonded to it, he didn't think they would be able to apply to get the training, as they couldn't leave for two years.

Munching on some appetizers, to last them the bit over an hour before supper, they chatted with the others who were there as well. Several of the off-duty people from his pack had come to relax if not in the pool, on the green grass which was around the pools and around the part of the greenhouse which was used as a relaxing area.

Many had heard about the weekly bonfire and asked some questions. Some were skeptical about the "rank-less" part but finding out it was mostly so all are welcome, and none needing to defer to another, they relaxed to enjoy it. Several asked about instruments, and Adam told them they could bring them, slightly gleeful about the music.

Heading in at supper time, seeing Rachel head in as well, Adam went over and wrapped an arm around her, "How are you doing?" he asked. Ignoring the momentary stiffening, before she relaxed into his embrace.

"I'm doing OK, Alpha." She said respectfully, and he could feel her slightly better over the bonds, "Thank you for introducing me to Piers and Eleonora. It is nice to know others who I can relate to."

Adam smiled, *Here one thing I don't want passed around; my father died just before I was ten, so I can relate to Jake quite well. If he needs someone, have him come to me. As long as I am not doing something which I can't be disturbed, I will be there for him.*

She was shocked at the admission, "I won't tell anyone." She promised.

Adam shook his head, "It's not needed to be kept secret from the pack, just not something which I care to discuss much, as it's been so long ago. Jake already knows and have told him something similar. If *you* need someone to cuddle with, as with the entire pack, my door is open as much as possible to all in the pack." He smiled, "Actually, any in either pack."

Rachel nodded, "I'll remember that." She said, before heading to a seat between her new friends.

Grabbing his food and making sure Charlie had some too, he sat down at the table. He had pulled on some warm leggings over a leotard and had a jacket. It was not quite spring during the day but was still winter at night.

Some of the wolves in his new pack had looked surprised when he wore Brook's clothes, but the looks were all he got, and it was just amusing. Most had stopped being surprised and were getting used to it. He didn't plan on changing or stopping anytime soon.

*****

Heading out after dinner, for the first time, he was in time to help set the fire up, "I expect many of my pack will be coming, so set the full size up." He advised the Theta who were working at it, before heading to the wood pile under its lean-to to help bring another armful of wood.

A couple tried to tell him it was beneath him, but they submitted at just a look. "I should never have a job I ask another to do, when I'm not willing to do it myself, nor is any job beneath me, even washing a toilet or floor. I will make sure all senior wolves in Wild Valley do that. If I don't know what the job entails, I have no way to know who to assign there, or who would not be good."

The Theta wolves mulled it over, as Brook joined them, and started to set up the kindling, and small bits to start the fire. Jess tossed her a box of matches to light it and started working on the smaller pieces under the larger logs. All MacLaren wolves knew how to set a fire up, as they might be stranded in the wilderness, and need to shift to human. It was a skill which all were expected to master. The pups started to be taught in a class as they entered their second decade, while some parents started the education even earlier. By the time a pup turned eleven, they were expected to have mastered the skill to make a fire from nothing but the forest around them, and to have cooked some meat. The last few decades, they had done a hot dog, steak, or for those who wanted extra credit, a rabbit they caught.

As they lit the fire and started spreading it out to light the rest of the pit, the others started coming. As each came, Adam and Brook gave each a hug or a touch of some sort. Adam smiled and enjoyed the touching; he really was getting used to it, as a human he seemed to always crave it, more than most of those around him. Here, he felt much more comfortable, and enjoyed getting and giving attention.

Adam smiled as Alphas Gareth and Maria came, which was rare. He gave both a good hug, but no more than he gave to the others, as was the spirit of the fire. Someone, he wasn't sure of, started singing quietly, but as voices added their music to it, it grew in volume. Adam grabbed a mug of apple cider to keep his fingers warm and moved to sit with a couple of wolves he could sense were feeling a little down.

Wrapping his free arm around one, as the other leaned in against him, sharing the comfort of knowing their Alpha cared for them. Adam smiled as both stopped feeling stressed and started to relax. Others, seeing him give comfort to a couple who needed it—something their old Alpha thought was beneath him—were comforted as well. *I'm glad they are starting to trust we are doing what we said we were doing, and they seem to be starting to heal from the abuse.* He commented to Brook, while both knew it would take years, if not decades for all the wounds to their mind and spirits to heal, they could get the healing started.

She smiled and nodded across the fire, before going back to the chat with Kelsey and one of her friends. Both had changed and were feeling much more comfortable around others. They had learned the outfit they had been wearing had been at the orders of the old Alpha, and they hadn't worn it willingly. They had requested and been provided with new clothes, as they had none which they were willing to wear now.

Chapter 4 – First Elder Meeting

The next morning, Adam and Brook rolled out of bed, "I'm surprised for once we didn't have someone curled up with us." Adam commented, as they headed into the shower, knowing they had the meeting with their elders this morning.

"I think the fire last night relaxed many of them, as we both had many come to us for personal attention over it." Brook replied. She too had been feeling the lack of 'alone' time for them. She hoped once the pack relaxed more, and they got more used to them, and the new pack, they would have more time for themselves, even if the pack came first.

Heading into the Alpha's boardroom after breakfast for the first official meeting with their elders, as it was the most secure, Adam and Brook nodded greetings as the elders came in. All looked much older from stress and neglect. Several were using canes, others the arm of another wolf, who left after helping them to a seat. All six of them were moving slowly. To Adam, they looked like they were about ninety if they were human, while the MacLaren Elders appeared seventy for the oldest.

When the last one was seated and the door closed, Adam sat up at one side with Brook, while the elders sat on the other side, "Thank you for all coming. I am planning on scheduling this meeting for weekly, to make sure we all have the same information." Looking at the room he saw looks which ranged from startled to pleased. "We will consult with you when possible on major issues, but we will not allow you to dictate the decision. Brook and I are equal and either of us can be doing the deciding, and when needed, will work together to decide."

They were all smiles, "I think I speak for all of us, and can live with that." Elise commented, getting murmurs of confirmation from the others. "It is much better than the last three Alphas, who had refused to even listen to us, on the occasions which we decided to speak up." For her, several times she had been growled at, and the last time threatened with being challenged, even if it was against the Pack Laws.

It lessened the stress for all there; Adam was worried they would want more say than just advising, as seemed to be the case in Arctic Shadow. The Elders were worried about being told they needed to shut up, as the last Alpha had told them, and since he was Alpha, he would make the decisions.

"I know we are not much more than wet-behind-the-ears pups compared to you. You are a wealth of wisdom and experience, and we would be fools to not use it." Adam told them, "I love the saying, 'Those who don't learn from history are doomed to repeat it.' As I have seen it happen, where someone ignores the past and just thinks 'It can't happen to me' and when it does, they are very surprised. I want the pack to succeed, and flourish like MacLaren has."

The elders smiled, and Elise seemed to be their spokesperson, as she again replied, "It is a good way to work. Have you been reading pack histories?"

"We both have." Brook replied showing Adam wasn't going to be the only leader, "I have to say the restricted Alpha records are much more informative and detailed. Especially the reasoning behind some of the laws, and what happened before the law was made."

Taking a breath, "We are here to share some executive secrets. They are to not be spoken of to others, unless it is absolutely necessary. Several of them are of a personal nature, and don't see a need for the pack in general to know." Getting nods from the elders, he hoped they knew how to be discrete. He would need to just trust them, as they had decided to not make it an Alpha Order. For one thing, it would let them see how discrete and trustworthy the Elder actually were.

"The first thing is my wolf has some memories from a previous incarnation, as the previous Alpha of MacLaren Pack, and Alpha Gareth's grandfather, Ralph. He died about seventy years ago." There were several exclamations of surprise. A couple talked about another case, which strangely enough was also the last time a wolf had taken the Alpha at a young age, although it had also been kept a pack secret till long after his death with his mate, as the pack's eldest. The secret was kept to the Alphas and the Elders but had been spread to other packs as well. Adam and Brook just listened, not bothering to interrupt, as it was informative.

"It makes some sense, from your bonds with this pack, and with the ease the other Alphas have around you, when they usually would have their back up; they know you aren't going to challenge them for their position." Elise said, slowly as she thought it out. "How much does he know?" She asked, meaning his wolf.

"Not too much he shares with me," Adam answered truthfully, "When he does, it is for the issue at hand and usually is something which resolves an issue, or the comment gives me the information to work it out. I'm not going to push to have him share everything but trust he will continue to help me learn and grow as an alpha. I do know he has helped me gain the physical skills to perform."

"My wolf also seems at times to have an extra insight but hasn't ever told me she remembers more." Brook added with a shrug, "I just make sure I listen to her, and consider her thoughts, even if I don't follow them."

After giving a bit to see if they wanted to say anything else before continuing, "Second, not sure if anyone passed it on, but I was born human, and lived in the city east of here, on the edge of the foothills. I shifted for the first time at the Solstice." That surprised many, but several seemed to have known he had been turned, if not how short of time it had been. "I know I had felt the fact I was missing something, and it clicked when I met Brook." They all knew how if the soul was a Were, but was born human, they would feel something was missing, until they were turned.

"Next, my sister has turned out to have a Mate in the Longview pack, just east of here." There were some calls of congratulations, as there was less issue with their human family; even humans mated and not turned, they live much longer lives.

"My father died before I turned ten—" He had to stop while the elders howled in sympathy. He bowed his head in thanks, "My mother is still alive, and is retired. Not sure, but I suspect she will either move in with my sister, or once we have the pack house made, may move in with us. It is her choice, and I am trying to stay out of it. She and Brook's parents are arranging a wedding this summer, a bit outside the northern border of this pack. That is common knowledge in MacLaren and is one thing you can spread. Right after it, Gareth has scheduled and is hosting an Alpha Conference, and we are formally signing onto the Inter-Pack Treaty during it, which for us will have it considered ratified." Many knew of the conference and nodded. The treaty would give them a measure of security and protection. It had also been passed out they already had three packs who had written they had accepted them as part of the treaty even without the signing, giving them initial protections.

"Questions?" Adam asked. He was going to be as open as possible with them.

There were a few clarifications, especially since his two helpers called them 'Dad' and 'Mom' and weren't too sure about them. They explained what happened with Jess and Joshua, and there was a quiet howl on their behalf. Another when he told them about Toby and Robin. There were some laughs about the two girls and how they came to be in his care, although he kept it to himself they might be Mates, as he wanted them to still be pups until they came of age. From the sly smiles on some of the elder's faces, they guessed it anyways.

A few others asked him about Adam's background, and he shared some things of his life growing up. A few things he decided to not share. He did share more about what happened to have him advance so quickly. Once he was done, Brook shared parts of her life as well. Both felt it best to be honest and open with their elders, hoping it would be reciprocated, and would work out well.

The meeting went long enough they took a working lunch, as there were quite a few questions on how he wanted the pack organised and run. They also looked at those who were wanting to transfer packs. To lower his workload on decisions, those who Gareth approved to transfer, he was going to have the Elders read over and give a suggestion. Some he was going to approve, but others he didn't know well, were going to get an interview with one or more of the Elders before being forwarded to him with an evaluation. For the most part, this was mostly a formality, as long as they didn't have a history of severe punishments.

Eventually it was time for the Video conference, and they closed the meeting. "We will be wrapping up before lunch in the future, unless it is critical we have the item dealt with." Brook told them firmly, "I dislike having working meals when I can avoid them." The elders nodded, as they packed their notes up as the meeting ended.

Adam and Brook smiled as the Elders left the conference room as they held the door for them. Gareth had commented Adam and Brook had been using it more than he ever had, as he usually had meetings in his office. Not having a dedicated office, they were using it for the sensitive meetings.

Pulling up the video conference settings, he called Fossil Valley's contact, hoping Josh was also a little early, as they had a few minutes before Sarabeth, who he found went by Sara now, and Rene came in. He hoped to talk some tech.

*****

Josh had decided to use his office again since it had one of the secure video chat stations. He was sitting at the smart table along with Molly, Maxon, and Adam. They were reviewing the plans to find the pack of rogues. He was sure it wasn't the one they had taken out since he had talked to Ethan. They had all been wolves and no other Weres. When the call request came in, he blanked the screens other than the one for the pack territory.

All packs Josh knew of kept a map of their territory in plain view. It didn't show details such as patrols or sensors, but it let others know what they claimed. He wasn't worried about Adam or Gareth's pack deciding they needed more. It was a simple statement of what they called theirs. He almost had to smile since the government didn't know the country actually had several sets of claims on territory. There was the human claim, Were claims, and some of the other supernatural such as witches and elementals. As with many animals, they shared the lands, and didn't try to exclude everyone and everything else, unlike humans who got upset when predators didn't 'respect' their fence, and entered 'their property', even if the predators had been there for longer than the human farm or ranch.

He finally answered the request and nodded at Adam, "Morning Adam, do you mind if I just call you Adam? Just call me Josh. As you know this is my Beta Adam and senior enforcer Maxon. The she-wolf is Molly and helping with a current issue, so she is working with my team. Ethan will be here shortly." He took a sip of his coffee before speaking again, "I assume you expected this, but I have assigned Ethan to the Enforcer team for the moment to get him as ready as possible for your spring trials. He has a way to go since he has been alone for a while. That and he was under nourished though not badly. Do you have any questions for me before I call him in?"

Molly glanced up when the screen came on and even over the video could sense the other's dominance. She met his eyes before lowering them slightly. She returned to what she had been doing since it couldn't be seen from the screen.

*****

Adam smiled, "Afternoon; it's almost 1 PM here. Time zones are almost like time travel," He was always amused when time zones were involved. At least it was only he was an hour ahead of them. "I have no problems, as I prefer informal as much as possible. With your rogue problem, my proposal for the network linking is on hold?" He also would have just put off a tech change while his pack's safety was at risk. "Let me know if you need any assistance with that. We have a number of highly skilled enforcers who I could loan you."

He knew Gareth would have no issues with offering some assistance to another pack to deal with a Rogue issue. Usually they sent single wolves, so they could see if they could find a Mate. Gareth had commented when he asked, usually the larger pack released the wolf to join the smaller one, as they could more easily cover the loss, and also created bonds between the two packs. From the grim look, he was sure it was a major problem for them.

"Before we bring them in, now that you have had a chance to see Ethan working with your enforcers, how is he?" Adam and Brook were hoping he would be able to integrate well, or if his time alone would cause problems.

"Did he need any medical care? If needed, we can cover the costs." Brook asked, as both knew the costs for medical care and even basic supplies was very high. They didn't know the financial state of Josh's pack, so would politely offer.

*****

Josh grinned slightly when Adam mentioned the time there, "Time zones give me a headache not to mention the bloody time change twice a year. I wish they would do away with it and call it good. I swear half the time even with all the prep I have at least five computers which ignore it. Such a pain in the ass." When Adam asked about the e-mail about the tech questions, he became more serious, "I have started to talk with Andrew about it. In this case before we can do anything we will need to talk to our council of elders. If it was just between your pack and mine, it would be one thing but for a wider reaching network..." He made a slight face, "Politics is a pain in the ass at times. I will get back with you about that."

Adam laughed, "I just use a common synchronized time source, and with a modern Windows, don't need to worry about it, as long as the time zone is correct. I too think Daylight Savings is a pain." He nodded about the political issues, "Feel free to have them pass it on, along with the documentation I sent, as I would eventually like to have it global, and have a better flow of communication between all Were."

"As far as the rogue problem we are still looking into it, and I am not sure what the thoughts would be on importing outside help. There are several packs or prides nearby who we have talked to. I will send you updated information when I can." Rogues were everyone's problems and didn't respect minor things like national boundaries.

Josh glanced at Maxon, "Maxon will give you that information since he is in charge of him." He nodded to Maxon and let him start speaking about how Ethan was working.

Maxon entered a few commands on the virtual keyboard on the table and the screen behind him turned on. He called up the current progress notes and shared the documents, "Okay, this chart is specifically designed to show how he is doing based on your criteria. As of now he is at..." He discussed the fitness level, weapons skills, and a number of other factors, "I am being bluntly honest, he is not going to do well but I have a feeling it is due to his time outside a pack. Currently his dominance isn't very high and if he was a member of our pack, he would be a home guard. Don't take it in a derogatory way since guarding the elders, women, and pups is very important. It is simply where he is at currently."

He glanced at Josh who glanced at Molly when she indicated she wished to speak, "Molly wishes to speak to you about Ethan as well." He knew she had spent some time with him since he had been at the table Ashleigh and Kylie were at.

Molly met Adam's eyes again before lowering them slightly, "Alpha, I have spent time with Ethan since he tends to eat at a table with some of the junior wolves. He has been very respectful of them and has started to open up some. He won't talk about what he has been through in the last few years which they understand. We have a young woman who is in sort of the same position. He has talked to her and her potential mate some. He has even helped watch the woman's child and they appear to trust him as long as he isn't too far away. It isn't they don't trust him, but the human has had a bad experience with wolves. For her to trust him even some shows he is a good person." She glanced at Josh.

Josh finished, "As I am sure you know being at the ranks we are, in many cases we have to delegate. Maxon and Molly are trusted team members of mine, and I asked them to keep an eye on him. Maxon from the aspect of his being a pack member and Molly as to who he is. I have talked to him some as well and so has my mother, the Luna. She feels whatever pack he might end up in he will do well as long as he is treated with respect. There are going to be long term issues he is going to have but I have a feeling you understand that since you took over his previous pack." He finished and waited for Adam to speak.

Adam smiled, "That is better than I thought, I hadn't expected his skills to even be that high. I have found mothers have an innate sense of who is dangerous, and if he is being trusted with a child, he will do well. I have been watching many of the others of the pack and have gotten reports which are similar from them. It seems even they had been lacking good training and food for some time, so many will not meet the qualifications for their current ranks." He had to smother a growl, and Brook wasn't able to in time, "I do know their pack house had not had any significant maintenance in the last decade outside of the Alpha's area and the areas which his lackeys lived in. In the lower ranks, they didn't even have running water in most of the bathrooms. Our loft barracks, they thought was our Delta area, where it is used mainly for Omegas—and overflow for Thetas, or when we have a major influx of guests to house."

Adam sighed sadly, "I have to say most of my pack is healing from some sort of mental issue. I have several who have survived their mate dying even and have helped them set up a support group for each other, and even took in one and their pup from MacLaren who needed a change. I am hoping getting most of them working on the pack house to get it done as soon as we can, will help. I want to get the exterior completed before the snows in September, so we can work on it over the winter, to have it habitable as soon as we can."

Josh had to laugh, "Ashleigh was making jokes about the table she eats at having a game of pass the baby. Each day a different person holds Charles while Ashleigh eats. She was somewhat thin when she arrived. She has started filling in and one of our junior wolves is helping take care of her and the baby. Kylie has had some good things to say about Ethan as well. Not as a mate in case you wondered, simply as a good junior wolf."

He listened as did the others on his side. The four of them returned the slight growl at the idea of an Alpha treating a pack with such disrespect. When Adam spoke about the conditions Molly snarled, "Even our Thetas have better conditions than that. The rooms might be plain and shared bathrooms, but the barracks are good and solid." When she realized she had met Brook's eyes she suddenly lowered them, "Sorry Luna."

Brook nodded in acceptance, "He will get to contemplate his treatment of his pack for a very long time, as we have been told the ones from his pack found a deep dry crack to drop his body into. It is also at the alpine level, and they left him in a thick body bag, so will take decades to get down to bones, and centuries at least till the bones do anything, if ever." Her voice had a bit of a vindictive satisfaction tone at the end, but it wasn't unwarranted. "If he wasn't dead, he would have had several days of torture with silver before being allowed to die for his treatment, once it was all found, as was the wish of his pack."

Beta Adam spoke, "We are sorry to hear that, and we will howl to the Goddess for you." He met their eyes and lowered them slightly. Thankfully, the table was covered with a very tough plastic to keep them from damaging it. It wasn't werewolf-proof, but it was extremely durable. They often had to change it every year or so from the claw marks.

Josh cleared his throat, "If you need any tech, you might check out a Silver Fox Industries in Portland Oregon. They are Fox shifters, and we use them quite often for the sensitive electronics." Josh was sure Adam would understand what he was saying. Their sensors were custom made or heavily modified as needed.

Adam nearly fell out of his seat as he laughed, "We already deal with their Canadian arm, Silver Orca Sensors. They use many humans up here but know what we are. We even accepted two into the pack. One came with us to the new pack, and is wanting to be turned, just circumstances have been delaying it from happening."

Hearing a knock on their side, Brook opened the door for the two, and motioned them in. Adam had them sit in front of the screen, "This is Sara and their mother, Rene." He introduced as he moved to the side, letting them speak, without him interrupting. He had hoped they could let the three have a private chat.

"Thank you, thank you, thank you, for saving my son." Rene gushed, not even waiting to be introduced. "I had given him up as dead, and to find out you saved him from death as a rogue, thank you."

"Good afternoon to you Sara and Rene." Josh greeted, waving off their thanks, "No thanks are needed since I was simply doing my job as was my team. Ethan will be here in a moment. I will be in the room since this is my office, but my team will leave you as much privacy as possible." The others who could be seen walked out and the other screen was blanked out. As they were leaving Ethan walked into the room.

Josh waved him towards the video camera and walked out of screen to his desk and settled down to do some work. At this point it was for those involved to talk and say whatever they wished.

"Mom! Sara! So good to see you!" Ethan said as he sat down on the edge of the chair, "How are you doing?" Tears were falling down his face unheeded.

Tears were falling down both his mother's and his sister's faces as well. "We are doing much better now our old Alpha is dead." They refused to give him the honour of saying his name, as did most of the pack. That none lived who knew his given name, or none who would say they knew it, just what he demanded to be called was almost a blessing, as one form of death was everyone forgetting about them. They were already halfway there. "Alphas Adam and Brook care for us, and make sure we get good, filling food, hot showers, and warm, comfortable beds to sleep on, even if it is a barracks style room until the pack house is built."

Rene turned to Adam and Brook who were working on a laptop in the corner of the room, trying to give them as much privacy as possible. Nobody would come into the room while they were there. "When can you get him here?"

Adam nodded, "We are working to get him here soon. We are trying to do two weeks from today for arrival."

Rene nodded and turned back to talk with her son. She shared some gossip and answered his questions on who was still around and who wasn't there.

Ethen smiled wanly, "All those I dreaded meeting again are no longer around. But also, neither is my best friend."

Ethan still didn't say too much about what he did in the time since he was exiled. He didn't want witnesses other than his mother and sister when he said what he had to do to survive.

Eventually they finished, and knowing they had ways to talk, and the fact they were going to see each other soon, finished up the call.

Adam moved over to the controls, as Brook took the two over to their room, so they could have a safe place to relax. "How are the plans going at your side?" He asked Josh after the door was closed, "There is a pack where their territory actually goes over the human border, at Colville Forest, so there are no issues there. Once over the border, they are going to just drive him to us, about four hours on the highway. As it is major highways all the way until they reach us, our laws allow for free movement on them." Gareth had to deal with that pack, as they had refused to deal with them.

When Adam started talking, Josh moved back to the table, "So far it is looking doable. I will contact the pack in question and arrange for safe travel. I will have him up there in two weeks assuming all goes as expected. I might not be there depending on how my next job goes." Ethan didn't need to know about the other pack of rogues.

Molly had come to escort Ethan out of the room as he continued, "Dad is reviewing your questions about the network. I have tentative permission for a link between your company and ours but that is it. It has been forwarded to our council for review as well. I will tell you more when I can. Time for lunch and then I am going to be gone for a while. If you have any questions, call and talk to my father."

Adam was a little startled at the ending and stared at the blank screen saying *No Connection* for a minute, before it switched to *Saved* then back to being a virtual window, until he realised they had talked over what would have been their lunch break.

A hungry wolf is a grouchy wolf, Wolf-Adam mentioned, making his human half laugh out loud as he headed off to his room to meet up with his mate and the two for a quick debrief.

Looking at the clock, he realised the video conference had used almost two hours, although he wasn't too surprised. Heading into the room, he sat down with the others and took the last mug of tea—no small teacups for them—and just listened, as Brook helped them understand what they had to do to get Ethan back here.

As they were about to head out, "That conference was recorded," Adam told them, "There was an admin chat before and after, so I'll extract the part for you and send an e-mail of where to find it." They were quite happy with that. They were running back up to the new pack house area, so they could be ready for the ceremonial sod turning in the morning.

Once the door clicked closed after they left, Adam looked at his mate, "Werefoxes? Witches? Elementals? Why didn't you tell me about them?" He said in mock-anger but tried to hide the amusement from his face.

"It never came up in a conversation before. You never commented about the name of the company supplying the sensors." Was her mild response. "With all your training and duties, I guess you never got through the last two chapters of the basic training."

Adam looked sheepish, "Yea, never got to those two. I kept hoping things would calm down so I could. There was way too much on my mind to investigate it, beyond the fact they were trusted to know about us."

She laughed, "Well after the sod turning for our pack house, we should start turning Chris, as it will make us take a break while he goes through the first part of the turn. That should give you time."

Adam sighed, "OK. But tell me the overview."

"There are other kinds of Weres, they are all predators. Foxes are the next most common after Wolves, but there is Cougar, Leopard, Snow Leopard, Lynx, at least two kinds of tigers, and others. About half the Orcas are now Were, as the regular ones are hit harder by the pollution, as they lack our immune systems. There are some other dolphins which are Were as well. There is starting to be less separation between the species, and some hybrids are forming. If you thought humans had issues with skin colours, it was us between the types of Weres a few hundred years ago. It has been others are tolerated but kept separate."

Adam nodded, "What's your feelings about accepting other Weres into the pack?" He had not raised with intolerant views, but he had found there were still a few prejudices in his life as a human which he had to work to stop.

Brook shrugged, "I'd have no issues. Many of the cats though are loners, and don't really form groups. The Tigers do, but as they have different ways, most are not comfortable in a Wolf Pack, nor are wolves usually comfortable in their prides. If one wanted to join us, they would be good for the harder patrols, where they could spend most of the time alone."

"Elementals?" Adam asked; they had got a bit side tracked.

"Elementals have control over heat or fire, water, air, or earth, mostly using mental abilities. Witches use spells and specially prepared ingredients and symbols to do similar things. An Elemental can use some

witch's spells to enhance their abilities or for those who lack control or discipline, to use them as a cheat to learn the control on their own."
*****

The next morning, the two of them led those who were running to the Sod Turning, as the bus loaded up with mostly Thetas and Elders who wanted to be there. This was mostly ceremonial, but for many, it was the first chance to get out to see where they would be living. Everyone in the Wild Valley Pack was going to be there. Hopping up on a rock, he gave a short howl, *We will be setting a brisk pace. There will be a ten-minute break every hour or so at a creek. Try to keep up.*

With that Adam dashed off. There were enough Betas and Deltas to secure for the Thetas who had decided to run, along with some fast pups, like the four—Not counting Jess and Joshua, as they were no longer pups—he had in his care. Jess and Joshua were helping at the site and had gone up the night before with Sara and Rene.

Chapter 5 – First Shovels of Dirt

Arriving at the site for the pack house, a few of the wolves sprawled flat out on the ground and panted. Several of those who had been there already put bowls of water near their noses.

Adam and Brook padded around the site, seeing all the snow had been cleared, and the ground warmed up by covering it in thick covers to gather the solar heat. Even though it was technically spring, up at this latitude and altitude, it was basically winter still. There were heavy heaters to thaw the ground enough they could start digging the foundations with the heavy equipment which had been brought in, some was on loan from the packs around them.

Turning human, they grabbed their clothes out of their packs. Adam was giddy at getting to try out his new camera. The fact he had almost no expenses and had been paid much more than he made before taxes as a human, meant he had the money and had pre-ordered the new Nikon cameras which had just come out. This was going to be its first real outing, as it had arrived only a couple weeks before.

Both cameras were professional-level, with one using a so-called Crop sensor, the D500, and the other being a full-frame, the D5. Both were the flagship cameras for their kind. Along with the cameras, he had also got the professional lenses he had always wanted. The mount-accessories and professional level tripod he had ordered had arrived about the same time. Other than testing it out around the pack house, he hadn't had time to try it out. He had also got the vertical grip for the D500, as he had got used to having it on his other camera. The test shots had him almost dancing, from how well they had turned out. Once the pack house was built, he planned on getting more gear, including lower-level cameras for those who were just wanting to play around with it, so they were less worried about how much the gear cost if they broke it. He had winced a little at the price for the new memory cards, and the need to get separate card readers for them, but since they were a new specification, it was understandable. He had already felt they were worth the money, from the speed they had.

He had passed his older camera with a couple of lenses which were now low spec of what he now had to Jess, as he had been giving her tips, and she had been borrowing it lots. She seemed to be really enjoying learning and playing with the camera. It being digital, there was no cost to taking lots of photos, just the need for storage space for the images. As he knew others had their own cameras, so he had set up a public picture system, which allowed everyone to share all the pictures they took within the pack.

Adam set the camera up on a tripod, with the lens, and had tasked Jess with running it. With the arrival of the last of their pack, Brook howled loudly, calling everyone over. Others around them picked up the call and amplified it around them. Quite a few were still in wolf shape and didn't seem to want to shift back; they were given front-row space, as their heads were much lower. The elders moved to the side, and had the only seats, out of respect, although they were starting to look better and even younger. Most no longer needed help walking from even a cane. A couple still used the elevator to go up, but all used the stairs to go down in the pack house.

Grabbing a couple shovels, he passed one to Brook. "This is the start of a brand-new pack. We are placing new roots and hopefully something which will outlast the youngest pups, and their pups." He called out to the gathered wolves. Digging in the shovel simultaneously, Adam and Brook took the first chunks of dirt out for their pack. He had come across a 'ceremonial' gold-plated shovel but saw no reason to spend several hundred dollars on one, just for a photo. He considered it a waste of money. The shovels would be used by the workers once they started the actual work. He was amused someone had put pawprint stickers on the blades and had drawn and done some carving on the handles, but as it didn't cost anything, felt it was worth it.

The pack howled loud, seeing this as the start of their new pack. There was one Elder who stood up and walked over. Brook handed the shovel to him, "For the Elders, I am pledging our lives, experience, and knowledge for this pack, to help it grow and prosper in the years to come." Before digging in and removing another chunk of the ground.

Once the howl had faded, Adam smiled and spread his arms, "Come help us start the hole for *our* pack house." He told the gathered pack, as those few who had been told about the surprise came forward with more shovels. As the last pack house, the little he could find in the records, had been started nearly a century ago, there was very little recorded on the ceremony other than they had one, so he had to make it up. He hadn't told the pack, but he liked the symbol of inviting the pack to help dig a bit, showing they were making it together, not just Brook and him making it for the pack. By having them involved, it would also work as a team building activity. Where to dig was marked out with stakes and rope, and a white spray paint on the ground.

Those in wolf shape had a ball and there was lots of dirt spraying; rarely could they just dig without a worry about leaving a hole, since as most canines, they enjoyed digging. Some posed for pictures of it while others, especially the few pups, just had great fun digging and Adam took shots of them from various angles.

He planned on printing out many of the photos, and then having the pack come up with funny captions for them and writing them on the papers. For the next few hours, many had fun with the digging, until all those in wolf form were tired out, with a couple having made some tunnels where they popped out somewhere else, and others just flung the dirt around, making a crater.

Then the large excavators started in... Adam was amused, and they too had wolf shapes drawn on them. As the pack had acquired them from a company which was shutting down, it was permitted. He took a few more shots as they started to really dig, and with only a few buckets worth, they had already done more than all the pack doing it by hand and paw.

*****

Adam flopped down on the couch when they made it back to their room, after dropping the pack, and not bothering pulling on any clothes, "I am so glad that part is over." He told Brook and Joshua.

"With so many paws, once it's dug, I can see it going up well." Brook said. Most of the pack had opted to stay at the pack house site and help with the construction. Most would be sleeping as wolves, as the nights were still cold, even if they had tents to keep them out of the rain, snow, and wind. "I'm glad we had an early spring, so we could get a start on it."

"As am I." Adam agreed, "I am very happy to be able to put our wolves to work helping them. Several had commented if they can get enough skills, they might consider working for a construction company." They had decided those who didn't want to work for the pack would be permitted, although ten percent would be due to the pack, and would have to pay for their room, food, and small portion of the utilities if they lived at the pack house. Many had been very interested in being permitted to find outside work, and although none had asked about also living outside the pack house yet, he wouldn't stop them from doing so, and would negotiate the pack's share with them, depending on what the specific conditions were. It just was easier for having the one large building than lots of small ones.

Jess had stayed out at the pack house site to document it with the cameras. She was also being his representative while out there. He wanted to see how they felt about a female in charge.

After cuddling for a bit, Adam went and checked his e-mail. Seeing a message from Josh, he quickly opened it. *Sorry for the abrupt disconnect, the call was running into lunch, and I am leaving shortly for the rogue hunt. I will contact you when I get back. By then we should have something on the network question even if it is just between your pack and ours.*

Adam laughed and clicked to reply to it. *As my wolf told me 'A hungry wolf was a grouchy wolf'. I totally understand. I hope you are having a good hunt, and that probably was distracting you too. I'm attaching the specs for the secure connection, and the security information.*

Opening the information Chris had sent him a few days before; he turned on the interface which would allow them to connect. Attaching the security information, and public certificates for it, he reviewed the e-mail, as Brook looked over his shoulder at it as well.

The wolfsbane is done. It has been broken down and rendered harmless. Gareth announced, happiness lacing the thought.

That's great! One less thing to worry about Was Brook's reply, as Adam added a quick note to the e-mail, as they had discussed it with them, so none of the wolves there worried about them having it.

Quickly looking through the e-mails, there were several contacts from other packs already. Three had said 'Not now.' Two others wanted to see another pack or two before connecting, and there were three packs which wanted the full specs and contacts for supplies, as they were going to use this to upgrade their setup as well, so would be a while before connecting. He passed on the information of their supplier and asked them to mention the referral. From the size of what they were going to do, it was looking to give them a reasonable sized referral, and he knew the company paid out cash for referrals.

*****

They had Chris join them for dinner. The hall looked empty with so many patrolling the territories and helping with the construction. Their friends ribbed Chris that it was his last meal, when they heard Adam and Brook were doing the Turning the next morning. After dinner, they took him for a good run and a hot soak in the hot spring, before tucking him in between them. Both had come to care for him as a friend, and hoped he wasn't one of the few who died during the turning.

*****

The next morning, Adam and Brook got up silently and had Charlie and Chris' Mika come out with them, as Joshua stayed to guard their human. They went for a good breakfast and made sure the two dogs ate too. Mika ran back as soon as she finished gulping her food down, not begging for more as she usually did.

When they were done, they headed back and found Chris just stirring. Nodding and heading for his own breakfast, Joshua closed the door with a quiet click to a wolf, and silently to the human.

"Good morning." Chris said, as he stretched, "If I knew your bed was so nice, I'd have come for cuddles more." While as a human, he knew it wasn't 'normal', he did know the werewolves often showed affection and care with cuddles between friends and even just random packmates. He had got used to it, and thought even humans could do with getting more physical contact.

Adam chuckled, "Keep it to yourself, as if everyone knew we had a soft bed, we would have no room to move from everyone wanting to cuddle."

Chris smiled and nodded.

Taking a deep breath, Adam started, as Brook and him were going to share the turning, "Are you ready to become a Wolf?" he stated, having memorised the traditional words.

"I am." Chris said, sitting up.

"Do you agree to uphold the laws and traditions of the People you are joining, even when they conflict with the laws and traditions of the way you were raised?" Brook asked.

"I do," Chris answered, having already shown his willingness to live by the pack laws and traditions.

"You have been given what will happen once you are bitten, yet you want to be turned. Do any questions linger?" Adam asked. From the number of questions he had been asked, he sort of expected some.

"None. They have all been answered." Chris replied with a smile, seeing the relief in Adam's eyes.

"Once bitten, the changes are permanent and will exist beyond the end of this life. Do you wish for this?" Adam asked.

"I do, with all my mind and soul." He had felt a bit like Adam said he felt, the wolf completed him in a way even Brook didn't.

Brook smiled as she moved forward, "Then prepare yourself to be Turned." She intoned, ending the traditional sayings, before she shifted to her hybrid shape, towering over the bed.

From the look of Chris' eyes, Adam had to restrain his wolf from a fit of jealously and remind him he had agreed to this. There was no fear in his eyes, a bit of lust and longing, and also respect. The lust was quickly hidden, and none even showed in his scent. He reminded his wolf that while Chris may have the feelings, he would never act on them, and to take them as a sign their mate was desirable, she was all theirs.

While he watched, Adam remembered his own turning, and was startled at how little time had passed. He had been turned with the honourary rank of Beta, before gaining the skills to have the rank not be just honourary, then continuing to gain skills, earned the rank of Second to help lead when the Alphas were not available, and now to be the Alpha, with the responsibility of life or death of an entire pack and all the members on the shoulders of him and his mate.

He could smell her attention even as she bit Chris' neck. It was all he could do not to want to take her himself, but it was needed for the best chance of success, even if he was a bit territorial over her.

He knelt and petted Mika, as she shivered in reaction to her bondmate's pain but knowing to not attack the Alphas for any reason, *This is Good, this is OK. He will be OK.* he told her, as Brook worked him over the first step. At her look, he nodded, and took the two dogs out of the room, hooking a leash on to Mika for the first time.

She didn't want to leave, but they had to stay out, and she knew to obey the Alphas, so reluctantly followed, with many looks back at Chris. Toby and Robin were waiting outside the door to take control of them, as arranged. Toby took Mika's leash, and she stopped tugging as Adam ordered her to stay with Toby. They had been trained to listen to more senior wolves, and it mostly worked.

A quick order for Charlie to stay with Robin was listened to better, especially when Robin pulled out a ball to play with him. All four headed out the door as Adam hung a sign on the door, *Turning in Progress. Do Not Enter or Disturb.*

He let Brook help their charge, as he hung another sign on the patio door and adjusting the tint for privacy.

He watched as Chris passed out, pulling on some surgical gloves, and handing her some too, after she covered him up to his waist. Unsealing the sterilized first aid kit, Adam pulled out a non-stick pad to cover the bite, and some surgical tape to cover it. It should be a scar by the end of the day.

Adam nodded at Brook for her to take the first break. They would be spelling each other off till he was through the first part of the turn and didn't need to be isolated.

Putting a hand on his head, Adam could already feel him heating up, so he unsealed the first thermos of cold water and package of cloths, and pulled out the first of the cloth, getting it wet, folded it and put it on Chris's forehead. They had to keep the fever from getting too high, but he would already be able to stand what would need hospitalization in a human.

Adam and Brook talked in soft voices, discussing Adam's turn, and given the different conditions, suspected they would be double the times of him. Right on schedule, four hours after the bite, Chris opened his eyes and groaned.

"Welcome back, that is the hardest part; the clearing of your human immune system." Adam told him. Brook was off at the other end of the room eating her lunch. She would need to wash up before she could come close.

Adam poured some of the sterile water into a cup with a straw and held it up. Being the Alphas had a downside, as they were the ones who did this according to custom, the rare time they had someone not mated to turn and taught those in the pack. It was the one course which Gareth warned them to not delegate out. He had both groups of elders looking into why it was, and if it actually would be harmful to at least have someone they trusted instead of them staying with them. Or if it was only custom which was keeping the turning to the Alphas.

The healers had wanted it down in their area, but as tradition didn't have it in medical, and there not being enough facts, they hadn't agreed. The elders were also looking for if it was just tradition it being done in the Alpha's room, and the Healers were looking for more facts to support their side of it being done in Medical. Adam was leaning to it being done in Medical and hoped it didn't actually need them.

After Chris had the four mouthfuls they could let him have, he pulled it away, "You can have more in a bit."

Chris seemed not to have any energy and just passed out again, and they were back to working to keep him from heating too much, although his fever should break after a day or so; Brook told him his broke after only twelve hours.

He heard the shower going, and his stomach growled, *soon* he thought at it. He took a glass of the water he had for himself. Even his was the tasteless sterile stuff, but he had got them to add in a thermos with ice-cold one with some lemon, to hopefully help with the taste for Brook and himself; it should be to them mid-afternoon.

Brook smiled as she came out, in fresh scrubs, and smiled, "My turn" she told him.

He gave her a good hug, "I never realised how much work you did to help me over the Turning. Thank you."

She returned the hug, "I was very happy to do it; you are my mate, and I could see even the first time I shifted for you, the longing you had for a wolf form. I was glad to make it possible." Letting him go with a quick kiss, as his stomach rumbled again, "Time to feed the beast." She laughed pushing him away.

"Fine! If that's how you feel." He mocked offence, but knew she could feel his amusement, as he headed over to eat. Joshua was bringing anything they needed, but could only just put it inside the door, and they had to be very careful. They were clean, due to their werewolf immune systems, but their clothes might not be, so they would need to be careful.

I can't believe you did this all for me and are willing to do it for Chris; you're the best. Adam praised his mate.

I didn't need to be quite so careful; with the mating changes, you had some of werewolf immunities already, so it was changing it slowly, but would never have gained a wolf without the Turning bite. She replied, reminding him of something he had been told way at the beginning.

Eating the food neatly but quickly, he sighed, stacking all the used dishes on the cart and sliding it out the door of their room, so Joshua could get it.

Cart's outside the door, son. He advised him.

Thanks dad, Was the reply. *I'll get it soon, helping teach some pups how to wash a floor.* The thought was of several pups who had decided to have a water balloon fight inside, and now get to learn how to scrub the room with scrub brushes.

They definitely need to learn that, Adam replied, amused. He knew it was the pups from some who had been senior ranked and thought it beneath them and had refused to do it. After a lecture of not ordering anyone to do anything they were unwilling or had never done, as how would they be able to know they were the best qualified for doing it, and needed to know how to do basic cleaning, so he could give chores as punishment later. He didn't want it also to be a punishment for a Theta who had to clean up after them.

Heading over to his computer, he didn't find any new messages for any of the network, and seemed Josh was still out hunting Rogues. He hoped not to need to deal with them; at least the two pack attacks were mostly sane wolves, so their actions could be predicted. Rogues couldn't, and they never backed down from a fight, it was always to the death.

Over the next four days, they watched over him. He was awake enough to drink every three to four hours and they had him drink a cup or two then, before he passed out again. There were three bouts of nausea, and Adam was gagging each time from the smell, as he was still overwhelmed occasionally with his sensitive senses.

His fever broke right on schedule, and although high, never got to the level their Healer told them to get him if it reached it. It was slow to go down, but it was going down.

Just after both had finished their breakfast, almost exactly ninety-six hours after being bit, he woke. Again, Chris woke with some nausea. Adam passed the thermometer to Brook, and she checked when he finished heaving, "You are finally down to the werewolf's body temperature. Congratulations, you made it past the dangerous part." She told Chris, as he laid back with a hand on his head.

Adam passed her a fresh cloth, and she put it on his head. "Relax Chris, you will need plenty of sleep to recover." Brook murmured, knowing his senses would be sensitive.

Adam headed to the door, having alerted Toby to bring Mika. As her claws clicked on their hardwood floor, he saw Chris clapping his hands to his ears, and her instructions about his hearing. Seeing the relief before screwing up his nose as Mika hopped on the bed to curl up against him, Adam smiled, "Think of another dial for your sense of smell. You will want to not turn it down too much, but just enough for you to stand. You can turn it up when you get used to your new senses."

Charlie was not much behind her and whined at Adam, not liking being separated from him.

Adam filled a cup with some water, "You will want to drink this slowly." He told him as he took over from Brook, who nodded.

"How long?" Chris asked, his voice raspy, before starting to drink.

Adam waited for him to finish before answering, "Four days; it's Monday morning."

Chris groaned, "No wonder I'm weak." He commented before taking some more water.

He passed out again, but was awake about another hour later, and knowing he would be hungry, Brook went to get the soup they had asked for him, as Adam helped him with some water.

"You feel up for some soup?" Brook asked, coming back in with a bowl of Chicken Noodle soup.

At his nod, Adam helped him sit up, and got a lap table for him, before he slowly ate the soup. "Either the chefs made this much better than they ever have, or stuff just tastes better!"

Adam chuckled, "Some foods will taste better, but if you are out in human places, stuff which is highly processed, or has lots of artificial ingredients won't taste good. I can't stand store-bought potato chips, or any pop now. They taste disgusting to me." The chips, he was glad the pack made some with 'real' ingredients, and a lack of the processed and artificial ones. If he wanted bubbly, he was down to sparkling water, which was healthier anyways.

After finishing the soup, Chris was blinking sleepily. They laid him back down and let him rest. "When he wakes up, try to get him to have a shower, and then we can move him off to his room." Brook advised. "Between Mika for security and Koda for care, he should be fine."

Adam nodded. When the pack had heard about the turning, Koda had offered his assistance to take care of him, if they needed. They had accepted, for once he was stabilized enough to be moved to his room. Koda was one of the Thetas who had been in Night Depths, so the fact he was willing to care for Chris, who the Alphas cared for, would get him some exposure for the pack. He had commented he was one of the few who had any exposure to humans. He had no issues with one who was Turned, as to him it took guts to face the prospect of dying and giving up everything they knew.

*****

Chris didn't wake all day, but towards supper he woke again. They helped him sit up and had a bowl of beef chili for him. It was something which he could eat as weak as he was but was full of the protein his body needed to fuel the changes, especially with him having been out of it for a longer time.

Since he didn't immediately fall back asleep, "Feel up to having a shower?" Adam asked.

Chris nodded and lifted his arm to pull the sheet of him, and they slowly helped him sit up. After letting him sit there for a moment, they stood him up, and they had to catch him as his legs buckled.

"Why am I so weak" Chris complained.

"You are going through some major changes; you are basically becoming a different species. Also, you have basically just been laying on your back for four days, you are going to be weak." Adam replied.

Slowly they walked him into the shower and helped him get clean. He had got over the amount of nudity at a pack long before, and just enjoyed the feeling of others washing his body; just standing there was taking all his energy. Once he was dry, they sat him down in the wheelchair, as he would not even be able to stand the time it took to get him up the elevator, let alone the stairs.

*****

Koda met them at the door to Chris's room, which Koda had been taking the time to have prepped for him.

"Hi Koda," Chris greeted him. They had become friends, as they had several similar interests. "Thanks for offering to nurse me for the next while."

"You're welcome." Koda replied with a grin, as he helped get him settled in his bed, "Keeps me away from the construction duties, or just fetching. I'd take caring for someone turning over that any day. It will let me read up some more on the history of MacLaren Pack."

Adam grinned spying a history book on the chair, "That is one of the better history books. Let me know if you want more." He offered as he put the wheelchair in the corner of the room.

"Yes, Alpha. Thank you." Koda replied.

"Adam shook his head, "Call me Adam. Alpha makes me look for Gareth or Maria." He complained.

Waving a hand, they headed off, heading up the stairs to check on the wolves up in the loft. They found only the pups and those watching them, along with quite a few of MacLaren pups as well. As Adam and Brook came in, Jake was the first to notice them, "Alpha Adam" He squealed, as he ran to him, throwing himself at Adam for a hug.

Brook laughed as Adam caught the pup and held him close for a hug. Most of their pack's pups and many of the other pups came over for a hug and cuddle too from both of them. *I guess we will be here till supper time* She commented, amused. *I let Gareth know the first part of Chris' Turn is done,* It was rare to lose a new wolf, once their temperature had come down, as at that point the Were-healing started to kick in, and the rest is having their body adjust and get used to the new abilities.

I don't mind. It allows us to check on them, before we check on the rest at the fire. Adam replied with a mental shrug. *It will allow for us to relax and enjoy being with the pack* Some of the adults were still very stiff and formal with them, but others were getting better and relaxing in their care. They had discussed it, and some may take years to relax, from the way they had been treated.

*****

Following dinner, they checked on Chris and Koda. Chris was asleep, and Koda was sitting there, finishing his dinner and gave them a smile and wave, before they closed the door.

They both felt the stress of being cooped up for those last few days, and once they got outside, played a bit of tag, to burn off some energy, before heading off to the fire. Many were startled to see them.

"Chris finished the first part of the Turning today. He moved back to his room. It will be a long slog, and I think he will be up and about in a couple weeks." Adam told the gathered wolves. Many in both packs were quite happy he was doing well enough to free them up. Several squeezed together to make room for them.

As they moved to the seats, they gave a brush of a hand over the heads and backs of those in a furred form, a hug, or just a shoulder squeeze, showing they cared, and giving a little bit of attention.

Packmates passed sticks and some meat to roast, as everyone relaxed and enjoyed the company.

Chapter 6 - Arrival

Adam and Brook waited at the warehouse in town for the vehicle from Sentinel Star Pack to drop off Ethan. Looking at the clock, he sighed, "I'm thinking we're going to need to feed everyone. It's just about lunchtime."

Brook leaned against him, both were wearing some thick leggings and a T-shirt, with a jacket, although they didn't need it, since they could be seen by humans. They had run as wolves, as there were several vehicles which needed to go back to the pack's parkade which were there, they were going to help and take one, so they carried clothes which didn't take up much room. "Patience, my Love. We can wait." She told him, also wanting this over. It took a long time to arrange everything but took only a couple of days for Ethan to travel. Every pack's territory which he was to travel through had to agree to him travelling, and Sentinel Star had to be arranged to smuggle him through their territory, over the human border. But doing so as a wolf was easy, as the pack did move though it regularly, so one more wolf would not be something the humans would notice.

They had just been notified the Pack house's foundation hole was finally finished being dug and were starting the work to get the pilings for the foundation installed. They had decided to go overkill, so it would resist all movement and still be standing in a thousand years, according to the human construction company they were working with who had tried to talk them out of, since they couldn't understand they wanted the building to last even a hundred years. The foundation and structure were also designed that the fourth floor could be made a full floor, and even a fifth floor could be added, if they ever wanted it. Mostly the pack was doing the actual work themselves, but was getting supervision from the experienced construction workers, so they knew it was being done right.

The other buildings were now having their foundations dug and would be continued after the others. The Greenhouse was going to be started soon and would actually be finished before the pack house, as it was much less complex. They had decided on Lexan plates, instead of tempered glass, as they would withstand the weather and any impacts better, even if it was much more expensive, as there was good chance of hail. The wells for the hot and the cold drinking water had been drilled, with them both bubbling up naturally, they had temporarily redirected them to a creek, while they built the building, then would be directed into filling the hot pool, and the drinking water tanks.

Hearing an unknown vehicle drive up, they headed out the door. Seeing Ethan stepping out, both Adam and Brook smiled, "Welcome. I trust the trip back wasn't too hard," Adam said. Ethan looked a bit skittish to him, as if he expected bad things.

"Not too difficult, all things considered, Alpha." Ethan replied softly, keeping his eyes down.

"Are either of you hungry? There's a nice restaurant in town here, or we can see if we can get back to the pack house in time for the meal." Adam asked. He had not been to the restaurant in several months, as they rarely went into town.

The driver smiled, "I'm Ryan." He introduced himself as he stepped around the vehicle. "You must be Alphas Adam and Brook." He asked politely, keeping his eyes on their chins. He could feel the power radiating, even as they tried to keep it down, "I could do with some food," He replied to their question. He could see Charlie peaking out around Adam and was curious about the fact they had a Service Dog harness on a wolf.

Adam nodded, "Well, it's just around the corner, so we can just leave your vehicle there, and we will walk there." He knew if they fed him, Ethan's wolf would be much happier; it would show they were willing to provide for him. Most born-wolves knew it instinctively, but he learned from experience, sharing a meal was the fastest way to have a werewolf's trust.

Getting a slight nod from Ethan and a nod from Ryan, "It would give me a chance to stretch my body out before driving some more." He commented, "I need to head right back." His Alpha had ordered him straight home, as he didn't want him interacting much with the other packs. The order could stretch over a meal in town, but not much farther.

Adam turned and led the way to the small restaurant. On the way, he gave into the curious glances at Charlie. "This is Charlie." He introduced speaking softly, so the humans wouldn't hear, "He is not a werewolf, but one of the very smart dogs which we breed at MacLaren. Charlie is bonded to me, so comes with me all the time. They are registered and trained as service animals, so I don't have to leave him behind when out in human areas." As they were not Pack, they couldn't say too much about them.

As soon as the door opened and the staff caught his face, it was like he kicked an ant hill. They were quickly seated, and water brought out. *I guess the word that we are Alphas now has caught on even here,* Brook commented, amused as the owner came out to say hello and take their order personally. They were getting much more respect than the last time they had been there with a large group; the staff seemed to turn themselves inside out to get them served fast. They knew about the dogs they trained, as they occasionally had them come in. They provided a bowl of water for Charlie as well and offered some food as well, which they gratefully accepted.

As soon as she left, Adam turned to Ethan and Ryan, "Order whatever you wish, my treat."

Ethan stared at Adam in the eyes in surprise before wincing and turning his eyes back to the menu, "That is kind of you." He murmured, and even if there were wolves at the next table, they would not have heard him. He cringed, waiting for Adam's attack.

Adam just sighed and worked with his wolf to decide on what to eat. They settled down on an Elk burger, as they had a certain way which they made it that brought out the flavours even better.

Adam looked at Ethan, his wolf whining about how beaten down Ethan looked. "Ethan, Josh had kept me up to date on your training. I want to have you come and train tomorrow after breakfast, so we can see if you have any deficiencies."

"Yes, Alpha." Was his only reply.

"Ethan, call me Adam. I prefer to be much more informal." He suggested gently.

"Yes, Al—Adam, I'll try." Ethen answered, hesitantly. "When do I get to see my mom and sister?" he asked. He almost didn't want to eat; he was wanting to see them.

"We have them down for the afternoon. Mostly they—and most of the pack—are working up at the new territory on building our pack house. After the workout tomorrow, we are going to run up to the new pack territory, and let you see it, and meet some of those who were packmates. You would be welcome to stay there for the time and help on the construction, and get some training in, or come back to MacLaren's pack house, and we can find some duties for you."

Ethan nodded, "Seems like you have some plans for me." He commented, a little miffed at them trying to take control, before shrinking back, expecting a disciplinary swat.

Brook smiled slightly and explained, "Since you are not known, and don't know either territory, we are making them at least partly known to you, so you can be mostly left without supervision, and have the time to find out if you do want to stay or go elsewhere."

Both Adam and Brook could see the realisation dawn on his face; they weren't taking control; they were giving him just enough direction for him to learn and take control himself. Turning back to their food, they discussed some other less heated conversation.

Ryan stayed quiet and just watched how the two Alphas handled the skittish wolf he had driven up. Both seemed totally different than he expected. His own Alpha required respect and gave cuffs for the smallest infraction. Rumours within the pack had Alpha Tom didn't consider these two Alphas, as they were under a century. His wolf agreed while they were here, they would not consider even asking their age; they could feel the power just rolling off them, even as they tried to suppress it. There was no way they were anything but an Alpha. His wolf was thinking if either one fought Alpha Tom, Tom wouldn't stand a chance.

*****

The reunion of Ethan with his family was quite touching. Letting them wander off alone, and have the private time allowed them to deal with some paperwork. Gareth had finally approved them to set up a second area for the dogs, and eventually start working with them to train them. Since the pack had never thought about marketing the backpacks, so Gareth was leaving that one to Adam so the Wild Valley Pack could use it as income. Gareth had also transferred some of the invested pack money, which should keep a steady income, as long as they only used the interest not the principal.

Wandering off, they checked in on their pack, as until they did the spring trials, they hadn't formalised any of the ranks, so were having to do much of the work they would have normally delegated. Jess and Joshua were technically Thetas but had taken up the duties of being their assistants, a job often for a Beta, or at least a Delta, and were trying to help keep tabs on the pack.

The elders were not being given much work, as they were trying to recoup from the neglect of their previous Alpha. They were working with the some of the MacLaren Elders with the pups, especially the older ones who needed to unlearn what they learned at the old pack. Most were starting to look younger, as were many of their pack. Both had thoughts of relief as they stopped feeling the stress coming in through all the bonds.

*****

Getting breakfast the next morning, they nodded at Ethan as he came in, "Don't eat too heavily, you have training after." Adam advised, "There is always food out which doesn't suffer from staying out, so you can have more after."

"Yes, Adam." Was Ethan's reply, before he got his own breakfast, seeing they were following their own advice as well. He sat with his mother and sister, needing the reassurance he wasn't still dreaming. Both had shared how they were respectful and caring to all their members, but also supported them in their own decisions, if they followed the rules laid out. When they had to punish... the stories his mother and sister gave had him shuddering, but thinking about them, in all cases he clearly saw it was a punishment for the infraction, but also allowed for once the punishment was over, for them to return to regular duties for the most part. Some of the Betas overseeing the work had then required them to redo their training, but the Alphas clearly didn't involve themselves with it.

All too soon for Ethan, breakfast was over, and it was time for the training. He headed over, not really sure what they were going to do.

Adam moved first, tossing a staff to Ethan, who grabbed it out of the air, "This is a warmup." He told Ethan, moving to the ready position. Ethan nodded.

After warming up with some moves and practice strikes, they moved to testing with staffs, "I'm impressed. The report we first got from Fossil Valley was you were new to it." Adam commented. "I'm taking this as qualified."

Ethan was working to catch his breath, just nodded. "When you are labelled a rogue, you have to fight and win or die, there is no middle ground."

Adam nodded, "I put word out to the other packs when we found out what had happened to you. So far, I have found three who had been accepted into other packs, and seven more who had been killed who had been forced out of Night Depths over the last century. There is many more who either haven't reported back to me or are not certain of identification."

Brook passed Ethan and Adam each a water bottle, as Adam cleaned and put away the staffs, "Next is swords or knives; which have you been training in?" She asked. She still had skills in the knife and sword fight which gave her an edge over Adam, mainly due to active experience, not just half-remembered skills which were more instinctual than anything, and he still was working on his muscle memory.

"Knife."

Brook brought out a tray of knives, and offered them to Ethan, so he could make his choice. Once he chose two, she put the tray back and took her own selection. They moved more in exercises instead of attempting to actually fight, as it was fairly dangerous.

Brook worked him through many steps, but seemed he was a master of them as well. After a thought to consult Adam, both agreed it wasn't too unusual, as knives and staffs were easy to get, even if they weren't the high quality finished ones they had available in the training area.

Letting Ethan rest his body, they tested how much learning he had done on the pack laws, and they were surprised he had read through the information they had provided him. They promised him some more material but decided they couldn't give him much more of their internal details, unless and until he joined the pack.

Adam took over for the unarmed training and worked out he needed some skills to be upgraded there, as he was fairly weak. From what they learned, he was more advanced than the others from Night Depths, as they suspected it was to keep everyone weaker without a weapon in hand.

It turned into a training session, with four names of people for Ethan to talk to for more lessons by the end of it, but they did tell him, as he was not in the pack, they would not require him to train, just recommend he do so.

Ethan was shocked, but pleased they were leaving it to him to do the next step at his own pace. He knew the pack had the training requirement, but it wasn't just him, it was for everyone. So far, what he had seen, he liked... but he was waiting to see what was hiding.

By the time they wrapped up, there was just enough time before lunch for a shower, so all three headed for the communal shower in the change room. Both Adam and Brook tried to relax the wolf, giving him attention as they helped each other get clean.

Grabbing clean sleeveless robes off the shelf, they headed up and joined the gathering for the food. This time Ethan came to sit with them, asking politely to join them for lunch.

Both Adam and Brook were surprised, "Grab a seat." Adam invited, having gathered his whit's a little faster than Brook. "This is..." he started, introducing everyone at the table. All the pack had been told was he used to be part of the Night Depths Pack and was considering coming back.

Relaxing to have a good meal, Adam could see Ethan struggling to form a question, but not sure on how to say it, quietly replied to just him, *If you would prefer, you can ask it silently. If it is something personal, and don't want to answer it, we will just tell you, and not be offended with the question.*

Ethan seemed to relax, *I have several,* he started, speaking only to the two of them, *Why are you interested in me? Why do you care about me?*

Adam blinked, surprised at the question, *It's the same reason I am wanting to take care of those from the Night Depths. I care about all the wolves. Everyone deserves to have a safe place to live and be cared for. Both myself and Brook, along with Josh and his Alpha agree you were kicked out without cause and would like to give you a fresh start. The fact you have family who are in my pack, gives us the first chance, but is not your only option. Other packs have also said they would accept you, if you asked. I will not force you to do anything, but we are training you to succeed and be as strong as you can be. If only so you can better protect yourself when you leave our protection.* He decided to leave it there. Ethan should be able to feel how much they cared.

Ethan just sat there, fork halfway to his face for a very long moment, before replying with a quiet, *Thank you,* Which carried much more emotions of gratitude and relief. Their answer had not only answered his spoken question, but all his others. They were not trying to dictate how he lived his life, but instead were just trying to give him the skills to help him have the ability to survive better, even as he got to see how they led the rest of their pack. He could tell they wanted to have him in their pack, but it was his decision alone and were just leaving him to decide.

*****

The run was uneventful, even with Ethan, his mother, and his sister to run with Adam and Brook, and of course Charlie, tagged along. Last minute, Lea and Robin joined them as they were going to start training their pack on the tech, especially on the security systems. Adam and Brook paced to not exhaust Rene, even though she was regaining her strength, now she wasn't so stressed out. Ten years seemed to have faded from her face once she had the first video chat with Ethan.

Adam introduced Ethan to the trainers when they arrived, one was to teach him how to use the bow they had fitted him with before leaving, another was to keep him up on his knife and staff skills, and a last for him to learn how to lead. Adam had a feeling with the right encouragement and discipline, Ethan could possible be a Beta in a couple decades and had told him when they let him know what they planned for him, if he decided to stay.

Leaving Ethan being instructed by one of the crew chiefs in the construction, as his sister and mother headed off to resume their duties. They had let him know until he decided he wanted to leave, they would mostly treat him as a pack member, although some of the perks—access to the pack vehicles and leave to go into the nearby human towns—would not be permitted. As long as he was working and training, they would pay him like any other packmate, and would provide a warm, dry place to sleep, and good, filling food. Nor would they give him preferential treatment, although he would be discreetly watched and guarded, as he was a Guest.

They checked in on the various work areas, doing an informal inspection. The blocks which would form the insulated outer layers of concrete foundation walls were being placed, they also worked as the forms which the concrete was going to be poured between. It gave a good view of how the shape was going to be, and it seemed to be a huge area. It seemed so much larger now it wasn't just numbers on a table.

"I can't wait till we can start moving in! Although I hate moving; I'm glad this should be the last time we move for a very long time." Adam commented to Brook as they headed to look at the outbuildings. They had the greenhouse larger, as the new technology would allow them to have food which used to not be possible to grow in a greenhouse. Also, newer technologies allowed for it to be cheaper to make, allowing for the size to be larger without affecting the price.

Finished with the tour of the work sites, Jess caught up to them, as they relaxed in what was used as the dining hall, having some hot food before heading off.

"I hope everything is in order," Jess said, dropping into a seat across from them starting her own meal before the massed pack came for their break.

"Looks great, nothing to complain about from our end," Adam said with a smile, "How are you doing?"

Jess smiled, "Nothing I can't handle, and if I have anyone who complains about me, I have told them to contact you two, since you left me in charge. I love being in charge. It was just scary the first few times I had to give orders."

Brook shook her head, "Nobody has contacted us, so they must have deemed it not important enough to bother us over."

"I split the crews into three shifts, so we can work around the clock" Jess offered, a bit concerned.

Adam nodded after a bit of a thought, "That's why you are farther than expected. I forgot with wolf-vision it wouldn't be needing to shut down when it got dark. Keep your initiatives like that up. It will give you skills with this project for management." Giving a sly grin, "You may make Beta yet."

Both Brook and Jess laughed.

"I like being in charge and bossing everyone around." Jess replied with a smile, "The few hard heads who objected to me being in charge shut up when I set them on their rears when they first objected to something, using some moves you two taught me, and they have been good since."

Brook grinned, "Showing them the Bitch is in charge?" She joked.

Jess laughed and nodded, even if she hadn't been sure when she was first told she would be the one to stay but now was enjoying the control which came with being the one in charge.

After letting them laugh and joke some more, Adam broke in, "We brought Ethan up, so he can see how the rest of the pack is living. I would like you to treat him as much as possible as if he is Pack, and if he asks to join, let us know right away."

Jess sobered, "Yes, I will also make sure he has discreet watchers. I don't know how a pack could take asking for details on an order would count as insubordination." She said with a shake of her head, and a slight growl lacing her voice. "I would more likely commend him for making sure he did his work right."

They discussed the decisions which Jess had made, and other than one or two they agreed was the right decision, and even the ones they disagreed with, they decided to leave standing, as she was in charge, and didn't want to undermine it, and after her explanations, they agreed with her for the conditions.

Once finished the good meal as expected, since Lupita had taken over making the food, Adam and Brook decided to take some time to explore the territory. Heading off they started near the pack house but expanded their explorations of the pack's territory. As the Alphas, they should know as much of their territory as possible.

Finding many lookout points around where the pack house was located, they marked a few for building lookouts into the cliffs to keep a watch. They found a group of nature hikers, nearly blundering into them. Hiding under a bush in the shadows, the humans passed close enough they could have tripped a couple by extending a paw, and they didn't even notice! The couple of teens were complaining about not seeing any animals, which had them sharing some silent amusement as they blundered through the forest loudly.

If they were hunters, I would have done something about them, but since they are just taking pictures, as long as they don't go to the top of the ridge and into the pack valley, I think we should leave them alone. Adam commented, chuckling at how unobservant the humans had been, although it may have saved their lives, since they had packs, they would know they weren't just wild wolves.

The ridge was the edge of the property, according to the humans, but the other side was all public crown land and parks, so they didn't have a problem, and were getting signs up for 'Area is Under Video Surveillance', 'No Trespassing', and 'No Hunting' signs at the edge of the property, along with 'Guard Dogs on Premises'. As a joke, a second line of signs had, 'Trespassers will be put to Hard Labour for Life' and 'Hunters will be Eaten' were going to be added.

There were very few places which humans could even get through the forest at the edge of the property to trespass, as it was fairly rugged. Where there weren't very dense trees which could disorient someone, there was scree slopes of broken rocks, ready to move and cause physical injury or bury an unsuspecting human. And where there was neither, there were vertical cliffs. Signs had been installed at the bottom of any of the slopes and cliffs, to warn the top was the edge of private property and would be trespassing if they left the top of the ridge but had also posted signs of climbing is permitted but at own risk. They didn't plan on doing anything to climbers, as long as they stayed right at the ridge, especially since a couple of the cliffs were known in the climbing community, and blocking access would not deter many. They had also added

'No Trespassing' signs a bit back from the cliff face at the top of the cliffs too, and a couple even joked about putting a fence up.

There was a guard post at the road, but wouldn't really prevent someone on foot, they were to control and monitor vehicle traffic and right now to direct construction vehicles. The road, they were expecting it to not be passible in winter, unless they not only plowed their own, but the road leading up to it. Adam expected once they had the equipment, they would do some road maintenance, but unlikely the next winter.

There was a nice highway a ridge over, so they had purchased some land near it for a vehicle garage. It did mean a bit more work, as it was about a half hour wolf run from the garage to the pack house, as an average wolf or a couple hour hike along the road. It was fairly low on the priority, as they were leaving most of the vehicles still at MacLaren, instead of bringing them out. Right now, it was just a gravel pad.

*****

I smell sulphur Adam called out, as they were investigating a bit of a pass at the south and headed down into a valley. Taking the lead, he followed his nose to a hidden cascade of hot water. *We found another hidden hot spring* He chuckled. The whole area seemed riddled with them. This was the third they had found, and there had been other reports of them. Most were in areas which humans would have trouble reaching, even if they could find them. The ones which could be reached easily were within the pack's property, so it was even more likely they wouldn't find any humans using them, other than those who were part of the pack.

The hot spring cascaded through several pools, before reaching the edge of a marsh which upon investigation, had several other feeds of water, with only one other being warm, the rest being cold, crystal-clear water.

Investigating more, they could see several kinds of tiny fish, and even some garter snakes hiding around the ponds. Relaxing on some grass, *This somewhat reminds me of the Cave and Basin in Banff.* He commented, seeing spots which with minimal work they could make some seats for a few to relax. The Cave and Basin was where hot springs were first discovered, when they were putting the railway through the mountains, and resulted in the Canadian National Park program to protect them when the first commercial ventures were started and wanting to privatize the known springs.

Remind me to look into what species we have here. I know at Banff there is endangered species which lives in the warm water and no where else, and if we have them, might be able to get money to keep it natural. If they did, it was also one more way they could use to control human activity in the area.

That evening, they watched the sun set over the mountains, and enjoyed the time alone, well, with Charlie shadowing them, but he didn't count.

They spent a couple of days exploring the area, relaxing and enjoying the warm weather. They did find out there was a claim at the edge of their territory of an actual wolf pack, which Brook called 'cousins' and they respected their claim, letting out a howl to let them know they had new neighbours, and traded songs with them late into the night to both of their delights.

*****

Padding in before first light Monday morning, after spending the afternoon with their pack relaxing and finding out the minor concerns, and most of the night curled up with them before spending the dark hours after midnight heading back to MacLaren Pack along what was becoming a well-travelled route, and one which was now regularly monitored by patrols.

Shifting and tossing his pack to the side once they were back in their room, "As much as I enjoy my time as a wolf, I also enjoy having my Mate in my arms as a human." Adam told Brook, as she too dropped the pack, before being swept up for a good kiss and hug.

Reluctantly they separated, but stayed touching as they headed into the shower, sharing a very enjoyable time. Coming out, their stomachs traded growls, leaving them giggling, as they pulled on some shorts and t-shirts before heading off to breakfast.

Heading to their table with loaded plates, and Charlie chowing down on his bowl full of meat, they got a bunch of smiles.

"Look who finally surfaced." Martin teased, "I knew you were out in your new territory, but you two were moving too much to pin you down." The sensors were having a little issue, due to all the construction sending vibrations through the ground. The patrols would report the sightings, but those were even more rare.

Adam and Brook traded looks "Did the patrols report our mock attacks?"

Martin tilted his head, perplexed, "Mock attacks?"

Adam had a slow smile grow on his face, "If we came across a patrol, we hid, and mock attacked them. Several were taken by surprise, but many were vigilant enough that the attack would have failed." The grin turned a little feral, "They were supposed to report them in, so they would get harder, but as they didn't, we weren't able to test the second part of where there was heightened alert." Passing a sheet to him, "These were the patrols which were hit, and a quick note on what happened."

Martin looked over the list, "Hmm, I'm going to need to have a word with the patrols, as having Alphas mock attack is something *unusual*, and should definitely been reported."

Brook nodded, as did many listening in around them, "Tell them we're going to start giving out penalties for failures."

Martin gave a feral grin as he finished his breakfast, "Bathroom and garbage duties are going to be full of punishments shortly. Want me to start with these?"

Adam shrugged, "Up to you. I would go easy on them, as they were not aware they were being tested. Let's also give them an incentive, where if they successfully repulse us, they will get some sort of privilege or something special."

Martin grinned, "If they take you out, I'm giving them a week's vacation extra, and if they take you both, a month!" He knew how fast and strong they were. A patrol had one to four wolves and could also have up to six dogs in it. With those working together, it would still be a feat to take Adam and Brook down.

There was wistful looks on many of the faces around them who didn't do patrols, and hopeful ones of those who did.

Dropping his voice, so only the table would hear, "Don't tell them we're busy till tomorrow afternoon." As having about a day and a half of no attacks may put them more relaxed, but they shouldn't be. They should be vigilant when patrolling, and be at least detected and reported in. Speaking normally, "We're going to have fun!" He commented. Most wolves liked to play hide and seek, and this was much more fun.

The whole table burst out in laughter, with many nodding in agreement. This would get the patrols working better to protect the land by being more vigilant.

Chapter 7 – Cousin Wolves

Martin passed on some information which had come out after they left, as he walked them to the Alpha's wing, "We had Sentinel Star take over patrolling what had been the south end of Night Depths territory. We still patrol about two thirds of it, but it would have had us thin, if your pack wasn't helping out patrolling what is becoming Wild Valley."

"Good, they did take the offer." Brook commented. They had made a side comment when they were negotiating Ethen's travel about needing some more territory. They had offered it, but as they were going to be away from the human communications, and Alpha Tom was one of the sticklers for Alphas needing a century of life before they would deal with them, they had left it in the paws of Gareth.

"It still leaves us more than enough territory to set up another pack in, if there was a spare Alpha to lead it." Martin replied. It was one of the very old laws: each pack needed to have an Alpha lead it. If one without the Alpha's abilities tried to lead a pack, many would refuse to listen, and the pack would dissolve into chaos. It wasn't just skills which was needed, but the ability to have others want to listen to them, and it was a very rare ability. "Why didn't they take more of it?" It was extremely rare for an Alpha to become corrupt, unlike a human. Even then, when an Alpha became corrupt, the pack bonds still kept them thinking of the others in the pack, even if only to keep them in the pack. If there was another with the Alpha ability, it seemed to almost be a compulsion to take out the one which became corrupt, and with the pack supporting the other, they usually won, and with the win, the pack's loyalty moved.

"They didn't want more. They don't want to spread out any farther." Adam replied. It was understandable. The part they took was the area which was the farthest from them and the hardest to patrol, so they were quite happy to release it.

Heading into Gareth's office, Adam had one question which Brook and him had discussed, but didn't have an answer, "Do we have a Beta who would be interested in acting as an Alpha of a sub-pack?" He asked, thinking with everyone he was taking from MacLaren, there still was going to be a large pack, which could support having a second location, even if they still looked to Alpha Gareth and Maria.

Gareth shook his head, "I take it you have been told about Sentinel Star taking over the part of the territory, but leaving us with enough for another pack?" Taking their smile of conformation, continued, "I had the same thought. Not sure if both of my pups are wanting a pack, as far as I know both haven't found a mate, so are returning." He wouldn't put it past one of them to have found a mate, and if they were looking to come here, to have kept it a surprise. He hadn't told them about all the tech changes or how Brook was now an Alpha. "I want to get your pack firmly in place first, and they need to finish their training at the Academy. With you taking over the one territory, it gives us the breathing room to not have it critical to find more space, yet. We have the wolves to patrol the territories, although I am considering a cheap longhouse for what was Night Depths, as it would allow for some to stay for more patrols easier, than needing a long run home at end of every shift. I have been using it for some of the hunting, though. I don't want the other two areas to become over hunted." A longhouse design they generally used was shaped like a "T", with the top being sleeping space with the common/dining room and kitchen connected about the middle. The kitchen was generally on one side, with bathrooms on the other, and then beyond it being the common area. It meant the heat from the kitchens could also be used in the sleeping areas, but with modern methods available for heat, it was less of an issue.

Adam and Brook nodded, "That would work." Brook said for them, "It would give some of the younger ones a chance to get away for a bit while staying with the pack too. Or for the more senior teams to oversee more than a team."

"You could always see if there is another with the abilities who would want to take over it, as I doubt we are the only one in the area who has been having population pressures." Adam offered.

Gareth nodded, "And you have run into some who refuse to discuss with you as you are such young wolves." He commented, having noticed several times when having to pass over to him the other Alpha, who had called him a 'Jumped up Beta' was the kindest. It offended him, even if Adam and Brook hid the hurt with their refusal. They had been using him to pass the information to Sentinel Star, since Tom had refused to deal with them at all. When Adam had first called, Tom had just hung up on him, refusing to deal with 'a pup', and they knew the pack wouldn't speak to a female at all. He was glad they didn't need to deal with the Feral Star pack, as they were even worse.

"So, I know you were out to your pack house with Ethan when he arrived." Gareth stated, leading. These meetings had become weekly meetings for them to ask of him questions on leading, and for sharing between the two parts of the Pack. Those who had been Night Depths didn't think of him being their Alpha, so while they gave him the respect he was due when they interacted, they treated him as a guest Alpha, and they didn't go to him with issues but went to Adam and Brook. This time let them to make sure he was aware of any concerns or issues before they got too big. It also let them come to him for his opinion and feedback on their decisions. So far, he was proud of how they were handling it. There were occasional times they had to learn their own leadership style and solutions. Gareth planned to scale the meetings back to monthly once the pack house was complete, and they were moved in, and over the next few years scale them back to nothing, and just be available as a mentor if they needed it. But their work with the Elders showed they had learned one thing; the elders could help. Some Alphas never learned it.

"Well, Ethan seems as forthright as he seemed at the video conference." Adam started, "His staff and knife skills seem to be good, but his bow and unarmed are low. We have set him up with trainers to try to get his skills up and assigned him a work shift."

Gareth smiled, "Hoping to have him join?" At Adam and Brook's grin and sharp nod, "From what I have had reported from the afternoon and evening here, I would accept him without any issues, if he wants something different. He feels like a solid wolf. Andrew even emailed me to make sure if he decided not to join in two weeks, to let him know he could have a position down there too."

Adam laughed, "I'll let him know the next time we see him, he now has two other pack offers open for him. If he decides against them, we would be able to get him into almost any pack with that record alone." With three packs being open to him, showed any other packs without meeting him, he would be a valued member.

"The pack house is going along well." Brook stated changing the topic. They didn't need to spend so much time on one single Lone Wolf, when they had many other items to discuss. She did agree with the assessment and was hoping to keep the wolf. "Jess has them on three eight-hour shifts. They are ahead of schedule. With the revisions, it is possible by the time the snow falls we could be starting to close in the pack house."

Gareth nodded, "If it is the case, you could easily move most of the pack in on pallets and finish the inside while there during the winter."

Brook nodded, "Yes, and have a warm place while working as much as we can on the outside buildings. The limiting factor will be getting the foundations done before it gets too cold for the concrete to set correctly, or the ground starts to freeze. The final outside layers may be delayed to next spring, though."

Gareth nodded, "Do you have secure storage for building supplies?" It would limit their speed.

Adam smiled, "Jess is getting the workshops up priority, with a dedicated team, so there would have an enclosed and dry space to store everything which needs it, and one is even being insulated and heated for the stuff like paint which can't be allowed to freeze. She is coordinating with Rein and Mikan for supply deliveries, as there is space to store them. Right now, they have all the forms, with extras, to get the underground parts done, and are getting all the concrete floors installed. The pack house has mostly pre-cast, so they are coming in as fast as they can be made, which is limiting the building, so they are working on the other buildings when they run out of stuff to do on the pack house."

Gareth was impressed, "Excellent. The decorative parts?"

Brook shook her head, "We're going to have the pack make them, after the pack moves in; it'll give them another way to show pride in helping to make the pack house."

"Same for any art. Although, I will be making sure there are plenty of photos of the members." Adam added. They planned on having photos of them, the Elders, and the various initial department leaders as photos, and he planned on taking a 'pack photo' once they were settled and expected to borrow Lucas for it. Some pictures of the construction were planned to be done, and would be up for a while, but taken down for others in the future.

Trading a look and a thought and decided to share, "We decided when the pack house is finished, we will somewhat finalise the pack membership. It is because we have a secret surprise. We are going to take resin pawprints of all the members, mark them with names and ranks, and hang them around the balconies. We will then switch colours for those who are born or join after that and change the colour every few decades." Those where were members when it's finished would have one colour, and after that would be a different one.

Gareth leaned back with a surprised look which morphed into a very proud smile. "It is ideas like that shows me you are going to be great Alphas and makes me proud to know you and be honoured to be able to advise you. Once the other Alphas learn how good you two are showing, I suspect you will have many wanting to trade contact information and discuss ideas." He expected them to almost be regional leaders, with many packs looking to them for guidance of topics outside their pack, and maybe even inside them, as younger ones took over.

Brook and Adam looked a bit embarrassed at the feelings.

"So, that was Thursday. What did you do for the last three days?" Gareth asked, tilting his head slightly. He was very curious, even though as long as they keep their commitments and were available by mind speech for any problems, the rest of the time was their own. He could feel how happy and content their pack was through them, so there wasn't an issue there. He didn't need to nanny them, they were adults.

"Explored our new territory and had some fun with the patrols." Brook stated, with a matter-of-fact voice, as if saying they went the next block over, then laughed at Gareth's perplexed look.

Adam smiled, "We mock-attacked the patrols, to try to get them more vigilant. Also, found out mock attacks were nothing unusual, so they didn't report them, so we couldn't do the second part. Martin was going to deal with them. From now, there is going to be punishments of bathroom cleaning and garbage pickup for failures in the vigilance they should have on patrols, and a mock attack is not normal and needs to be reported in, otherwise it will be a failure. If when we mock attack, they can take one of us out, the patrol will get a week of extra vacation, and if the unlikely happens and they overcome both of us, he is giving them a month."

Gareth nodded soberly at the reaction and smiled at the punishment, and laughed at the reward, "I think those are good incentives. I take it you're holding off for a couple days before you start, not that they will know?"

Giving a feral grin, Adam replied, "Tomorrow afternoon we plan on starting. We'll be having everyone take the afternoon and night off Thursday from construction, for the full moon. We'll take everyone who is up at Wild Valley, even if they are MacLaren, so you can send some up."

Gareth gave an equally feral grin in return, "Do some of my patrols on your way back up there. I have noticed the patrols have been stood down a little too far following the taking out of Night Depths. The two packs are not the only concerns out there."

Both young Alphas gave a sharp look, "What?" Brook whispered.

Gareth sighed, "Only rumours and circumstantial reports there has been some bad rogue activity which has been moving towards us from central US; several deaths and missing humans who are believed to just not have had their bodies found, which human law enforcement have reported as large dogs or even bears being the cause. Nothing has been fully documented. At the speed they have been seeing it move, if it arrives, will be a while, likely years, but there have been more minor reports all over. Following the attack and turning of a boy who was out running, almost a year ago, there is now a DNA record of the worst one, with a Kill order attached." He was annoyed the report had taken about nine months to arrive, but it was partly due to a lack of international couriers, as there wasn't much traffic between the packs which had a council looking over their shoulders and those which were independent. After a comment during the chat with Alpha Andrew, he had received a large packet of all the rogue traffic they had dealt with, and even the rumours of others, and more about his current issues. He had happily paid the courier and had sent a response to keep him updated on anything new, as the courier was heading straight back south, but with a few side stops on the way to the border for him.

Even Adam looked pale, remembering how hard his own turn was, "Is he OK?" he asked quietly.

Gareth sighed, "The report was the rogue pushed him onto a road where he hit his head, then a car ran into them both, pushing the rogue away. It seemed to save his life, but he was in an induced coma for three months while he turned. Adding to it, his parents were killed, and a sister hurt in a car accident while they were heading to visit him."

Adam and Brook both gasped in concern, close to tears of sympathy. While they were with just Gareth, they didn't have to hide their feelings, to always show their strength.

"Apparently," Gareth continued, "They have an uncle who is a born-wolf, and both been taken in by the Mac Tire' Dona Pack. I'll forward you the entire reports, so you can be briefed as well."

Brook shook her head, "Poor pups. I hope they can settle into their new world." It would be hard for the injured sister, as she was still human, but hard for the boy as well, as he came to understand his new urges. Looking up, "So nothing close or immediate. Rogues are always an issue."

Gareth sighed, "It seems there is many more rogues out and about in our area. It may be many of those who got kicked out are now actual Rogue, not like Ethan. Most run as soon as they are spotted, and few are very aggressive."

Adam sighed, "That's not what I wanted to hear. Has Martin been advised?"

"He will be." Gareth confirmed. "His meeting is after lunch today. I'll discuss the testing of the patrols with him. I'll tell them to say they are going to be starting tomorrow morning."

Brook laughed, "He's saying they're starting after lunch today."

"We want them random, so they aren't expecting them." Adam added.

Gareth nodded, "I think I may have others do them too. Keep the patrols on their toes." He made a note to discuss it with Martin on who else to have do it.

They discussed the decisions they had made over the week, and Gareth gave pointers on how they could have done things better, or just differently, as a learning exercise for them to understand what could come from their decisions. In no case did they have any changes to the decisions they had made.

Both discussed any details they had heard from other packs, so they could make larger plans. Both packs were right now mostly patrols, constructing the new pack, or the various support duties like hunting and cooking, or maintenance. The ones who worked for other companies were the least impacted, and even then, most volunteered their free time to the pack to help with other tasks, to free others to travel to the Wild Valley pack, to help out there.

Gareth was still handling most of the discussions with the other packs, as many still refused to acknowledge Adam and Brook as Alphas, although some were changing as word of their deeds reached them. They were going to deal with many of them in the summer, and since both were busy enough as it was, they were leaving it be.

*****

Bounding up to the gathered wolves gathered for the moon hunt that Thursday night, already shifted to his wolf, Adam let out a loud howl, with Brook coming in almost immediately after, to be joined with the entire pack letting out a howl of 'gather!'. *I have just got confirmation; we have permission for fifteen deer tonight. I want to target twelve, but if we find an extra one or two which needs to be taken out, we can.*

It surprised most of the pack into another howl of appreciation, as it was enough to have fun and help control the population. Weak deer which never got hunted tended to get sick easier. They also often got too many, with many humans blaming the wolves, just so they could hunt them. They were working to change it and having the key people aware there were werewolves who would protect their lesser cousins, and they needed to stop the inhumane wolf hunts.

Adam had got the e-mail of what was approved for their area from a human "Wildlife Management" point of view. Those in that department who were aware of them were a mix of Were from the packs in the area, and humans who had been let know of them. They knew they would be able to keep a better knowledge of what animals were in the area and manage them.

The howl got the nearby wolf pack going with a howl of their own. Many of the werewolves listened to their wishes for a successful hunt with a smile and replied with their thanks.

The wolves may become curious enough to come seek them out, or just stay in their territory. The werewolves and the actual wolves both acknowledged kinship, and while they had limited contact, the wolves knew the werewolves would protect them if needed, and there were cases of them helping and protecting an injured werewolf, especially a pup.

Come, lets run and hunt! Adam called, starting to pace forward, leading the hunt this time. Brook paced at his side, as the pack was learning she was no soft Luna, but an equal Alpha with Adam. Both could be soft when was needed and do the hard jobs. Jess joined them, staying just beyond his tail-tip, ready to break off and help lead another part of the hunt as needed. Ethan had been invited, as normally visiting Lone Wolves were not permitted to join in the hunt, as it was a pack bonding time, but as he was more of a prospective packmate, they were having more privileges.

Adam could feel the pride and joy from many of the wolves for a nice hunt. From what he had learned, it was a very long time since Alpha Night even showed his nose on a full moon, not caring to mingle with those of his pack. When he had heard the comment, he scared the one who said it with a savage growl; it showed how out of touch he had been. After apologising to them, he had giving them a hug and let them know they would always be leading the hunt as long as they were able.

*****

Waking up the next morning surrounded by packmates in the field near the pack house, his mate snuggled against his furry side, her muzzle tucked into his neck, with his own head across her shoulders, was blissful. Adam didn't want to move, but they needed to check on the patrols and if they had time, say a hello in person to their neighbouring wolves. His wolf wanted their scents.

Standing up with a yawn and a good stretch, woke her up, *Another successful hunt. You are getting good at them.* She told him, sending affection at her mate.

I had a good teacher, Adam told his mate, sending affection and thanks back.

They picked their way through the sleeping wolves, with the occasional one starting to wake up. They had taken out fourteen of the weakest. Two old bucks past their prime, two sick does, and three which had injuries were ones he noticed himself, the rest he wasn't sure on, other than one which looked like it had been bitten then escaped from a werewolf. None of his wolves had reported an escaped one, as they would sicken from the bite, even though it couldn't turn them. He suspected it was one of the lone or rogue wolves they knew were outside their territory.

Heading off towards the valley the wolves claimed, they circled outside their perimeter scent marks. Once they had circled it, back to the side facing their own territory, they relaxed in the shade from the late afternoon sun, panting a bit, as it was getting unusually hot.

They had stashed their packs fairly deep in the pack property, and running as wolves, for the chance encounters with humans, as they were still learning where they often were. *It would be easy to extend the actual pack territory to surround them and protect them.* Brook commented. *It's little but would allow us to monitor if the humans tried to kill them* The last had an undercurrent of a growl, as the BC government had done some 'culling' of wolves, where they used a collared wolf, and took out all the others of the pack, leaving that one to find a new pack, and repeating the killing. Both had agreed it was inhumane, and they would use the radio collar to disrupt the hunts if they came close. They were said to be done to help the caribou herds, but 'predation' wasn't the issue they had, it was the encroachment of human industry, and the fragmentation of the wilderness. If they didn't have all the logging or Oil and Gas industries, or climate change disrupting their sessional migration routes, they wouldn't be having issues. The issue was the human industries had a voice, and neither the caribou nor the wolves had one with the decision makers.

Hearing a howl from the pack, *"Where Cousin?"* It called; it seemed their circuit around the pack had them wanting to come meet them.

"Here! Come Cousin!" They howled back, keeping it simple. The wolves could understand them but would not understand a complex message.

The wolves approached from downwind, the Alpha male moving forward stiff legged, to touch noses and sniff them. Brook sat back and shifted to human, which startled the Alpha into jumping back, but as she sat back down beside Adam, who stayed wolf, moved forward and sniffed her again, before giving her a lick, the Alpha moved forward, and accepted a pet and an ear scratch before wagging, and allowing the other four wolves to come forward to greet them.

"Leaders?" The female alpha wolf yapped with a head tilt after greeting the two after her mate decided they were safe to meet. Brook could understand them, but human mouths couldn't respond in wolf sounds easily.

"Yes; Leaders of great many." Adam yapped back in agreement, knowing they would not know numbers as large as the number they had looking to them. *I never thought I would be talking to actual wolves.* He commented his awe to his mate. He wished he had his camera with him!

It's rare, Brook agreed, *But these wolves seem to be fairly smart. Sometimes a Lone Wolf will join with our cousins and teach them some. From how smart they are, I suspect a generation or two ago at most.*

"Give help?" Barked the alpha female, who was actually the leader, and chose who the male they would mate with and make the protector of the pack.

From how she said it, was looking for a promise to protect them than needing help now Brook offered. She didn't understand much more than Adam, as MacLaren didn't have a pack of them.

"Yes," Adam whuffed back, *"Give help/protection."* He agreed, *"Keep cousins safe."*

"Good." The female gave, imperiously, tail up like a flag.

"Making Safe Den West." Adam offered, knowing they understood directions, *"Protection when needed there."* He offered. He knew they were wild and wouldn't want to stay unless they had to. That he was accepting them as kin and offering them a safe place if needed would help them.

"Good. We hunt." The female said, heading off with the rest following. They had no words for goodbye, they just separated.

Jess, have the word spread, we just took the wolf pack under our wing and protection. Adam called, passing the scents of the pack, so they can know they were permitted to approach. *Have them extend the sensors around their territory* He passed a mental image of the map, with a marking of the territory they were accepting, *No Were packs in the area, so we don't need to deal with them. Brook and I already scent marked the area.*

OK. Jess said shortly, a bit surprised, *I'm a bit busy right now* She said, before fading. It was one problem with distance communication, didn't know when they were busy.

*****

They panted laughter the following Saturday early afternoon, as they padded into MacLaren's Pack house. They had caught an entire patrol of four Weres taking a nap in the warm sun. They had found a bunch of pups having some hunting training and had co-opted them with their instructor's permission and had the pups take down the patrol. The pups trotted right behind them, with heads held high and tails up, proudly. Their trainer was padding beside them, also looking amused.

The four of the patrol followed them in, heads down with their ears back, and tails tucked, knowing they did wrong. When they shifted to human, Joshua tossed them clothes, having been given a heads up. Martin and Gareth were standing there waiting for them, arms crossed, and stern looks on their faces.

The four shifted human and kneeled, after pulling on the clothes, knowing they were in very big trouble. They hadn't returned fast, and with them returning with the pups looking proud, and the patrol looking dejected had word arriving much faster than them, so they had a fair number waiting, especially when the Alphas came out to wait, and looked annoyed.

"These four were tasked with patrolling the pack to keep us safe, but while on patrol, decided to take a nap, which is permitted, as long as there is one awake to keep watch." Adam stated, ignoring those who gathered, speaking to the Alpha, but doing so loud enough all could hear. Allowing them to rest and nap on breaks helped to randomise the patrols, which made it more difficult for someone to get a schedule and work between them, but they needed to have one on watch for them. Pausing as the part of the pack gathered, and started to murmur, "They failed to do that. We have been doing tests to see how good the patrols are doing, and they were aware of it." The pack started to growl at the failure of the patrol, and all four blanched. It was one thing to be caught with a surprise check, another to know they were doing random ones, and to still be caught. "We took them out with a group of four young pups, who haven't been able to take out anything bigger than a *rabbit*." He nodded to the four standing off to the side, looking pleased and very proud to have been given a task to help the pack. He didn't need to mention they had been told by their instructor they were still learning how to take out rabbits and had a low success rate. Being easier than a rabbit hunt would be even more humiliating to the enforcers.

It made the four Enforcers go red with humiliation as the pack laughed at the idea a patrol was so stood down to have been detected and then had the pups brought in and enough to have simulated a take out without any waking up.

"If they had been rogues, we would have had the four dead, and the only warning would be their death hitting the rest of us." Adam growled and was joined by the rest as displeasure rolled through the bonds.

"We think they should be de-ranked, to start." Brook stated, "Waste and Latrine duties after house-arrest, then if they want to go back to be an Enforcer, have to retrain and qualify again."

Gareth gave a feral grin, "Agreed." He accepted to the satisfaction of the pack. "You will be publicly announced about this at dinner, and I will announce the length then. Don't be late." He told them before turning away.

Martin gave them disapproval look, from his place at the side of the Alphas, "If it was up to me, you'd be whipped and locked in the Rogue cells for a year. You have been reassigned to Theta rooms. Follow me, as you are to stay in them till dinner. Internet and phone access to those rooms has already been disconnected." They had only a copy of the pack laws, rules, and some histories which Adam had requested for them, he knew they would be about what happened to others in similar cases.

The four nearly crawled up under the disapproval growls of the rest of the pack. They had failed badly. That they weren't being kicked out was the only thing which was keeping them going; all were old enough they should know better but were under a century. Their excuse to Adam and Brook was they were deep in the territory and were at a low-risk status.

The entire trot back Adam and Brook had lectured them as just a warmup to soften them up for the encounter with the Alpha. The disapproval given by the pack would cut deep. Brook had liked the idea of lecturing, so both had been reading all the histories they could, so they could give more return.

Walking into Gareth's meeting room, Gareth and Maria were there, along with both pack's elders, as they had requested.

"Why did you want to keep the four disgraces of a wolf here?" Elise asked, "I say they should be Omega, if not kicked out." Several other elders murmured agreement or nodded.

"First, the conditions: They were inside the 'safe' perimeter, where taking naps is permitted. They just missed the part where they had to have one on watch. They were waiting for their next scheduled run, but they were to start about five minutes before the pups pounced, putting them late." Adam told them, not bothering with sitting. While technically they were late, they had a twenty-minute window to start, as another way to randomise the patrols, so they still had five minutes left to start.

"The fact they were so out that four pups could take them out without any waking made it hard to let them off for it. The other fact they knew we were running tests but decided not to follow the rules to the letter and spirit. They should not have been so stood down even in the 'safe' area is why we are punishing them. If they were that tired, they should have called it in for relief, as they would not be an effective patrol." He had to stop, for a moment to let it sink in. The pack would have had no issues with it, as they were doing a double shift, and sometimes the first one was enough. They had teams on call for those times.

"The other thing, I have found the patrols in general are lacking awareness," Gareth told the elders, "This hasn't been the first patrol which had been caught napping between two patrols, but a general complacency of the patrols. So, while I feel this patrol needs to be disciplined in such a way it will make them an example for the other patrols in both packs, of we cannot tolerate inattention when they are the first line of defence, even if the sensors are there to assist them. Their example will show all the Enforcers we are serious about enforcement of the rules, and hopefully it will not be needed any further." He added. Several looked thoughtful.

After giving them a bit to think about it, "Although we will give them a good punishment, I don't want to make it a permanent punishment, which ranking as Omega or kicking them out will do." Adam added, "I would prefer to give them another chance, since all four have had spotless records before now. Also, since the patrollers have been generally too lax, I don't think a permanent punishment for them is warranted." He didn't think any of them had asked to move packs, he was going to double check, and if so, it was going to be denied.

Most of the elders were nodding in understanding and agreement, finally understanding what he was trying to do, so Adam sat down and pulled out his laptop, "Now, what we have an hour before supper to figure out how long to have them punished?"

Chapter 8 – Punishments

Walking into the dining hall, the four were standing at attention, right in front of the Alpha's spots. As much of the pack which could make it was there, still leaving it fairly empty feeling after getting used to having extras there. Brook and Adam followed behind Gareth and Maria. They had given the recommendation, and had led the meeting, but Gareth and Maria were the Alphas of the wolves in question, so they got to hand out the punishments.

"Before we start to eat." Gareth said into the expectant silence; he didn't have to do a thing to catch everyone's attention, "We have a punishment to dole out."

Looking each in the eyes till they submitted, "Ardolf. Connor. Kurt. Tate." He gave, naming each to the pack, not that it was needed. "You four have been found to have failed in your duties to the pack, due to your negligent actions. Your inaction could have put the pack at risk. It did put yourselves at grave risk." He didn't need to give them disapproval and sadness that they failed; the pack was doing it for him. "As such I am within my right to have you banished or ranked as Omega." He stopped and let them digest his statement and see them pale. If he had the right to do them, death was also on the plate, as those were the three most severe punishments, and if one was permitted; all three were almost always available.

"For your sake, we have decided on lesser punishments." Gareth could feel a large amount of relief from the pack, with some disappointment flavouring it and even a few being upset over it. "You will be marked with red collars, to show you are being disciplined. Until your punishment is complete, you are not permitted to remove them, except within your room. Also, you are stripped of your ranks and seniority. You are now ranked at the bottom of the pack, below the Thetas." As they were employed by the pack, it would mean they had their pay suspended while they were on punishment duties. Adam and Brook moved to the wolves and clipped bright red nylon dog collars around their necks. "You will first serve two months of house arrest. You will be permitted an hour of supervised exercise of your choice, outside or in the gym, and will require you to have your meals with the pack. The rest of the time you will be restricted to your rooms. You have each been provided with reading materials which you will be expected to know at the end of the house arrest." He didn't bother telling them they would be tested on their knowledge then or failing the test would have their punishment time reset and would have to redo the first part. He did plan on weekly quizzes and would be told they needed to pass them. They wouldn't punish if they didn't pass the first quiz but would be told then as they wouldn't know of the punishments for failure.

Gareth gave them a feral grin, liking the touch Adam had given him; using the punishment to educate the wolf in why the rule is there and a reminder of the rules which are in place and including the *why* and case studies of what happened to others and their packs following the similar failure. He was thinking he would use it in the future. Now that the pack laws binder was electronic, Adam had gotten a bulk order of waterproof e-readers and were-resistant cases for the pack, so they could load them up easily and have as many copies as was needed. They had more on order; enough so eventually everyone would have a reader and their own copy of the laws and history. The elders had been all for it, as it made sure the knowledge was available to all. With the pack having the printers too, any who felt they wanted a printed one instead, could make it.

"Once the first part is complete to my satisfaction," he told them, and the pack, "You will then serve a year dealing with the communal garbage and cleaning the Theta and Delta bathrooms." Since those were shared use, some got really well used, and always needed constant cleaning, sometimes multiple times a day.

Gareth wanted to smile at the disbelief and horror look on their faces; once again Adam had found exactly what the worst punishment the wolf needed, "Once that year is up, your work will be evaluated. As long as your supervisors and I are satisfied you did your work well, you will be released to the final stage, where you will be given other jobs, but still ranked the lowest of the low for an additional two years. The elders, myself, and my mate will review your work then with your supervisors, and if satisfied, will release you from your punishment. At that point, if you wished, you can re-apply to be Enforcers, although Martin has said you will have to go through all the training again."

Gareth looked over the pack, and most had a satisfied look on their face. While being punished, they were also not permitted to participate in the spring trials, and this year they would not even be able to attend, as they would still be on confinement. *That is much more complex of a punishment.* Gareth told Adam and Brook, *I would have given them a year of confinement, but it can cause wolves to go insane. I have to say this will be much easier on their mental health, even if it is longer.*

I had noticed our wolf half can't stand long periods of being cooped up, and the smaller the space, the shorter the time. Adam replied. He had found himself couldn't stand more than two hours at a stretch in a vehicle before he needed a break. *It is why there is the hour of exercise and the meals with the pack. It punishes them, but also shows them they are still part of the pack and lets them have a chance to maintain their pack bonds.* Wolves were much more gregarious and needed the touch of their packmates. He wanted better wolves out of it, not wolves which needed mental help getting their centre back. If one of their friends wanted to join them for the night, it would be permitted as well.

"Are there any who want to comment on what they are receiving?" Gareth asked the gathered pack, to with there was silence, or shaking of heads. After giving a long couple of minutes for any to decide to speak up, "I am calling this punishment assigned." He turned to the four and dismissed them, "Go eat, then return to your rooms." They quickly moved to get out of the direct sight of the alphas, even if the acid-burn of the disappointment of the pack still burned in their mind, over their actions. The few points of wishing for a harsher punishment had disappeared, even before the last stage was announced.

The pack seemed to all have a single topic of discussion: the punishments which had been handed out. From the complexity many could see Adam's hand in it, even from his short time, they had noticed how he usually did multiple stage punishments. The troublemakers had found to their disappointment he seemed to know how to tailor the punishments to the individual crime and wolf to get the maximum effect out of it, while not placing a burden to the pack to see it happen, nor to cause major long-term scars to the wolf, once they had served their punishment. Most approved of it, especially those Thetas who got a reprieve from having to do those very dirty jobs, they had smiles on their faces.

Chris had made an appearance to the cheers of the pack, having been cleared by medical, he was done the most critical part of the turn, and now it was waiting for his wolf to awaken and start talking to him. He and Koda sat down beside Adam. He looked a little pale, and was a little shaky on his legs, but it was just due to mostly being bedridden for three weeks. Adam gave a good hug to both, before they sat down, welcoming them.

Brook returned with a plate for both of them, heavy on meat. Placing them down she too gave them a hug, "Glad to see you up and about, Chris."

Chris gave a grin before starting to dig into his meal. Koda smiled at his Alphas, acknowledging his good job as he dug into his own. Chatting with the others at the table, they all thought the punishment fit the crime, although they were going to be ribbed for a long time they had been taken out by pups. Adam hadn't told anyone, but they had taken a picture of the four pups pouncing on the patrol. When they complete their house arrest, a copy will be in their e-mail box. He was going to wait for the Alpha's approval before distributing the pictures or making any prints.

Chris sat back with a satisfied smile, his plate almost licked clean, "I have no idea how I ate all of that!" he said, surprised.

Everyone laughed, and Koda murmured, "It's your Werewolf metabolism kicking in. You'll probably be hungry in two to three hours."

Adam smiled, "Tomorrow, Koda, take Chris down to the gym and start working to train him on his new body, slowly." Turning to Chris, "Your muscles are going to be much stronger, and your endurance like an athlete at the peak of their game, so you will need to re-train yourself on how much power to use. Then you need to start training to werewolf standards. You have a year, and I expect you to pass the Delta trials." He held his eyes till Chris dropped them.

"Yes, Alpha. I understand." He replied. He had seen the level needed and didn't think he currently even could reach the Theta level which was expected of all. But since Adam expected he could, he would try his hardest.

"I will make sure you have the duties to get the leadership skills, starting this fall, once you finish turning." Adam added quietly. Some resented being under the supervision of a human, even if they are turning, so he wasn't going to put him in that position. He had enough to learn as it was. As soon as his wolf started talking to him, he would be gaining some more access, and the last once he turned for the first time.

Adam had found out after he finished turning, as the few thorns he had to deal with had become happy to do his requests and became good workers. They felt he didn't understand them enough or the right to be over them but respected his fighting skills so didn't challenge him.

Taking his used dishes, he gripped Koda's shoulder for a moment, *Keep him out of trouble, and help him learn to be a wolf,* He asked, his mind voice laced with the trust they were putting in the wolf and thanks for his work so far.

I will do my best. He has been reading all the information you left him and asking questions. He wants to move up to the new pack house as soon as he can. Koda told him.

Adam shook his head, *He can't until his first turn. We have no facilities to house anyone who can't shift.* It still got cold enough at night most slept as wolves for the fur coat designed for the conditions. *We will take both him and you up then. Till then, use the time to learn and train*

Heading out the door, Steve caught Adam's attention, "Could I speak to you two privately?" he asked respectfully.

Nodding, they went into a small meeting room and sat down, "So, what did you want to speak to us about?" Adam asked when Steve didn't start speaking. Both Brook and him thought they knew what he was going to ask.

"Can I be turned?" He asked, speaking very fast.

Brook shook her head, "No." She answered firmly, "You disobeyed when you were joined to the pack. You are going to need to either find your mate or wait a decade to be turned." At his disappointed look, she decided to elaborate, "I looked it up when we first realised what you did, expecting this request eventually. The pack bonds seem very strong, but they can be brittle, especially with human minds. To put it one way, you cracked your bonds when as they were first forming you used the drugs, and it takes a very long time for them to heal fully. If you change, it will stress them, as will changing packs, and I have read of cases where they have snapped badly. I will not take the risk."

Steve sighed, "At least there is a reason why, not just that I am being turned down. I can wait."

Brook smiled at Adam, who had sat back and let her deal with him, "If you do find your mate, as soon as your mating bonds have completed, you can be turned. The changes from the mating would heal the issues, so there would be no problem then."

Nodding, Steve stood up and gave a hug to the two who had helped him find his place with the pack, "Thank you for supporting me joining the pack, and I am still sorry I caused problems. Hope you two have a good evening."

Adam laughed as he traded a heated look with his mate, "We will, oh, we will." As he closed the door and placed the "In Use" sign beside the door, so those would know it was available.

Taking his mate's hand, they quickly went to their room, where the clothes were nearly ripped off. They hadn't had a bed or sure privacy since they headed out Tuesday after lunch, four days before.

*****

They spent Sunday catching up on all the paperwork which seemed to pile up, with many Alphas requesting meetings with them. Some came in as requests to find out when they had time to meet, to a demand they present themselves to the alpha in question at their pack on such and such date and time. The nice ones, they commented they were overseeing a pack split and building a new pack house, so wouldn't have time to meet one-on-one, but sent invites to the Alpha Conference, where they could make time for an hour private meeting while there.

Many sent confirmation of their going, and those they passed to Gareth. It was turning out to not be the small gathering he expected, but a major one. "I'm glad we're not hosting it!" Brook commented after the fifth one commented about them going. Some of those going were packs they had to look up, as they were from farther away than they expected, and it was either their actions or the wolfsbane which caused enough of a stir for them to want to attend.

Those who gave demands as if they were theirs to command, got their generic answer which Gareth and the Elders had worked with them on, of "No. We are not yours to command. You are welcome to meet us at the Alpha's conference, but as we are very busy overseeing a pack split, and the construction of our pack house, you will have to wait. We will let you know when we are willing to meet with you." They would meet with those ones one-on-one once they were more entrenched in their position, and the construction was done, and it would be the leaders of those packs who would travel to meet them.

They didn't have to answer to anyone outside of the treaties, and there was nothing in the treaties about how often each Alpha had to meet with others, if ever. Courtesy was you answered requests with arranging something, but most Alphas ignored the demands of their peers who treated them like subordinates; they could put off without reprisals or set the terms they would be willing to meet under. Adam grinned as he signed off on the third letter in their pile as such, putting it in their mail bag after sealing it. Some of it was because of their bonds with Gareth and Maria and the MacLaren pack, they could use them as a buffer as well. Any attack of them would automatically be an attack on MacLaren, and as had been shown with the two recent packs, only a pack which was suicidal would attack them. With the absorbing of all the new members into Wild Valley, and them training them to be a force not to be trifled with, it was likely they wouldn't have problems, once the realisation got out.

Adam got savage pleasure from being able to refuse their demands, and not deal with them until later. It seemed many Alphas were planning on being there for the Alpha conference. A few had been invited to the wedding just before it. They had decided against a honeymoon trip, as their pack needed them, and they were just satisfying Adam's human relatives. A honeymoon he had found was a fairly new concept anyways; before that, after the wedding, they would just get back to work as farmers and start trying to make a family. The richer ones would go on a tour to visit those family members who couldn't make it to the wedding, often to show off their wedding outfits. As like the engagement ring, it had been started as a way to make money, and the marketing inferred how 'everyone was doing it' to get it into the culture through a peer pressure. As such, both felt there was no need; if they needed a break, they could relax somewhere in the territory, to be out of immediate reach, but still close enough if there was an issue to be there quickly, which was what they had planned.

They had received several congratulations, notably from Arctic Shadow, and Longview packs for accepting the Alpha position and confirmation of representatives at their wedding and requests for meetings at the conference. It gave them two packs who were there to support them. The requests for meeting privately were scheduled after the signing, where the treaty would be an additional point of protecting them against any threats.

Joshua rolled a cart with food in at dinner time, causing both Adam and Brook to stop and take a deep breath as the food smells hit them. They stood up and headed for the food, as if magnetically attracted to it. Toby and Sam followed them into the room.

"You have been working so hard, and I didn't see you out for lunch, I thought you might have lost track of the time and need a break." Joshua commented, as they started filling their plates, and they joined them. "I thought we could have a family dinner – well, of those who are here, anyways."

Adam smiled and waited for the two youngest to get the first choice of the food, for good manners, even though he was nearly growling in hunger. Placing his food on the table, he gave all three a good hug, "I am glad you could. We have been busy and did lose track of time."

Brook nodded, as she started eating; they had totally missed lunch.

So, how has your training and work been going? Adam asked, as he started to eat, switching to talk silently, since he was hungry.

Been good. We have passed the unofficial details and want to try out for the Spring Trials. Toby said, before both him and Sam gave him puppy dog eyes.

Adam sighed, *I have no problem letting you. But Sam, you need to get permission from your parents. You are both very young but seem to have the skills to succeed.* Both nodded and looked excited, *Even if you do qualify, it just means you will get a few more duties for training. The rank will not really effective till you become adults.*

Both nodded and looked excited.

I did notice your book learning has been good too. Adam told them, pride showing in the talk. The two blushed with pleasure. They got reports on all four of their learning and training, and mostly didn't see anything they would change, as all of them worked hard.

Brook smiled at Joshua, *We also noticed you have been given the supervisor job for the others in this wing. How are you liking that?*

Joshua smiled, *I'm enjoying it, especially when you two are away, and I don't need to worry much about cleaning here!*

It had them all laughing, as it sent the mental picture of them coming in dripping of mud, leaving pawprints everywhere, and covering everything in it, but also the undertone of joking.

Seriously, I like the fact I get to boss other around, and make sure they are doing a good job. Mostly they are, and I don't need to do much, although I have to make sure they have all the supplies they need from the stock Rein keeps. I also like the feeling of others trusting me to look out for them. Joshua answered.

I'm planning on having you and your sister switch after the Spring Trials, so you can get some experience there. Adam commented, and when he looked at Brook, she smiled in agreement.

OK. Joshua replied, reluctantly, not wanting to change already.

We plan on switching you two every two months, until we start moving everyone up there. Adam advised him, *It allows for you both to gain similar experience, and for you to sleep in a bed about the same.*

Seeing as to why they were doing short periods, Joshua nodded, agreeing with it. He knew his sister would like to have a bed too.

Turning to the younger two, who were working with security in addition to their regular education, *I plan on having you two move up, once the security is starting to be installed. You will help supervise the install and setup of the security systems. As long as Martin agrees, once you are of age and qualified, you will be in charge of the Pack Security.*

The two just stared with big eyes, surprised at the trust he was giving them.

I wondered why Martin was having us shadow him more and having us do almost every duty. Sam commented, *He's training us to do his job!*

Adam nodded, as he finished his food, and sat back content, "Yes, although he is arranging a mentor for you two to be the one actually in charge till you are of age. Till then, you cannot technically be in security. Also, you have to be fully qualified at Beta before you take over."

Brook chuckled as they were again frozen in shock, "It is part of why we are letting you test early, so you can get used to the format and how they test early and see what you need to test on. I know you are helping train other pups with weapons, even though you haven't been certified as trainer levels. That you can get right away. The laws and inter-pack stuff can also be done early. The leadership will have to wait."

Adam added, "Once you have Trainer status, you won't need to be supervised while you train the pups, although you can't do adults, which will help take a load off the other trainers." Seeing them smile, he had to add, "When you come of age, you will have to retest to show you are still at the levels and get the Adult Trainer certification."

*****

The next morning, Adam and Brook sighed as they flopped on the couch in Gareth's office, each having a coffee in a travel mug and a bun full of meat. They had been chatting late into the night with the three of their family who was here, so didn't get to sleep until late—or was it very early morning—and as such missed breakfast, other than taking what they could eat on the run.

Gareth chuckled, "I heard you had a family evening and night. Must be hard having it split."

Brook sighed, "It is, but at least we are still able to mind-speak. I assume the greater range is due to us being Alphas?"

Gareth nodded, "Yes. When you two met, if you weren't so injured you were fading in and out, you could have called me or Maria for help, and we would have heard you. As it was, I knew you were injured, and you were on the eastern edge of the territory, but hadn't been able to pinpoint your location, and had alerted patrols, but before they could find you, Adam called in with you, and knew you were closer to Longview, especially in a vehicle."

Brook was startled, "I didn't know that." She said quietly.

Gareth smiled, "Us Alphas need to keep it quiet, so others don't find out we have a much greater range to talk. If I strained, and Grant or Louise were listening for it, we could talk, but it is easier to do it on the phone, especially now it's secured."

Brook and Adam nodded, "I guess there is no full list of abilities?" Adam asked.

"Nope; we have kept it mostly self-discovery or another Alpha training to do it." Gareth replied, "You're welcome to write the book, but only Alphas would be allowed to read it."

Sitting back to relax, Adam asked, "So, the four miscreants, how are they doing?"

"Bored out of their minds. They should be starting to read the information this morning, then howling bored by tomorrow afternoon." Gareth said with a chuckle. "We put them in the best insulated rooms, so to not disturb the others." Getting serious and looking at Adam with respect, "I think the having the meals with the pack will help keep them sane and show them—and the rest of the pack—they are being punished, but they are part of the pack. I'm not going to have to work to re-integrate them when the isolation is over, and they still have more of the punishment, dealing with items which most wolves find distasteful!" He chuckled, "They are going to be well chastised when done!"

Adam laughed, "That was the plan; have them well punished but help the pack by having them take distasteful duties. I plan to do it myself, either distasteful duties or the least valued shifts. I prefer not to just have them sitting around doing nothing."

The three shared a chuckle over the punishment, before settling. "Before I forget, John and Bri are coming back on Wednesday, and will need you on hand here, as I need to introduce you to them. They are finally done their training."

Adam and Brook nodded at his request.

"It has been quiet without those two leading the pranks." Brook commented. Adam looked confused, "Before they left for their training two years ago, if they got bored, they would start pranks. They were never harmful, but more just to shock someone."

Gareth chuckled, "They sure kept the patrols on their toes; neon pink paintballs." Looking at Brook, "I wonder how they got those, and paint guns..."

Brook just looked away, not saying anything. It was known she helped them with some of their pranks, but nobody knew how or who helped them with their supplies for sure. Many suspected Brook, but there was no proof as when she was asked about it, she sidestepped it, never actually saying yes or no to it. The most the Alphas had gotten was, she *could have* got them. "It did keep them on their toes and taught them how to dodge bullets." She commented, "It may have saved lives, even with the recent attacks."

Gareth looked thoughtful. "Hmm, I may put them to work thinking up stuff and continuing the patrol *testing*. They would have loved to be there when you took the four down with pups."

Adam pulled out his tablet and showing the pictures he had taken of the takedown, clearly showing the four sleeping, and the pups creeping up on them, and one even of the four in the air pouncing. The next showed the shock on two of the patrol's faces; the other two were facing away.

Gareth roared laughter, till tears ran down his face. "I want a big copy of the pounce for the pack, and I want a smaller for my office here."

Adam nodded, and after discussing what sizes, sent the commands to have them printed. "I'll get them to you by supper, framed."

Brook smiled, "There has already been a laptop placed in each of their rooms for them, with the initial logon. Have them let us know if they needed any other software for it."

Gareth smiled, "It is going to be a big surprise for them. They have been bugging me about upgrading, and I haven't told them about any of the networking changes, just they could talk to you about what they want done when they get here."

Brook shook her head, "I hope they didn't stop at an electronic store and pick up a laptop on the way home."

"Nope," Gareth said, "They have no access to any money till they are back here. There was no need. They *did* ask about getting one, but I said we'd discuss what they need when they were back."

Looking at his notes, "That is all I had, you have anything?" Gareth asked.

"Only that the pack is working hard, and they are making noticeable progress on the construction. They are limited by the speed the concrete is setting and can't go any faster. It just is having them be ahead of schedule on the other buildings. The temporary storage rooms are done, so the supplies are being moved in. The wind turbines and solar panels at the storage rooms, which will be the workshops are now almost done. They are finishing up on the power centre, getting the battery banks ready, so they can shut down the temporary diesel generators. The natural gas one is just about ready for certification." Adam rattled off.

Most wolves would be quite happy when they could shut down the noisy portable generators. Next was to get the big permanent air compressor system installed in the shop complex, as it was much quieter and hidden away, and would much reduce the construction noise. They would run temporary pipes for the air lines to where they needed, with extra accumulator tanks. The natural gas generator was much less smelly and had a much higher efficiency than the temporary diesel ones. He was crossing his fingers they could get most of their power from the solar, wind, and the bit of hydro which they were planning. They didn't want the cost of hooking up to the power grid, but they might need to. They had everything they needed in the power room, if they did, they just needed to trench in the wires into the capped access hole and connect to the input disconnect to do it.

He had considered geothermal, but the costs to get it going and run it was too high. He had left space where they could have three additional sources of power without any issues and had been built individual shut offs so they could get them going without needing to shut down the central main bus. There were more spaces for three more outgoing connections as well with large breaker spaces.

Looking at the clock, "Well, you have two hours before lunch, to go catch up on your lost sleep." Gareth told them with a nod, as the two yawned.

They smiled and headed out, taking his suggestion.

Chapter 9 – Returning Heirs

Monday afternoon they trained hard with Joshua, Toby, and Sam. The Spring Trials started the next Sunday and went as long as there were any who needed testing. Usually, it went for a week or two, but the number who were looking to update was almost everyone who qualified and weren't on some sort of punishment which would preclude participation.

The MacLaren Elders were grumbling, as it meant much more work for them. For the Wild Valley Pack elders, this was a whole new experience, which at their age was a treasured thing. The last time their pack had the Spring Trials was long before they became Elders and was in a much different format, so they where quite happy to learn what to do. They were working with the MacLaren Elders to get the preparations going, and there was going to be enough who were available to be race monitors. They ended up having to agree to use some who had finished their testing for the later time, to switch out the earlier ones.

The training areas were packed, so much so Adam grumbled, and headed off with the others to a more remote clearing, where they set up a makeshift circle to practice.

Joshua sighed, as he stepped into the circle, "I don't know why we need to work this hard." He complained, getting the staff up in time to block Adam's.

"Rein, Mikan, Brook, and I," He commented, with a strike with each name, before letting Joshua strike at him, "All believe you and your sister can be the Maintenance Managers for the pack, but we have to get you up to a Beta level to be qualified for it. If we can get you to at least a Delta, we can qualify you as a trainee for the position."

Adam grinned, and lightly tapped Joshua's chest, as he stood frozen, "You need to not get distracted, even as we talk." He rebuked.

Joshua looked at Adam annoyed, "Yes dad." He said, as they continued, "That is just so surprising. Growing up, the highest dream we had was of us taking care of the Alphas. We had no thoughts we would even be permitted to become Deltas, let alone *Betas* and never in a leadership role."

Adam smiled, "I think my leadership abilities are rubbing off, and you are excelling. I know we will be watching the others closely at the trials to pick out those who will be offered senior spots or supervisors. As such, they have Sunday for us and Gareth's pups, so all can see, then Monday for key people, like you. Then the rest start Tuesday."

Joshua was silent as they worked more. A few times he was nearly able to hit Adam and got grunts of surprise. "It's never been like that before; everyone is jumbled together." He complained.

"You've never had Alpha levels doing their initial qualifying. Most want to see it, so are doing them separately." Adam advised. "We not only have myself and Brook, but I have heard John and Brianna are trying for it too."

Joshua nodded, starting to be winded, as Adam sped up on the movements. After a bit of Joshua keeping up, he starting to make mistakes, so Adam called for a halt, as Joshua panted.

"Your turn," Adam called to Brook. She smiled and called both Toby and Sam up.

"You two need to learn to work together. You two are together against me." Brook told them.

At first the two worked separately, and Brook kept ahead of them, showing her longer amount of training in it. Adam didn't think he had the experience to handle it without some extensive work for it.

Brook was able to mostly defend herself against the two, as they were only barely working together. They were working enough she couldn't separate them, and guarded each other's backs, but not enough to attack together.

Brook stopped them once they were dripping sweat, "That was OK, but you two need to start working together to attack. You did do a good job of staying together to not let me separate you and protecting each other. When you have the last down, it makes it much harder for one to defend against two."

Both panted, nodding.

Adam looked up and estimated the time from the sun, "We have time for a quick jog before heading to supper." He told them, heading to jog along the trail. The others quickly followed. They kept it fairly slow, to use it as a cool down, taking side trails which looped and took an indirect route back to the pack house.

We're heading back up to Wild Valley tomorrow evening. Brook advised, *We're going to continue the patrol testing, and give John and Bri a tour.*

All three laughed, *So far, few of the patrols even bother reporting the attacks.* Sam mentioned. *Link us and we will let whoever is in the office know, so they can watch with the surveillance systems, and we can deal with them if they fail to report it.*

Martin has been telling us stories about John and Bri before they went off to the training. Toby commented, *I did like the story of paintballs. Could we do that now?* he asked

Brook laughed, *I had forgotten what John and Breanna had done to keep the patrols on their toes, until Gareth reminded me.* She replied, *I have ordered some paintball guns and pink paintballs earlier today. Should be arriving in a day or two*

They all laughed; the patrols were going to be sporting pink spots when they did.

I ordered four guns and plenty of ammo. Brook added, *John and Bri I think will definitely be interested in helping us keep them on their toes, as it seems they have started getting lazy.* With the Alpha's approval, she had been able to get much better weapons than the basic ones they had before. These ones had much more range and were more accurate even at a distance.

*****

Supper was talk about the two returning, as it seems the word was out. Most were looking forward to them returning and were wondering if they would be coming with a mate or not. Adam was taking all the stories and trying to put together a picture of them, as they hadn't been back since the short holiday at the autumn equinox before he had joined the pack.

Brook was helpful in describing them to him and thought they would get along well. Even he was caught up in the excitement. There was betting on who would succeed and be named Next Alpha, as both couldn't be. With Mark and Ben being the Seconds, since Adam and Brook were basically only honourary now, as they were Alphas of Wild Valley now.

Heading off to the firepit that evening, there was far fewer people there; he realised after a moment most were up at the other site. *Next Monday evening, I think we need to spend it at the other pack, and make sure the pit is ready, so we can have time with them, not just here.* He told his mate, not wanting the others to have it even cross their minds he didn't care about them.

I agree, although make it the week after. They will be here for the Trials. Brook replied, *Well, other than the patrols, and even those will be scaled back.*

Getting swept up with the others in the songs and camaraderie around the fire, he brought his mind to the now, instead of letting it wander. As usual, there were many wanting their personal attention.

Adam, and his wolf were quite happy to have the pack come to them for care and comfort. They didn't want to just be known for their punishments, but the fact they were getting to be known for being fair, just, and inventive kept most from wanting to find out what their own punishment was.

*****

Rolling out of bed the next morning, with a groan, then a thud as he rolled literally out of bed, Adam groaned, "Can't we sleep in today?" They had only got two or three hours of sleep that night. Brook only growled her annoyance about being disturbed and her reluctance to wake up.

Joshua slipped in, "Yes Dad, you can." He told him, "I was just asked by the elders to request to cancel their meeting, as they are busy preparing for the Trials."

Adam opened one eye, and crawled, literally, back into bed, and snuggled his mate, who appeared to already be asleep again with Charlie against her back as he did occasionally, "Granted. Wake us in time for a shower before lunch." He instructed, before closing his eyes and embracing sleep. If Joshua gave a response, he didn't hear it.

*****

After dressing nice for the two returning, and a nice lunch, they joined many who were off-duty, or could get away, to welcome John and Bri back.

Stepping up beside Gareth, "They just are parking, and will be taking a walk outside, as they have been driving for the last six hours." Their flight had got bumped and had taken one up to another city instead of the nearest one; they had enough notice to have a driver with a vehicle to get there in time. He murmured quietly, "They should be here in about ten minutes."

Adam nodded, "At first, I had thought you had no pups, although there had been off hand commented here and there. It took me a while to connect and find out what they were doing."

Gareth smiled, "We were lucky they both qualified for The Academy. It is an honour to the pack they got to go. There are rumours out they are looking for a new location which is low on human activities. They have found the European sites are being encroached too much and looking at moving over here."

Adam smiled, "Oh? Maybe invite them to the Alpha's conference, and we can show off the area here. We have plenty of room, and with mountain parks around us, it is very unlikely to be seen."

"They already requested to come, which is how I knew about the issue. They plan on coming to see it, not sure on anything farther."

A howl of greeting came up, as they could see two people walking up, each with a large backpack.

A grin lit on their faces, as they walked up to Gareth and Maria, and gave them a big hug.

"You know Brook, this is her mate, Adam." Gareth stated, leaving their rank as a surprise.

John gave Adam a hug, as both had their wolves come forward to take in the scent of the strange wolf. Adam could smell their Alpha in potential, but not totally there yet.

He'll be Alpha within the next decade, His wolf commented, as John seemed surprised, and took a second, and a third sniff.

"Alphas?" He commented, releasing Adam, "And partly of another pack?"

Adam nodded to both comments, with a smile.

"Why didn't you tell us?" John declared, annoyed at the smirk on his father's face.

Gareth laughed, "I thought it would be a nice surprise. After the greeting, take your stuff to your rooms, and come to our living room, and we'll get you up to speed on the changes and what has happened in the last few months."

"You mean like all the sensors and cameras in the forest?" He asked under his breath, going to give Brook a good hug too. "Congratulations on finding your mate. I had high hopes for my favourite trainer. You seemed to just be coasting and not trying to push yourself."

Brook laughed, "And my mate has really pushed me too. I hope you like the surprise in your room."

"What surprise?" Bri commented, not sure how much more she could take. The pack house looked the same, but there was almost a waiting energy moving through the pack, and many more voices in the bonds, even if many seemed muted.

*****

Adam and Brook flopped on one couch, as Gareth laughed as he sat beside Maria in another.

The two burst in almost the same time, "New laptops?" They exclaimed together.

Motioning to the third couch, while laughing, "You will want to sit down for this." Gareth told them.

Sitting down, they described how Brook had found Adam, and how they started to get the pack internet. John and Brianna's smile grew with every comment.

"This exceeds what we had at training!" John exclaimed, "Cool! I don't need to try to talk dad any more to finally get him to let us join this century!"

Adam and Brook laughed with John and Bri, as Gareth gave his son a glare, before thinking for a moment, "OK, I agree, I was resisting changes. It was for a good reason though."

It made them laugh even harder.

Once they calmed down, "You already noticed the cameras, but there is a whole set of sensors which blankets the territory, and a little beyond it. Also, in the common areas, there are cameras inside the pack house."

Bri commented quietly, "What caused such a shift to the thoughts on the security? Even when we were last here, there was no way it would have been permitted."

"We had a scout get in," Adam stated, "The Now-Nameless Pack which had been north of us," As was normal, the pack's name was not spoken, would know them by where they had been located, "Wanted to get back Duncan and Keanna, not only at the pack house, but up in their room. I was able to chase him off, but not catch him, that time."

He had to stop at the growled outrage from both of them, both had just met them at the equinox, but their parents had told them about the accusations which had followed them and how they were being permitted a new life. He waited for them to subside, nodding to Gareth to continue, who shook his head, he wasn't going to take over this part of the briefing.

"Following chasing him right out of the territory, I lost him, and the pack stayed at heightened security. That got me the permission to get the security upgrades I wanted." Giving a half-smile, "I didn't know then, I hired a Were-owned company to help with the upgrades. Over the course of the phone conversation, there was enough keywords and phrases dropped which I was able get into the group which knew of us, so I knew they were cleared."

Smiling, "Good thing too, as they needed to send techs on-site, and it was much easier we didn't need to worry about hiding from them. By the end of it, we had two techs who requested to stay and join the pack. One has requested and got permission to be turned. The other isn't eligible, since he decided to take something for the post join headache."

There was an annoyed glint to their eyes as they nodded, "I hope he was punished."

Brook laughed, "Steve was well punished, first by being bedridden for a day, then by me; I did a round of staffs with him, and by the mental displeasure of the pack."

Both John and Bri winced, "Ouch. I assume he had to be carried out?"

Brook shook her head, "No, I took it easy, as he was just a human. He was able to crawl out but was bruised nearly head to foot the next day."

Adam smiled, and added, proudly, "She didn't even take a touch herself, winning me a bet with Martin, and took an idea I had of lecturing him at the same time, of why he shouldn't have done it, and the worst cases we could find."

Both winced, "Yup, he was well punished. And advised he can't be turned without a mate for a decade?" John asked.

"Yes," Brook confirmed, "When he asked to be turned, after Chris was cleared from isolation." Letting them know obliquely the other human had decided to be Turned.

"Soon after we had the sensor network up, the pack decided to attack in retaliation for chasing the wolf away—" At the snarls, "Let me finish!" Adam demanded, "They attacked, but they were still preparing, not knowing they had triggered the sensors, and we *surprise* counter attacked before they were ready."

He had to take a breath, "Good thing too, as they were packing bullets with a concentrated Wolfsbane liquid in them. As it was, we lost three."

"Who?" Came the sad reply, "Who did we lose?"

"Kyle, James, and Jason." Gareth replied.

Bri had tears, "Oh, no! Jake!" She said, as she stood up, knowing James had a young pup. She could barely feel both of them in the bonds.

Brook caught her in a hug, "Shhhh, He's doing fine, as is his mother."

Brook sat down with her arm around Bri, who was still teary-eyed, but nodded.

"They ended up having basically all of their fighters in that fight. We took many alive, and they were dealt with." Bri gave a sharp nod, so he continued, "There was a Triad of packs, and decided to dissolve the pack. Brook and I had the task of clearing the pack and finding out if there was more wolfsbane."

Both gasped and turned white at the dissolving of the pack. Adam gave a grim smile and a nod to their reaction, "We liberated the rest of their pack, and many have been integrated here into MacLaren. Others

Brook and I took a group to Longview, and others went to other packs. During the clearing, Arctic Shadow gave us some help and turned out they had some spies and traitors." He growled, hating the entire idea of being a traitor to a pack. "Turned out the wolfsbane was a barrel which Night Depths had provided. When they found out we had taken it, they gave an ultimatum for returning it."

Both were growling under their breath, "Following that eventually they started to attack, but the patrols were alert enough they picked them up from a change in the wind. That fight lost us Ali and Tyron."

Brook was in tears, still missing the bubbly Ali. Bri gave her a good hug, as she sighed, knowing Brook and Ali were year-mates and had been close friends when they were young, even if they had drifted a bit apart as they got older.

"Part of the fight, I had fought the alpha, to the point of disabling him, and instead of taking defeat, he took his own life. Those there declared me their Alpha," He was still a little miffed he was thrust to being Alpha, instead of being able to learn it first. "It is not fun being Alpha without all the training and experience."

"You're doing fine," Gareth remarked, "Go on."

"We also counted; they lost eighteen. Another I had to kill when we went to the pack house to gather the Thetas. The rest accepted us, with a brand-new set of pack laws, many were from MacLaren, but a few were re-written." Adam smiled, proud of that accomplishment. He had also simplified the laws at the same time.

"We had been planning on using that pack's pack house for the new pack, but the conditions are horrible, and the Night Depths' buildings were in even worse shape, except for the areas of the Alpha and the few senior-most. We moved them in up in the loft here, and the Omega quarters were better than their Deltas!" He growled. "Now, we have most up at what is becoming the Wild Valley Pack; led equally by Brook and myself." He told the last with pardonable pride.

Bri gave Brook a side hug, and congratulated her, that they were taking a pack. John gave a sigh of relief, "I assume that you are also taking some of MacLaren with you?"

"Yes, it is going to give much relief to the territory here for hunting. What Gareth wanted to wait for you two, was to decide what to do with the territory which was Night Depths. As it also is now ours." Adam replied. "We also are planning on taking you two, starting after supper, up to the other pack, so you can be introduced to them, at least."

Bri groaned, "Not more driving!"

Brook laughed, "No, we're running there, as it's much faster. The pack house is even more remote than this one! It's a lovely view and nearly unspoiled land."

"And they are taking Ralph's ideals and vision to the extreme to keep it that way." Maria added.

John smiled, "It sounds nice." He commented, before yawning, "I need a nap first." Turning to his father, "I assume it's all learning the new wolves, and training for the Trials, so we can be confirmed as Alpha status?"

Gareth nodded, "Yes, and you will be working with Brook and Adam, so they can qualify as well. The first day is booked exclusively for you four, the next day, for those who are being looked at for senior positions in the Wild Valley Pack, and then the rest. They would be the ones who can bring you up to speed the fastest."

"Since the ranks were more on the butt-lickers than anything in both of the packs we took out," Adam growled in annoyance, "For most of them, their ranks were dissolved, and are being qualified under MacLaren standards, which has already been ratified for standards of Wild Valley as well."

They stood and traded hugs, before heading out, "Sorry it is going to be hectic, but we have only days before the Trials begin. Once they are over, things will calm down, and you can relax."

"Take a pack with clothes for a few days, and the laptops. We can show you some parts when we're out there." Adam advised the two.

They had finally got a temporary Wi-Fi link over to the pack house, using some relay hops along the way across ridgetops. He was glad the Wi-Fi gear used very little power, so they could use a solar panel and a deep cycle battery bank to get it going.

The fibre line was run, but the termination couldn't happen till the pack house was complete, and the data centre built. He was very glad for the extra infrastructure they had done to the cave spot, so they could install the extra antenna dishes there to start the relay hops.

They let John and Bri head to their rooms, as Adam and Brook headed to theirs. A large box was sitting in the middle of their room, with a long thin one on top.

Brook squealed like a little girl, "It came in time!" She said before starting to rip it open, as Adam sat back and rubbed his ears.

"Ouch! My ears!" Adam complained, rubbing his ringing ears. He moved to look over her shoulder, smiling as she unpacked the four paintball guns from the smaller box. Opening one for her, he found several large hoppers for the ammo.

Brook opened the largest box, it being high enough to be a table for them, and a cube in shape. She smiled down at the fact it was stuffed with neon pink paintballs. With an evil grin she started filling the hoppers with paintballs.

Adam laughed and moved to help her fill all the hoppers, before grabbing their packs, and noticing Brook or Joshua had already added a sleeve to fit the guns into, along the spine, and pouches to the chest for the hoppers. He put two hoppers on each of their vests and fit a gun into the pouch for it on both of their packs.

Remember the games we had before you went training? Brook sent to John and Bri, *This time we have official approval to do it, and unlimited supplies.* She sent, including Adam as well, the grin still plastered to her face. *I have new gear. I'll have Joshua grab your bags as you head to dinner. Come with us after dinner to our rooms, and we can add the gear.*

Adam laughed some more, "I have an evil mate!" He teased, "But it just makes me love her more!"

You do? Bri replied, sounding as excited as Brook, *Awesome!*

Martin, Adam called, *Start watching for pink dotted wolves. They need a reprimand or something. I don't want it known there are four 'hunters' here.* Amusement flavoured the sending.

Martin's wordless reply of acknowledgement was flavoured with surprise and amusement. He had agreed when they discussed it, that they wanted it to be a surprise of how they were going to do the testing. If they really felt the patrols were needing some discipline, they would let him know, otherwise would be minor issues, like made to stay wolf and show off the mark to show they failed at staying 'alive'.

While he was letting Martin know, Brook had contacted Joshua, to get the packs at the start of supper, as they could leave from their room after dinner, and see if they could catch any patrols not doing their job.

Adam and Brook chatted with the two over mind links, discussing the strategy they were going to use. They were thinking of a long jog as humans for most of the night, as their attacks up till then had been during the day. Adam was planning on also doing some photos as the sunset, if they caught anyone, maybe some dark sky shots, or of mountains with stars, and then at dawn.

The shots he had got of the pup-pouncing had gone like bacon at breakfast. Many of the wolves liked the startled expression of the wolves. Even the wolves who had been subjected to it were now laughing at it and were full of chagrin; each could see how hard they stood down, and while they were being punished, they would be able to recover from it fully and there wasn't anything lasting. Each had the best picture of them being pounced on large sized, and the others in smaller on their walls, to make a point they had let themselves be 'taken out' by pups, and they knew it was not acceptable. As they saw how they had failed as Enforcers, they had to decide if they wanted to go through the training again or do another job. They had years before they needed to decide, and were grateful they could fully recover from the momentary lapse in judgement.

*****

John and Bri laughed when they saw the colour of the paintballs after dinner. They had gotten away as soon as they could, as they were wanting to reacquaint themselves with the territory and get to know the new areas.

"Those are even brighter than before!" John exclaimed, "I almost think they glow in the dark!"

Brook shook her head, "I decided against *those,* as they could put them at risk of a real attack, and would glow in our hoppers, giving *us* away."

"Good point." John said, pulling the pouches on his harness. "You said we have approval?"

Brook nodded, "Not only Gareth and Maria approved it, but Martin is also supporting it *and* will be the one handing out the punishments for those we tag. He has said he wants to know conditions behind each hit though, so we have a little work, to let him know." It was the easy part; choosing the punishments was going to be harder and luckily, they didn't need to worry about it.

Adam patted a tablet in a rugged and waterproof case on the front of his harness, "I'm doing the notes tonight, and since we will be basically running close to where the network link is, we will have points of service where the e-mails will send." He had placed a third antenna at each relay point, which did some spot service, even if it wasn't too far, at least it was there.

John eyed the tablet, "I want one of those!" he said, enviously. "I need to talk to you about some more tech, even though the laptops are excellent."

"Erin is the lead of Tech here, and she will be staying after the split." Adam advised, "You can discuss it with her, and we can sit down up at Wild Valley. I also plan on a stop at one of the network relays, to show it off. They are portable enough for a couple of wolves can carry an entire kit at once." The thing which was the limiting factors were the bulk of the solar panels, and the weight of the lead-acid batteries.

Both girls were giggling as they headed out the door into the evening, the guns hidden in their packs, so those around the pack house wouldn't notice and tip off the patrols. Even the boys were grinning, as they were going to have a fun night, even if the paintballs were *pink*.

Chapter 10 – Hunter Captured

As soon as they hit the trees, all four went silent. They switched to chatting over mind speech, and Adam was pleased to find he could relate to both of the Alpha's pups. Through his wolf, he could almost sense a kinship, but knowing where the spirit came from, decided to put it aside, as an elder had taken him aside and let him know he should make new bonds, rather than use those 'ghost bonds', although they would make it easier to forge new bonds of friendship. His wolf agreed then, but now was whining about it.

They ghosted up behind half the inner patrol, not seeing the other two, thinking they were going to get the drop, only to have sticks lightly tapped on them behind, and all four of them being tripped as the two turned the tables on them with a grin.

Once the shock wore off, Adam started laughing. "We ourselves got a little complacent," He commented. "We could see two who seeming were inattentive and fell into a reverse trap."

The leader offered his hand to Adam, "It would work only once, and I wanted to get the time off which was promised." He commented with pardonable pride.

Adam took it, and used it to pull himself up, "You got it, Kevin. Although, you will have to wait until after the Trials. We are stretched a little thin, as it is."

Martin, not sure if you were watching, Adam knew he had the control room tonight, *But we got taken a little complacent ourselves!*

Martin's amused reply came right back, *I was watching, and was nearly a perfect takedown. They will have their month off, but what should we do for the fact not only they took you two down, but the other two Alpha pups?*

Brook smiled, *We will have to discuss it. Not too sure right now. We are a little smarting on our pride.*

Adam smiled, "Martin saw the take down, and said it was near perfect. You did take all four of us out, in addition to your month off – arrange it with Martin – what would you want?"

Kevin blinked, "What do you mean by more?"

Brook laughed, "The week was to take out Adam or myself, a month to take us both out. You did that, but also too took out John and Bri. I forgot you hadn't been introduced, they are Alpha Gareth's two pups and are presumptive alphas." Having them decide what else they would like, meant they didn't need to think of it.

Kevin shook his head, going a little white, "I didn't realise it..." He trailed off at Bri's laugh and John's amused expression.

"I take it you are new?" John asked.

Kevin nodded, "Barnet and myself follow Adam and Brook, and are in the Wild Valley Pack, while Nina and Blake are MacLaren, and were from Sh—The nameless pack."

Both Bri and John pulled the four in for a hug, and to get to know their scents.

"Welcome to all four of you." Bri commented, "One of us will be taking the Next Alpha role and be our father's heir. We decided between ourselves to wait to see who does better, and if one doesn't want it."

"We *had* been considering the other to do the Second, but not sure as there is a new one training." John added.

We don't have a second, yet, Brook added silently, not including the patrol, *We can discuss it later.*

"Can we think on it?" Blake asked.

Brook nodded, "OK. Let us know, no later than the end of the Trials, then."

Kevin nodded, as they continued their rounds, and the four headed back onto the trail, this time keeping an eye out for anyone else trying to get a drop on them.

*****

They tried to sneak up on the next patrol they came across, but before they got close to getting into position, Martin called, *You're caught! The patrol just called in an alert. They caught your movement. They are a new patrol, and only qualified as a team three months ago!*

They sighed, *Give them an elk steak dinner in town on me for that! If they caught us, they are being very sharp.* John called out, and the other three nodded, surprise and respect showing on their faces.

They left the next two patrols alone, as they didn't want them talking and finding out they were hitting them all.

Reaching the top of the ridge, Adam showed the layout of the system for the relay. There was a U of pipe, with a baseplate of a thick piece of steel which had sockets for the pipe to be bolted into. On the baseplate, a box with several heavy batteries, and rocks held it stable. On each of the two vertical posts, there was a radio dish, and both connected to the cast aluminum box which held the radio cards and router board which controlled the radios. On the top of the loop, the solar panels were mounted, with a reasonable angle. There was also a third antenna connected to the box, but this one was smaller. It was to provide hotspot service for the area, for those like Adam, who needed to upload reports to have it send.

"If the fibre isn't online by the fall equinox, we're going to need to add battery blankets to keep the batteries from freezing," Adam told them, "We can install them if it comes to that. I think we can at least get enough done we can plug it into a temporary setup, so we don't need these."

"Why not keep them?" John asked, "It would be a backup link between the two packs. You know how fibre sometimes gets cut accidentally."

Adam nodded and agreed, "True, but they are too exposed and are on public property. It needs to be better protected and would prefer fewer than the four hops. It can be done, just needs more research and planning. I'll be doing it once the pack house is done."

"Why not leave this until that one is ready then?" Bri asked, "Then you have the backup link 'til the permanent one is done."

Adam grinned, "I like that idea. It means they will definitely be needed at least this winter. I'll get the battery blankets ordered, then we can have them installed slowly."

"Incoming," Brook called, just in time as a patrol came up and each touched their nose to the four and woofed.

Caught ya! Called the team leader.

Adam chuckled, "You caught us, which means you get a free pass, and we won't bug you tonight. Stay vigilant." Reaching into his vest, he tossed each a good strip of buffalo jerky. They may be intelligent, but their wolf-side would happily enjoy the treat.

They scampered off to continue their patrol, each gnawing on their treat.

I take it, that patrol isn't getting anything else? Martin commented, *It is a boring night, so keeping an eye on you four.* It was also easy with the system locking into them on one screen. It would be a good check to make sure they had enough cameras in the area between the two packs.

We are going to take a run; see if you can track us! Bri called back, before stripping and shifting to her wolf. The other three were quick to follow, stuffing the clothes into their packs.

They ran through the thinly patrolled route between the two territories, until they came to the edge of their own pack area. There they shifted back and pulled out the paintball guns.

They gave each other a savage grin and started to move with lots of stealth.

Hold up, Brook said, as they were coming near a patrol, *I smell a human.* They quickly moved together. They were on the land which they were working through the painfully slow human government to transfer ownership, and to make 'Wild Valley Land Trust' to control it. They hoped by mid-summer it would be done. Luckily, they still had enough elders who had signing rights from the old 'owners' they could do so.

Jess, are there any humans authorised on the territory? He called. He didn't think there should be, but as she was in charge while they were away, she could have let one on.

No. There were some deliveries which we let in this afternoon, but they were cleared out before dusk. She replied, startled.

Bringing in Martin, *Sound a 'Watch' alert. We are smelling a human up at Wild Valley. Within the restricted territory itself.*

Acknowledged. I just had a slight ping on a sensor but thought it might have been you four. They are within one-hundred meters of you and are extremely light on their feet. The IR sensors and the cameras aren't done in that area, yet.

Moving with even more stealth, they followed Brook, *Booted feet. Sounds like combat boots.* She commented. Moving, up, they spotted them, wearing heavy camo gear, with a gun they could now see, not just smell.

Sharing a thought, they moved around to surround them, alerting the patrols in the area.

Now! Called Brook, as all four moved forward, "Drop your gun. You are on private property!" She called out, keeping her paintball gun up; in the dark the human might mistake it for another rifle. Adam had shifted to his bow, and John had pulled out a dart gun, with a human-strength sleeping agent.

Shit! Martin called, *I missed him! He IS on the camera… he just was so blended, I missed him on the daytime cameras!*

Adam smiled, *Well, it is good; more evidence for us. Gather all the records and generate an official copy to turn over.*

The human started, but refused to release the gun, "I'm a taxpayer, I can hunt what I want where I want!"

Bri moved silently behind him, with all his attention on Brook, slapping the gun out of his hand as she spun him around and cuffed him, in a single motion.

Brook lowered her paintball gun, and the others moved in, as the human started to struggle.

"You are under arrest for trespassing and illegal hunting. This is not public land, and you passed through two sets of No Trespassing and No Hunting signs." Brook told him, as he continued to struggle in vain, as the patrol came up, panting.

The human paled as he was surrounded by the wolves.

"They are one of the several layers of security we have." Brook told the human, as Adam called Jess for a vehicle to the nearest point and RCMP at the gate, "Now, walk, and don't try to run. They would enjoy a chase." She told him.

There will be a RCMP to take the human at the gate. Jess told them, *ETA ten minutes.*

Thanks, Adam replied, letting the human only see the two girls, as him and John paced out of human sight, as the four wolves of the patrol formed up around them. Adam had picked up the gun as they had passed. It would be handed in as well.

*****

They reached the truck not a moment too soon for John and Adam, as the human had spent the entire time insulting and making noise about how his rights were being infringed upon.

Brook opened the back door of the crew cab so hard she nearly ripped the door clean off. "Get in." she ordered him, with a growl and a tone which was hoping he'd refuse so she could fling him in.

The human had regained his colour on the walk, but was ashen with her tone and with help, climbed in. Bri climbed in the other door, putting the human between them.

Adam climbed into the front and nodded silently to the driver, *Take us to the main gate, as we have a RCMP to take this sad excuse for a human.* He told him, silently, knowing he would be growling, if he opened his mouth. He had been trained it was also normal for them to not speak around a human, except to give commands for the human, as it reduced the amount of information the human would learn.

The driver nodded and headed out. John had jumped into the back, and the patrol had melted back into the forest as the doors were closed.

With the ride only a few minutes, the wolves saw the flashing lights of the RCMP pickup just outside the gate.

The barricade was quickly moved so they could park beside the RCMP. Adam jumped out and opened the door for Brook. The human jumped out and tried to run as Brook stepped out, but Brook's conveniently placed foot prevented it, as he slammed into the gravel driveway. It wasn't the first time one had tried to run.

Brook picked him up, and with Adam on the other side, both laughing in their head, "Like I said, don't try to run. We will pass you over to the nice officer, and if needed, will see you in court. We have video of your trespassing, and our actions."

Brook was even kind enough to point out the camera, which was covering them right now, since it was not one of the hidden ones. The fight just seemed to go out of him, as he realised he was caught.

The cop added his own cuffs then John removed the first pair before he was put in the back of the police vehicle and belted in as he was read his rights.

After closing the door and stepping away from the vehicle, "I was read into the 'Wolf Team' just last week. Didn't think I'd need it this soon." The officer told them quietly, and the werewolves relaxed. He didn't bother telling the werewolves he had been stunned for a day, then going online, had realised just how much information was out there, even if there was a fair bit of contradictory information. The RCMP had officers who had been told about them, to smooth interactions in areas near the wolves, even if most of the government wasn't aware of them. He knew they were generally respectful of the police, as long as he was respectful. To never lie or badly shade the truth during a questioning, as the werewolves had ways to tell, and if they felt they lied or shaded it enough anyone would infer the lie, likely would not say anything further and refuse to do anything further with them, which was why the last person was moved and he got the position. If they demanded their Alpha, to just have the Alpha notified of the request and wait for them, and usually the pack's lawyer, even if the laws allowed them to continue questioning, or even pre-empt it and have the Alpha there for the start of the discussion.

Also, for many issues, just turning the offending wolf over to the Alpha, with all the raw evidence proving the issue, and they would be in for a much harsher sentence than the human legal system, and it would be assigned with within days, without any of the court's costs, and no technicity getting them out of a punishment.

Adam stepped forward to stand with Brook, "You can let those in the know, know we have had some actions, and the old pack which had been here, and Night Depths pack no longer exist, as we police our own." He wasn't going to go into it with the police; he didn't need to know there had been many deaths, and several times actions with guns were used, and everything else which happened.

The officer looked a little confused, "Then what pack is here? I thought it would be the Shadowed River."

Adam smiled and introduced himself with pardonable pride, "I'm Adam, and this is my mate Brook, and we are the Alphas of Wild Valley Pack." He didn't bother commenting about the other pack's demise, as the officer didn't have a need to know anything except it wasn't there any longer.

The officer had been jotting notes down. Adam passed a business card over, "We were doing some random patrol testing, to keep them on their toes, when we came across the human within our property. He refused to leave on his own, so we apprehended him." Passing the officer the gun and the ammo from it, "This is his gun. Once he was apprehended, he started to become belligerent. He had passed two levels of no trespassing and no hunting signs to get where he was." Taking a breath, and collecting nods from the others, "We do want to press charges of trespassing and illegal hunting."

While he was talking to the officer, Brook pulled out her cellphone, and ended the voice recording, and emailed it to the officer after he told her where to send it and sent Martin a copy as well to attach to their own incident report. "I just e-mailed you a voice recording from the time we approached him, and I forwarded it to our security manager so he can also get you the video of it as well"

The officer gave a slight smile, "It sounds like you've done this before. It sounds likely of a conviction. You are leaving it in our hands?" He sounded curious to why they had even turned him over. He had been told usually the pack here just handed in the ID and they had already dealt with them, and not to ask questions. Their policy for that was to have the ID for when the person was declared missing, and to not get the search parties out, but a week later the person reporting would just be told they found only their ID and considering them dead. This way was more work but didn't need to hide anything.

Brook smiled, "I have, but with MacLaren Pack. We prefer to let the human courts deal with the petty criminals. If he had shot a pack member, that would be a different story. We try to catch them before it happens, as it gets very messy."

The officer grinned, "I can see three cameras here, and if you have videos deep in the forest, it seems you really want to keep encounters down."

Brook and Adam nodded, as Bri and Joshua had let the truck go, as they could continue their fun from here. They were lounging inside the guardhouse, chatting with the guard, who was one they knew.

"There is a wolf pack east of here, which we have taken under our wing." Adam told the officer, "Make sure the local hunters know not to go after them, as if they do, our werewolves will treat it as if they went after their children. We protect our lesser kin, and they are smart enough to call and run to us for protection." He had always hated how hunters considered the predators as competition to eliminate, which was not the case; they helped take the injured and sick, which the humans rarely went after.

The officer paled, "Understood." He commented, knowing they would be lucky to get a positive ID for the unlucky human if they did, as the pack would likely dispose of the body, and they would never find it. "Do you have a map of their territory, and what you claim?"

Adam nodded, "I'll e-mail it to you. I'll let you know the wolf territory is within what we patrol, so make sure it is passed on. They do count some park areas and will be placing passive sensors and cameras around them. We too would prefer to prevent, rather than react. Most areas we have no issue with hikers, or other uses which respect nature but not hunters."

A convoy of six large cement trucks rumbled past and were waved in, making the officer eye the trucks, and looked curiously at the two leaders.

Adam nodded, "The existing structures were what would be considered condemned condition if anyone was to inspect them, so we are building new structures. They should be done in about a year." He wasn't going to go into details, but Shadowed Valley's pack house had several structural defects which was putting the building at risk of collapse, according to their engineers.

The officer nodded, "I wondered at all the large construction equipment rumbling through the town." He passed him one of his cards, so they hade his e-mail address.

Adam nodded, but still didn't invite him to visit, feeling a bit territorial. "Anything else you need, let us know, and we will let you know when we have a moment." He advised, with a tone he wanted to get going.

The officer nodded and headed to the vehicle. The wolves could hear the hunter's screams about false arrest and his rights about hunting, but the officer winced when he opened the door, before hopped in to take the hunter to the station.

Both Adam and Brook heaved a sigh of relief when they lost sight of the patrol car, and they re-entered the pack property. *We're finally done with that issue,* Adam told Jess and Martin, *He knew of us, so Martin, make sure he gets the videos, as we are going ahead with charges. Jess, have a note made to look into beefing up the edge security.*

As they nodded in greeting to the security guard, John and Bri joined them as they padded off into the forest, to look for the patrols.

*****

The patrol they came across an hour later, were also napping, but with a sentry keeping an eye out, as they should.

Shoot one shot onto the tree around them, give them two seconds then start shooting them. Brook told Adam, as it wasn't nice to just fire at the sleeping wolves.

Adam nodded and took aim, just above the wolf's head, and pressed the trigger. Before he had counted one, all four were awake and up, looking for them. The four of them started firing, and by the time they were done two had only a couple of spots, but the younger had a spotted complexion. Martin had also let them know they had also called in an alert even as they started to respond.

Pink? Whined the youngest, who looked to just be of age. *Why did you have to use pink?*

Brook laughed and smiled, as they came up to the patrol, and petted the wolf's fur, who leaned into the attention, ears back and tail tucked in embarrassment. "Because it's visible on all fur types. We are trying to get the patrols more alert at all times, and train you how to dodge shots, like those two did," She replied, nodding at the two with a satisfied but still annoyed look on their face. "Your actions were what you are supposed to do."

Adam nodded, "You four responded how we expected for tonight." Turning to the older two, "You need to teach the other two to dodge."

Yes, Alpha, Came the relieved reply. They had heard of the other team and were glad they weren't getting a punishment, even if three had been sleeping.

Adam nodded, and led the others back into the forest, this time, heading for the hot spring. They had already spent most of the night, and a hot soak sounded nice for a way to relax. Hopefully, it would get the stench of the hunter off them.

*****

"I'm going to be jealous you have this!" Bri commented, as they sprawled in the hot water, as the sky cleared and they relaxed, staring up at the night sky unblemished by lights. The only sounds were of Adam snapping a few pictures occasionally, spending a fair bit of time setting up each shot.

"Why?" Don't you remember the one I took you to?" Brook asked, surprised.

Bri turned and stared at Brook, before smiling, "I had forgotten, as you had sworn us to secrecy."

Brook smiled, "As far as I know, very few people know of that one. I have barely ever smelled any other wolves there, and never had another join us."

Bri perked up, "A private pool, basically? Awesome!"

All four laughed, with John looking satisfied as well.

They spent the time discussing their ideas for the future of the packs, and Adam and Brook told them about the conditions for the other two packs, and they agreed they were going to need the soft touch, to get their recovery going, and to learn to trust.

"I'm saddened we had not one but two Alphas who abused their position for personal gain, instead of care of those who looked to them." Adam reflected, "But I am glad we were able to take them out and save most of the packs."

"It was a high price, though." John commented. "We lost some good wolves."

"What help has Jake been given?" Bri asked, being concerned for the pup.

Adam smiled, "I'm personally keeping an eye on him and his mother." He said to her evident relief, "They did need a change of scenery, so with their approval, we have transferred them into Wild Valley, and Rachel has been assigned to care for the pups."

"She's looking and feeling so much better." Brook added, "It seemed she wasn't able to handle doing the same patrols as she had before. I think also being able to be around Jake, instead of leaving him with another is letting her heal. If she decides to go back to being an Enforcer, she will have new territory to patrol as well. And she knows it's still an option for her in the future."

Relaxing in the hot water, they watched the sun rise over the mountains.

"Well, guess it's time to get moving." Brook said, pulling a towel from her pack, and drying off before dressing. Passing the towel around, they quickly set off to check on the patrols a bit more, as they headed for the pack house.

*****

The next patrol ended up finding them first, and although weren't able to catch them unaware, they impressed them enough to earn a treat of some of the jerky they still had.

Coming up to the next one, Adam smiled, and pulled the trigger, catching the leader right between the eyes. They yelped loudly, and played dead at the amusement of the four, once the surprise wore off, as they speckled the others while they were frozen with surprise, with paintballs.

No report called in this time. Martin advised, *Although the leader's fake death was fun!*

They wandered up to them, and smiled at Ryan, "Nice acting. I had to check the bonds you weren't actually hurt." Adam commented, amused.

I remember you three doing this before. I had never had a chance to try it, but it worked well! He commented, pulling his paws in from the sprawled position he had fallen into. *I saw the paintball gun just as you fired, but not enough time to dodge.*

Adam shook his head and passed the last of his jerky to the wolf, "You deserve a treat for the amusement." Turning to the others who were well peppered with pink now, looking disgruntled, "You three just froze when he went down. You should have gotten yourself to a hiding spot and called it in."

Brook gave an evil grin, "Your punishment is to spend the next week in the time you are off, until the start of the Trials, reviewing the rules for what to do when the leader goes down." She told the three. They all had their ears back and heads low out of embarrassment.

Yes, Alpha. They intoned. Before heading off, following their leader.

The four chuckled more as they headed into the tent which contained their field kitchen. Flopping down beside Jess, she grinned in greeting, "John! Bri! Welcome back from your training, and welcome to what will be Wild Valley Pack."

"I heard Adam and Brook adopted you, congratulations!" Bri said in response, "I'm loving the location, and I'm almost jealous I'm not part of the Wild Valley pack and will get to live here!"

Adam and Brook laughed, as some food was brought over to them, and they murmured their thanks for the service. "After the food, we can go for a tour of what's here." Adam offered, pride showing in his eyes.

*****

As they were looking at the sites, mostly just foundations of concrete still curing, Jess came running up as someone let two long blasts of an airhorn sounded an alert but not an emergency, "We have a convoy of five vehicles which refused to wait at the gate. They just said, 'Adam had better be waiting for us when we arrive.' When they stopped for a moment, before crashing through the gate." She told them looking panicked.

Chapter 11 – Unexpected Visitors

Adam nodded, "Any idea who they are?" He had an undertone of a growl from his wolf; their territory was being violated.

Jess looked a little pale, "Not yet. Martin is running the plates and the faces the cameras captured. The guard did scent they were wolves."

Brook growled, "Break out the weapons. We have no idea how many are there, but this is no friendly visit." She ordered those around them.

Jess howled, calling the pack to the defence, and ran to make sure they were in place. They had five minutes till they arrived.

Adam turned to John and Bri, "I want to not announce we have you here, unless it is needed." Pulling his mate close, "I hate not knowing who I'm facing, so if we are taken, I want you two to protect our pack and get them to safety."

John showed steel in his eyes as he met Adam, before submitting, "Yes, Alpha. We will have your backs." He could feel the alpha in the other, and his wolf submitting to him even as he doubted they would not be victorious over the invaders.

Got them! Martin called. *They are from the Feral Star, and Alpha Tyler is with them.*

John growled, "That pack is a very traditionalist offshoot of Sentinel Star. I am surprised they are even arriving in vehicles. I heard they are for no contact with humans and refuse any new technology." Turning to look at both his sister and Brook in turn, "They also are cave-wolf in ideas of women: they are required to be subservient to the males in all ways."

Adam snarled, "They also were one of the packs which had sent a letter demanded I go to them and submit myself for their inspection. I refused and said after the Alpha Conference I might meet with them." He remembered it clearly as it was full of commands. It was more strongly worded than what he used to assign punishments.

Prepare for an unhappy Alpha in the vehicles arriving. Adam called out to his pack.

Jess, secure the gate. Stop all deliveries there, and just tell them we have a situation here, and it is unsafe for them. Brook called.

Already done. I also have a couple calling the supply companies to have them call the drivers, so they don't even get here. I want to keep the humans out of this. I have called in half the patrols, as that's where the Beta fighters were for the most part. The rest have been put on alert for attacks. She replied.

Gareth called in, *Got the alert for you. We're too far to assist, but I know Tyler. Treat him with respect but don't bow down, and maybe he'll respect you. Adam, he is one of those who won't accept you as Alpha, due to your age, and the fact you were turned. I have heard any turned are treated less than Omegas. Brook, he won't accept you at all for the fact you're female. They are a tiny pack, of about fifty, last I heard.* The thought also had an undertone of he didn't think their reported number was correct, as like others, they didn't count some of the lower ranked wolves, and in this case, maybe they just counted the males.

Adam and Brook growled, as they headed to the edge of the road, to be there to defend the pack. He considered making the Alpha come to him in the mess tent, but decided against it, as the highest ranking were female here, and he'd probably attack them. They both pulled on their packs for the weapons and the protection the armour gave them.

We're taking command of the defences. We have them secured and with clear view of all the area. We will keep the pack safe Bri called out; it came with a steely base of they would protect the weak with their lives.

Some of the pack moved to their Alpha's back, as they waited beside the road. The bonds shared the feeling that these Alphas were worthy of their help and to guard their backs as they protected the pack.

Adam closed his eyes and breathed deeply, calming himself. He wanted to try to look as casual about this he could. With the Alphas he had met, looking as casual and relaxed seemed to the belligerent as an insult, as if they were that casual and relaxed, they clearly weren't worried about them attacking, or if they did attack, weren't worried about winning. They didn't like being thought of as not needing to worry about a fight.

I'm glad I'm done turning. Would he be able to know I have turned? Adam asked his mate.

Unless he knew you had been turned, at this point, he won't be able to tell. Your reactions and body language are those of an Alpha who has lived as a wolf all their life. She didn't bother adding 'and has the clear loving support of the pack.' As both knew it was there, and was something they always worked to cultivate, as they had seen what fear-respect gave when they were down or not there; the pack turning away. Was her reply, *I hope you can keep up the relaxed view.* She worked to follow his lead and hide her nerves.

The large SUVs skidded to a stop, throwing a dust cloud and gravel at the gathered pack, with no care for how it could leave a rut, and was extremely disrespectful. The first vehicle boiled out several wolves in human shape even as it stopped, but several shifted to Were, shredding their clothes as soon as they were out of the door.

The back door of the second was opened by one from the first vehicle, and the large male got out. Everyone could feel this was the alpha, "Where is he?" He roared. "Where is this wolf who refuses me?"

Adam smiled, "Greetings, I am Alpha Adam." He called out, not moving closer, forcing Tyler to make the first concession by coming to him. Nor did he move to meet as equals halfway.

As Tyler locked eyes with him, Adam forced his wolf to not to attack, sharing his plan with his wolf got him to calm down enough he wasn't having to work harder. Eventually Tyler came stalking over to him with a growl. *I won the first exchange.* He commented to his mate, amused and trying to break the tension, as Tyler used his movement to look around at the gathered wolves. None of them looked happy to see him.

"You? You are not even in your third decade. You cannot be the Alpha." Tyler declared, "Where is the Alpha?"

The pack growled at the insult to their Alpha. Several of the visitors started to look nervous, at the numbers who were gathered around them, and were now looking insulted. Just the sheer number would be able to take them down.

"My age has no determination of my ability. Night Depths fell when their Alpha was defeated by me in a challenge." Adam held up a hand, and the growls from his pack subsided. "What brings you to our pack, unannounced, and in such a hurry you failed to wait for permission and had to break through the gate?" He asked, as if he was asking someone how the drive was, to make small talk and didn't really care what the answer was.

Alpha Tyler growled at the perceived disrespect shown. "You refused to meet with me."

Adam shook his head, "No. I refused to respond to your summons, as if I was yours to order around." Motioning to the construction which would be their central buildings, "As you can see, we are hard at work to build our pack buildings. In the letter, I said I would contact you after the Alpha Conference to arrange a meeting."

"I demand a room and rooms for my wolves." Tyler demanded, ignoring the comment.

Wild Valley Pack laughed, to the annoyance of the Alpha, "Rooms? In what building?" Brook asked, "We have no rooms here for our pack! They sleep as wolves under a tarp."

Tyler growled, "Be silent female!"

Adam snarled, causing many of the guards Tyler had brought to step back at the contained power it showed. Adam stared at Tyler in his eyes, in a clear challenge, "You will leave now. You insult me, which I can deal with. You trespass without leave; I was prepared to have some words. But you insult and disrespect my mate, who is also an Alpha? I am *not* going to stand for it." He held up his hand as Tyler tried to speak, "I have nothing further to say. You have five minutes to leave, or your lives are forfeit as I will consider you as invading trespassers."

"The Inter-Pack Treaty demand more respect." Tyler growled, now seeing armed wolves move into sight, as the unarmed ones stepped back to pick up more weapons they had out of sight. All the weapons were pointed at his wolves. Even if his wolves each hit with a kill shot of the upstart pack, there was more than enough to take his out. A breeze tickled his nose, with the scent of silver, showing at least some of them were armed with silver bullets.

"It also stipulates how you are supposed to interact *before* entering a pack's territory by getting permission to enter. *And* how you are to respect other packs while on their territory *as guests*. Neither of which you are following. Nor are you following the rules for the Guesting Rights." Adam replied, before he gave a feral grin, continuing to stare. "Until the conference, and we are accepted, the pack is not officially part of the treaty, so *technically* neither part is in effect. The moment you stepped on my territory, by the old laws, you were mine to deal with how I wished. I still could do so, including killing you, and scattering your body for the animals. Night Depths honoured those laws, which is how we became their Alphas—and I do mean 'we', as I stipulated they would accept my mate Brook as their alpha as well before I would accept them, which none had any issue with."

He turned his back, and started to walk away, showing graphically he was done with them, also showing he wasn't concerned or worried about him attacking.

Tyler gave a snarl, and reached for Adam, but stopped suddenly, as Adam had pulled his sword as he had spun back to face him. The sharp tip was a finger-width from his nose. He was nearly cross-eyed as he stared at the sharp tip which could easily take his life before he could respond.

"I don't have the time to teach you some manners right now." Adam growled, "If you continue to push me, I will be forced to make the time and will also show you my displeasure at the interruption. I could also count that as an unprovoked attack as well, under the treaty, you keep saying gives you the right to force yourself on me. *Technically*, I could take breaking of the gate as your first attack on the pack and have been within my right to not have even let you say a word, either. I could have just had the pack shoot you with silver bullets."

Tyler stepped back and stalked off to the vehicles, realising he couldn't think of anything which the pup couldn't take as an attack, meaning his allies would turn their back, and he'd be on his own. Slamming the door after climbing in, the rest slipped into their vehicle, and they raced away, throwing more gravel.

Adam slid his sword away, and sighed, unbuckling the pack, passing it to a random pack member. Brook came up, and gave him a hug, tucking his nose into her neck.

Eventually John and Bri came up, after calming the pack down. "I can't believe he left without a fight." John commented.

Adam smiled, feeling better for the contact with his mate, "I think he realised I would just remove his head. He seemed more bravado than brains. I almost hope he challenges me at the Alpha Conference. Give me a chance to knock him down a notch or two as I beat him in the challenge circle. I don't want to take his pack; I'm already feeling a little over my head! A year ago, I was just a human computer tech, and not even a supervisor!" He whined. They already had a large pack; they didn't need more.

Jess came over, looking white. Adam pulled her into his arms and held her, listening to her racing heart slow as he could feel her breath on his neck. Brook slid behind her and hugged her as well. It would have been very stressful, as she was the one to deal with them if they had arrived when they weren't there.

Martin, I want some more defences on the gate, as soon as they can be done. This will not happen again. Adam called, with an undertone of a growl.

I thought you might. Already ordered. Will be there as soon as they can. May need to work over the Trials, but Rein, Mikan, Kuri, and Evan have already agreed to be there, if they do. Was the reply. *I knew you'd not want a repeat of this.* The silent though of them also having Gareth's support for it as well.

Once Jess was calmed down, "We are going to beef up the border protections immediately. We will be staying within the territory till the Trials as well."

John and Bri nodded, "We had plans to go look at what had been Night Depths but decided it can wait till after the Trials." Without words agreeing they would be there too.

Adam smiled, "This won't happen again; the border security is being beefed, including better defences at the gate. Crash barrier will be installed. It will keep unwanted vehicles from successfully ramming through. They will be done by the time we are done the trials.

Everyone who was still there looked relieved the issue was being dealt with immediately.

Adam smiled, "Pack dismissed! We have to work hard! We are stopping Saturday, so all but the minimal patrols who volunteered can head back to MacLaren for the trials. I need a good sleep Saturday night in a bed!"

A happy howl broke out as they headed back to work. They all wanted to be there for his and Brook's trials, to see their Alphas qualify and to show he has the skills to protect the pack.

Wandering back to the dining tent, where they had placed his pack, he slid out the hard case which contained his laptop and plugged it into the convenient power strip on the table.

He smiled and hit the connection to dial his sister; it was her birthday, and he *had* to wish her a happy birthday.

"You're late" Tara said as she connected the video link, "You said you would call me half an hour ago." She grumped.

"Sorry, we had a situation here." Adam replied, "We had another Alpha decide he wanted to give me 'what for' in relation to not giving into his demand for an immediate meeting with him."

She looked at what she could see, "I don't see and bruises. You must not have fought him." She looked bit relieved.

Adam smiled and told her innocently, "I just had him at sword point and ordered him to leave when he tried to disrespect Brook." At her surprised look, "He's from a pack which treats women as property, and humans—and those turned—as below Omegas." He could hear her growl which was good for one who hadn't been turned, "Although he didn't know I was turned, and I have enough experience, I have been trying to live as a born-wolf he didn't notice. I think he had enough when he realised he had no grounds for being on my pack territory, I wouldn't be bullied by his demands, and I had every right to not let him leave."

Tara seemed satisfied by the response, "OK, pack come first; I've learned that already."

Adam smiled, "So onto the reason of this call: Happy Birthday!"

Brook sat down and smiled, "From both of us." She commented.

Tara blushed, "Thanks."

"So," Adam started, "How's life in the pack for you?" He wondered if she had any questions he could answer.

Tara nodded, as her mate sat down beside her, and gave a slight head bow and a quiet "Alphas," in respect.

She leaned in when he wrapped an arm around her, "I've been learning it. So far, I have been liking how everyone shares the work and cares for another. I have been working to get used to how open everyone is, and the fact nobody really cares to even try to keep secrets." Taking a deep breath, "I have some questions for you about turning." She asked quietly.

Adam nodded, "I'll answer from my experience, we also helped one of our humans turn already. The other will have to wait, due to some stuff we're not going into." She had no reason to know Steve's issues for turning, and they were not going to give it out.

"Do you think it is worth it?" She asked.

Adam had to sit back for a moment, "I'd have to say overall: yes. The fact I have to eat much more to not feel hungry and have to snack lots is a bit to get used to, same with a warmer body temperature. The ability to go out in colder weather and not need a jacket is nice, though. I have noticed I have a shorter temper, and stay angry longer, unless I work to calm down with my mate. You do get hot a bit easier. I don't really like the need to hide, but the positives greatly outweigh the negatives. The better immune system, better senses, and longer life is the biggest. The fact I get a wolf in my mind, so I'm never alone is nice, and I love being able to shift and run as a wolf."

Tara had listened, "If you had to do it again, would you?

Adam smiled, "I would. The first part of the turning is painful. The learning the new abilities which come with being turned is very annoying, and also painful at times, but I think it's worth it."

"What do you think mom would say?" Tara asked.

Adam shrugged, "She has been nothing but supportive for me. I don't know. She may want to move in with one of us, if you do turn. You may want to talk to her, but the turning is between you and your mate, and even then, it is *your choice*."

Tara nodded, "So you have barely replied lately, been busy?"

Adam smiled, "Very busy. We're working to be ready to qualify in our Spring Trials on Sunday, and we need to hit the Alpha standards. On top of that, is caring for our pack, overseeing the pack house construction, and testing the patrols. Those which are lacking are getting paintballed with a neon pink."

Tara started laughing at the last, "Sounds like you're having fun!"

Adam smiled, "It was a fun night, although now I'm introducing John and Bri—Alpha Gareth's two pups, who just got back from a two-year training program—around to many of the wolves who have come since they last were here."

Tara continued to laugh, "I suspect you four left several spotted wolves behind?" She laughed harder at Adam's nod.

"If they were able to catch us, even if not get us before we saw them, they were left alone." Adam added. Failing to suppress a yawn, "Sorry, was up most of the last two nights, and just got some sleep yesterday morning."

Tara shook her head, "In that case, get some sleep. If I decide to turn, I'll let you know."

Adam nodded, and they signed off. Packing up the laptop, he yawned again, and Brook yawned in reply. Wincing as some diesel engines revved up, they shared a thought.

Jess, we're going to go check on the cousins. We are going to take a nap there, and then do some more patrols. Call us if you need us.

OK. She replied, *I understand it's going to be hard to sleep here. Most go off a bit into the forest to sleep, so I have several patrols split in half and doing close and fast patrols.* Her mind voice sounded anxious about the last part.

You're in charge. If you feel it's safe enough to let them sleep like that, and have more patrols out, then it works. If you want more, you can arrange with Martin to have some of the dogs out here to help beef up the patrols. You already know we are going to be doing our own breeding of them eventually Adam replied, feeling agreement from Brook.

He could sense the relief, but still, some stress from the decision. It was a stressful choice, so he could give her some support, but he wanted both to have experience as the lead, although he didn't think they would be able to fill in as Seconds. He silently shared his belief and trust in their decisions.

They shifted to wolves after stuffing their clothes in the packs and securing them. It would take them about an hour to run it. They howled for permission to enter the territory, which the wolves happily gave them. Padding in, they noticed there were a couple yearlings, but no pups this year.

Flopping down in their clearing, they release their packs and left them to the side, which the wolves sniffed, but at a slight growl, didn't do anything more to them. When they flopped down after a wolfish greeting which even included Charlie, the two Alphas joined them, then the rest of the pack and Charlie arranged themselves around them. From their expressive ears, tails, and faces, all the wolves were happy they came to see them, even if it was for a nap. Falling asleep, their wolves kept an ear cocked for trouble but relaxed to rest.

*****

Waking up late afternoon, Brook could hear faint crying. She nudged Adam awake, *I hear a human crying,* She explained, turning her head to locate the sound, trotting into the woods.

Adam? Brook? You awake? Jess called.

Just woke up. What do you need? Adam called, as he tossed Brook's pack on Charlie, and pulling his on, but only getting the neck strap done up on them, doing them up was hard without thumbs.

The RCMP officer just called the main number which is currently routed to me. Apparently, there is a child lost out in what we sent him was the cousin's territory and they were getting ready to send in a rescue party. Jess replied. *They were seeing if we had any concerns about them doing it, or if we would help.*

Adam panted wolf laughter as he followed his mate, *Umm... have him give us half an hour, as Brook already hears crying. We may already have located them. Make sure to thank them for the heads up. We'll let you know as soon as we know anything.* He was quite happy they were willing to contact them, even if it was just a heads up about a lost child.

His wolf was forward and wanting to run faster to the pup. Brook was racing ahead, and they were just following her trail, with Charlie and a couple of curious wolves following.

Coming up to tall ridge, they could see her way below. *Found her.* Brook called out, almost a half hour later, *She's at the base of a ridge. The wind must have brought her scent and sound to us. It's going to take an hour for us to make our way to her.* They would basically have to go around the entire mountain to get down to where she was. *Tell the RCMP to meet us...* With their sense of direction and the wolf's ability to keep a mental map, they knew the closest spot which they could meet up with a human, who didn't have climbing gear.

As they travelled around the mountain, they worked out a plan, hopefully to keep their secret. The two wolves they had ordered back, as they were heading outside of the wolf pack's territory, and into the edge they patrolled.

As they came up to her, a patrol had beaten them to her, and the little girl had her arms wrapped around one young wolf who seemed to be trying to cuddle her tightly, with his head on her back. The rest of the patrol was standing at a distance in the trees, clearly on guard, waiting for them. When they had called in the report, they had been notified to just wait for the Alphas, as they were already on their way. The girl would not have seen any but the one young wolf. Their careful plan was totally destroyed, since all were wearing packs, but since they were dealing with a pup, they weren't too upset.

As they came up, the one wolf looked guilty, and they could see he was still underage but was helping with the patrol. *Cody, report.* Adam ordered, gently. He realised who it had to be, as there was only one underage who they currently training as an Enforcer.

She's my mate. He stated quietly, *I heard her crying, then when we got closer, I could smell her, and realised she is my mate.* His surprise at finding his mate this young was evident. Him being only sixteen was shocking.

Brook chuckled in his mind, *Jess, have her parents and only one of the read-in officers at the meeting. We are at the girl, and other than being a little cold and scared, she's fine. Apparently, a patrol-trainee is her mate. We will need to discuss with her family.*

They could feel Jess' surprise at this turn of events. After a bit, she returned, *Her name is Amber. She has only a mother, no other family,* Was the quiet reply, full of pain, *Apparently the father walked out on them, and the rest of the family disowned her when she wouldn't get an *abortion. They were on a hike and the girl got separated. It took several hours before they could call for help. She's only eight.* She stopped for a second, then sounding a bit confused, *The officer said to tell the girl 'Wolves have four paw drive'*

Adam laughed, *It's a secret phrase which parents use now so she will know her parents know us, we are safe to go to, and we aren't kidnappers. Apparently, she or her mother really loves wolves.* It should make it easier for them to be comfortable with them.

Adam shifted out of sight of the girl, and slid Brook's pack off Charlie and onto his mate and strapped it on, as while Charlie could carry both packs, it would not be comfortable for long, and pulled on some clothes, before walking up. He sat down beside them, and pulled off his pack, and pulled out a warm fleece hoodie, which would be huge on her, "Hi Amber," He said quietly, "Your mom is very worried about you, and we're going to take you to her. She passed on a message to say, 'Wolves have four-paw drive.'"

Amber shrank into Cody, "I can't talk to strangers." She said, as she shivered in her t-shirt and shorts. This part of the forest was in the shadow of the mountain, so it was already dusk, and the air temperature was dropping. Adam realised while he was comfortable in t-shirt and shorts, she clearly wasn't.

Adam nodded, "Yes, you shouldn't. It can be bad. I wish I could get your mom on the phone, but you will have to just trust us. Didn't I have the right message?" He said quietly, not sure how to get around the conditioning to not to talk to strangers.

Amber nodded, and thought for a minute, "She said if they knew that, they were OK to be with. I guess you're OK."

Adam slid closer, and as Cody seemed to get concerned, told him, *I'm only slipping on the sweatshirt, then going to put her on your back. It's a half hour wolf-run to the pickup place.* Cody's wolf calmed. Slipping the sweatshirt on the girl, she giggled, since it was so big on her.

She squealed in surprise as he picked her up but was quickly cut off when she was placed on the wolf.

"Hold him here, tight, you won't hurt him," Adam told her, having Amber hold Cody's scruff tight, just above his pack. It would also help keep her hands warm.

Rest of you, finish your patrol, I'm taking Cody with us. He told them, and they headed out. They knew the Alphas would protect the pups with their lives, if necessary.

Follow Brook, I'm going to shift and be tailguard. He told Cody. Since he was in Wild Valley, him, his very young human mate, and even her mother, were theirs to protect.

"He knows how to get you to your mother, and I'll see you there." Adam told her. He could see her starting to shiver, even with the sweatshirt and sitting on the warm wolf. She was too young to let know about werewolves, unless she was living with them. At her nod, Cody started to trot, before speeding up to the speed he could take for hours, as Adam stripped off his clothes, and repacked them, and slid back into his furry, four-paw drive wolf. His wolf was howling in their mind over the joke, even if it was true. It was one they would have to remember. Taking a cartoon image from his human's mind, they shared an image of a wolf with their paws moving so fast they were becoming blurs of wheels.

Charlie and Adam caught up before they had gone far, and they kept a watch on the back-trail, trusting Brook to keep the front clear. They didn't want to meet up with a grumpy bear waking up, or especially not a mother with cubs. He could smell them in the area, too.

Chapter 12 - Rescue

Reaching the clearing without seeing any bears, they had Cody head in with the girl on his back, as Adam and Brook shifted in the trees to their human, and pulled on clothes, Adam grumbled about human modesty and the need to keep the shifting secret.

Stepping out, they smiled at the reunion, which a wagging Cody was included in the hugs, as they got the helicopter ready. The same RCMP officer who they dealt with for the hunter was there, trying to herd the two humans onto the helicopter. Amber refused to let Cody be left behind. Adam and Brook walked up, with Charlie padding beside them, and with realization of what Cody was, the officer nodded the two of them and stopped trying to separate them.

He motioned them all into the helicopter and sat them down. Cody sat with his head in Amber's lap, as Charlie lay on the remaining floor space, having been trained to do it in an aircraft, as the adults belted themselves in.

"The nearest emergency room is thirty minutes away." The officer said, as soon as they had their headsets on, "Do you know of something closer?"

"Do you know where the MacLaren Lodge is?" Adam asked, using the human name for it, as their own medical wasn't built yet, so they didn't have the resources to deal with them there.

"Yes," the pilot said, as he brought them up, "But it's restricted airspace."

"Head there, on my orders." Adam said decisively. "I will make sure it's all good."

Alpha, we are in a helicopter heading in with a human pup and her mother for medical. We need landing permission. Adam called out at he played with his phone, for show, as if he was contacting someone.

Granted. Helipad lights will be on momentarily. Gareth called out. *I'll alert medical.*

"Landing permission is granted, helipad and approach lights should be on, and medical has been alerted." Adam told them.

"Got it. Hang on, we're heading down to it." The pilot called, relieved he didn't need a long flight.

Turning to the silent officer, with a relieved look on his face, "I take it you need to get statements?" Adam asked.

He nodded, looking a bit pale, "Yes, and I hate flying." He replied shortly.

We also have an Officer who knows of us who will be taking statements. Adam called to Gareth, before pausing for a moment, *It seems the girl is a wolf-mate as well. Her mate, Cody, is underage as well.*

Gareth seemed to take a while to respond. They were down and unbuckling, as their healer and a nurse rushed up the ramp to them with a gurney. *You really know how to pick them.* He chuckled, eventually.

They quickly placed her on the gurney, and she cried about losing the wolf. Adam stepped up opposite her mother, "He's right here, and he'll be staying with you, don't worry."

Silently he passed on the fact of the two being mates to the medical staff. The fact she calmed down as soon as she knew she wasn't going to be separated confirmed for them it was true. As soon as they were clear of the helipad, the copter left and headed home. When it was clear, the exterior lights clicked off, bringing back the normal darkness of the spring evening.

Sliding her into a room for a checkup, with Cody moving to lay in her sight, to keep her calm, Adam tapped the mother's shoulder and motioned her out. Leading her into a consultation room, while Brook stayed with the pups, he closed the door.

"I have something hard for you to understand, just try to keep an open mind." Adam said, trying to stay calm. This was the first human they were telling, and even though Brook agreed, he was also putting MacLaren at risk.

She nodded, "I'm Karen, and you are?"

"I'm Adam. The woman with me is Brook."

She smiled, "Nice to meet you. Thank you for saving my daughter. Sh-She's all I've got left." She started crying to how close she came to losing her.

Adam sat beside her and wrapped an arm around her. She leaned in, feeling the protection and comfort an Alpha brought, surprising Adam. He had been told only wolves would feel it, giving a silent inquiry to Gareth with the fact she smelled only of human.

She may have a wolf ancestor. Since she smells human, she may not know of us. He replied.

When she was calmed, he noticed the officer had slipped out, leaving them alone. Charlie he could feel had gone up to their room for a sleep. He hadn't even followed them into Medical.

"I have something to tell you, and it may be hard to believe." Adam started. At her nod, he took a breath and continued, "We're werewolves."

Karen stared at him for a long minute, "You are a werewolf?"

Adam nodded, letting her work it out before saying anything.

"You can actually turn into wolves?"

Adam nodded again.

"Can I see?" Karen asked quietly, as if not sure it was one question he would answer.

"OK." Adam replied, after a quick discussion with Brook. Moving to the middle of the room he pulled off the bike shorts and plain t-shirt he was wearing – it was easier to carry them for shifting and were cheap if he had to shift in them.

Karen smiled, and seemed to appreciate his body, before remembering her modesty and averting her eyes.

"Please don't scream, and especially don't run." Adam asked, before starting his shift. His body had the normal momentary numbness as the bones shifted, and once he had finished shifting to his wolf, he shook his fur out, and padded over to Karen, who had a smile on her face.

"Grandpa's stories were true; he was raised by wolves." She whispered to herself, confirming Gareth's thought. It had been a very long time since she thought of the old stories he had told them as kids.

It was rare, but did happen, and it seems they were having long odds, as having two under-age mates find each other was very rare too.

Shifting back, he stumbled, but caught himself, waving off her help, "Too little rest, and too many shifts in too short of time." He commented, as he pulled his clothes back on. Looking at her awe, he sat her down, "I heard you say your grandfather was raised by wolves?"

She nodded, "You have good ears, Mr. Wolf."

"All the better to hear you with." Adam joked, before laughing. "What stories did he tell?" He coaxed, wanting to know.

She shook her head, "He mostly just teased about being raised with wolf siblings. He always was very tactile, and what he called wolf-ish in his mannerisms, but he tried to hide it. He always refused to talk about growing up, as if it was a secret. My daughter is just like him that way; she loves to curl up and cuddle and hugs." She paused for a moment, "It always seemed to cause him pain when others pulled away." She added. "He died shortly after she was born."

Adam nodded, "Well, it is a secret, but one we are going to let you in on. In your case, he is most likely he was born to a wolf and a human who hadn't been turned. Very rarely, there is one born as a human to them, and are not turned, or the turning doesn't take." At her nod he continued, "For all intents and purposes, they are human. If they didn't find their mate, they tended to drift away from the wolves, and join the human society, and live their lives out there, usually never returning to their wolf-family."

Karen sniffed away tears, "He always seemed sad when we asked, so we stopped asking as kids. He seemed to quickly fade after his wife died."

Adam nodded, "That is normal; losing a mate tends to have the effect of the remaining one loosing interest in life, especially if they have no responsibility to keep them grounded long enough to heal, like a child which needs them."

Karen shook her head, "But why am I being told?" she asked.

Adam smiled, "First the wolf who rescued your daughter is one of my pack."

"You're the Alpha!" Karen exclaimed, connecting the dots of how him, and his mate she now realised, were deferred to by the medical staff. She jumped to her feet, as she had read enough stories Alphas were kings in all but name. They had the power of life and death over their members, the same way medieval kings had it.

Adam sighed, "Karen, please sit down." She sat with a thud.

"The wolf is a werewolf named Cody," He said slowly. "He is your daughter's mate."

"But she is only eight! She's way too young!"

Adam nodded, "Yes, but both are too young. Cody is only sixteen; he's too young right now, even if his mate was of age. It is exceedingly rare for underage wolves to find their mates. They will have to wait till both of age to mate. Of age for us is two decades—twenty years—old."

Karen nodded, accepting it.

"What Brook and I would like to offer, is a home and family. I have heard you two are all alone, since your family disowned you. Since Amber is going to want to stay close, and you need to stay with her, we are willing to extend the offer to you both."

"Yes!" Karen answered, throwing herself on Adam, hugging him around the neck, "I just got laid off before the trip. I didn't know what to do." She sobbed.

Adam held her and let her cry herself out. *She accepted.* Adam told Brook, *It seems she just got laid off too.*

When she was calmer, but still clinging to him, "What sort of stuff do you like to do?" he asked gently, wanting to fit her in.

"I love to cook. I was a waitress but was spending some time learning the kitchen." She told him.

Adam laughed, "We have openings for you to work in the kitchen; most wolves can't be trusted, as they will try to sample all the food, instead of sharing it."

Karen smiled, "I like that!"

Adam nodded, "There is a few things I need to tell you about..." He told her about the fact the pack was splitting, and right now they were building the new pack house. How they didn't have facilities for anyone who wasn't a wolf, yet, so until they did, they would be staying here. She would be helping with the kitchen here, learning more skills of how to feed the wolves.

Brook knocked, and slid in to join them, "Amber was borderline hypothermic, but is doing fine. Cody and her are sleeping. His warm body will warm her slowly and safely. We are letting them recover before telling her about us, in the morning, at the healer's recommendation. The healer is wanting to keep her here over night, for observation, anyways."

Karen nearly went limp from relief.

Brook passed an e-reader to her, "We would like to invite you, and your daughter, to join our pack. But before you decide, you will need to review the Pack Laws and what you will be agreeing to. Even as a human, the joining the pack will change you a bit."

Karen smiled and nodded.

Adam smiled, "Until you decide to leave, or join the pack, consider yourself our Guest. Did you want to stay down here with your daughter, or we can show you to one of the guest rooms?"

Karen smiled, "Thank you for your hospitality. Could we look in on my daughter, then go to the guest room?"

Adam nodded, and held the door, as they let her look in at the two. Cody was sprawled on the bed still in wolf shape, with Amber cuddling him, with an arm around his neck and her body pressed to his belly with his paws also wrapped around her. Both were under the blanket, with another folded and over Amber.

Standing there for a bit, Joshua padded in silently and handed Adam a camera and a Wi-Fi phone. Adam smiled in thanks, clipping the phone to his waistband, and quietly took a picture, before they stepped out.

"I'll get you a print of that tomorrow." He told Karen, as they took her to security for a visitor ID.

Showing her to the guest room, her jaw dropped. "This room is bigger than our entire apartment," she whispered.

Brook smiled, "All our guest rooms are large. We often have important visitors who expect them."

Karen nodded, as Adam headed out, leaving Brook with her, to show her the room.

"We pulled out some basic clothes from our stores, till you can get some for yourself. I hope they fit." Brook offered, as she showed the closet, "And you have your own bathroom."

Karen selected the sleepwear of a soft pants and shirt, "When is visiting hours?"

Brook shook her head, "We don't keep set hours, and the healer didn't set any restrictions. They are only keeping her to see how she reacts, although with her mate, it is going to help her be relaxed. We'll discuss it in the morning. The officer is also going to need to take statements too." She told her about the dining hall, and how she could get food at any time, and she could ask anyone for help, before leaving her to rest for the night.

*****

Adam tracked down the officer sitting at a table in the dining room, finishing a late meal. Adam grabbed some food which was left from dinner, and sat across from him, "The girl is being kept for the night for observation, and the mother is relaxing. Would you be able to stay the night and deal with them in the morning, Officer Smith? Or did you want us to drive you somewhere?"

Officer Smith looked surprised, "This is the first time I have ever been offered a night to relax. I would need to check in, and we are out of radio range."

Adam grinned, and pulled a Wi-Fi handset from his belt, and place it on the table. "Hit three to dial out. If you want to do it in private, there are small meeting rooms just outside this room, just pick an empty one, and set the in-use indicator."

Officer Smith shook his head, "Don't need to do that," He said as he picked up the handset, and started dialing. "This is Officer Smith checking in. I have been offered a room for the night..." And he had a short conversation with his dispatch, so they knew where he was and was technically off-duty till morning. Adam agreed when asked to arrange a ride back to the office when they were done.

Brook had sat down as well, just as the officer hung up.

"Thanks to you both for your hospitality and care for the child." The officer said. The room was mostly empty, as it was past dinner time. "From my reading, and the way that wolf and girl acted, he's her mate, right?"

Adam was surprised he noticed, "Yes. But they will not be able to fully mate until both are twenty, which is the age of majority for wolves."

Officer Smith sighed, "Did it get passed on the two are alone and are not even on speaking terms with the rest of the family?"

Brook growled, "Yes. To us, family means everything. Pups the most, but the rest of the family as much, and pack is family." Taking a breath, "We have offered both of them unlimited Guest stay." He had no need to know they had offered pack membership to Karen, since Amber was too young to decide on her own, after she read all the details, even if he likely would learn more later, they still didn't fully trust him with their secrets.

He nodded, "I can see you are deciding to take care of them." Both nodded. "Then I have one last question, "I'm wondering on the relationship between the two packs, as you say you are Alphas of the Wild

Valley pack, but we are clearly at the MacLaren Pack, yet you still seem to have high seniority." He had seen how they were deferred to, and how the others acted around them.

Both laughed, "The simple answer is we are an offshoot of the MacLaren pack here." Adam told him, "We are in the process of splitting MacLaren, as it is getting too big." The officer had no need to know there was nearly three hundred in MacLaren, or there were other packs recently absorbed, nor he had defeated Alpha Night, who decided to kill himself rather than live with having been defeated. He also didn't need to know further details on how the pack was splitting and decided to not say anything further about it."

The officer nodded and covered a yawn. "Come," Adam said, standing up, "We'll put you in a visitor's room for the night. Come back here for breakfast. There is hot food made between six and nine. You're just getting the leftovers from dinner now."

Officer Smith smiled, "If this is leftovers, I wonder what the fresh tastes like; I may not want to leave!" as he stood and followed Adam.

"Well, if you are still in the office, once the new pack house is built, we could arrange for you to be permitted to come visit." Adam said, "It is always nice to have an in with the law enforcement, for the times we need to deal with it." He felt this officer would be someone to cultivate in the future as a contact, especially since he knew of them, but for now, they were not saying too much, as Gareth was using his contacts to learn more about how trustworthy he was.

"Like dealing with that trespasser, who when he was presented with the videos of trespassing, pleaded guilty, and we are skipping the trial, going straight to sentencing. Did you want to have me let you know when the sentencing is?" The officer offered, as Adam let them through the first door into the guest wing, and opened a locked cabinet with another card swipe, pulling out a one-night generic visitor card, before closing and locking the cabinet.

Adam shook his head, "No thanks, it's small enough I'd prefer to just let the courts handle it, we are busy this summer as it is."

Leading him to the door to the second guest room, Adam swiped his ID, then the visitor one, activating it for the room. He handed it to the officer, "This card is now active. It'll let you into this room, and the wing, and the main doors for the building. It will deactivate at 6pm tomorrow. Leave it with the guard at the gate when you leave." Pushing the door open, he showed the officer the weapon locker in the closet, so he could secure his weapons.

Officer Smith shook his head, "I have had hotels which are not as well set up."

Adam laughed, "Also, if you are hungry at night, there is a light buffet kept running all the time of foods which aren't harmed by being left out, as often we are out at all hours." He didn't bother saying anything about their hot spring in the green house, as there wasn't any need.

The officer nodded and yawned again. They traded good nights as Adam stepped out of the room, closing the door with a sigh.

Heading to Gareth's office, he knew he'd be there for an hour or two more working. Knocking on the frame of the open door, he stepped in, "The girl, Amber, is OK. She was borderline hypothermic but will be recovered by morning and is in Medical for observation for the night. It appears she is a mate for Cody."

Gareth stopped his typing, "Cody? The pup Cody? Just started being a trainee patroller?" He was very surprised. They had another older patroller called Cody, but he had seen him at the pack house just after the call for permission and needed confirmation.

Adam nodded at each of the questions, "I know, the one we accepted to Wild Valley. He's sixteen, and Amber is only eight. We are waiting till morning to do much with her, as she was not in the right mind to discuss anything. I did talk to her mother, and her grandfather had some stories of being raised by wolves, so she is one of *those*." He had been told about humans who had some wolf ancestors. The more wolf-ish one was, the more likely they were to find a wolf mate. But look at him; he had his family tree compared to known wolves, and so far, have not found any trace of a link to any known packs. A copy had been sent to their friendly packs, to see if they could find any farther links, or cross-reference his older records which Adam had from the early 1700s, which was easier for a wolf, which there may even be an elder who lived the times. They didn't really expect anything of it, but they would be diligent to look as far as they could.

Adam sat down, "Apparently, Amber's father walked out when he was told about Karen—her mother—being pregnant. Her family turned their backs when she refused to have an abortion." He nodded sadly at Gareth's growl. "She had been just making ends meet, but recently got laid off, so Brook and I have decided to offer both pack membership and passed her a copy of the laws and what she is agreeing to."

Gareth smiled and nodded, "And extended Guest Rights to them till they decide to join or leave on their own." He stated. It was within Adam and Brook's rights to extend it to them on behalf of their own pack, and technically could with their authority here, even if he could override it here, and ask them to leave, although he doubted he would ever need to do it. With it involving a pup, let alone one who's family had discarded, he would support however was needed.

Adam nodded in confirmation, "It is only right, Karen was a server at a restaurant but was wanting to be a chef. Cody refuses to be separated from Amber, not that Amber will let him out of her sight."

Gareth laughed, "If Karen wants to help out in the kitchen, she is more than welcome to do it! We always are short handed there." Getting serious, "If Karen would permit it, there is a way to resolve it, Cody could bite to turn Amber. Since she is so young, it would take up to a year to do it. It would also cause a partial mate bond between them, and would settle both down, and let them act mostly as normal pups."

Adam blinked, "I thought mating and turning wasn't done for pups." He was a little confused.

Gareth nodded, "Normally that is the case, but there is a condition where if a pup has their guardian find a mate, or they do, they are allowed to be turned. In her case, Cody must be the one to do it, as the bond helps it. She will appear to be down with the flu for a week or two, as her immune system is rebuilt, but after that, it is a very slow and gradual change." At Adam's surprised look, he nodded, "I was told when there was one similar, soon after I became Alpha, and haven't done it since. There, a sibling had the care of the pup and had found their mate. The mate had brought both in, not sure what to do, since they only had an older uncle who they were not close with, and an elder told me about the unwritten condition. The pup was turned soon after the sibling finished their turn. Both are quite happy as wolves." He didn't see any reason they needed to bring up an old fact. For both, they were indistinguishable from those born-wolf.

Adam nodded, "The Mountie is staying the night, too. He knows of us and wants statements. I promised a ride up to his detachment in the town nearest to Wild Valley tomorrow, so we could let the two rest tonight." Mountie was old nickname for RCMP officers, as they had been the horse-mounted police force for the western part of what became Canada, even before Canada was a country, and still were in all but the larger cities, as they were often contracted to handle the local policing in the western half of the country.

Gareth nodded, "That's fine with me. I had a vehicle which needed to go up there this week, anyways. It has some kitchen stuff which Lupita requested."

Adam smiled, "Well, that was all for now. Brook and I were going to take a short night to sleep, and then play with the graveyard shift of patrollers before breakfast."

Gareth waved him out while he laughed, not saying any more.

Adam headed to his room and found Brook curled up with Charlie. He sighed, stripped down, and slid behind her, and curled up against her back. "Good night, love." He whispered, kissing her neck before putting his head down and sleeping, surrounded in her scent.

*****

Getting up very early in the morning, after having the afternoon nap with the wolves had them wide wake. They were snickering as they refilled their paintball hoppers, taking several pouches of more, and packing up about half the rest for John and Bri.

Sitting on the computer, they got the patrols and where they should be, so they didn't have to search for them.

Heading out the door, they slipped between the trees, wearing dark clothes. Slipping up downwind of a patrol, they fired one shot each before they seemed to disappear, even though there wasn't much undergrowth. *Where—* Adam started to say before yelping and rolling, as a tongue swiped across the back of his neck. Rolling into a crouch, a wolf panted laughter right where he was, the tip of his ear pink.

He heard Brook curse, with her on her back and getting a tongue bath to her face.

Adam pushed the wolf off his mate, and laughed, "One hit, and then they turned the tables..." He shook his head and sent off a message the Martin; he commended they had only got off two shots, total. "Special dinner for the four of you, my treat. Martin will arrange it, and any other commendations for it he wants to give. If we were attackers, we would have been down."

The leader panted laughter, *At first, I did think it was an attack!* He shook his head, his other ear was notched, *I have had a bullet hit my ear and it felt the same! By the way, the other hit a tree.* He cheekily threw over his shoulder as he padded off, tail held high.

Brook growled, not liking being taken down. "We have time for the other home patrol, before heading back for food."

Adam nodded and had her lead. They came across the other one taking a break. They seemed to have caught some rabbits and having an early breakfast. Adam's first shot missed, but hit a rabbit dead on the head, as the wolves scattered. Brook's hit a wolf she wasn't targeting as it ran in the line of fire, on the rump, getting a yelp of surprise.

They moved to cover each other, and as the wolves tried to slip up to them in another counter-attack, got off more shots, and at most splattering the wolves as they came close to hitting but missed.

Truce, Adam offered, after taking several shots at the wolves surrounding them, putting his gun into his pack.

Brook smiled and did the same. "Sorry, Jesse!" she called out, as the offended black wolf came up to her, "I wasn't even aiming at you, and especially not at such an undignified spot."

Give me some of the elk jerky in your pocket, and I'll take the apology. Came the reply as Jesse leaned into Brook's petting.

Adam and Brook passed out the Jerky to all four, before letting the wolves head back to their breakfast and leaving them in peace. Adam pulled his tablet back out and sent another message, for more commendations, as even having a break the only shot was a fluke, and because one accidentally pushed another into the line of fire, otherwise all six would have gone wide.

"Well, the inner defences are very much up to what they should be. We just need to get the other groups to their level." Brook told her mate, as they headed in for a good meal, before they sat down with the two prospective packmates. It was surprising, as the inner patrols often were younger or less experienced, as help was much closer.

Chapter 13 – Talks

They knocked on the door to the room Karen was in, to have it yanked open almost instantly, "I was just about to look for breakfast," Karen said with a grin.

Brook smiled, "I was just coming to get you for it." She said before turning to show Karen to the dining room, "We do three meals. Breakfast is six to nine, then lunch is eleven to two, and dinner is five to eight. Between meals, there is food out which doesn't spoil being left out for hours, as we can't always make the regular meals. We also keep a selection of drinks made."

Adam waved them to a table, where Martin and several other Enforcers were chatting with Officer Smith at one end about policing. Karen sat beside Brook as she cuddled into her mate's arm.

Karen moaned around a mouthful of pancakes in pleasure, "They are delicious! I haven't had them done this well in a very long time!"

Adam laughed, "Wolf senses are much better, so we don't use many artificial ingredients, as we can taste them, and they don't taste as good as the real ingredients."

Karen nodded, "They always do. It's just they are very expensive."

Brook grinned, "It is why we have a greenhouse, and a garden. We grow lots of our own spices and herbs. Along with fruits and vegetables. We don't have the resources to have fields of grain, so we trade with other packs for, and most of the livestock are raised by other packs. We trade to have them. When they are near ready, they are brought here, and we let them roam till we need them."

Karen smiled, "It sounds like you don't go grocery shopping often?"

Brook shook her head, "Nope; it would be too expensive to do that! We also prefer not to have as many chemicals in the food, so it is healthier. Much of our food is made from scratch."

Finishing up the breakfast, they stood up and motioned for Officer Smith to join them. They headed out, "We booked a meeting room which is in the medical wing for the day," Adam said, leading them down the stairs and into the medical wing. "I'll get Cody and Amber. Brook will take you to the room."

Heading into the room, waving at the nurse on duty, he smiled as Amber was feeding Cody some of the ham from her plate, as she giggled, he was eating it as daintily as a wolf could.

"OK, you two. Time to come have a nice talk with the police officer." Adam said.

"Do I have to?" Amber asked. "I don't want to leave Wolfie!" Cody just sighed and nodded.

"His name is Cody, and he is coming too." Adam told her, smiling indulgently, *Keep acting as a wolf, and don't shift yet. We are planning on telling her about werewolves soon.* He told Cody privately.

Yes, Alpha. He answered, *Please be soon. I want to be able to talk to my mate.* Standing up, he hopped off the bed, and Amber quickly followed. Standing, with his head up, both had their heads at the same height, which amused Adam.

We are going to be discussing it after we all give statements to the officer, including you. Adam told him.

Walking down the hall together, Amber had her hand entwined in Cody's scruff. "Mommy!" She called and ran to her. Cody let out a sub-vocal growl, at seeing another touch his mate.

Enough. That is her mother. You will not growl or snarl or show any displeasure for attention between them. Adam reprimanded, directing most of the order to the wolf half.

The growling subsided immediately, *Yes, Alpha.* Came a furry version of Cody's voice, showing the wolf half got it, as he was the one causing the problem.

Brook and the officer were nowhere in sight.

Karen smiled, "Officer Smith wants to see us separately, you first, once he's done with Brook, then..." She trailed off, nodding at Cody.

Adam nodded in reply. He had Joshua bring a pair of shorts in Cody's size for him, for the officer's modesty more than anything.

Cody sat down beside the two and relaxed, being able to be near his mate.

Brook came out shortly, and Adam went in. He covered from the time they woke up till when they got to the helicopter on the record, leaving out the fact they had been wolves at the time, to leave the assumption of being much closer than they had been.

The officer leaned back and turned off the recorder, "Off the record, is it normal to invite people into the pack who are human?"

Adam shook his head, "Not at all. It is very rare but is becoming more common in some packs. We have had two recently, and Alpha Gareth has said the last one was about fifty years ago. Those two were here for a business purpose, and already knew of us. Both seemed to have a wolfishness, and they fit into the pack already. There were several wolves who were willing to sponsor them into the pack, as well." He had no reason to say what they were there for, and after saying it, thought he did say a little too much, as the officer was easy to confide in, but knew he needed to learn to be less giving of information, even if it was off the record.

The officer nodded, "But what about Karen?"

Adam smiled, "That's an entirely different case. Cody is a pack member and is claiming Amber for a mate. We do have a custom of if they have dependents they are invited in as well, or when they have someone close who would be left without anyone. It usually helps both settle into the pack, and they tend to find mates eventually, anyways."

Officer Smith frowned, "How are mates found?"

Adam gave a sad smile, "We just know them, mostly by scent. I can't say any more without going into pack secrets. Some of what I have said already is stuff we don't want to spread around."

The Officer nodded, "It was off the record, mostly to clear up some stuff in my mind, and I'll keep it to myself, as you wish."

"Thanks. We are very protective of our pack, which is basically family to us." Adam commented.

"Enough to kill?"

"Enough to kill, if necessary, but also enough to sacrifice ourselves so the rest can live." Adam countered.

The Mountie sat back stunned for a moment, before seeing the sad expression on Adam's face. "You've had fights and had some die in them?" he asked quietly.

Adam nodded, "I can't say any more on the subject. Did you have anything further to say?"

After thinking for a minute, shook his head, "No. Could you send Cody in?"

"He is underage, I hope you don't mind me sitting in, as a guardian. His parents are a four-hour run away." Adam asked, as he sent the request to his mate, so they could distract Amber while he was in the room.

Cody was soon in the room, and head butted the door closed, before shifting, and Adam tossing him the shorts Joshua had grabbed him.

"Cody, I want you to be truthful, and not leave anything out, as long as it is not a pack secret." Adam ordered, "I will let you know if the question hits on a secret which can't be revealed."

Adam moved to a seat against the wall, as Cody sat across the table from the officer, and they took his statement.

"OK, we're done. Now I need to take Amber's statement." Officer Smith said, looking at the mulish look on Cody's face added, "If you change back to your wolf, I don't mind you staying with her."

Cody nodded with relief, before pulling the shorts off, and shifting back to his wolf. He would be considered a yearling, but was already larger than a regular wolf, and was heavier, due to denser muscles.

Karen led Amber in, as Adam stayed in his spot, not saying a thing, having pulled his tablet out to review and approve some documents and approve payment on some bills. Several made him wince at the amount, even though he knew they wouldn't even make a dent in the interest they made that month. He just wasn't used to dealing with individual bills which were larger than his entire yearly salary before joining the pack, and the before tax amount.

"OK, Amber," The officer asked softly, once she was sat down, with Cody's head in her lap, "We need to go over what happened yesterday. Your mother said you got separated?"

"I saw some nice flowers at the side of the trail and went to look at them. When I turned around everyone in the group was gone, and when I called, nobody answered," She looked to be nearly in tears. Cody whined as he could smell how upset she was, and she started petting his head, which helped calm her down, "I tried to find them and get somewhere high to see if I could see them, but then found myself at the bottom of a mountain with trees all around, and remembered mommy said if I got lost, to stay in one spot if I could."

The officer nodded, "That is exactly right, go on." He asked her gently.

"I was there a very long time, and it was getting cold. Then Wo—Cody came right up to me and stayed with me, till he came," She pointed at Adam, "Then he gave me a sweatshirt and had me ride Wo—Cody till we got to mommy."

The officer offered her a smile, then nodded to the adults, "I think we're done here." Looking at Adam in the eyes, before dropping them to his chin, as he had been taught when he was read into knowing about the supernatural beings. "Please arrange for my ride back."

Adam smiled, "Martin is waiting outside, to escort you to lunch and then will get you to the vehicle. If you need to contact us, you have our numbers."

The officer nodded, "I take it you have some more to discuss with these two?"

Adam nodded and opened the door, "Thanks for your help." He replied as the officer passed him.

"Just doing my job of keeping the peace. No, thank *you* for the speedy help in finding the girl." Was the reply, "It seems you will be doing more for her, and I thank you for your kindness. I had been warned you were hard and wouldn't do much, but I'm glad to be proven wrong."

Brook smiled grimly as she joined her mate and elaborated, "If you met the other two packs, then *that* is what you would have found. Nor would they have helped, just grudgingly given you permission to search for her. Enjoy your lunch."

Martin smiled at the officer as he led him away, and they seemed to restart their chat from the morning.

Adam and Brook went into the room, as Amber cuddled into Cody, "I don't want to leave Cody! Can we stay here?"

Karen smiled and stroked her daughter's hair, looked at the Alphas, "I already see the care you give for both of us, and the others have been nothing but friendly. Can we move in? I'm still reading what you gave me, and you said to read it before deciding to join the pack."

Brook nodded, "Yes. You can stay. We will arrange to move your stuff here, and you can stay."

Adam moved to Amber, "We need to tell you a few things, for you to stay," At her nod, he continued using his Alpha voice, "You cannot tell them to anyone, they need to stay secret."

She nodded, "I promise." She answered, not realising even if she tried, she wouldn't be able to say a thing.

"We are werewolves; we can turn into wolves. Cody is one of us." Adam told her, finding kids could understand much more than some thought.

"Why does he stay a wolf then?" She asked, "Why isn't he gone human?"

"Because you didn't know, and until you were told, he could only be a wolf around you, it is our rules." Adam replied, before turning to Cody, "You can shift now."

Cody slipped out of Amber's hold, and shifted, grabbing the shorts when Brook tossed them over, pulling them on. He knelt down in front of a wide-eyed Amber, "Hi Amber, you can call me Wolfie all you want, I don't mind." He said opening his arms to her. She threw herself into his arms, "Thank you for saving me." She said into his chest as she clung to him.

Cody sat down in a chair, holding Amber possessively, "You are very welcome, Amber."

"Can I become a wolf too?" Amber asked, looking up at Cody. He just looked at the Alphas for help, he didn't want to tell her she had to wait till after they mated, and that couldn't happen until they were both twenty.

"You want to?" Adam asked her, kneeling in front of her, "If you do, it is forever and ever, you can't ever become human again, you will always have a wolf in your mind, even if you look like a human."

Amber nodded, "I have always had dreams of running as a wolf. I want it."

Brook had been talking to Karen, who sighed, "I'm not happy with it, but I'm not going to stop her," Karen agreed finally. "As a baby, she barked and played a bit like a dog, or a wolf. She seems to be very wolfish as she has grown, just like my grandpa. I shouldn't keep her from what clearly is her destiny. I had my parents try to dictate something I felt strongly about and ended up putting a wall between us. I don't want that with her."

Cody looked confused, "I thought the laws were we had to wait till we were adults?" They had told him to keep quiet about being mates for now, and he and his wolf had agreed; let her be just a pup till the time was right.

Adam shook his head, "We can make exceptions." he told Amber, keeping it simple, *It's because of the bond you two share, it is possible.* He told privately to Cody, since the mate bond was to be kept quiet, till she noticed it. "I thought it might be the case. We are going to be having tests and games, including running and fighting starting in a few days. We will need to wait to start it till it is all done, as you will be sick for a bit, and you don't want to miss it."

Amber smiled, "As soon as they are done?" She asked, wiggling a little.

Adam nodded at Cody, "Yes, Amber, we can. Cody will make sure you see some of what is going to happen and keep an eye on you. If you need help, come to either Brook or I, or if you're here, Gareth or Maria, although any adult here is safe and will help you."

Amber looked to her mother, who nodded, "Yes, all who are here right now are good, and you can go to." Karen confirmed.

"Cody, why don't you go pull some clothes for her from the stores. Amber can stay with you, and we will get Karen a room too. I'm putting you on leave from patrols, till after the Trials. I want you to get her settled and start teaching her the rules." Adam told him.

"Yes, Alpha. Thank you!" Cody said, clearly surprised but grateful. Standing up, he carried her out the door on his hip, to find the healer and make sure she was cleared to leave. He silently asked a Theta friend to grab a selection of clothes for her and put them in his room.

Karen had a furrowed brow, "You're not worried about him taking advantage?" She asked, once the door closed.

Brook shook her head, "Since they are mates, it is extremely unlikely. I have only ever found one case of mate abuse, and that was one who was borderline insane. It was over three hundred years ago. Normally, mates are not able to knowingly harm their mate in any way; he is more likely to spoil her than to abuse her. He's not going to be alone; We have several keeping an eye on them, and ready to step in if needed."

Karen nodded and looked relieved. Writing down her address, which was a fair distance away, and passing her key, "We are renting a townhouse, and have only a month left on the lease. We are a month behind on rent..."

Brook nodded, and picked it up, "Do you have much?"

Karen shook her head, "No, the place came furnished. The furniture is theirs. Just our clothes and such. A few pictures. It all would fit in a car, if I had one."

Smiling, Brook gave her a hug, "I'm going to send a truck and a couple wolves to pack you up, if you don't mind? Then you can stay here and continue learning."

Karen nodded, "I think that would be best."

"Now, sleeping arrangements," Adam started, "Right now, Wild Valley has the loft. There are a few rooms, but most of the pack prefers to still wolf-pile and curl up together."

Karen was surprised, "Sleep all together?"

Adam nodded, "Even we joined them the first few nights. Being able to curl up with another helps to de-stress and helps the pack bond together. Other various wolves from MacLaren have joined in, especially the pups. I suspect Amber will join them, and you will be welcome to as well."

"What about getting cold?" Karen objected, mostly thinking it was fine; she always liked when Amber crawled in to cuddle. Something she missed from her ex.

Adam smiled, "Wolves are warmer than humans," He said, showing it by placing his warm hand on her, "We are like curling up to a big, heated pillow."

Karen smiled, and hugged Adam, holding him for a minute, "One which cuddles back" She said with a smile.

*****

Leaving Cody and Amber was hard, but they had a job to do. They had introduced Jake to Amber, along with Sam and Toby, since they were there. Cody knew them, but they hadn't talked, as Cody felt he was too low for them. Both showed they didn't care what rank their parents were and introduced them to other pups, especially those around Amber's age.

They headed back up using a different route, which was an extra hour of running but would let them see more of the land between the two packs. They tested several more patrols, and found most were adequate, with only one which came close to catching them. Several were able to escape with minimal hits, but then lacked the skills to get them back, now they were watching for it.

Jess smiled when they came in at supper time, "How's that girl doing?"

"Amber is doing good. Turns out Cody beat us to her and is her mate. Both are now at MacLaren relaxing." Brook replied.

"Cody..." Jess asked, "The Trainee?"

"Yup," Adam replied, sitting down for food, and switching to a private chat, *Gareth let me know there is a way for Cody to start a slow Turn, and to have just enough of a mate-bond to keep them happy when they separate.*

I take it they have been told of us and are joining the pack? Jess asked. Personally, she was thinking they needed some fresh blood, as they were starting to get too close in MacLaren. Those from the other packs would help too.

They were offered it and asked to read the details before deciding. Adam elaborated, *Although I am certain they will both be joining us eventually.*

Once they were done eating, after restocking John and Bri for the paintballs, they wandered a bit, checking on the wolves: chatting for a minute here, a hug there, and answering some questions there.

At random times, they moved to test the wolves. These tests were testing skills which were hard to test during the trials. They were going to work with Martin to use them to choose the new enforcer patrol teams, so they had a balance of those who were able to completely dodge, and those who barely even moved when they were hit, once they figured out which pack the wolves were going to be in. They also made sure they got enough time to sleep and relax as well.

Saturday morning came around way too early. Once everyone had breakfast, Brook howled to gather everyone at the edge of the space. The night shift had been tasked with securing everything and making sure all was locked down for the time with almost nobody around. The re-tractable crash barriers at the gate were installed, as was boulders to pre-vent vehicles from off-roading around the gate. There was one line of boulders going to the cliff on one side, and the river on the other. They planned to also place more, both in the first line, and to add a second line, but would take more time to do it.

"We are heading back to MacLaren for the Spring Trials. Enjoy your relaxing afternoon or getting some last exercises in!" Brook called out, getting a good cheer for it, interspersed with howls of those already shifted. They were all running, as few had decided to not test, and the few who were from Shadowed River or Night Depths either had been given a field rank, and would test the next spring, or were from Ma-cLaren and were happy with their rank. A few others would be relieved later and be down for part of it.

Brook shifted and nuzzled her mate, who had arrived from doing a final check, and both howled the start of the run. With them leading the run to the pack. John and Bri had offered to do sweeps at the back, and they had the Betas running at the outside, protecting the Deltas and the Thetas.

Adam and Brook had to keep their speed down, otherwise they'd outpace everyone else. They took hints from Bri and John as to when to have breaks and rest, as the slower ones started lagging, which often was the Thetas.

Arriving just in time for lunch, some were looking exhausted, while Adam, Brook, Bri, and John were looking only a bit exercised. Others looked happy to be done but were not exhausted. Even Charlie wasn't looking more than pleasantly exercised as he panted.

Arranging for the exhausted ones to get some food later, they left them resting on the grass around the pack house. As they headed inside, they checked them off to make sure they were all there. When John and Bri arrived with the last of the exhausted ones, all were accounted for. They brought bowls of water out to the wolves, so they could at least get a drink while they recovered.

Everyone had the afternoon off, as Adam had found was traditional. Once they had their busy day of tests, they would be quietly observing the rest having their Trials. With the slow, for them, pace getting here, it had been what they would have called a leisurely morning.

Walking into the dining hall he winced at the noise. It was full and then some, and noisy with the excited wolves.

Grabbing a plate and filling it, they quickly ate their fill, Adam and Brook headed into their room for some peace and quiet. "Tomorrow is our big day," Adam commented as they curled up together for a nap.

*****

They went for a walk after dinner relaxing and enjoying the brisk evening air. Gareth and Maria found them on the edge of the hill, looking at the stars to the east. They enjoyed silent companionship, none wanting to spoil the mood.

"Karen has started working in the kitchen. Apparently, she just walked in and asked to be put to work." Gareth said after a while, "I admire her courage to do it. Since then, she has impressed Ben for how diligent of a worker she is. He has put her on a schedule today, since she has spent basically entire shifts doing what needs to be done."

Adam laughed, "I was going to start her after the Trials, but guess she got bored."

Gareth chuckled, "I have had good reports about asking intelligent questions about the laws and joining. So far it seems she's taking it to heart about it."

"I have had reports she is getting to know those few who had stayed behind, and Cody is helping Amber start learning the ways of being a wolf; both are puppy-piling with my other pups." Adam replied. "Karen has mostly been sleeping alone," He added, "But in the same room as the others." Curling up in a group is something totally foreign to most humans so he wasn't going to force it.

Eventually they went into bed, knowing it was going to be a busy day the next day.

*****

"Good morning!" Gareth called out, the last few were running in, having finished their breakfast late. The weather was perfect; cool, but not cold, a slight breeze, and sunny, with patches of clouds. "As you all know; we are doing a slightly different method this year. We have four who are testing for the Alpha level, including Adam and Brook—" He had to stop there to let the howl die down, "Along with my two, John and Brianna," Again there was an enthusiastic howl. "As they are much faster and will have to do other tests other wolves aren't required to, we will be doing them today, so all can see."

Maria stepped up, "We also are using the trials this year to help decide how to split the pack, and what positions each will have in the resulting packs. Since so many are wanting to do the trials, and see about qualifying higher, instead of just using your last one, it looks to be a long Trials. The schedules are up inside. Tomorrow, we are looking to test those who have been asked for senior positions, but don't be discouraged, any who does well, may also be considered!" Often, they would also be wanting to fill leads for the shifts, who would report to them, and/or Seconds, so they had enough who had the skills, since they had enough members to do so. It often helped when someone wanted to change jobs, as often another was already skilled and could just take over with minimal time to get them up to speed.

There was a louder howl, full of hope.

"The first test is the run, in human shape." Gareth stated, as the pack turned, "Runners, are you ready?" He called out to the four, who were at the start, behind the gathered pack. "You have two hours to meet the Alpha standard. Go!"

The four took off running faster than any human could maintain amid howls of encouragement. The route was 50 km long. The rest of the pack dispersed a bit, with some following the four as wolves but would be mostly back here when they got back in a couple hours. Between the three major test runs, they were doing the mental tests, to give their bodies a chance to rest.

Both Brook and Adam had worn matching 1-piece running suits, of tight shorts and an attached tank top with a back zipper. Brook hadn't told her mate when she had ordered them, she had ordered both of them the female version, but Adam just smiled when she told him as they tried them on, when they had arrived a few weeks before. She had ordered custom ones with "Wild Valley" across the chest in purple and were a black colour with almost flames on the sides.

*****

They're almost back Was the call from the track monitor to all the packs, when they were passing the 48 km mark. It was the call to gather to watch them arrive back.

The wolves howled and shouted encouragement as the gathered wolves at the end caught sight of them, with not much time left. Many didn't think they would make it, as they couldn't themselves run to the finish line within the time left.

Chapter 14 - Trials

Adam and Brook put on a last burst of speed, and pulled ahead, passing the line at five minutes under the two hours. John and Bri were not far behind and got to the finish with seconds to spare.

The howl was deafening, as all four had passed the test, and could be clearly seen. They were wrapped in towels to dry their sweat as they gulped some water and did some cool down exercises. By the time they reached the deck, they had cooled off and were ready for the first mind part. They had to recite the main laws which the packs had, and each had to detail one law. Since John and Bri were doing the MacLaren, and Adam and Brook were doing Wild Valley, they were being tested separately. They discussed it as they stretched, and had Adam and Brook go first, as they needed the time to finish catching their breath.

The human run, while the shortest, was the hardest, as they tended to shift and run as a wolf, instead of staying human when they needed to go any distance. The test was to show they had the power and endurance, even in the human form. There were times it was needed to hide the fact they were able to shift from humans, was one reason for needing it.

Reciting the laws was easy for all four, as they used them all the time. The detailing of the laws, Adam had chosen the one about new members and membership transfers, knowing it had some quirks which he wanted to say to the wolves. Brook had chosen the one about the duties a pup can have, including about underage mates. She had found it hard to find which one to give in detail, till Cody had found his mate, and started reading up on it.

Taking a break for a shower then lunch was nice, as the four were given their lunch in private, with an elder to watch, as they 'weren't to discuss any of the mind parts. Adam shook his head, as they could discuss them silently, and privately, and the Elder wouldn't know. He realised part of it was on their honour they would not do so. They discussed the plans for the Wild Valley pack, and Adam shared some of his memories of growing up and living as a human.

After lunch, the other two were tested on the laws. John had chosen the one about the creation of sub-packs and splitting, so all knew the rules they were following about it, as it included timelines for how long to give members to choose which pack to belong to (five years minimum), and what it needed to form (An Alpha, an Elder, three Betas, nine Deltas, and fifteen Thetas minimum among those who had at least two decades of life), and how to declare it to the other packs around them, which was a part of the Inter-Pack Treaty which had to be written into the pack's laws, although generally packs had already had rules like it which predated the treaty, it unified them.

Bri had done the one about how to change ranks, including how it was permissible to challenge someone to a fight, if they didn't like a decision, or if they felt they could do the job better. When they had discussed it, when they were working out what to say, Bri had said in their pack, it was rare, but in some other packs, it was the only way someone advanced. Here, they usually could work it out, so some who wouldn't stand a fight, could go far on a job which didn't need to be strong.

After the elder announced all four passed the part, they stripped for the Were run. After shifting, they lined up near the start, and they were off after being told they had two hours to run the distance, which was twice that of the human one. The gait was a really bouncy movement, due to the digitigrade footing, giving them basically another joint in the leg.

Most of the wolves stuck around and chatted while the four did the running course, with some obstacles to make up for a slightly shortened route. On the way back, John had taken the lead, with Brook and Adam able to stay with him.

They reached the end with a few minutes to spare, arriving all as a group. Shifting down to human, to give their wolf-halves a break, they pulled on a robe, they sat at the edge of the deck, and they had their activities listed. All four had had sworn statements for fights, instead of having to fight today, or to demonstrate their skills with the weapons.

"Do any of you dispute the findings in these reports on the fights or weapon skills? Do any feel they need to challenge them to see if they are worthy?" The elder asked the gathered pack, who were silent, or shaking their head. The details in the reports were extensive; if they challenged it, they would be declaring they wanted to fight them to prove their worthiness. "I, Elder James, Head of the MacLaren Elders declare all four have passed the required fights and have the required fighting skills." It would make for a long day, if they were challenged, but one which an Alpha was expected to be able to handle.

"All have given disciplinary actions, and us elders have confirmed they still stand. Do any wish to review them?" Elder James asked. Again, nobody wished to bring out the details; generally, they just accepted the elder's word for this part.

It was the same for their leadership test, all felt they could lead and didn't need a demonstration of it.

"Next, each will list three contacts they have in another pack. Each contact must be in a different pack, they cannot be in the same pack."

Brook went first, "Alpha Grant, of Longview Pack." She had known him since she had first gone there, as a pup. "Beta David of Forest's Edge Pack." She used the manager of the restaurant they had gone to for Adam's mother's birthday. "Beta Mike, of Mac Tire' Dona Pack." The last one gave a stir, as the last pack most didn't know. She had just got the note they were accepting the invite to the Alpha Conference, and he had chatted with her about what they needed to bring.

"Where is Mac Tire' Dona Pack, as most don't know." The elder prompted, with a smile.

"Oregon, US." Brook replied, which got gasps of shock before a cheer. Having wide contacts like that was seen as good.

Adam was next, "Alpha Oscar of Forest's Edge. Alpha Rufus of Arctic Shadow Pack." Both packs were closer to their pack, and would be ones which had offered their support, even without the signing. "Beta Josh of Fossil Valley Pack – also in Oregon, US." It got some murmurs, as both had a contact of a pack in the US.

John and Bri gave their names, mostly of contacts from their training. They were even farther reaching than Adam and Brook's. Both had a contact from European packs, and one from the US, and one from Eastern Canada. It got an even louder murmur of chat among the pack as they were all well connected allowed for an exchange of ideas to and from other packs.

"Any doubt the contacts given?" The Elder stated.

"I challenge Adam's contact in Fossil Valley," Was the reply, which surprised them all. When the voices quieted down, "He is Next Alpha, not a Beta." The wolf replied.

Adam stood up to meet the challenge, "Yes, he is the next alpha, but down there, they do not have a separate rank, nor do they use the rank 'Second'. Thus, Josh holds the official rank of Beta, even if it is a very senior sort. Part of it is due to the size of their pack being much smaller than us, and as such have less structured ranks." Was his reply. Part of the reason, the packs had much smaller territory, and thus he had found that almost never was a US pack even at 100 members, with most in the forty to eighty adult member range, due to there being many more humans, and there not being as large of areas they could run in without being seen. Adam thought the tolerance for the cold was another reason he had found the wolf population ratio was skewed as well. He hadn't bothered looking into it, but he had wondered if the Councils also made sure the packs didn't get too large, either.

The wolf smiled, "Thank you for the details; I retract my challenge." He knew him through a cousin who moved into a neighbouring pack. He had known Josh was to be the Next Alpha, but not his official rank was Beta; now it made sense. It also did show they actually knew them, not just giving names.

"Anyone else?" The elder asked, waiting for a short time. "I declare all four have passed."

There was a loud cheer, with many howling.

"From our knowledge, all four have had key roles on inter-pack negotiations. For John and Bri, during their training away from the pack, they were the mediators between two packs, and were able to resolve an ongoing issue, preventing it from escalating to pack war!"

There was a gasp, as they had kept that part of the training a surprise. Both nodded and smiled at the pack.

"Adam and Brook negotiated the movement of a former Night Depths pack member across five packs in the US and Canada, and the settling of the Nameless Pack members in several packs." The elder told the gathered pack.

"Are there any who dispute the fact the four completed the inter-pack negotiations or want further details of what they have done?"

Pure silence was the answer. Adam and Brook were relieved to be in the clear. Many were curious about the work John and Bri did, but not enough to want to delay seeing them test their wolf's speed in the last run.

"The last item, other than their wolf-run, is have they lead a pack hunt?" Those who had been around before John and Bri left nodded, as the elder paused for effect.

"To our records, all four have led successful hunts. Any dispute this?" There was a bunch of shook heads for it as well.

"Well, now it's time to the last task!" The elder called out. Normally the Alpha did the actions, but because his two pups were being tested, he had to step back, so there wasn't any hint of bias. He had started the first run, but with others watching, it wasn't an issue.

The four stripped again and shifted to their wolves, ready for the final run. The pack made plenty of noise. They had been waiting for this test.

"To meet the alpha level, this run needs to be done in ninety minutes." There was a bit of a surprised murmur, as some didn't realise how short of time they had to do the run, but Alphas needed to be fast. When it had died down a bit, "Go!' Called the elder, getting them running.

Adam and Brook were off like a shot, and the other two were nearly as fast. Although Adam paced it nearly all out and was working to get Brook to stay with him, he continued running the trail, thinking it was much easier than the other time they did the run; there was no slippery black-ice coated rocks to watch out for, and the dirt provided even more traction than the snow did. They didn't need to try to see the loose stones under the snow before they stepped on them, they could see them clearly.

The gap between the two pairs just got bigger, even though both were moving very fast. They passed the halfway point with over ten minutes to spare, while John and Bri made it at the normal time.

Hitting the homestretch, Adam and Brook almost overran some before they could clear the trail.

Brook had finally got Adam to not pace her a bit past the halfway mark, and he zoomed over the finish line, and had trouble slowing enough to not run into the spectators and to turn without tumbling. Lapping around the pack house a couple times to recover, he saw his mate join him after the first lap, and completing the third one, sat down near the end, waiting for John and Bri.

They passed the line with a couple minutes to go.

What kept you? Adam teased them, as he panted a bit, and lapped water from a bowl in front of him at times. *You seemed slow on that run*

Where did you get the rockets? John joked back, *I don't see or smell them, otherwise I'd accuse you of cheating!*

I should have you tested for performance enhancing drugs, Bri teased; they all knew the drugs wouldn't work on them at all. Even if they were taken, they could be detected by their scent, and they wore off very fast. Having a chat with her father the evening before, with details of how he had run down the white wolf, wasn't too surprised on him being fast.

It was extremely rare to have a wolf able to take enough to boost their ability at all and not be scented at the start or end of the race, at which point there was large penalties, often with being ranked Omega, or if the Alpha was feeling kind, lowest of Thetas for a century or two. Also, they would likely never be accepted as an Elder, even if they lived that long, nor was it likely they would ever be trusted with a sensitive or senior position. Many wolves would turn away from one who cheated, let alone for something this important, as it was breaking a major trust. With those penalties, most didn't feel it was worth it, as those who would cheat usually were the lazy ones, and the higher ranks had more responsibilities and duties to go with the privileges, and there was a greater chance of needing to fight to defend the pack. Lazy wolves often were happy to stay as Thetas and the non-combatants.

The Elders conferred and double checked their times. There was a hush at they stood on the deck, "We have a new track record!" He called out to get a good howl, and waved to get the attention, "Adam ran it at seventy-four minutes, forty-eight seconds. Brook ran it at seventy-nine minutes, and John and Bri at eighty-eight minutes. All four have passed to the Alpha Level." The howl was loud enough it bounced off the mountains, making them seem to howl in celebration as well.

Gareth smiled and took over, "The chefs had no reservations about them passing. We will be having a celebration with their good food at dinner!" There was another howl for that, as when the chefs decided to celebrate, even the wolves had trouble eating all the tasty food. They reserved their tastiest choices for those nights.

Adam padded off to his room, with Brook at his side. They had a bounce in their steps, as they headed in. Jumping up on the bed, Adam sprawled out as flat as he could, all four paws outstretched, not bothering to shift. *Nap time,* He commented sleepily to Jess, who walked in behind them, as Brook hopped up and flopped beside him, doing the same pose, with a long sigh.

Jess laughed, as she took some photos of them, "I'll wake you in time for dinner, which is a couple hours away." She closed the door as she walked off with a smile. They both needed their sleep, as they had a very hard day, but they were Alphas.

*****

Adam and Brook walked into the dining hall, hair still damp from a shower, the hall went silent for a moment, before the noise picked up. Gareth motioned them up, to join him, his mate, and the other two, John and Bri.

Gareth howled to get everyone's attention. Almost instantly it was given.

"The elders tell me never before in MacLaren, The Nameless Pack, *or* Night Depths has *four* qualified for Alpha level. I even talked to Alpha Ranulf, in Glenshee pack, and he found the last time was in thirteenth century there was that many who tested, and then only three passed. Both of us have had four try individual tests, but not the set all at once." Glenshee pack was the parent pack in Scotland and named for the glen which formed one of the original pack boundaries; it was part of the required reading on the history of the pack.

The pack was looking shocked, before breaking out in a happy howl: they just did something which the packs haven't done before. For those in or wanting to join, it was a nice legacy for the pack.

"With that, I am pleased to present the four with their Alpha medallions." Gareth stated, opening the first box. Inside was a bright gold wolf head, howling with a Ring around it, and was about 10 cm diameter. The details on each wolf matched their own wolves. There was an embossed *Alpha* and their name on it along with their pack name. For Adam and Brook, they had *Founding Alpha* on theirs. He placed each of the four around their necks and gave them a hug.

Once all four were placed, they stepped up and a loud howl broke out, to congratulate the next leaders.

Adam and Brook went to their usual spot, Jess smiled and held up the camera, "Got it!" She said, as Adam plucked it from her grip, and looked at the pictures.

"Excellent!" He praised, showing the shots to Brook.

Before they could go get some dinner, Joshua was there with plates of their favourites for both of them.

"Thanks, I'm starving." Adam replied, sitting beside Amber and Cody, giving them a bit of attention before digging into his dinner. After eating their first helpings, Jess brought them seconds, as they started chatting.

"Cody was telling me you're the fastest!" Amber stated to Adam, wide eyed. He smiled and shared a mental chuckle with Brook; they both knew he could have run it even faster but hadn't want to leave her to run alone. They would keep the extra speed a secret; it would give them a surprise if needed to fight an attack.

Adam smiled, "I train really hard, to be that fast, so I can go help whoever needs it."

"Like you came to help me?"

Adam hugged her, "Yes like you." Changing the topic, "So, did you enjoy yourself today?"

"Yes! Although it was boring when you were out running." Amber replied.

The table laughed, "Well, you two can sit with Brook and I, while we see a bunch do testing." Adam offered.

"Yes, we will!" Amber agreed. Cody just ducked his head and blushed in pleasure. The fact the Alpha was inviting them to be with him showed some favouritism, which in a wolf pack was normal, and expected. He just never expected to be noticed by the Alphas. The others just expected him to not ignore the rest of them.

Adam talked to the two pups. He hadn't had any interaction except when Cody and his parents joined the pack. They had all been ranked as Omega, as the pups of Omegas were automatically Omega. Adam thought he may even be Beta material eventually. The had removed it totally from Cody's record without looking into anything, and after reviewing it, had found it was simply his father had embarrassed the Alpha to another Alpha by losing a bet by submitting in a fight, instead of fighting to his death, so he was given Omega, and his wife was also dishonoured when she disputed the charge.

When he had found Night Depths had pups who were forced to be Omega at no fault of their own, just they were born to an Omega, it was a good thing they didn't know where the body of the old alpha was, or by now it would have been shredded into little pieces from all of the issues they had found. Both he and Brook had the thought it was why he decided death was preferable to them finding out about it while he was alive; from what he sensed from the pack the first few days, most would have wanted to tear him to pieces and leave them for animals to scatter.

Eventually the party broke up. Adam had seen Jess and Joshua, along with Toby, Robin, and their girlfriends – who had permission from their parents to do the Trials – head off early, to get a good night's rest before they had their busy day. He hoped for the best, and same as Gareth and Maria the day before, him and Brook couldn't work any of the tests they were participating in, so there wasn't even the appearance of favouritism.

*****

"Go!" Called Gareth, sending the first batch of those running the wolf run as the first test in the morning. Sam, Lea, Toby, and Robin were off like a shot, outpacing everyone even before they were into the trees. Jess and Joshua were next; they were going to give it their best, but Adam had let them know he would love them the same, no matter what the outcome was, nor would it really affect their jobs and what they were having them do, the ranking was so they would have the clear authority from the seniority to deal with any issues. That had helped some of their nerves, this being their first time testing since they became adults.

The young four wanted to prove to their Alphas and the rest of the pack they were worthy of the attention, and the jobs they were being trained to do.

The next group was starting to get positioned, they were running the human run. Some of these were people Gareth had picked out to take over the positions of people who had requested to move to Wild Valley. They mostly had the ranks, but wanted to better the times, or were a skilled Delta and wanted to advance to Beta.

Brook called out for those to start. Adam shook his head from thinking, moving, as it was his turn to start the race for those in the Were shape, although there was fewer of those. Betas had three hours to run the Were, but Deltas and Thetas didn't have to even test, as there were some who didn't have the mental discipline to get to the shape. Some because they never bothered to try, as almost all could eventually get the mental discipline to get to the shape, it just took more time to learn the skill, since it was a careful balancing of the wolf and human minds, and they had to work together to access the form.

"Go!" He called out when it was time. They spaced the starts out to have the wolf runs out first, as the fastest were nearly back already. The Human runners would be back next, then the Weres. They had agreed to allow for switching days, if they wanted, so they weren't doing all the tests the same day.

Alphas were expected to be the best, so they had no choice, and were expected to be able to do all the tests in one day. He stepped back, letting the elders run the tests. He joined Brook beside Sam and Lea's parents, and even Toby's birthmother was there; the first time he had seen her in months. He heard she had been living as a wolf. She was human, but her eyes still showed her hurt. He casually wrapped an arm around her and worked to send his support and care, and she leaned into him, radiating sadness of her lost mate.

You can talk to your pup, and your nephew, He encouraged, *I would never keep you from them, even if you gave them up to us.* He'd not push, but realised they needed to keep an eye on her. She was silent but could feel the fact he had no hard feelings to her was surprising. She turned up for her shifts in the laundry, and did what was requested, but refused to say anything except what was absolutely required. He had passed it onto her, through her supervisor, if she wanted, she would always have an open door to move packs, but they were aware she didn't want any change right now.

He smiled as all four came back together. When they passed the finish line, the elder shook their head with a grin, as they gave the time.

Adam shook his head, *Already checked all the records I can, and they are the youngest to qualify in three centuries.* He told her before stepping down from the deck and moved when they were going to just fall down, "Don't stop; keep moving." He said falling into step beside them, making them follow as he moved to go around the pack house. "Do a couple laps. Go slow on the second, and if you feel stiff, don't stop." He told them, as he went with them around the first time, setting the speed a slow trot, as they panted. When they were halfway around, *You took off way too fast, you should have paced yourself a little slower* They nodded in agreement, having realised it about half way.

He joined the adults again, with Brook now having her arm around Toby's mother, *Thank you for giving them a chance. It seems you were right. I'll see them later.* She sent privately to Adam and Brook, slipping away before anyone else noticed her. She knew her pups were skilled, and would be able to protect themselves better, even if she wasn't able to handle changes now.

He watched as Jess and Joshua made it for Beta level as well, along with several others. He guided them to not stop, when several wanted to collapse, ending up needing to use his alpha voice to keep a few moving. The other four had stopped when they had got around, but he was picking up more when they finished one lap, working with each group on the first lap.

The elders had not wanted the Alphas doing too much with the timing of the races, as there was much in seniority up for grabs, and they didn't want a chance of challenge over bias. Challenge fights often were nasty, and sometime both wolves were badly injured if something went wrong. Helping them *after* they crossed the finish line, to get them properly cooled down was totally all right, and showed he cared for their well being.

There were several sets of races going on. Another would start once everyone was past the three-quarter mark, to try to prevent different groups lapping another. They also tried to group ones aiming for the same level together, so there was less spread. Adam thought about ways the races could have been automated and worked to make better times for starting and finishing more accurately. *Next Year,* he thought to himself. It would help take a load off the elders but would take a bit of learning first from them. He would just suggest it and let them decide.

For a bit, there was humans and wolves coming in, since the wolves were running three times the distance, and then the fastest Were were added in with the slowest wolves and humans.

Reaching the last, they were holding the next group till after lunch, as if they were running to have lunch right after, was asking for trouble; either they might go after a hapless live meal or get cranky with the others running with them.

Adam flopped down, feeling like he had run a race himself, and started to munch on the food. Once he finished his first plate, he looked up and smiled, "Sorry, it is lots of work to get them to cool down correctly, not just lay and pant then wince in pain for the next day from stiff muscles and take a while to get fit again." Getting a second helping, he came back, and smiled at the pups, "I hope your other tasks go as well."

"Human run is this afternoon." Jess offered. They were eating a bit lighter, as was good before the hard runs, and knowing that, there was some more selection of foods in warming trays during the day for those who couldn't make the meals. They would have more to eat after the run.

*****

Again, the four pups took off, but slightly slower. It seemed they took his thought to heart to pace themselves slower at the beginning, slightly. They still were the fastest there.

Jess and Joshua were closer this time, having realised they could speed up a little. The rest were out behind them. Adam had switched to taking pictures, as he wanted some records of his pups. He was having fun with the new Nikon D500 and D5 he now had, and he was loving how fast it could take pictures, and he had got a better lens. He ended up giggling as he checked out how sharp and clear the photos were turning it out, even without using a tripod, as he grinned. He was taking them not just of his pups, but of all those running. A few seemed to wonder if he was going insane, but most of them realised

"Here they come!" Someone called out.

Adam smiled as he looked up: the four were again running together and were getting close; he didn't know how long it was. It can't be much longer till the time ran out.

Chapter 15 – Surprises

Again, after they passed the elders conferred, but for a much shorter time. They smiled, "Again, under the time for Beta."

The gathered pack howled in pleasure. There was a rumour floating around that the pups were being marked for senior positions in their pack. Adam and Brook had agreed they would neither confirm or deny it to anyone, as they were waiting till after the trials and would decide with the pups what they wanted to do.

They still had some tests to do to qualify, even if they still had to wait until they were an adult to be allowed to have the full duties. Even if they didn't this year, they still had several years to qualify.

Adam just glared with his arms crossed at the runners who wanted to collapse, and they started doing the cooldown laps, as Brook passed them water bottles with cool water to sip as they cooled down. Wolf-Adam was panting laughter in his mind, it just took just a pose and a stern look to make them cool down, not needing to lead them directly.

Between runners, he had pulled out a laptop and was trying to respond to all his e-mails. He had over five hundred messages which he had to get through. Most were other Alphas starting to find out they passed and congratulating them on passing their testing. There were many packs who did some sort of trials, but others used different methods to test and rank members. Universally, the Alpha tests were very hard, and while they varied, most packs acknowledged those who had passed the tests as Alphas. He was hoping some of the Alphas who had disparaged him would now treat him as the peer he was, even if he was very young to be an Alpha and as a wolf at all. It amused him how fast they were learning of it.

Several Alphas who had ignored the Alpha Conference were now replying and enquiring about attending. Those he had forwarded to Mikan, as she was handing the organisation for their stays. She had said they would arrange for latecomers till they ran out of room.

The ones who had really surprised was Josh from Fossil Valley had messaged him about attending when they were discussing Ethan and had commented about the conference, along with a Beta from another pack from their area. Beta Mike, when he was contacted, said he wanted to bring team of pups, as they were out of school. Luckily, they could be roomed together. Since it was international, he was the one they were talking to, instead of someone lower. To make it easier for the pups, he was having them come a couple days before the Alphas arrived, so they could get used to the differences. He had passed the pack and inter-pack laws they would be expected to follow while here to both of them, to make sure everyone was familiar with them by the time they arrived.

Gareth was ecstatic; he had never been able to get any good meetings with the American wolves, only been in contact when there was a problem. Even then, most of the contact had been with the councils, and it always left him growly, as they seemed to think because they had authority over the packs in their area, they had authority over him too. At best he was willing to treat them as equals, even if many of them he felt were just in the position for power instead of being there to help, as few had any actual ties to the packs they had under them. Adam agreed with Gareth when they had discussed it, and preferred to not have someone above an Alpha, and instead where the packs were independent.

Jess and Joshua passed the finish line within the Beta time, with a bit to spare. He gave them a smile and a nod, showing he saw them come in. He was very proud of them. He had hoped for them to qualify at Beta, as he had told him he was looking at having them be responsible for the domestic side, and basically be their estate managers. The kitchen was

Lupita's domain, along with the menu, the food they grew, and the grocery shopping. They would oversee the maintenance, cleaning, and care of the pack's land. They would also be their event planners and hosts. He had his eyes on some for being security managers, and then with all the tech they were doing, they would need someone to manage it too. The Alpha duties are taking up enough of their time they were not able to do anything else.

Once everyone was in, they started to prepare for the tests with the weapons. With many looking to test for trainer, which was a harder test to pass. For weapons, they had to be more on form and not have any major mistakes and had to fight for a longer period. They also had to do a written test about the skill and pass it with 90% or better on the test.

They randomly selected names for the four rings. Adam and Brook tested some of the MacLaren wolves for their tests, those who were not considering changing packs. They were tough testers, and a few didn't pass. It was always disappointing for the wolf, as they would need to wait till next year to test again. An elder watched each test, and they were the one doing the scoring. Adam didn't bother using his more advanced, nor did he use much of his speed, and did very little of his strength.

Usually those who failed were ones who had decided the two would not be totally at the Alpha's level or due to their age, would not have much skill, and hadn't prepared enough to be ready for it. Several were shocked at how skilled both Brook and Adam were. By the end, they were disappointed with their own performance, and the failure rating they were given. All had been told that to pass they didn't need to win the bout, but just do well enough against them. Even getting a single touch would almost certainly gain them a pass. As they had trained their six for quite a while and Brook had been one of their instructors for years, they all passed the trainer level for the tests, but being underage, they were not allowed to train adults; until they had re-tested as trainers when they were of age, until then they could only train pups. All six had picked Bow, Staff and Sword trainer levels, in addition in hand-to-hand. They would need to re-test when they came of age, to maintain the trainer status, and Adam was toying with the idea for all trainers to need to retest to maintain their Trainer status, at least once a decade.

All six had to do the fights, which were going to be in the evenings starting tonight. They had many who needed the competition fights to show they had the practical skills. For Betas, it was two wolf and two as human. They were permitted a staff for the human fights, but many chose hand to hand. It was until disable, submission, or first blood.

They had been watched, and while their groups were of pups, they showed the needed leadership skills. All six had given disciplinary actions to someone recently, which surprised their parents, they were issues which was in their scope of duties and had been confirmed by their supervisor. For Sam and Toby, it was for their organising older pups to watch some younger, who then failed to take their duties seriously enough and hadn't bothered turning up for their shifts. They had arranged with Ben to give them a shift of dishes: an afternoon of being stuck in the kitchen while they smelled the cooking food, even Adam felt was sufficient for a first offence of missing a shift.

Lea had caught one pup who downloaded a report instead of writing one, with the teacher's permission, giving them a much harder essay in reply to write, and had them sit on a day off to write it in front of her, while she did a computer training with other pups, on how to play on the internet, without giving away what they were, and how to recognise and mitigate the occasionally slips. For part of it, the pups were permitted to play their choice of a list of games, while the one in trouble had to work on the essay. He felt that one was light, for someone who was trying to cheat, but wasn't going to do anything further for that case. He did send an email to all those who did some teaching, including the elders, and to pass on how much he hated cheaters, and how downloading a report was to him cheating as bad as using drugs or some other means of cheating during the Trials. The tests and projects were to show the pup knew the topic they were learning and knew how to apply it. Pups, he would mostly be lenient with, but repeated would get much tougher.

Robin had been doing an unscheduled inspection of the computer room and had found some wolves who were eating at the stations, and one had just dumped a mug of juice into the keyboard while trying to hide it. All four he had kicked out, and gave the keyboard to them, telling them not to come back till the keyboard worked, or paid the penalty. So far, they hadn't been back. Adam knew of that issue and Robin had then pulled a spare and replaced it, from the billing the four for the penalty, which far exceeded the $10 value of the keyboard. They would be paid off the penalty in a month or so.

Adam smiled, as he wished he had been able to do that before coming here. Here, he would have also put them all to work cleaning all the keyboards, including popping the keys off to get the crumbs out of each and every one. With 104 keys on a standard keyboard, it got tedious to pop them all off then clean, then having to put them back on in the correct order. Also, the keyboards could get really nasty under them.

Discussing the pack laws and inter-pack laws, it didn't really surprise anyone till Robin had brought up the most recent rules, related to the not eating in the computer lab or in other critical areas. He held up the laptop one Beta had killed, showing the damage as the reason why: there was a big pile of corroded circuits from the liquid, clearly showing for the least techie member why to keep liquids especially away. The wolf who had caused that issue had immediately owned up to it and had paid for the replacement out of his own pocket. For that, they had not given them any further punishment.

Discussing the inter-pack laws, the pups didn't do too much, and there were no surprises. The four were excused from the needing a contact or participating in an inter-pack negotiation. Both Jess and Joshua were helping Mikan with the organisation of the Alpha Conference, and nobody challenged the decision to accept it.

All six had worked with pups to do scent tracking, part of some of their duties. Adam linked the Elders, as he never had to do it. *You were excused, by unanimous vote of us. You are a new wolf, with enough duties* *and tasks already on your plate to have to do teaching of it. You were tested for scent-tracking and passed by the fact you led a pack hunt.**

Brook had taken Jess and Joshua on a couple of hunts with a few others, letting them lead, knowing they needed that part. The other four were excused till they were of age.

When did you do that? Adam asked. He didn't remember when she had been away long enough, and him not being aware of where she was during enough time to do a hunt with each of them since they met; they had been that close.

It was before you met me. I often took eighteen- to twenty-year-old pups on their first solo hunts, with their parent's consent. I have many requests, but we have been too busy to take them, so it never came up. Was Brook's reply. **I took Jess and Joshua on theirs at eighteen, and on last joint with just us three about a month before we met. I was one of the favourites to go out with, as I was fairly lucky. It was rare to not get a chance at a deer or elk with me.**

Adam just sighed; he agreed with his wolf about having a family hunt. One hunt on the full moon was not very satisfying. **By fall it should be calmed down and should be able to do it.** He told his wolf, reassuring him, eventually they would have time. It hopefully would calm him down enough to survive.

*****

Four days later Adam howled, catching the gathered packs attention mid way through dinner, "We have several very special promotions to do. First, we have two who had been ranked as a Theta in MacLaren, but now have passed all the tests, and the elders now confirm they are Beta rank!" There were some gasps as many others sat in stunned silence; it was a massive leap in seniority. "Jess and Joshua step forward!" He called out into the silence.

The two sat stunned for a moment before they were urged forward. There was a howl of appreciation from many voices, as they came up, blushing. Those who could reach them gave them a touch or pat on the back. There were many feelings of 'about time' and how they deserved the rank floating through the bonds.

Adam placed brand new insignia of being a founding Wild Valley Pack member and ranked Beta around Jess' neck, and handed her new ID, as Brook did the same for Joshua. *We will discuss any new rights and responsibilities after the end of the Trials,* He told them, it being laced with how proud both Brook and him were of their accomplishments.

"MacLaren and Wild Valley Packs: meet the newest betas!" Brook called out, getting a loud howl of greeting and happiness.

"Next, we have four pups who have also astonished the grouped elders, enough for each had two timers for their races." The smile on many faces, there was no secret who the pups were. "Toby, Robin, Sam, Lea: step forward!" Adam called out loudly.

The four were ready and smiled as they walked up, hands out to accept touches from the many gathered wolves. "They have passed all the tests they were given, even though they are designed for mature wolves, and passed the Beta levels, some almost reaching Alpha levels. If I didn't know better, I'd think they would have designs on my position!" He joked, getting a good laugh from the pack.

"In discussion with the few other senior members, and the elders of Wild Valley, Alphas Gareth and Maria and the leadership of MacLaren, we have decided to have a *Junior* rank for those pups who also pass the qualifications in the future, as it is not fair to not offer it to all pups." There was much whispering from the pups, till he sent a glare their way, "You will need to get agreement from your parents, along with a sponsorship of a Beta, Elder, or Alpha, before you will be permitted to try out. If you have questions on what is required, talk to Brook or myself. We do plan in the fall to make the requirements, and which test you would not need to do. Remember, many of these tests, you are qualifying to the same levels as the adults. It is for those who are wanting to help the pack, not just to get more rights, as there is much more duties and responsibilities which go with it." He could see quite a few eager pups who were looking interested. "Also, when you come of age, you would need to re-test to maintain your status." He added, showing there was more work for them.

Pulling them close, and wrapping his arms around them, "All four of these pups have qualified at the *Beta Instructor* level! They were excused from the Inter-pack negotiations or needing a contact outside of the pack. Teaching will be limited to pups and will need to re-qualify the Instructor Levels when they are of age. Being so young, there hasn't been a chance to have them lead a hunt. As their Alpha, we do guarantee they will have a chance before a year is up to qualify that part, and the elders agree they will be successful."

The instructor level was a higher level than just Beta, and was mostly with the weapons and fighting skills, where they had to have enough proficiency to teach others.

The pack nodded. They could understand that part, and nobody was interested in challenging it.

Pulling out the new insignias, they were more generic ones, so they could reuse them, they didn't have their names on it. When they were of age, as soon as they qualified for the last parts, they would get the full beta insignias. Adam and Brook smiled and gave each a hug and kiss as they bestowed them on them. Maria had been tasked with getting some photos, since it was a surprise for Adam's usual photographers.

Gareth and Maria then took over, having a few who needed special recognitions as well for their pack. There were others who had passed beyond what was expected and as such were being singled out for the recognition. Gareth and Adam had done a coin toss to choose who was going first, both wanting to go first.

Once everyone had been recognised with their new ranks, Gareth nodded at Ben and Lupita, who were just outside the kitchen, they nodded back and headed into the kitchen.

"In celebration, we have some cake for everyone." Gareth told the gathered wolves. There was another howl, as almost all wolves had a sweet tooth, same as humans. The two chefs, with their helpers started to bring carts with slabs of cake out to the various tables.

They celebrated, but not too late, as there were still plenty doing the various trials the next few days, as they had yet to even get through half the tests. They were getting to the lower groups, so they were getting bigger.

Adam had asked all of his wolves who had transferred from MacLaren to test in addition to those from the other packs, and Gareth had asked those who recently joined, to test, so they could get a baseline for them, as they had found they could not trust the records to be correct, as they had found the close to the old Alphas they were, the higher they ranked regardless to their skills. Those who didn't suck up were ranked low, even if it was more from wanting to be fair, and not try to suck up. Some were forced to do the duties of a position much higher without the official rank and the privileges to join the duties and responsibilities, and since they were already doing the job. As long as they passed the tests, they would retroactively have all the new members ranked to what they qualified at, with it being back to when they joined the pack. He wanted it to be so all were ranked equally.

There were a few enforcers who had been excused from the tests this year, so they had enough doing patrols. They had unofficially demonstrated their skills, to get an interim ranking and would be testing the next year or two to be confirmed before the pack.

*****

"Is there anyone who is left, who has not done any of the trials they wanted to take this year?" Elder James request at the end of lunch three weeks later. They *finally* had run out of participants. It was the longest Trials he had ever done. He was tired and was glad it was finally over. He had asked it every hour since the beginning of breakfast, and still had none asking.

The pack was silent or shaking their heads.

"Then I declare, as the Head Elder, this year's Trials to be over!" He said to the gathered wolves, who howled in appreciation of the effort of the volunteers and the elders in their work to put on the trials.

"We will have the results posted by the start of dinner tonight and will give out the new ranks tomorrow. Martin asked if anyone wants to update their ID photos, and will be getting a rank change, to visit security before dinner tomorrow, once the changes are posted." The elder advised.

All the wolves were glad to finally start to get back to their schedules. A few wolves had moved back to doing patrols, and others rotated back in.

Adam stood and howled to regather their attention, "Gareth and I have decided we will be finalising for the next year the two packs in two weeks. You have till then to request a transfer between our two packs. Once we do it, you will have to wait till next year's trials to request transfer, unless you feel you need to be an exception, which will be rare." He advised. "We will be doing the same for the next four years, so in five years we will basically set in the packs. This is to allow both packs a sense of stability. We will permit those who tell us they considering transferring packs to move between the two pack houses, so they can see if it's a better fit before the actual changing of the bonds. If you are interested, have word sent to us within the next two weeks, even if you would prefer to not do the change for a few months." He advised, giving the bad news they didn't have what they wanted to do and have a long choosing time. A few who had stated interest were four to six months before their relief was ready, but he didn't mind; they could work with them, they just didn't want the requests constantly coming in.

Giving the good news, "Also, we have been discussing it with John and Bri, in addition to Gareth and Maria, we will be working to maintain close links between both packs, and with open doors at most times for visitors between them. Saturday, we will be restarting the construction on Wild Valley's pack buildings." He had to smile at the enthusiastic howl, "We will be doing a wolf-run again after breakfast. We will *try* to pace it a little slower, this time." He stopped for the laughter of the pack, now knowing they were the fastest wolves around; the four-hour run they could do in two hours if they pushed it. "All who don't have duties are welcome to join in and help with the building, from both packs. Talk to an Alpha, so you are known to be running with us, if not already on our list, which will be posted shortly."

Sitting down in his seat, Cody and Amber had become regular members of his table. Cody had got late permission to test, and had qualified as a Junior Delta, although he hadn't been confirmed as one; he would be listed when the results were posted. Of the three other pups who were at least fifteen from his pack, another had also qualified as a junior delta, with the other two asking about next year. Although both he thought they were going to just go for the Theta, as they were fairly passive, and were just going for confirmation of their skills.

Both Amber and her mother had joined the pack two weeks ago, which gave the ability to mind-speak with others. Karen didn't use it much, but Amber used it all the time, where she would whisper before, knowing the wolves could hear the whispers.

Alpha, Amber asked, *When can I become a wolf?* She asked softly, as he knew Cody had been teaching her what it meant to be a wolf, but as she was still human, was much slower, weaker, and took much longer to heal. She also had been chosen by one of the dogs which wandered the property before they had a chance to introduce her to any. Orca was her constant companion, and to be a help for her when Cody had to do something. Like her namesake, she had a white belly and a black back. Gareth had been annoyed at Adam over the loss of the most striking one from the kennels, but Orca had been the one to choose Amber.

I keep telling you to call me Adam, he told her privately, teasingly. *How is Monday afternoon?* he sent to both her and Cody. He felt agreement from both, and also from Brook. *Monday morning, both will need to rest, and then no lunch, and only a light breakfast. Make sure to get fully clean before I meet with you.* Cody was going to be staying with her over the first part, then it would be just a waiting game.

Make sure you pack your gear in that new pack Adam told Chris as he watched the new-wolf head out of the dining hall. He had finally turned on the last full moon, a week before and had been learning his wolf body. He had enough control and speed to do the run now. Brook had been around when his wolf first talked to him, as he happened to be in the middle of testing some wolves for their weapon skills.

~~~~~

Brook saw Chris grab his head and be looking around. She quickly grabbed his arm and took him to their room for some quiet, "What's wrong?" she asked concerned, at his sudden alarm, thinking she knew what it was.

"Hearing a new voice in my head. It sounds young..." He complained. "It keeps wanting a mate."

She smiled, "It's likely your wolf." She stated, startling him.

Sitting him down on the pad in their living area, as it had become a crash area for pups who needed to be near an alpha, not that they generally cared, "Look inside, and meditate." She told him softly, sitting in front of him, "I will be with you, but you have to link to your wolf."

He nodded and closed his eyes, as Brook took both of his hands in hers. Suddenly Chris was inside his mind, and he could see a wolf who he didn't know, with light grey, with bold black markings.

He is your wolf, He heard Brook say, and suddenly she was beside him, with her wolf beside her.

The wolf ducked his head in respect, **Alpha,** He acknowledged, knowing it was their alpha. He also knew this wolf was not their mate, which was disappointing.

Wolf-Brook licked the wolf across its muzzle, accepting his respect and deference.

Touch foreheads, as you have been taught, and share your memories. Brook advised. Stepping back, she watched the two start to join before giving them the privacy of their mind.
~~~~~

Sitting down, she let her mate know where and what she was doing, as she sat there petting a stressed Mika, as she could sense the stress, but didn't know what to do to help.

It was about an hour later Chris opened his eyes and smiled, "Thank you! My wolf is more than I ever dreamed he could be." He had tears of joy in his eyes, "I'll never be alone again."

~~~~~

Adam smiled at the memory of the thoughts Brook had shared, as both needed to know. Brook had been exactly right also on him turning at the start of the Full Moon howl the week before. They had been howling for the start of the run, having started it at the back of MacLaren's pack house, with Chris there, since Brook had thought he'd turn for the first time with the howl; she had been right.

~~~~~

Even having been told and expecting it, Chris was surprised when the wolf in his head joined the howl, and he felt his body go numb. He could hear the joints popping as they changed but was unable to feel them. Next thing he knew, he was shaking out his fur – his fur!

Adam and Brook had then howled again in welcome and had him run between them as he stretched his legs as a wolf for the first time. He had even been given a taste of the freshly killed deer, and in his wolf form, it tasted better than any steak he had ever had, something he didn't think he could even bring himself to eat before his wolf had come in his mind.

He didn't know how he had got back, but he had woken up snuggled against Kelsey. Both were nude, but he had been getting used to the casual nudity around the pack. From his senses, he could smell they hadn't done anything. Since his wolf had started speaking, he whined about any action which wasn't with their mate. He wanted to wait for their mate before doing anything.

Chris hoped they found her soon, as he missed getting some action, but was totally willing to accept the wishes of his wolf in this.

~~~~~
~~~~~

Adam felt Chris' surprised acceptance of the order, but also the surprise and pleasure; he hadn't been allowed up at the Wild Valley pack site. *You asked to go,* Adam told him mildly, *And we promised as soon as you turned, we would let you up there. Having one who knows humans well at each site permanently will be good, for any interactions which need to happen.*

This time, Joshua was going up to take over as the manager, instead of Jess, although she was coming for a day to hand over. She'd be running back with them when they returned Sunday afternoon.
*****

The run was easy for many, but Chris was a new-wolf, and such Adam, who was doing sweeps, paced with him, sometimes a bit after even the Thetas. Lupita had set up, made lunch, and most had cleared out after eating by the time they had come in, with Chris utterly exhausted; he didn't even want lunch. Jess showed him to a tent which they had set close for him, and after lapping some water, and having her pull his pack off, as he hadn't mastered doing it as a wolf, collapsed without shifting and was asleep in moments.

Adam smiled as both he and Brook would check on him later in the afternoon, "Chris is probably going to wake at dinner, and be ravenous." Adam commented, "It was a hard run for him, even if it was almost a stroll for me.

Brook laughed, "I think being here will be good for him, though. He has been feeling a bit forgotten, from what I heard."

Adam smiled, "I'm planning on having him in charge of getting all the sensors going, and then be in charge of maintaining them."

Brook smiled, "That sounds perfect!"
*****

Just before supper, they woke Chris up. He growled at being woke up, but it instantly turned to a whine of apology when he realised it was his Alphas.

"Time for supper. Did you want it as a wolf, or as a human?" Adam asked, stroking Chris' head-fur, letting his wolf know the apology was accepted.

Human. He said before standing and stretching before shifting. He shivered as he pulled on the clothes, "Man, that feels strange. Going from being nice and warm to feeling the cold air on the skin!"

Adam laughed, "You'll get used to it. Be glad you're not learning in deep winter, like I did!" He advised, as they headed to the dining tent.

"Give Chris some extra," Adam mentioned to the server filling trays with rations. "He needs the protein, and he missed lunch."

"Yes, Alpha." Was the simple reply, as they added extra meat to Chris's full tray.

Sitting down, Adam and Brook smiled as Chris nearly inhaled the food, seeming to barely stop to breathe. The Alphas weren't even half done before Chris was literally licking the plate clean.

Adam laughed, and took it away, "Need some more?" he asked, amused. A theta was already there placing another tray in front of Chris, before taking the tray and dishes from Adam with a grin.

Chris blinked a few times before shaking his head, "Wow I seemed to lose control of my wolf there." He started to eat the new plate at a much more leisurely pace.

Brook shook her head, "Adam did a couple of meals like that. The wolf felt very starved, so took control till the meal was done. The longer you're a wolf the better control you will have. It is one reason you are restricted to the property and will want to not run alone."

Letting out a burp as he finished the second plate, "Well, he's very satisfied now. It was a hard run we did." He shook his head when the Theta asked if he wanted any more, "I think I'm good for now, but may want something later, thanks."

Adam grinned, "I stroll just slightly slower than the speed you run." He teased, "You need to build up your wind and stamina. I want you to take daily runs with a Delta or Beta which are at least an hour long."

Chris nodded, "Yes, Alpha," he replied, hearing the order, as it would get the others helping him too. He wanted to be able to qualify the next year, at least as a Delta.

*****

Sunday afternoon, Jess, Adam, Brook, and the ever-present Charlie ran back down to MacLaren, and pounced on an inattentive guard, while the rest of his patrol silently watched. The jokes the rest of the patrol would have on his behalf of being pounced would keep them attentive. They didn't need to give them any punishment and did let them silently know.

They chatted with Cody and Amber that evening when they were back, just to make sure she knew what she was getting into. They had discussed with her mother, and she had come to the decision it was better to Turn her now, so she could ease into her new abilities, rather than have her play catch up later. Looking at older records, due to her age, by the end of a year, she would basically be indistinguishable from a born-wolf pup and would gain abilities like one. Amber's mother agreed it was for the best, and she thought back to a few of the comments her grandfather had made, seeing them in a new light.

They left the two of them curled up with Jake, having a good sleep. Amber was going to just skip breakfast, when they talked about what would happen, since it was safer.

*****

The next morning Adam awoke before his mate, and he knew they had a busy day, even if he just wanted to go back to bed.

"Morning; we have a meeting, and a Mating/turning to do." Adam said, as he pounced his mate, kissing her well. For once, they were the only ones there; even Charlie was off somewhere.

Chapter 16 – Meetings and a Turnings

Adam smiled as Brook kissed him back wrapping her arms around him lovingly.

"Morning!" She replied once they separated, reluctantly. "Breakfast sounds good." She commented, slipping from under him and heading for the shower.

Chasing her into the bathroom, they spent some time getting a shared shower, before pulling on some comfortable clothes and heading out for breakfast.

*****

Gareth waved them into his office when they arrived after another delicious breakfast, finishing his chat with John and Bri. "I'm having them sit in on the meeting, as one will be the Next Alpha of MacLaren." Gareth told them.

"Which one, and what's the other doing?" Brook asked, catching the note.

"They have yet to figure it out, although both have as good of position of taking it here, they are both very young." Gareth replied. "I will be easing them into doing duties I don't like, or don't have time for, which includes Monday night fires."

"We were hoping one would find a mate when we were at training," Bri replied, "As we had agreed before we left, they would join whatever pack their mate was from, and the other would be the Next Alpha."

"Assuming they were the Next Alpha for their pack," John amended. "If not, we were not sure what would happen."

Adam smiled, "Well, even with Wild Valley, we still have two good sized packs. We still have control over much of the territory which was Night Depths; one could train to take over it, as another pack in a few decades." It would also give a good use to the currently empty territory.

Everyone looked at him like he had horns growing from his head, they were shocked.

"I like it!" John replied. "We just have to figure out which of us inherits."

Adam nodded, "With that territory bordering two packs where females are still not considered equal, my opinion would be for you, John, to lead it. It would give a buffer to Bri leading MacLaren." Both Sentinel Star and Feral Star Packs, Brook had told him, wouldn't deal with her and as such didn't want to try to deal with them and would leave it for him to do.

Gareth laughed, "That's perfect! Although I think we'll have both of them ranked 'Next Alpha' till they are a century." Getting nods of agreement from both his pups, "I think we will start the construction once yours is done, so we don't slow it down, and we can get the room back here the soonest."

John smiled, "I'll see about reusing the existing building till then."

Adam shook his head, "Don't bother. Other than the Alpha's suite and his lackeys, the rest would nearly need to be rebuilt to get it even what I'd consider habitable."

John nodded, "Take it you have been there?"

"Just briefly to gather those left behind when becoming their Alpha." Adam confirmed, "I didn't even need to step inside to smell it. I have no idea some wolves could be that bad." He had first thought werewolves were more like wolves, and were much cleaner than humans, but from the other few packs, it seemed not to always be the case.

Bri shook her head, "If the senior ones show no care, the Thetas usually don't bother cleaning the higher ranked areas, they in turn think cleaning is beneath them. There was a few like that at the beginning of the training. They either left or changed their tune quickly."

"But how to keep the area in use? I don't want a pack thinking it's vacant." John replied, thinking this would get the three eventual packs down to the point they would be able to not worry about splitting even at their record-setting growth in their lifetime.

"Use it for a training area," Adam replied, full of ideas today, "Even if it will mostly be a training area for you on being an Alpha."

Moving on, they discussed who they wanted for senior positions, and Adam took only those who had asked to move already, leaving now quite a few, for John to start with. Picking some names of those he knew and more he only had bare notes on, and comments from the four who had met them, he made a list to interview and see if they would fit in the pack he was wanting to make.

"I would give them the word first and organise them to make sure they are fully trained and experienced over the next few years." Adam suggested, "Let the packs know, so they can find out if they would like to move eventually. Doing it now, allows those who were considering Wild Valley to have another option in a few decades."

John thought for a minute, "That sounds perfect! Get the key positions filled and trained, so we can flesh out the pack from them." He looked at Gareth, "Sorry dad, but I'm thinking your pack is going to be much smaller."

Gareth smiled, "I keep thinking I would love a smaller pack, and it will be easier for Mark to be the Second while Ben stays in the kitchen, as he wants. I will still have him train a replacement which will go with you. You can discuss it with him."

John nodded; you never wanted to get on the Chef's bad side, or you'd just get the burnt scrapings! "Often the way to a healthy and happy pack is through their stomachs; give them good filling tasty food and generally they will be happy." He said, quoting one of the instructors from their training. "Luckily, we did have a class on how to set up a pack, and what skills are essential." Turning to Adam, "Think you could get your design team to help do another pack?" he asked.

Adam smiled, "I'll let them know when they are done assisting the building of Wild Valley. About two thirds are still in MacLaren. I will get Steve to start designing the sensor and defence network. We should get the bones in before it gets cold."

John smiled like he had been given a gift, "It means we can get the defenses up before anyone is there; great! I want a network like we have here, too." He begged. He had been shocked at how fast and rock solid it was now, and all the features he had not even thought to wish for, and now had access to.

Adam nodded, "Sure, but not quite as extensive. I think the secondary datacentre could be for all three packs, to cut down on the cost, and have the systems back up to there. I do want a backup link to here for security. Building another data centre there could be done later." When looking into it later, he would find out there was much smaller server unit to run the security systems, which worked as a relay to the full server they already had, which could later be replaced with the full one.

Gareth nodded, "That is fine."

Most of those who were requesting to move to Wild Valley had already gone up, and they would just have to arrange the actual bond transfer. The numbers up there made it easier to get the work done; so much so they were ahead of schedule, but with the extra long Trials, they lost most of the time they were ahead, other than the outbuildings are being done in parallel to the main, instead of waiting till after.

"Just in time," Gareth told Maria as she slipped in. She sat on his lap and gave her mate a kiss.

"The work to get the Alpha Conference working is coming along." Maria shared, "I don't see any issues. We are going to be stuffed, even with many who are up at Wild Valley, and not coming down during it, and giving permission to use their rooms or having even had it cleared, with their stuff in storage waiting for the new pack house is ready for them to move in."

"We're hosting a conference, here? Anything we need to do?" John said, not having heard about it. Bri nodded and looked interested. Alpha conferences were very rare and happened at most once in a decade. It was a big honour to be able to host one, although it was much stress as well.

"After our wedding, we are signing the Inter-Pack Treaty for Wild Valley, and the Alphas decided it would be perfect for a conference." Brook replied, surprised they hadn't heard about it. "They are also wanting to discuss the fact two packs have disappeared, directly involving our actions."

"The actions of those packs mostly just boiled over with us," Gareth mentioned, "They have been building for decades. It was bound to happen even if you weren't here. The fact you took direct control of one group and were key in the other is making many leaders who want to meet you face to face. The issue there was also the wolfsbane concerned many and have a talk about it."

Everyone nodded. Wolfsbane was one of the few things which could outright kill a werewolf. It was left unsaid but was felt it was the key reason for the US wolves coming up. Likely their council had their paws in it too.

"Please tell me the facility was destroyed." Bri asked, concerned.

"Totally." Adam confirmed, "Both the instruments, and the records. I made sure they were destroyed personally and made sure there wasn't any copies elsewhere in the pack house."

"So, when are you planning on moving into your new pack house?" John asked. Having two packs in one site makes it complicated, and lots of wolves in the same location made for chances of squabbles to break out. With werewolves, those tended to turn into fights and repairs needed to buildings.

"We're trying for the fall." Brook replied, "We need to have the basic building done, even if the inside isn't finished, we can wolf-pile in the common area while we finish the rooms. We too want the pack together. The biggest was the little ones and elders are here, not with the rest of their family."

Adam pulled out his tablet, and looked at the project chart, "Looks like some of the outbuildings, like the gym and the greenhouse will be built before the conference but will still need to be outfitted. The gym still needed the wolf-grade exercise equipment, and which are being made to order, they had quoted end of September for delivery. The mats are also scheduled for September, and the weapon racks would be made in the workshop, so should be about then too."

"The greenhouse is getting the fruit trees beginning of August and will be planting most of the rest by those with green thumbs. The play area will be sodded at the same time but would still be the fall before it is usable." Brook added.

"The outfitting for many parts are scheduled for September, along with the deliveries of the stuff for them. The tech stuff can be done once the snow starts, as long as we can keep road access." As long as they could clear the road and the hill spots didn't get totally iced, they should be able to keep it open.

"Back to the conference," Maria started. "John and Bri, we will be having you handle the pack for the time, so you can get some experience, and we can take a break and be more involved with the conference."

John and Bri looked startled, but nodded after a moment, they had received training as they grew up then intense training at The Academy over the last two years.

They brought John and Bri up to date with the state of the packs, which was taking a while. By the time they finished up, it was lunch time. Together they headed into the dining hall, and sat to eat, discussing items which didn't need privacy.

*****

Cody held the door to his small room, letting Adam and Brook come in. Amber was grinning, she finally was to be turned! Adam and Brook had moved them into another vacant room in the senior Beta wing, across from their own room, as it shared a bathroom with an unused room, so they would have the isolation needed for the turn, and it put them where they could watch them easily.

Adam and Brook tested to make sure she understood what she was getting into, and she knew it could be a while before much of her wolf-ness appeared.

"Are you ready to become a Wolf?" Adam asked, formally.

Amber stilled, "Yes."

"Do you agree to uphold the laws and traditions of the People you are joining, even when they conflict with the laws and traditions of the way you were raised?" Brook asked, not sure it really applied, as she had started to learn, but was still a pup.

"Yes!" Amber answered.

"You have been given what will happen once you are bitten, yet you want to be turned. Do any questions linger?" Adam asked.

"Nope!" Amber answered, with a shake of her head.

"Once bitten, the changes are permanent and will exist beyond the end of this life. Do you wish for this?" Brook asked, knowing the answer.

"Yes!"

Adam motioned Cody forward, "Prepare yourself then to be Turned."

Cody moved and helped her to remove her shirt. He had been taught how to partly shift, to do the turning bite. He shifted, this time his wolf-head sat on a human body. Turning to Amber, he lapped at her neck, as she giggled and tried to hold still. Adam and Brook watched but didn't need to intervene.

Cody bit, and Amber screamed, as Cody held her for the right length before releasing the bite, his head quickly shifting back to human, "Sorry, sorry, sorry," He kept repeating, tears running down his face, knowing the first part was painful, but didn't like the fact of his mate being in pain and especially from pain *he caused*. They quickly lay her back in the bed, as the first of the changes happened. She seemed out of it but hadn't passed out.

Brook tucked the thought away; it was a good sign of her being fairly senior, if she could fight passing out, as was their custom, but it wasn't always true. Some senior ones still passed out, and others were just so mind-strong they didn't.

Adam murmured instructions to Amber, about ignoring her body, eventually she opened her eyes, and groaned. Adam nodded to Cody that it was ok now to touch, and he quickly snuggled down beside her.

"Welcome back. That is the hardest part." He described where she was, but she just sighed and closed her eyes to sleep. Cody looked alarmed, but Adam reassured him, "This is normal. She will be sleeping lots for the next week or so. You two will need to stay in the room till we tell you. Even a mild cold could be dangerous to her."

Cody nodded, and snuggled tighter as she shivered, and seemed feverish.

Placing a few sealed containers of water on the table, "Try to get her to drink a couple sips at a time; not too much or it could make her throw up, as you have been taught." Brook offered. "We'll leave you be but call us day or night if you need anything."

Closing the door behind them, they placed a hanger on the door *Do Not Enter—Turn in Progress* to warn everyone away.

Adam sighed, "I have been wondering why there aren't more pups around." There were about forty for the MacLaren, and eighteen in their pack, not including the two inside the room.

Brook cuddled into his side, "Firstly, it is almost unheard of to conceive without your mate. Second, we have a harder time conceiving and during the first month of a resulting pregnancy. If the female is at all unhappy or stressed during the heat, the chance of conceiving is unlikely. During the first month, spontaneous abortions are common. I think it is somewhat a control since we have such long lives. Having four separate whelplings in a life is considered a large number, although having a litter of two is common, and three is not unusual." He already knew they carried the pups for a shorter time than humans, and often they were born smaller, they quickly grew. "Also, Thetas tend to have more pups than the most senior ones." She sighed, "Alphas usually have one or maybe two sets of pups." She had wanted lots of pups, but being Alpha meant it was very unlikely.

Adam pulled her close as they went to dinner, having left a covered tray for Cody, since Amber wouldn't want anything for a day or two, from his experience. *Well, it doesn't mean we can't try lots.* he sent, letting her know he loved her greatly all the same, *And we already have four of our own, with three more who are nearly as close.* Even his wolf considered the four their pups, even if they hadn't been conceived from them. All it lacked was the formal bond for the other two as well.

Brook smiled and gave him a kiss, *And that is why I love you!* He could sense he had pulled her out of her feeling down, *I think we may be picking up a couple more. I can feel the bonds to those two pups forming, as well. They feel the same way as Jake.*

Jake had been coming up behind them, and they pretended to not notice, even though he tried, he was loud on his feet. Just as he got close, Adam turned and bent down to catch the young pup, pulling him up for a cuddle, "You need to learn to be light and quiet on your feet. I could hear you coming!" he told the pup as he pouted.

Jake wrapped his arms around Adam's neck relaxed in 'his arms as Brook got the plates of food and carried all three to a table. Adam sat with the young pup in his lap and chatted with the other wolves at the table. Several of the pups came over for a quick hug and to eat with the Alpha. Those who were not from MacLaren loved the change; they could go bug the alphas for hugs at any time they wanted, or even go in and curl up with them at night if they were scared. Unlike their old alphas, they cared about the next generation and would help the pups all they could.

Adam and Brook very much cared for the pups, even though they currently had twenty of them in Wild Valley, with the addition of Amber. The pups were all starting to learn to relax in the pack. Their four who had qualified as Junior Beta had been put in charge of them, so were keeping a pair here now, with Willow, who had qualified as Junior Delta, being there to help them as well. The others all seemed to look up to the five, although Daniel and Kyle had already asked for help with training to qualify the next year. He smiled at those two, who were helping the youngest with their food.

Wolf pups were much cleaner eating than human toddlers; it seemed they knew food belonged in their stomach, not on the outside. Nor did they play with it. They just sometimes lacked the coordination to get it in, but they were trying. With a werewolf's immune system, they didn't need to worry about dirt, so the pups would eventually eat the stuff which landed on the floor, if one of the dogs didn't get it first.

Toby and Sam were down right now, and he had tasked them to help Daniel and Kyle learn the basics, since it showed he was taking their instructor level seriously. Several other pups were getting some lessons as well. He wanted them all to be able to be able to defend themselves until help could come right from the youngest. It would also give them some pride, and for those from Night Depths, where only the fighters got any training, a way to know it would never happen again to them.

"Not tonight," Adam told Jake, who asked when the next pup play time would be, "How about tomorrow afternoon?"

All of the pups, even the oldest at the table smiled and nodded.

Looking at the pups, now the meal was basically over, and they were just relaxing near them, "Go tell the other pups. They will want to go too." Almost immediately the pups were gone, following the request to share with the others.

Gareth smiled as he walked over, "Seems like you made some happy pups." He tried to do the play time, but he had trouble making time. "Enjoy it, as soon you will be so busy you can't do it."

Brook snickered, "You need to learn to trust those under you, and to delegate." She teased, "That is what Senior Betas and Seconds are for; to make your life easier and less busy."

Gareth shook his head, "I always prefer to do it hands-on, and not step back." He told them, *I have never been good at delegating.* He did admit to the two silently, along with the thought he wasn't going to change in the near future. A faint thought of giving some of the tasks to his pups though, did tag along.

Adam laughed, as they stood to head out to the firepit, remembering he should have been out to the one for Wild Valley, *Joshua, have them know we are going to move the pack fire up there till Friday.*

An amused mental snicker was Joshua's reply, *We were betting you wouldn't make it. There was a pool going on if you'd make it, or when you would make it. I'll pass it on. Have fun at the one down there.*

Adam shook his head at Brook's amused look, "You were in on that," He accused, as he picked Jake up again, slinging him on his back.

"Nope," She replied, "I just thought it wouldn't work, especially with needing to be here for the Elders tomorrow but didn't join the pool." Those who had been organizing the bets had refused her, stating she was too close and could unfairly influence it.

They headed out to the fire, doing a fast run when Jake kept saying "Faster!"

Rachel laughed as they showed up, "He said he wanted a ride,"

Adam grinned, "I don't mind, my pack is as heavy as him." Sitting down randomly, he pulled Rachel under an arm. "How are you doing?" he asked her.

Rachel leaned in and sighed, resting her head on his shoulder, "A bit better, Alpha. Thank you for letting me change."

Adam hugged her, feeling her relax into him. Around them those who were here gathered. They all could feel she needed the Alpha's attention. They kept the songs happy and light, and many sang along with them, sharing the comradery of being together.

*****

Uncurling from his mate the next morning, he could smell several of the pups with them. Quietly, he and his mate moved to have a shower and leave the pups sleeping, *Willow, when you come down, please wake *the several pups who are sleeping in my room, so they are up in time for breakfast,* He called as they left for an early breakfast. It was nice to have some pups he could use to get the rest of the bunch in line. They left Charlie napping with the pups, on guard to watch them. Adam didn't have a need to have his back guarded, as he could do it better himself, so had Charlie often do fetching or guarding duties.

Yes, Alpha. Was the reply, the warmth of given a task from the Alpha to do. Being trusted to do a task for a pup, especially for one as responsible as Willow was a validation of all their hard work and discipline.

*****

Brook sighed as both Adam and her slumped down at lunch, "It feels like all we do is move from meeting to duty to meeting now," She complained to the amusement of their friends at the table. "I want some time to relax and enjoy my mate!" Not much was discussed, and no decision was made, but it took all morning to do it.

Adam laughed, "I think our job is to be bored all day long, so the rest of the pack can *do* stuff." Looking around the table, "Anyone want the job?"

There was several 'No!' or other refusals, and the rest look shocked or horrified.

Adam sighed, "It was worth a try!" He said with a straight face, before him and Brook burst out laughing. "That was a good one!" He told her, as they enjoyed the looks the others were giving them.

Martin laid his head in his hands, "Why do we have such horrible friends?" He groaned, "Brook was bad, but with Adam they are much worse!"

Several muttered agreements, "At least their jokes are funny!" Jess commented as she sat down, laughing. "Is it quieting down for you now?" she asked, after she stopped laughing. She needed to stay on top of their schedule to help them.

"Next major thing is the wedding." Brook commented. It was more a show for the parents, and human family. For them it was just something to be endured. She was getting a very nice dress out of it, though.

"After that is the Alpha Conference. We have quite a few packs confirmed coming, with others yet to full confirm, and two additional packs from the US are coming up. The two from the US includes a few pups and are arranged to come up a few days early." Adam replied. The two US packs were related to their contacts, so would be nice to see them.

"This afternoon we are having a pup playtime." Adam replied, nearly forgetting about it. Many of the wolves smiled, fondly. A few volunteered to help, as playing with the pups always relaxed a wolf no matter how stressed.

Meeting the moving ball of fur which was nearly all sixty pups from both packs. He was glad for the volunteers, as he hadn't expected they would be released from their lessons. The few instructors were there to help, all had impish grins on their faces.

Leading the way, he took them to the nearby meadow, so they could play. Usually, the pups were not allowed this far without an adult, so it was an extra special treat, as the grass was tall enough to hide all but the oldest, and the pups seemed to enjoy a hide-and-pounce game, as the adults moved to ring the meadow to keep an eye on them all. Adam knew Martin had also tasked a couple patrols to ring them, and make sure nothing got close to them. He could see several relaxing at the edge of the meadow, staying alert.

*****

They headed back up to Wild Valley after napping the evening and early night away. Playing with the pups had been relaxing, but also exhausting. The inner patrol had tried to pounce, as they pretended to not see them, but the wolf which tried for Brook just got a face full of dirt as she darted to the side at the last moment, and the two who went for Adam, he was able to time a limb of a tree to catch them in their mouth, and give them just a jaw full of twigs and leaves.

The last one aborted her attack, knowing they had been had!

Nice try! Brook consoled, *Try to stay down wind!* She advised, but changes did happen; it was how they caught Alpha Night.

The wind shifted and let them know just before the trap was sprung. They knew wolfdogs were off limits for the play-attacks, as they didn't always understand it was a test and not real.

Heading out, there was now regular patrols along the space between the two territories, as there was seemingly a steady stream of wolves moving between the two areas. Moving along, they were able to catch a couple wolves before their patrol-mates were able to warn them, but it seemed the patrols were wary, as they should be.

Catching a deer, they had plenty to eat, even when a patrol moved in to join them; respectfully waiting till the Alphas had eaten their fill. The deer also let them work out a bunch of energy and frustration.

The next patrol was not so lucky. Adam and Brook shifted to Were and grinned as they climbed into the large trees, using their claws. They pounced from overhead, catching the patrol unaware of the attack from overhead, even if they were watching the ground level. They were having to be inventive to catch the patrols at all now!

Reaching the pack, Ethan was waiting for them, "Alphas," He greeted, showing his neck in submission, "May I speak with you?" He asked quietly.

Chapter 17 – Finally Married!

Shifting back to human, "Sure, Ethan." Adam said, as he pulled his pack off, and his clothes on.

"I want to join, if the offer is still open." Ethan replied softly. "I can't stand being outside looking in a day longer." He sounded almost desperate.

Brook smiled and gave him a hug, "You read the rules and responsibilities?" She asked.

Ethan nodded, "Much better than the old ones." This one he could easily see was geared to support the pack, not just have them as the lackeys of the Alpha. Also, they were enforced as they were written, not on a different way. He had heard everyone was getting an ereader with a copy of the rules too, and even copies of all the treaties with other packs, once they were moved in.

Adam shook his head, "Night Depths as a pack died with Alpha Night. We are a new pack called Wild Valley. We may have had most of the former members of Night Depth, but it is not Night Depths." Technically, they were an offshoot of MacLaren Pack, but most considered it an entirely new pack.

Ethan smiled, "The feel is so different, I won't have trouble remembering that." Here, there was no stink of fear, it was the nice refreshing scent of happy wolves. The leaders of the pack used love-respect, not fear-respect to keep the pack in line. He had no issue with the punishments, as they fit what he thought was right for what happened. Disobeying orders had it even noted "Asking for details or elaboration of assigned task or tasks is not disobeying, nor is if vague orders were given and while they did the letter of the order, they didn't have the desired outcome." There were several examples given, and they made sense to him.

Adam nodded and led the way to one of the sleeping tents, "You will need to sleep after, as you will have a headache as the bond forms."

Ethan nodded, "I called my sister to be my witness, if its OK?"

Brook smiled, "That's fine."

Both Alphas greeted Sara as she came in, standing to the side.

"Ethan, do you wish to join the Pack?" Adam asked, placing his hands on Ethan's shoulders, starting the Oath. Ethan had a smile ear to ear as he answered the questions; he had been looking for a hidden side, but seemed these Alphas liked a happy pack, and he could live with it. The elders he had spoken to had described two kinds or respect: the kind which was from fear he knew well, but the kind which came from mutual care and loyalty was one he was only starting to see. "Fear was easy to do, but gaining loyalty is much harder to get, easy to lose, and had to be continually maintained." They had told him, "But in the long run, loyalty and caring makes for a much better pack." He could see it in how everyone was working hard, not lazing about when the supervisor was not looking. It was also clear in how the workers had offered to split into several shifts and were now working around the clock, and he kept being told they were ahead of schedule, and were having to wait to proceed, and to move to another area.

"Welcome to the Wild Valley Pack, Ethan." Adam ended happily, "I hope now you can heal fully." He amended softly, before touching his forehead to their newest packmate. As Ethan staggered, and both she-wolves caught him, and laid him down on the bed, they could feel the welcome through the bonds, and a loud howl of welcome from the werewolves in Wild Valley Pack. It was soon echoed by their wolf pack cousins also welcoming the newest member. Even if they didn't have bonds like the werewolves, they too knew the joy of gaining a pack member. Ethan fell asleep to the howls of the cousin-wolves welcoming him, with a smile on his face, as his sister curled up with him.

*****

"We are formally introducing you to the newest member," Brook called out that evening, as they had a short break between shifts a few hours later, at Ethan's request. He had recovered from the pack bonds forming. "You all know him, but only as a visitor. Ethan decided he wanted to join the pack!"

The howl this time reverberated through the air in welcome. All who had met him thought he was very special to have lived through being branded a Rogue and being caught with some actual rogues.

Ethan smiled and stepped off their makeshift stage, a stack of plywood sheets ready for doing parts of the construction. Ethan mingled, feeling the welcome. He had passed word to the elders and others down at MacLaren. When they headed back, he would join them for a small gathering for the few left behind, so they could welcome him too.

*****

Friday evening, Adam and Brook found their pack had worked out a plan so everyone who wanted to go, could attend the fire without needing their involvement, without any of the work slowing down. Some were working a double shift who didn't want to come as well and would get a free day as another traded with them another day so they could be there for it all.

Both Brook and Adam were impressed, as were many of the crew leads who approved the changes. It was done worker to worker. Some would be there early, but then need to leave to work later, to let others come. It had ended up having all who wanted to go able to make it, while the work wasn't even going to slow down.

For their wolves, Adam and Brook would make sure they stayed till the last. They had even helped in the tent which served as the kitchen, and made some food for the wolves, as this fire would double as their meal break for some. The kitchen had also supplied some raw meats which could easily be cooked on the fire, along with some whole pota-toes and ears of corn wrapped in aluminum foil, to roast in the coals.

Most of the wolves had made it to one or more of the other fire gath-erings, so were quite happy to help those who hadn't been to one. There was some overlap on songs, but most were not repeated. There were sev-eral retellings of how Adam had handled the Alpha who decided he was at his beck and call but left with his tail between his legs, with some ex-aggeration, but not much was needed, as it was funny now. Along with it was a retelling of how he took out the old Alpha.

Adam just smiled, and snuggled against Brook, as they enjoyed the pride of their pack in the strength of their Alphas. There was only one or two who grumbled to themselves about how they were too young and lacked the experience to handle a pack without a mentor. Those wolves had been gently but firmly told 'no' to the idea of a mentor, so they just grumbled to themselves which they mostly ignored and de-cided they would only deal with if it started to undermine the pack, but it seemed they didn't care it enough to ask for a different pack, so both had decided they were the ones who weren't happy if they couldn't complain about something. Others reminded them they did have a mentor, in the form of Alphas Gareth and Mara; just the mentors didn't have veto powers.

Only the Elders knew Adam had a mentor in his head, in the form of his wolf remembering his previous incarnation. Even Brook had con-fided to Adam hers was starting to offer suggestions, so she was thinking she remembered more than she had ever let her know about. Both had decided it wasn't something which they needed to pass onto anyone.

*****

Adam grumbled as he was fitted for the Tuxedo on Saturday after-noon when they got back to MacLaren, he had been trying to avoid it, but there were only six weeks left till the wedding and the wolf who worked as their tailor had cornered him.

He didn't realise it before, but one of his wolves had worked as a seamstress for the old Alpha. When Brook's mother had found out, he heard she had given a bit of a dance. Her parents had talked to Brook and him, and had decided to move into their pack, to be closer to their only child, but with the understanding she was the Alpha, and could not use the fact of being her parents to influence the decisions, which was his only concern. They agreed immediately, which laid the concern to rest, and he happily accepted them.

"Susanne," Adam started, trying to distract his mind from being poked and prodded from the outfitting, "What are you doing now?"

Susanne ranked only as a delta, but she seemed happy at that rank. "Right now, I help in the kitchen, and work in the laundry." She said with a sigh. She had noticed the current Alphas rarely dressed up, preferring comfort over style. When they did, they weren't hard on those clothes, most of the time. But like any, sometimes they just shifted, often tearing the clothes. The old Alpha kept her busy between washing, repairing, and replacing his clothes and that of his favourite Betas. After a couple of starch filled underwear, the Betas learned to respect her, and to leave her alone.

"What would you like to do?" He prompted, hearing the dissatisfaction in her voice.

She smiled up, "I love sewing and working with clothes. I loved being a seamstress." She told him. "But there's not enough work to keep me busy, so I do other jobs."

While she worked on his outfit, they chatted. One of her dreams was to have a shop to do fancy clothes, including custom work. They discussed how the pack was planning on making the backpacks, which also had a fair amount of stitching, even if it was of materials nobody would really want to have in their clothes.

Adam smiled, and after sharing some thoughts with Brook on the idea, they agreed to let her do it. "I think we could let you do that, if you wouldn't mind sharing the profits with the pack, we could help you get a start. If it gets busy enough, might even be able to have a packmate or two work with you."

She was nearly in tears, she was so happy, "I don't know how to thank you!" She wanted to hug him, but knew it wouldn't be good to do so, with all the pins.

Adam smiled, "You can thank us by being successful, and bring in some money for the pack. If possible, I would like to wait till we have the pack house finished first."

"Of course," She replied with a smile, as she finished pinning the adjustments. Waiting till they were moved in would let her see if there was a place in town she could get for a storefront, as he had no issue with her not being limited to the pack. Once done, she helped him out of it, so she could do the stitching. "Tell that mate of yours I'm ready for her."

Adam smiled, *Your turn to be stabbed with little pointy things and fingers for a while.* She had wanted to keep her dress a surprise. Adam had agreed, as he loved nice surprises.

He gave her a kiss as he passed her just outside their room. "Love you!" He called as he went off to check on their wolves, and make sure all were happy.

*****

The next few weeks went by fast, with Brook and Adam splitting their time between the two pack sites. When they were up at Wild Valley, if they had nothing else, they helped with the construction. It really helped speed the work, as the wolves loved it when they got to work alongside their Alphas, as they took the dirtiest and hardest jobs which they could.

They had all of their pack join together at the Wild Valley site for the full moon and the Solstice, which happened to be the same day. It made for an even bigger party; they had stopped work mid afternoon before the solstice, and it went till about noon the next day, to let those recover who were working on the pack house. The Elders were astonished at the size of the building, and how fast it was going up. The majority had not been up since the Sod Turning at the beginning of the construction.

They had set some new traditions, with a pack-romp in the afternoon, which included all wolves who were able—including the pups and elders, and a pack fire gathering at the end, towards the end where the pups were put to bed, under the watch of a few volunteers who were not joining in on the hunt. They were not sure they would do it for every moon, but definitely at the seasons change.

They also had been helping with the training classes which were still going on. Many wanted to advance further now they saw the tests were run impartially, with no favouritism or slight fudging of numbers, or had only partly qualified at the Trials. There were a couple they had their eyes on for advanced training skills. A few times, they had stated the person had a provisional rank, with the requirement to make the mark the next year, but for the most part, those were the ones who either had previously had the rank, or the elders agreed with the Alphas they just lacked the time to get the training time to qualify.

*****

All too soon, and yet what seemed like a long wait, was time to head up to the wedding. There were several wolves taking vehicles there with the large, bulky tents and other heavy things, as it was nearly a seven hour drive due to the round about route they had to go. They left the afternoon before and spent the night at the nearby lodge or under the stars, as they wished. They had to go nearly two hours south, then east by an hour just to get around the mountains. Running, they were only about an hour run north from the MacLaren pack house or about two and a half from Wild Valley. They even had a hiking trail which went basically straight from the territory to the area.

Their clothes had been sent in the vehicle, so they didn't need to worry about them; they had their usual light plain stuff with them if they needed to shift, and since they were trying to pretend to be humans, they had brought shoes, although good ones were with their good clothes.

Smiling, Adam and Brook shifted to their wolves, then headed out the door, meeting up with those who would be going with them. Many of both packs wanted to attend, and others were just shrugging and not caring about it, as it was a human custom; they knew Adam and Brook had a bond which was much tighter than the piece of paper they would be getting. Those they could spare from both MacLaren and Wild Valley had open invites to go. Some wanted to go, as they had never been to a wedding.

Heading off at a slow run, they enjoyed the trails and the exercise to run off the nerves and excess energy.

*****

Adam and Brook ran up to the pavilion tents they had set up for them to get ready in, sharing a nuzzle and a lick to the muzzle before separating to their own tents to get ready. Brook still hadn't let him know anything about her dress, other than it was white, so he was looking forward to the surprise. There was a larger tent for the werewolf guests running in as well, so they could shift and dress. Many had sent their clothes as well, since packing a good suit or dress into a wolf-pack would probably wrinkle it.

Others had taken the long drive as humans in the vans and were helping set everything up.

Most of the wolves arrived early to help with setting up the site, as they were only able to book the park for the day. The ceremony was late morning, with a lunch being held under a large tent, for if bad weather came, otherwise the sides were strapped back to keep it open and just the summer sun out. After lunch, there would be some dances, with several wolves providing the music. Lupita had taken control of the meal when she found out, and nobody had tried to stop her. She had been down for a day at Longview, cooking up a storm, and generally annoying their cook, it being the closest pack house to the site when driving. It still was an hour and a half drive away. They had set up a field kitchen to roast the meat, so it would be hot. One of her helpers was here dealing with it, as she did the finishing of the cake and other more delicate stuff.

Adam had decided on Joshua being his Best Man, and Toby and Robin being with him as groomsmen. Brook had Jess as the Maid of Honour, and Sam and Lea as Bridesmaids. Everyone had gone up with them, so they split by gender, to get ready. Neither had bothered with a stag, as they had been Mated for a while now, and preferred to spend the night together.

They had booked Lucas as the photographer, so they could get some wolf shots later as well. He had been honoured for the ability to pay them back for the chance at being promoted. He had accepted before they had even said what they were paying.

*****

As Adam had promised at Christmas to have some assistance there for his grandmother, Evan had agreed to carry his grandmother, but also had an Argo there for her to decide.

He had seen a couple pictures of her, so when Angie and Misty showed up and parked in the handicapped spot reserved for them, he was at the door to help her. "Welcome," He said with a smile, as he stared at her dumbfounded face, "I'm Evan, and Adam asked me to assist you today, Misty." Both he and his mate, Kuri, had a great laugh when they described the argument, and how Adam had resolved it.

She was elderly, for a human, so he did provide the assistance with the deference due to an Elder. When offered to carry her, or for the ride in the Argo, she took the Argo, seeming to not want to have the view of being carried and was taken aback it was offered.

He quickly took both her and Angie close to her seat and walked them straight to her seat. He mused about the fact none of Adam's other grandparents being alive and was quite happy he should be around to see several generations of his pups find their mates.

The day was warm, but with the slight breeze it was a comfortable temperature. It seemed even the weather wanted to be good for them, making a good omen for those who were superstitious, or it was part of their religious beliefs. The view behind them was of the Upper Kananaskis lake, with mountains surrounding them. There were some deciduous trees where they could get light, among the slower growing coniferous pine trees which blanketed the mountains all around them, but with the tops of the mountains rising enough they were bare limestone rock, showing.

Adam stayed in the pavilion for a while, getting some of his paperwork done, but was soon out greeting many of the humans who had made the trip.

He greeted Misty, "How was the trip?"

"Fine. I never said I wanted to be carried." She complained. He shook his head, "I distinctly remember offering a ride or 'A strapping young man to carry you' at Christmas, and you couldn't decide then." He replied with a grin. His wolf was still put out over her trying to get them to stay apart till tonight, but the human half had got him to agree the amusement at her expense would be much better than biting her, which would cause many issues. "I was following through on my word. You wanted to decide today. Evan did agree to help you however you need today." He advised, before walking off to greet some others he hadn't seen in years, not waiting for her reply.

"You are looking much younger," One aunt and uncle who lived in another city several hours away commented when he greeted them, "How did you do that?" Adam hadn't been up to see them for a couple years before he had met his mate.

"I could tell you," He replied, "But then I would have to take you into protective custody." He replied with a straight face, as he had been replying to everyone who asked questions he couldn't answer. "How was the trip?" He asked, changing the topic. With his wolf hearing, those not in the know, were commenting they didn't know if he was joking or not. He had been serious; if he told them, he'd need to protect them till he knew who was safe to tell.

Eventually it was time. Gareth was officiating the marriage, and he had been delighted when asked. They had invited a few Alphas, and they had brought a few more wolves. Others had declined. He was glad Alpha Tyler hadn't been invited, as he'd probably give away the secret, and try to subjugate the humans there.

Looking over the mass gathering, well over half were wolves. Adam had basically cut ties with his human friends as he had moved to the pack, and he'd not talked to most in months. So, other than his family, with several uncles and aunts, there were only a couple cousins with their spouses. For the werewolves, there were many from Wild Valley, to support their Alphas. MacLaren had lots, as Brook had shared her many friends with Adam, and were there to support both. Longview also had more who had come. Some were ones he had met or had done the run with, but others were just curious. Alphas or Elders other packs were there too. A couple had commented they had never been to a human wedding before, either, while for others it had been several decades since the last one.

Brook's Îyãħé Nakoda Elder friend, who he was amused to find out went by they name Wolf Friend, and another elder were there as well. She had personally made sure they were invited and arranged for their travel.

Charlie was wearing a simple service dog collar, as they had left off his harness, and looking put out about it but had also been washed and brushed till his fur gleamed with health. He hadn't cared for the wash but had enjoyed the through brushing afterwards but was still annoyed. He had to stay beside Adam, and no rolling, until after the event.

Eventually it was time, and he headed up to the stage which was set up, with a beautiful mountain vista behind them. The stage was mostly boards leveling a slight rise in the ground, with them framed by the lake, from the view of everyone else there. There was a patchwork of fluffy clouds, like balls of cotton in the sky, which would make for great pictures and help from letting it get too hot. He mostly ignored Lucas and the clicks of the camera.

He was glad the clothes were made light, and while they fit well, didn't feel hot, and he could tell he could move well in it. Susanne had also made it with a secret which had been passed to her from her mother, on how to make the clothes tear a single seam out, so they could easily be repaired and didn't get stuck, if they shifted.

His outfit would become his most formal outfit. He planned on asking Susanne to make them some other formal wear, as the first jobs of her new shop. She was making some business stuff for the Alpha Con-

ference in under two weeks; he was much more nervous over the conference, than he was over the wedding!

He preferred close-fitting clothes which stretched nicely. She was
making some which looked really nice and flattered him but didn't
make a statement of how they moved. He had agreed to it when she
asked, even as she started on the Tuxedo, which was made somewhat
like it.

Several Alphas had inquired on who his tailor was, and smiled at the
complement, and advised it was a pack member. Many were interested
in seeing if they could arrange for some work. It sounded like Susanne
would be getting some orders, even before her shop was even opened! It
meant it was possibly the pack could have more money flowing in.

He promised he would let the pack member know to talk to them
during the conference.

*****

Brook chatted as the four females got ready in their dresses. Since it
was outdoors, they didn't have a train, as it would get caught on everything or get horribly dirty. It was a simple A-Line dress, in a traditional
white which went down to mid calf, keeping it clear of the ground.
What set it apart was the strips of embroidery on it. It was of many
wolves of all sizes, and of paw prints. They were in eggshell and ivory, so
they were visible, but kept with the white.

Susanne had smiled when she presented the finished dress and said
she had started the embroidery pieces long ago, and they were stitched
to the dress. She felt well rewarded for the many years of effort which
had gone into it by the thanks and feedback. She had confided to the
Alphas that for once she was quite happy to have a commission appreciated and felt the pack's leadership was worthy of their loyalty.

For once, Brook and the others had used a little bit of scent-free
makeup, but still not too much.

Amber, giggling in her new dress and having some light makeup on.
She had commented she had never had such a nice dress before. As with
all the dresses, it went down to mid-calf and matched the bridesmaids;

those dresses fitted each of them and were similar and had a little bit of embroidery, but not as much as Brook's did. Amber was passed the basket of native flowers, as she had been made the flower girl, which her mother was very honoured about. Initially, they hadn't planned on having one, since they didn't have any young she-pups they were close enough to involve, but after checking with Susanne to make sure she could get the dress ready, they had offered it to her and her mother.

She knew Jake had also been tasked with being the ring bearer, and him being responsible enough, both Adam and Brook had entrusted him with their rings. He had been very proud of being given the duty by his Alphas. A loop of white ribbon was tucked into a slit in the pillow, to hold the rings in place, but to also be easily undone when it was time. It was something Susan had provided as well.

Amber and Jake had come up earlier with Cody in a vehicle and had napped before everyone arrived, so they would not be tired when they had guests. To the wolves, the involvement of the two pups also said they were close to and under the protection of the Alphas.

There were more wolves hiding in the trees around the clearing, as they didn't want to overwhelm the humans with all the wolves who had come to watch and functioning as additional security for the event. Many could see well through the leaves, even if the humans wouldn't see them. They had already run off a grizzly which had been attracted to the food, without harming it, with the humans none the wiser. Some had even gone off farther and were on some lookouts farther away, not having wanted to be too close to the humans. The nearest wolf pack was their own, and they listened to Adam and Brook reasonably well, although they didn't mingle with the pack, other than the occasional howl or sharing a kill near their own territory.

The group of wolves who had brought instruments started up, including some who had bagpipes and were in traditional Scottish dress, giving the cue for everyone to stand. Adam looked up as Jake and Amber started down the isle. At that point, all the guests disappeared as he saw his mate in the most beautiful dress he had ever seen.

He had known they were in a traditional white but had not known any more. The bands of embroidery around it, had wolves seemingly dancing on it as she moved towards him. They seemed to frolic around his mate in celebration as she slowly came up to him. The neck was open enough to show off her mating mark, showing to the wolves she was mated, and not available. He lost all track of anything else till she was standing in front of him.

His wolf was forward and agreed she looked beautiful, if anyone looked closely, his eyes were showing flashes of his wolf. **Ours** he said, nearly drooling over the fact the most beautiful she-wolf was theirs and theirs alone. He couldn't suppress the possessive growl from coming out, but he was able to keep the volume down to one which the humans couldn't hear but saw many wolves smile as they heard it, understanding the meaning of it.

Thank you, Brook simply said, *You make it all worth all the work and bother.* She could see the comments he would say about beauty and love in his eyes and didn't even need the bonds to tell how deep his feelings went. She herself just wanted to take her handsome mate away and ravage him. This was for their parents, and for his human family. *You clean up well.* She teased.

Both mothers were crying as she came up the isle and holding onto each other, as *their babies* were married! Both knew they were now Alphas, and had been Mated for months, but this was a clear indication of their growing up.

Tara and Ryan were beside the mothers and were trying to ignore the sobbing mothers. Jake and Amber's parents, along with Cody and his parents were also in the front row. Behind them were his human family and the families of those who were in the wedding party. A few other humans were behind them, but not too many. He didn't know when they had been invited, but Officer Smith and three other Mounties were a splash of red, with their dress tunics on. From the rank insignia, a couple were fairly senior, and he thought it might have been his bosses who tagged along. There were a few other law enforcement people there as well, including a pair of Alberta provincial Conservation Officers. He almost expected to have some military show up too, but he didn't see any.

On the other side, were all the Alphas, with Alpha Maria, Longview's Alphas Grant and Louise, Forest's Edge Alpha Oscar and Luna Olwen, and Wildpaw's Alpha Richard and Luna Elizabeth, in the front row, as they were the ones who made it there. He knew there were some Alphas and Seconds in the second row, but he didn't know them personally, several were from east of the mountains and had packs in the foothills. Behind them, the Elders who had come from even more packs, and they filled several rows. Behind them on both sides were the rest of the packs who had come.

They ignored the grumbles of a few older humans about the dress not having a train, nor a vail, or about how they were too young—they both looked to be early twenties, even if they knew their true age—or the wind was too soft or too strong or about it being too hot or too cold. Others grumbled about how it wasn't in a church. Along with all the awe and comments about how good she looked by the wolves.

Standing up on the stage, a mere step above those gathered, they both barely heard the words being said, they were just so happy to be together. Both had agreed to not have it be religious, but have the ceremony be secular instead. The most they commented on was the spiritual connection or with nature.

Eventually they gave their "I do" and kissed to a thunderous applause. If any of the humans thought about the daytime howls from the trees, they didn't make a comment about it. Neither would remember anything of the formal ceremony, just the look of their mates, and how good they looked. Lucas had one of his pack videoing the ceremony as well, so they could look at it years later, if they wanted.

Stepping down, they smiled and did the pictures as they signed the marriage license to appease the human legal system which currently didn't recognise a mating bite. Next, they quickly took the pictures of the families and introduced Misty to their adoptive four and gave the details on the others they had part of the wedding party. Everyone had been warned she had not been told about being wolves, and they planned on keeping it that way. From the way she offended his wolf, likely wouldn't see her too often, nor was she likely to live for more than a decade more. His wolf was still miffed and shared the thought it couldn't happen soon enough, even if he wasn't going to attack the human elder, unless they attacked first.

Misty did turn to Brook, and congratulated them, having decided she didn't like the nearly seven months without any word on anything, and realising she did want to be involved at least a little.

Once the shots with her and the other human family members were done, Evan provided his arm for her as he led her off to her seat for the lunch, as those part of the wedding party stuck around a bit more.

They finished the shots with their human shapes and shared with the wolves and those who knew about them, that after the reception, they would slip out for a bit and get more pictures. Lucas was grinning nearly ear to ear, as he got to take the pictures. In preparation, he had taken a course and read lots up on how to take the wedding pictures. He knew he hadn't had to worry too much about them being upset if he missed specific shots but had asked for which ones they wanted to make sure they got and had everything documented.

Settling down for the lunch, Adam caught sight of the massive cake: it had two wolves standing instead of figures of the bride and groom, each in their colours, with them nuzzling the other's neck. Both snickered silently, and just smiled at those who complained about the breach of tradition it was.

On the tier below were icing of their four pups, and the other four who helped out in their wolf forms. Those eight were the closest to him, and it warmed his heart Lupita had known him enough to do it. He could see on the back, one of Charlie, who was rolling in some mud, which was a patch of chocolate icing, and there seemed to have been 'dug' a hole in the cake beside him. Below them on the side of the tiers and on the lowest tier, there were a multitude of wolf pawprints, to represent their pack. He didn't bother counting, but from the numbers, he expected it to be as many as they had of members.

There were other wolf shaped items around. Adam shook his head and wondered how many humans would think something was up about it. The few who asked, he just said both him and Brook loved wolves, and the parents had chosen it as the theme. When they saw their rings, and how they were paw prints themselves, just smiled and stopped asking questions. It wasn't like the theme was oppressive, nor was it done without taste. With it having been done out in nature, it actually fit, too.

*****

"Where are you going?" Asked Angie as Adam and Brook tried to slip away later the afternoon. "We have some stuff to do privately." Was the best he could say, "Then we are taking off for the week." They were not doing any sort of formal leaving in a vehicle... as it would just have been more of a pain.

They moved into the trees, the last to escape who needed to make it for the pictures. Angie tried to follow, but by the third row of bushes, they had lost her, and they suspected she had lost her way too.

Kuri? Could you head south into the woods and collect my nosy aunt, please? He asked, exasperated. *She tried to follow us to our wolf-photos, but she doesn't know what we are doing, and I don't want to have her know.*

Well, I guess I could... She said slowly to tease them, before pausing for a bit as they worked their way through the trees, mindful of their clothes, for once, *Found her.* Was the eventual reply, *I'll get her back to the others.* She replied, and both let out a sigh of relief.

Adam's mother, sister, Amber, and Karen were the only humans there. The rest were all werewolves. Most had already shifted to their wolves when they arrived for the second set of photos. The few left, had some more pictures with them in their 'good' clothes, before they used trees to hide behind, in respect for the three who were not used to a wolfpack, with Susanne there to take possession of the clothes to take back.

Lucas even had a few where they had Amber and Jake riding both Alphas, and several of both pups cuddled down with them, to everyone's amusement. Others were similar, where they had Mary and Tara with them, and with the other close relatives.

*****

Finally! Adam replied to his mate as they loped off into the evening. Others had taken their good clothes, and after cleaning, would have them put away. Once the pack house was done, they would have them up for display for a bit, so the pack could see them. They even considered having them up on display when Susanne's shop was started. Her shop was also going to be their front for selling the custom packs but would be displaying only the most basic ones. Adam was finished with being in photos for the next while. It was one reason he preferred doing scenic photos; he didn't annoy people with all the work to take photos.

Lucas knew he had the week to get the photos done and was going to get the best printed for them and would be waiting for them when they got back. He had done a selection of the best photos as a slide show during the lunch and the short dance after on a TV they had brought. The human photos along with the videos of the ceremony and the speeches were available openly for any to order. The Werewolves would get an email with the expanded selection, if they wanted. Lucas was happy he was going to get to make money doing this work, even if processing all the photos was going to be several days worth of work.

Adam and Brook had a few quiet spots in their territory they wanted to spend some time. They had arranged for some camping gear near one of the hot springs, for if the weather turned bad, along with some food so they wouldn't have to hunt it all, although the coolers were strung up between trees to keep them out of reach of any bears, if the wolf scent marks didn't keep them away. John and Bri had offered to keep an eye on their pack, so they had a week to themselves. After the week, they would have to start getting ready for the conference.

First thing they did, was have a nice long hot soak in the spring, and cuddle as the stars came out. They had helped keep the rabbit population under control on their run, which would keep them happy till later.

They were both nearly asleep when a cat's growl woke them from a doze. They growled back, with a sub vocal of being the alphas in their territory. The cat's growl stopped, and a single cougar stepped out of the bush.

Chapter 18 – Cat!

The cougar shifted and stood up, "Who are you?" She growled. "You're not of Shadowed River."

Adam and Brook stood hand in hand, as they growled back, "We are the Alphas of Wild Valley Pack, and you are in our territory. Who are *you*?" Adam growled, glaring at her, holding the excited feelings of finally meeting another kind of Were in check; he had to deal with the threat to his territory, and possibly his pack first.

The cat looked shocked and confused, "This is the edge of the territory claimed by Shadowed River Pack, although they never come here. What happened?"

They relaxed a bit as the cat, standing warily but also dropped the ready-to-fight tenseness, willing to discuss. "Almost six months ago, *that* pack attacked MacLaren Pack." Brook replied, knowing the cougars were mostly like their wild cousins, and were mostly loners. She probably didn't know. "Since it was unprovoked, and they used Wolfsbane, a council of packs decided to dissolve the pack under the Inter-Pack Treaty, which they had been a part of. MacLaren decided to take the territory for an offshoot pack." She worked to not say the pack's name.

"I never liked that Alpha, he never even bothered giving me his name, although he did permit me to pass through. I'm Serena." She replied, dismissing the old pack, losing most of her wariness, and smiling a little before starting and getting wary again, glancing off to the trees.

A patrol ran up growling, making her drop into a fighter's stance and growl back.

What are you doing here? Adam asked the patrol leader, stepping between the cat and the patrol, ignoring the fact he was naked and dripping water.

The sensors detected a disturbance, and we were to investigate it, Alpha. He called back as he cringed at the force behind the sending, *I had not been informed you were in the area.*

Well, you can go back to your patrol, and we can deal with the Werecat He said, making it an order. He didn't need the patrol here to deal with the single cat.

The patrol ducked their heads and scampered off.

Tell whoever is the dispatch to check with us before dispatching a patrol to where we are in the future. He called out after the retreating wolves.

Turning back to the cat, he could see she had slipped into the pool, and Brook was updating her on all the changes.

Serena shook her head, "That is too many changes in the last while. I am glad I'm not Pack." As she relaxed a little. She did like how the Alpha stood to protect her, a stranger, when some of his wolves misunderstood the scene. She greatly liked seeing the wolves running off with their tails tucked. Especially since she didn't have to fight. It would amuse her for a while.

Adam smiled, "It keeps our wolves on their toes."

Serena laughed, "That it would."

Looking between them, "Would you be willing to give me free passage?" She asked hesitantly, now knowing her permission had expired while she was elsewhere. They might want to deny it, from how she had immediately been ready to fight them.

I'm for it. Brook offered, *Cougars are Loners, and prefer to keep to themselves.*

Brook's comment meshed with what his wolf was telling him and Adam gave mental agreement of the approval to his mate.

"We can agree to permitting you passage rights, but I will request you check in with the nearest patrols entering and leaving. There is a network of sensors and cameras, which is why the patrol showed up. It will prevent misunderstandings." Brook told the cat.

Serena nodded, "I can agree to that." If they were going to be more vigilant over their territory, checking in was reasonable. She put the changes down to wolves being wolves.

Adam and Brook smiled, "Then it's settled. Were you just passing though? I'm Adam, and this is Brook." He realised he never actually gave their names.

Assured she would be able to continue on her way, she didn't stick around long after getting caught up with all the changes around and had decided to leave the area before the conference started, not being at all interested in being even nearby with the number of Alphas coming.

Adam and Brook napped and relaxed for a couple days, before Adam pulled out the paintball guns, a little bored, and with a gleam, "I wonder if the patrols are taking it easy or keeping up, knowing we are taking the week off."

Brook gave a feral grin as he tossed her the other one, "Sounds like fun! Our pack should know better than to let their guard down."

They quickly tidied their campsite, making sure everything was secure and the fire out, with the smelly stuff up a tall tree, out of the reach of anyone, and with Charlie slinking behind him, having learned how to travel as silently as any werewolf, they set out to track the patrols.

The first patrol they found smelled them before they got close and were waiting for them. The second had responded correctly when they fired their warning shot and were good. The third patrol was just coming off shift and was tired. They got the team with one shot before they were in hiding. They had got an alert out, which Martin acknowledged, but had caught sight of the prowling Alphas first, so he didn't pass it on to the others, as it wasn't needed to be.

Stepping out, "You four are out, but you did get an alert out, I would call it understandable for an end of shift. Make sure you start getting more sleep, as I would rather you respond a bit faster, and not get taken out." Adam told them.

I thought you were on holidays. The leader commented, surprised to see them, ears partly down in chagrin of being caught.

"We were bored and felt stalking patrols would be fun." Adam told them with a smile.

The wolves panted laughter, *I hope you have fun with another patrol then, we're done!*

Adam nodded, "Go then, and enjoy your leisure time." He watched the patrol pad off, heading in for a well-deserved meal and rest.

Adam yawned, as he wrapped an arm around his mate, "I feel like some company, want to join the pack for a meal then a run back to camp?"

Brook smiled, "That sounds like a plan!" This was the longest either had been away, since they got their pack, and were starting to miss it.

They shifted, and quickly caught up with the patrol. They gently bumped them, *Be glad we don't have the paintball guns out! We weren't even trying to be quiet, and you didn't notice us till we were among you!* Brook scolded, *You need to be aware all the time!*

Yes Alpha, Was the embarrassed reply from the leader; he never thought they would have the Alphas come after them right after doing one. It really showed they needed to keep watch as a real attack *could* have come after a mock one.

*****

They walked in at the end of their week, to check in with the Wild Valley, and flopped in their tent, for a night's snuggle. They would find out how much work had piled up in the morning.

The next morning, they found a pleasant surprise it wasn't as bad as they expected and over the next three days, had dealt with everything they needed to deal with. Much was reviewing the work done, but the work now to get ready for the conference was heating up. They would be heading down to MacLaren now they had finished up here with getting caught up. He was glad he had arranged for the US wolves to arrive a couple days before the start of the conference, so the pups could get settled before all the Alphas and those they brought with them arrived.

*****

The pack jewellery Zane's Uncle had got him was a heavy chain with the pack emblem on it as well as an earring. It was designed to remain in the ear even through changes. It had a wolf's head designed to look like Zane's wolf on it. To make it look even more like his wolf, there had been light enameling on it to give hints of the colour of his wolf, of his white fur and a single black ear. The others had similar jewellery though his was heavier and clearly more expensive, since he was the team leader and expected to become a senior wolf.

Since they were going to be up north for several weeks, they had a fair amount of luggage with them. Mike was driving one vehicle while Malcom was driving the other vehicle. It was going to be a long drive, but they all had things to keep occupied with. It also helped they stopped reasonably frequently to visit some of the sights. It wasn't till late in the day when they finally reached the Fossil Valley pack and pulled up to the gate.

Mike had the window down already, "Afternoon, Beta Mike from the Mac Tire' Dona pack. Here to see Beta Josh." He flashed his credentials for the wolf at the gate to see. Moments later the gate opened, and they were directed towards the pack house, as they were expected and Mike knew where to go, as it hadn't been the first time he had been there.

As they were pulling in, the kids were looking out the windows, "Man this place is flat. Where are all the trees and stuff?" Olivia asked since she hadn't realized parts of Oregon were fairly flat. She had expected more mountains and trees. To her, wolves seemed more at home in mountains and forests than anything else.

Mike laughed at Olivia's question, "Not all of Oregon is mountains. We even have a desert, believe it or not."

When they pulled up to the house everyone gave it a good look. From what they could tell this pack tended to have one or two main buildings they lived in. With their pack a fair number lived in the pack house but most of those were singles. Families tended to live in either an extended house or a normal house. With a shift in the wind Zane made a face, "Great, cows. If anyone even considers suggesting we help with them, they will regret it."

Rico and Melody both gagged thought since they had all been cycled through the animal pens last year. It had been nasty and horrible work. In some cases, it was considered a punishment detail dealing with them, "I will help you bite them." Melody muttered.

Mike laughed even as he climbed out and moved over to Josh. He gave him a good hug, "Good to see you and if you need some helpers in the cattle pens..." He winked before looking over his shoulder, "This is my niece and nephew as well as his team. Olivia is going to need to go in and relax. Her leg started bothering her not long ago." Since it was summer, she had shorts on, and the scars showed.

Molly had noticed a junior wolf helping the girl who clearly was injured out of the car and moved towards them, *I will take care of her and her protector.* She could see how the teen was almost hovering over her, "Afternoon and welcome to the Fossil Valley pack. I am Molly and a friend of Josh's. If you come with me, I can show you where you can relax."

Zane met the woman's eyes and mentally tested her dominance as he had been trained to. Based on what he was sensing she was reasonably dominant, "Thank you and while Uncle Mike and Beta Josh talk if you can show us to our rooms, we will drop our overnight bags in there." About then several teens their ages hurried out of the house. Instinctively he moved in front of Tessa, Oscar, and his sister.

"Josh, thanks for having some of your pack come and get what we need. If they can show Zane to the rooms, I'd appreciate it." Mike felt his reaction, *Relax Zane, they aren't a danger. This is a pack we have close ties with.* He knew telling Zane to trust them wouldn't help since he was still very protective of his sister. Mike knew Olivia thought Zane had backed off some, but he really hadn't. He had just become subtler about his over protectiveness. His fears were still there even if they were less obvious to her. Some of it, he had been accepting of Oscar's protection of her, while he hung back, or hid it in protecting Oscar instead of just her.

Zane met the other pup's eyes, and his wolf was pleased when they lowered their eyes. It was obvious they were lower in dominance than he was, "The small bags in the back of this SUV are the only ones we need. Mindy, would you show them please? This is my sister Olivia, and she is human. Be careful around her." He kept his voice reasonable as he was speaking.

Josh gave Mike a questioning look. When he did Mike mouthed back a 'later', "You ready to go tomorrow? I decided to bring this lot along to give my mate a break. They have been occupying our house for the last few weeks."

The junior wolves grabbed the bags and Molly waved for the others to follow, "I will let you know which lounge we end up in Josh." She led the troop inside, "Zane if you want, Jeffery will show part of your team to a lounge so Olivia can relax. Once you know where your rooms are I will show you to the lounge. Beta Mike explained Olivia still has problems with stairs, so I am going to show you an elevator she can use. You have rooms on the second floor of the guest wing."

Before Zane even had to say anything, Melody and Rico peeled off and walked with Oscar and Olivia. Tessa was next to him with his arm around her. She wasn't his mate, but he was making a point she wasn't to be messed with, "Thank you ma'am. That is greatly appreciated. Would it be possible to shake our fur out and even run nearby?"

"Call me Molly. I will have a few of the more dominant pups change and run with you. As far as how far you run, we do have many miles of property. It would take you a while to leave the property. They can show you as well." Once the bags were in the rooms she had to smile slightly since the girl with Zane had her bag put in his room. Zane had Oscar's bag put in the room for his sister as well.

Once they were done, she showed them to the lounge, "Alfonzo will be here soon, and he will take you for a run if you are ready. The other pups will remain here or with you, so you don't get lost in the house." Nobody would be hurt but it was a large house.

Zane gave her a grateful smile before settling down with Tessa. Just to make a point he gave her a good kiss, *Not going to have someone trying anything. I expect they are well trained, but you are my team member and my girlfriend.*

She leaned into the kiss and sighed in contentment. Tessa could tell he was still feeling stressed from the visit to his aunt. She had a feeling it wasn't just worry about the she-wolf but having those memories brought back. *Not worried Zane and love you.* She nuzzled his neck as they relaxed.

*****

Mike flopped down in Josh's office on a couch. "I take it you didn't read the report my pack sent out about Zane being turned?" He commented.

Josh shook his head, "I haven't had a chance. I did read the details on the Rogue but nothing beyond that."

Mike nodded, "To summarise, it the attack was about fourteen months ago. Zane was out running in the evening and going through the edge of a wooded area. Unknown to him, there was a Rogue on the prowl. It attacked him just as he hit a road and threw both of them in front of a car, which then hit them. Likely, it was what saved his life, as the rogue ran off. The hit from the car did cause him to get a concussion and was taken to the hospital." He sighed and looked at Josh.

Josh swallowed his growl and nodded for Mike to continue, as that was not even close to the amount of information in the report.

"Zane was put into an induced coma, so he could heal from the concussion and leg being run over." Mike said, before starting to have tears fall. "His family were coming to see him and were hit by another vehicle. My half-brother and his mate were killed, and Olivia was badly hurt."

Josh moved to hug the other Beta, not knowing what to say. Both knew he was just offering comfort, unlike humans who would interpret it in a sexual way, seeing two men hugging.

Mike took a big breath and let it out before continuing, "One thing not in the report, after they were moved to be near me, I was called away on a mission for the pack. It took several days before I could get back, and by then Zane was awake." Shaking his head, "After that, it was mostly Zane dealing with the total change to his life and learning his place in the pack, and about his wolf." Shaking his head, "The few issues stem from them being teens more than anything. I am not sure why we were asked by name to come."

Josh smiled, "Partly was from me. I had a captured rogue wolf who was acting more like a lone wolf which had been accidently captured; he was wary but respectful and answered the questions. Getting information from Canada, since they don't have councils meant contacting a random pack which we did have contact information for. Lucky for me, I had been routed to Alpha Adam and was able to rectify the issue. When a detail about a large amount of Wolfsbane came up, our council wanted better relationship, so when I heard of this, I asked to come, and seemed Zane's Rogue turn report had even made it up to them, and Adam asked questions about it, and when he found out I knew you, he especially wanted to meet him and his team, so I had a formal invite passed on.

Mike growled, "If something happens, I'm going to take it out of you!"

*****

The next morning everyone climbed into the SUV's again and a third was added to the convoy. What Zane found confusing was Josh was being called a Beta but so was Adam, even if he clearly submissive to Josh. Molly appeared to be in some relationship with Josh, but he wasn't sure what her dominance level was. He considered asking but decided not to. Instead, he pulled out the briefing papers Mike had made for him and his team. It listed the major players they were going to be seeing, *Remember to check the stuff Beta Mike gave us. Don't want us looking stupid for not knowing something.*

Some they had decent relations with, but others sounded... Well to be honest like they had a bad case of cranial anal impaction. The reason he was given the information was so he knew who it should be safe to be around and who might cause problems. They didn't have a great deal of information, but they had some. Based on the notes they were going to the MacLaren pack where the meeting was going to be held. There were several other packs nearby which were on good terms with that pack. They would be passing through one pack's territory to get to the MacLaren pack, but the major highway was considered neutral territory, and didn't need to check in, as long as they didn't leave it.

The trip had been arranged several months ago. Eventually he closed the binder and leaned back to think about what he had read again. By now he had most of it memorized, "Uncle Mike why are you bringing us with you? Shouldn't it just be you, Malcom and maybe Abby or Brandon?"

Mike was wondering how long it was going to take Zane to think of that question, "Because eventually you will be an enforcer. It might be in our pack or possibly even a different one. The more you know about the other packs both near and far the better you can do your job. It isn't the only reason, but it is a good one. Also, I want you and your team to meet and get to know the pups of the other packs. Figure out who they are, what they are like, and if they might be good contacts in the future. Consider this the next step in your training." He didn't bother saying anything about Alpha Adam wanting to meet him, and having the invite extended. Generally, when an Alpha asked for a meeting, unless there was a very good reason for it to be declined, it was accepted, even if the Alpha wasn't even in their area. That the council had also pushed for them to go annoyed Mike. It did mean the Alpha requesting generally did pay for the costs of the one they requested without any real issue as well, so this whole trip was going to be billed when they got back. For them, it also included almost a regular wage, not just the food/fuel for the travel.

Zane chewed on Mike's reply for a while before speaking again, "So… try and figure out who might have an impact on our pack and the others nearby? That and figure out those who might be of some benefit?" It was what it sounded like. All of his team had been well instructed on the rules the Canadian wolves had. They were similar to the ones in the states though there were differences.

"Pretty much. There are other reasons but that is for me to worry about Zane. Don't ask since I won't tell you." They were going to talk about possibly considering an exchange of pups for part of the year, as a suggestion from the Council. It would help strengthen pack bonds, but before it could happen, they needed to know the packs. The council was all for any links with the Canadian packs, as they refused for the most part to deal with the councils directly. The councils knew, but usually didn't acknowledge, it was because the Canadian packs refused to accept there was any higher position than an Alpha. The reasons why seemed to change alpha to alpha, but both sides knew the Canadians were willing to fight to maintain their independence, and many packs would join in to prevent the council from winning too, to the point it was a warry truce. Some packs refused to deal at all with the Councils, and only would deal with the other Alphas.

Zane sighed, "Great, at least I am not a cat, so my curiosity isn't going to drive me nuts wondering." It was a lie, and everyone knew it. Zane was being taught to start questioning everything. If something didn't feel right, pay attention and see what was off.

Crossing the border wasn't bad though it was a pain since it took time, even with them having left their guns at home. Thankfully, they weren't selected for an 'enhanced security check'. Once they were through customs, Zane relaxed back in his seat and hoped they would be somewhere soon. The scenery was nice, and they had things to do but being confined in a vehicle was annoying. Even his wolf was starting to get grumpy with the lack of movement.

*****

Eventually they reached the warehouse in town they had been instructed to head to. Once there, a wolf was waiting to show them to the MacLaren property, and they had the security card. The drive to the garages was interesting since it was on what Mike would call an unimproved road, it being just a single vehicle wide gravel track into the forest. Once they arrived and climbed out, he stretched before looking around slightly confused, "Where is the pack house?"

"The pack house is about two kilometres from here," Alpha Adam said, stepping out of the shadows, "When it was built, horse-drawn carts were all there was for vehicles. The way at times is too slippery for using vehicles, and there are several rockslide and avalanche areas the road passes through, so we park them down here, and walk in. There is a secured tunnel for bad weather but thought you might enjoy seeing the pack house from the outside first, along with a chance to shake out your fur."

When a wolf stepped out of the shadows Zane immediately stepped forward. It placed him in front of his team and especially his sister and junior wolves. He met the wolf's eyes and instantly knew he was an Alpha based on his dominance. After a moment he lowered his to show he wasn't a challenge. As he had been trained, he rested his vision on the man's chin.

Even as he did so, Josh stepped forward and met Adam's eyes. Even though he was working as a Beta for his father, he was an Alpha, so he didn't bother submitting, instead met him as an equal. He might not have a pack as of yet, but he was an Alpha. He did break eye contact first, as was expected of visiting Alphas. Eventually they would split the pack, or his parents would retire and he would take over, "Greetings Alpha Adam. It is nice to actually meet you face to face. This is my Beta Adam," A slight grin crossed his face, "And team member Molly. Thanks for the invite."

Alpha Adam grinned and gave Josh a good hug and sniff, "Greetings, I am glad to finally meet face to face. It's not the first time I have had the same name as others." For several years growing up, he had another Adam in class... one who didn't bother putting his last initial, so constantly was getting his stuff too. He controlled his wolf at the failure to submit, reminding him they were equal, as they could feel the Alpha inside Josh. He greeted the ones introduce with a hug and sniff, before turning back to Josh, "I could show you part of the network, but some we would have to run as wolves, and another is up in the cliff behind the pack house. We will also have to track down Ethan, so you can see how he's settling in."

"Thank you, Adam, I would like to at least check on him. He was shaping up to be a decent wolf while he was at our pack. Don't make a big deal about it since he doesn't need an alpha making a big deal of it." Josh was hoping the man was settling in well.

Mike moved forward and after meeting Adam's eyes he lowers them slightly, "My pack also thanks you for the invitation. I am the Beta Enforcer Mike Duncan, and this is my assistant Malcom. This is my nephew, Zane. I will let him introduce his team to you."

Alpha Adam nodded, "Welcome." He again did his usual greeting; his wolf memorizing the scents.

Zane moved forward a bit more before briefly meeting the Alpha's eyes, "Afternoon Alpha, I am Zane and the team leader. This is my assistant Melody, team members Simone, Rico, and Mindy. My junior wolves are Tessa and Oscar. Olivia is my sister and Tessa is my girlfriend."

Adam gave each of the pups his usual greeting, so he could know the scents. He knew what he called Thetas, were called Juniors in their part of the US.

Zane glanced around, "How far is the pack house sir? My sister has a problem with her leg and can't walk long distances." Even if she hadn't had a problem there wasn't any way she could keep up with wolves at full run.

Adam looked concerned, then at Mike who looked down. "I had assumed you were all wolves when Mike passed the details for the IDs I have up at the pack house for you, as nobody had told me otherwise. I have an Argo which I was going to haul your luggage on, but I will be right back and get its trailer so it can haul your sister, and anyone who wants to ride there. I had placed your team in one of the guest rooms, with several cots, and the adults in another beside you, as we will be nearly popping out the windows with all the packs which will be coming. The rooms are on the first floor, but I will have Olivia registered for use with the elevator, if she needs it."

Zane nodded as well, "Thank you Alpha, a single room for my team and sister will be fine and if needed Olivia and Oscar can use the bed. As a wolf, the floor will be fine for me and the rest of the team." Being a wolf had some uses though he had gotten used to sleeping with Tessa in his arms. They were growing closer and eventually they would become seriously involved.

Mike had figured they were going to be strained for room, so it wasn't a problem, "I thought it had been mentioned Alpha, sorry if it didn't come through. As long as Oscar and Olivia have a bed, they can use, it is fine. First floor is fine and thank you for the offer of a ride for my niece." He watched him vanish even as he smiled slightly at the pups' reaction.

Adam used the stealth training he had been working on since qualifying to slip back into the forest and quickly attached the trailer to the Argo before bringing it out and stopping before the visiting wolves. Hopping out, "Gear in the trailer, and who is wanting a ride?" He didn't move to help Olivia, knowing she wouldn't want to show her disadvantage.

Zane moved forward and before he realized it, he gave the Alpha a light hug, "Thank you sir. Olivia and Uncle Mike are the last of my blood family, other than my aunt. My team is family but thanks." He moved back and looked down since he hadn't been expecting his wolf to react affectionately to a stranger, but for some reason felt right. He turned to his team, "Get the bags and load them up. Oscar, help Liv into the thingy and remain with her." He went to get the luggage as well.

Adam sniffed out of habit when Zane gave him a hug, hugging him back. He could smell a trace of a rogue on him which he didn't get the first time, **Only an Alpha would smell it; he was force-turned by a rogue, and the rogue still lives. The rogue might try to come after him.** His wolf told him, and he gave an internal growl. *Let it try; we already have six Alphas here, and more coming to keep the pup safe!* The human side told his wolf silently.

Beta Mike, Zane was turned in central US, correct? Adam asked, and at the affirmation didn't need to know more to tell the sadness and hurt in his scent was from losing both his parents, while he had asked, it had included 'Or a representative who knew the details' so wasn't sure if they would permit him to travel. *I will need to speak to him and introduce him to a couple of the pups I have adopted. They too had suddenly lost their parents, one lost both, and the other lost only one.* Toby and Robin would understand somewhat where Zane was coming from. *I was turned by my mate, so would know what it feels like to be a wolf now is warring with a human upbringing and had lost a parent when I was a pup. I had seen the report months ago but forgot or I'd have had them here to greet him.*

Mike gave Adam a slow nod, *He was, and his parents were killed in a vehicle accident. It was the same one which almost killed his sister. We were able to have a Lycan surgeon look at her and repair most of the damage. They lost their parents, and I lost my brother and sister-in-law.* He slowly inhaled at the momentary resurgence of the loss, *That might help, thank you, though I will warn you he is still holding people at an arms distance. His team and our family are one thing but others? He is very prickly and distant even now. He is a good kid and has stepped forward even when he was trying to push people away. It is how he ended up with his team. If you have questions, later we can talk.* Even he had been surprised with the hug in thanks.

Adam helped balance the load, so it wouldn't shift while on the trail as they talked. He sent a mental hug to Mike and agreement to talk later; he could offer to help Zane, but even if he wasn't ready, he would have the contact to do it later. Once they were done, he secured the webbing over all the bags. He hopped in and started it up.

Zane didn't know what was being said and glanced at his team, "Shift and we are going to run with..." He didn't know what to call the thing Olivia and Oscar were in. It had lots of wheels and looked like it might even be able to go over water. After stripping and changing Mike took a moment to hand their clothing to the two pups in the Argo. Once they were ready, he and the others changed and set out with it. The run more of a jog for him and it felt good to stretch their legs.

Adam kept it at a reasonable speed all the way up to the trail, slowing down then stopping just inside the trees from the pack house. "The pack house is just past the trees, but I have to go around back to get in. My mate, Brook, is waiting at the door for you, with the IDs, and I'll have your bags taken to your rooms."

Mike shifted back, "Zane's team can take care of the luggage. If you just have someone show them to the rooms and then to a lounge or even show them around." It was later in the day but there were a number of hours left before the sun would be near down.

Adam nodded, and heading around to the back entrance, moving slow now, due to the number of people around. As Zane and his team grabbed the bags, Adam led them into the pack house, and into the large central hall. As Brook walked up, he smiled and introduced her, "This is Brook, my mate, and Co-alpha of Wild Valley Pack." Pulling on his wolf's memory, he introduced everyone by name and rank.

Brook gave each a hug and gave them their ID. When she got to Olivia, she quietly added, "Yours has access to the elevator, if you need it. I'll show it to you later."

Olivia leaned into the hug from Brook and smiled at her, "Thanks, I am sure my brother heard, but I will assume he won't say anything. I can walk but it can start aching after a while." She had most of the movement back from her damaged leg. There were times it bothered her but normally it was only after a long day.

Leading them into the guest rooms, "I have the pups in the first one, and the adults in the second. There are already additional mattresses placed for all of you." Seeing they had pared off a little when they had arrived, he had two of the smaller mattresses swapped with one larger one, and the bed was still the king which was normally in the room. "The guest IDs will open the wing, and your rooms. They also have access to the common areas, like the gym downstairs and the greenhouse, which has a hot pool." Looking at Mike, Adam added, "I added you to the pup's room, as you are their guardian."

Mike glanced in the room and nodded, "Works for me and will keep them out of trouble. As far as us adults, not an issue. My mate is at home with our pup, so I won't be getting involved with anyone." He wasn't sure if they knew he had a mate or not but wanted it known.

Josh grinned, "Molly is working on..." He had to grunt when she punched him in the side, "She is working on trying to tie me down. I am holding out, but my wolf is being a pain. He likes her and her wolf. I want a really good dowry from her, but they aren't playing fair." His face was neutral as he was speaking.

Beta Adam blatantly laughed at him, "Accept the fact you are going to mate and deal with it. I, however, am free to play the field. Well, me and Malcom as well though he is trying to seduce the Nova he is currently working on..." The car Ash had arrived in was being a pain in the ass even as Malcom was working on it. He kept finding repairs which weren't very good. One had even been duct tape, another baling wire.

Once they had placed their bags, Adam offered, "You must be starving after the long drive. Come, I'll show you the dining hall. We dine together for meals, as it helps keep the pack tight knit." He went on to tell them about their normal three meals, and the buffet which was kept between meals.

At the mention of food Zane's mouth started watering. He was starving and he figured the rest of his team was as well, "Food sounds good sir. If you show us where it is, we will try to keep from a search and eat mission." It was silly but as they were walking in the food had smelled good.

Mike looked at Zane, "Remember flowers are not wolf food. If you see any leave them alone…" The damn joke had entered the lexicon of the entire pack. He knew Zane even now was tempted to go and tear the flower bed up.

Letting them fill their plates, Adam directed to the tables he had reserved for them. He sat with them to keep the curious pack away till after they had their fill.

Adam smiled as the wolves went back for seconds and finished it before sitting back to relax. Sending a mental link to Jess first, he introduced her to the visiting wolves. "She will be able to find me if she can't get it herself, for anything you need."

For the pups, he introduced them to his four, Toby, Robin, Sam, and Lea, whom he had made sure would be down for the conference. Adam wanted to make sure they would be here to help the pups have a good time. Just from the way the two pairs acted, it showed the others they were hands off for anything but friendship.

Zane quickly introduced his team and sister. He figured it would be obvious who were together, so he didn't think to mention it. His pack knew so it never occurred to him if part of the pack hadn't seen them, they might try and say hello. Part of the issue was the food was killing him and his wolf. It was obvious he was distracted by the food placed out.

Olivia grinned since the other wolves were looking much the same, "Thanks for the intro and ignore my brother. Food is his second love. He hates cows unless they are just off the hoof and mooing." She made a face when he grouched at her.

Adam laughed, "My sister is the same as you. If you like the beef, wait for the first night of the conference. It is planned to have some elk steaks and elk burgers out then. There will be some bison at some of the meals too. Bison are leaner, and there was more of it on a single animal. They also reproduced as fast as regular cattle, but needed less resources, and aren't as hard on the environment. In winter, they know how to take care of themselves, where the cattle lacked the brains to paw through the snow to the grass."

Zane still had to make a face, "It isn't the meat... It is the taking care of it. We, the pack, own a ranch. Last year my team and I had the fun of being dragged through the muck and mud of learning about it. Taking care of the rabbits, goats, cows, and other animals. My wolf was horribly offended by the stink."

Adam smiled, "If you want, I could take you to a feedlot the humans use. Here, mostly we do free-range." He was having fun teasing Zane, as he saw much of himself in the pup. He hadn't been near a feedlot as a wolf, but as a human, it reeked even a mile or two away; he'd probably need nose-plugs to protect his sense of smell. Especially on "cleaning day" where they tilled over a lot after the cattle had been moved out; it was a good dieting tool, even as a human. "We keep about a dozen free-range on the territory here, before we kill them for the meat. There is more Bison here, as they are native to this region, and we take one or two down a month. Living, they have a much sweeter smell than cattle."

Zane closed his eyes and held a hand up as his fingers started flicking. He was frowning before he started speaking, "We have a large herd of free-range cows but there are a number of large barns with an open side for the winter months. We also have a barn for cows who are going to deliver as well as for dairy. The occupied barns have constant maintenance. Driving a skid loader to scrape stuff off the floor stinks. Even my junior wolves wouldn't come near me until I was sanitized. Now if you don't mind Alpha, I would prefer not to think about it and focus on the food." He opened his eyes once he was done speaking.

Adam smiled and nodded, enjoying the relaxation after eating a good meal. Looking at Toby and Robin, "Why don't you take Zane and the other pups to the room and introduce him to some of the other older pups there."

The pups took Zane and his team, along with Olivia to the living room the pups tended to hang out in, as it had the gaming systems hooked up to one large TV, leaving the adults to talk.

Zane had to admit the food was damn good and he had probably eaten more than he should. He just sat back and watched the movie on the TV. Even his wolf was sated from all the food. Before he realized it, Olivia was quietly snoring on Oscar's shoulder, "Time for bed, I think. Thanks for showing us the lounge." He nodded at the four teens who had ate with them. He helped Oscar stand before letting him carry Olivia to bed. She had to take one of her pain pills after the long drive. When they didn't do anything but give her slightly concerned look, he gave them a thankful nod. He followed the rest of his team towards the guest section.

Chapter 19 - Preparing

Adam smiled as he headed to their room. They had the space, so several wolves had moved in, to give them the space to fit the visiting wolves. He sighed at the lack of privacy but knew it would be only for a week or so.

Luckily, it was wolves from Wild Valley. The Elders had moved in to double up with MacLaren Elders. Toby, Robin, Sam, and Lea were sharing the one room, with Sam and Lea's parents sharing the other. Jess, and about half of the pups were staying in their room, with the other half and their parents in the vacant suite beside them.

The others of Wild Valley who were down at MacLaren for the Conference were bunking with friends, which freed up the entire loft to put the guards and others the Alphas brought. The Alphas themselves were going to be in the Guest rooms, with others attending in Beta rooms on the second floor. Maria said there were a few independent organizations, like the training program John and Bri had just finished, which had representatives who were coming, mostly as observers. In addition to the two American packs, there was an American council representative as well, but only as an observer, since none of the Canadian Packs enjoyed dealing with them. Often the council members tried to dictate the terms to the Alphas, and while the American Alphas had to listen, in the past it had cause issues, as the Canadian ones didn't acknowledge their authority and felt it was a challenge to their autonomy. It was part of the reason the US councils didn't have contacts with the Canadian packs. Those packs which had contacts south of the border often dealt with at the Alpha or lower levels and ignored the councils as much as they could, and if an agreement required their approval, it would be left to the US pack to contact them.

Many other wolves volunteered their rooms and were doubled up with friends. Most of the single wolves were hoping to find their mates, as this was one way to meet wolves they otherwise would never get a chance to. Brook had commented to Adam, when the two were different packs, usually the male moved to the female's pack, but often it was decided between them and the Alphas of the two packs which way they go. Sometimes, the one losing the member received another wolf or two who was wanting a change in exchange. They would not stand in the way of wolves leaving, except in very few cases for key positions, they would have to wait for a replacement to be ready.

One of the outbuildings had been hastily turned into a conference centre, with several boardrooms in addition to the main conference room, and some small rooms which fit maybe four people, and a gathering lounge area, which had food brought over from the pack house for the lunch break. Several packs and organizations were using this conference as an opportunity to have discussions outside of the main agenda, as it was a secure but neutral location, where neither had an advantage. Adam was glad he wasn't involved with it. He and/or Brook had several one-on-ones with some Alphas, but most were only a short fifteen or thirty minutes.

He smiled at Willow, who was in charge of the pups. Between her, Karen, and Jess, they had the pups taken care of. Many had shifted and had curled up in balls of puppy fur. Mixed in was the few others who hadn't shifted. She nodded and closed her eyes, curled protectively around the pups as a wolf. It was a great honour to be in charge of the pups, and protect them, even if it was just as they slept in the Alpha's room. She could rest easy, knowing the Alphas were in the room too, and would definitely give their lives to protect any pup around them.

Sharing a fond look at Brook, they quickly got ready for bed. *Tomorrow, we have to make sure everything is ready. Some of the Alphas are going to be arriving early.* He replied silently, as to not disturb the fur pile, as he snuggled, with Brook's head under his chin.

Yes; we will be thrown to the wolves! She said amused at the human saying.

I was, and I'm now leading many of them! Adam replied, laughing in their minds, remembering a quote he had come across. *We'll be fine. I know we have MacLaren, Longview, and Arctic Shadow's full support. Between the four packs, it is a force others would have trouble standing against.*

*****

They spent the next morning shuttling their vehicles out to a field they owned, to allow for the use of the main parkade for the visiting VIWs – Very Important Wolves – as nobody had time to do it yet. Before he went for lunch, Adam felt he reeked of exhaust fumes, and Brook agreed. They had just finished getting them moved and enjoyed a cold soak in a brisk stream on their way back. The deeper spot had been dug and lined with sand, for the pack to use. Helpfully, there was even some biodegradable soap there too, to scrub the oily, burnt stench off their skin and out of their hair.

They were all driving in, and various Deltas had been tasked with meeting them at the warehouse, to lead them to the hidden entry to the parking, and to swipe them in. An extra early breakfast had been organised for them, so the first ones could be ready.

They had decided they were not going to be telling the other packs about the tunnel, and have them taken either walking, running as wolves, or in the Argos. An additional blast door, which was designed to blend into the walls around it with the edges matching into expansion joints, had been closed, so with the cover over the controls looking like a service panel cover as well, unless someone knew it was there, it was unlikely to notice it.

Robin and the other three were tasked with showing around the visiting pups. The four of them looked to be about the same eventual seniority as Zane would have, so they treated him as equal, and the other pups well, knowing they were Zane's team, and protected them from the few pups who hadn't been schooled by Adam's zero-tolerance of bullies.

The bullies didn't want to mess with those four after the demonstrations of their skills which had surprised the adults and even the elders. With passing the Trials, the four had the rank to give any pup punishment duties, the few who looked to start trouble usually stayed away from them, when looking for mischief generally, but knowing they had many senior wolves as guests, and their actions would be punished even more severely, they mostly were trying to stay out of the way.

*****

Flopping down for lunch, Adam and Brook smiled at the fact there were other pups who were chatting with those from the US. If they could get more cross-border communications, it would make for more flow of ideas.

"I'm already wanting this conference over, and it hasn't even started," Adam complained to those at the table.

"Could be worse," Martin said, looking tired, "Could be having to deal with all the security! Even with having Chris, Sam, and Toby helping out managing it a bit, it's a lot to organise."

Adam nodded, "Feel free to pull from my pack as needed."

Martin looked sly, "Already have pulled all I can, without impacting security of your pack, and all the wolves need a bed here, and I have already maxed it out, with doubling and even hot bunking with two and even three shifts!" He shook his head, "That just made more work to do! And now Toby and Sam are helping out with the pups, so are unavailable." Some had even offered to bunk down with others, or as wolves.

Adam nodded, "I thought it best. It gives the four some pups from another pack to get to know and gives the visiting some security assigned to them."

Martin smiled, along with several others listening in, "I agree, and would have been where I put them too. It'll keep them out of trouble and provide a bit of downtime they deserve and saves me from having to assign guards to keep an eye on them. What are you up to this afternoon?" Unofficially, he had asked the four to be their guards too.

Adam sighed, "I have to test all the computer gear for the conferences, to make sure all is working as expected. I want to show it off to the wolves, since some are still used to flipcharts at most! I have two sets of replacements for everything." He had found the items he didn't have spare of were often the ones which went down, if it wasn't just the one running the presentation not knowing how to do it.

To pre-empt the issues, all the tech in the room had spares in a nearby storage room, as they were either for another room, or would be used in the new pack house once it was done. He had decided they were not taking any chances of anything failing without multiple spares nearby. He knew each of the rooms had an assigned tech-pup who was trained to help, and at the beginning of the event would be there to make sure there was no issues. Once the sessions started, there were two who would stick around, and Erin was scheduling the rotation of them. One small boardroom had been put aside for them, for them to hang out, so to deal with walk-ups. If not needed, they were allowed to play on a computer, read, game, or just chat together, but needed to stay in the conference centre. A couple of comfortable recliners had been brought in for them to relax in too.

Two Thetas had also been assigned to float around, and to refill the carafes of hot water and coffee in the boardrooms, make sure the small buffet in the central area never ran out, and would check on them for anything they needed.

"Gareth and Maria are thinking we may just leave the building as a conference centre, which could give a neutral meeting place for other packs to come to in the future, although they might turn one or two of the rooms into dorms, for if they need to be isolated from everyone." Adam replied to Martin's horror.

"They wouldn't!" Martin exclaimed. It would make an ongoing headache for him to deal with at times.

Adam gave him a sad smile, "Won't be decided till after the conference, and not without discussing it with you."

Martin looked relieved, "OK, I have a chance to talk him out of it!" He would make suggestion they have it at Wild Valley instead, make it Adam's problem instead of his.

Adam grinned and turned the discussion to what others were doing. Many were picking up extra shifts with helping the Theta with laundry or cleaning, as with the visiting Alphas, they wanted the pack to look good. Even the tops of pillars and ceiling fans were dusted in preparation.

*****

"Welcome!" Adam said with a smile, as he greeted the first arrivals the next morning. They had a board with IDs grouped by Packs just inside the front door. He was the greeter for the arriving packs. They had extra spare badges for if they needed them and would be used until they could get one made.

"Rufus of Arctic Shadow. You must be Adam." He said in his voice which sounded like a growl, even when talking nice.

Adam nodded, and they shared a hug and a sniff, getting each other's personal scents.

"This is..." Rufus went on to introduce the three other wolves in his group. One she-wolf was a personal assistant, and the other two had been for security and to drive. When he said they were coming, he had offered to have them in one room, and with bringing such a small group, they easily fit in one of the guest suites. He gave each the specific IDs as they were introduced.

One guard growled, "Why is such a pup greeting us, not an Alpha." As Adam went to greet him.

Adam glanced at Rufus, who nodded permission, he could school the wolf. Rufus had chatted a bit over the phone and got to know the youngest Alphas in living memory. They knew they were young, and while they did have good ideas, they were willing to listen to others, and to find out the *why* behind traditions before doing away with them. They also didn't have any issues with showing respect to those who had been in roles for decades if not centuries, unlike many youngsters who had an overinflated sense of importance and skill from getting a senior role young.

"Because that 'pup' is one of the Alphas of the pack south of you." Adam growled back, letting his Alpha influence come out a little, and wash over the large man, as he stared him down. "If you wish, we could step around back and have a bout and show you why." He had learned how to supress the influence, as he really didn't need to use it to keep his pack in line, for the most part.

The guard looked a little pale as he could feel the power and looked at his Alpha. Rufus was standing with his arms crossed, looking amused. "Feel free to provide some entertainment, if you wish. You will still need to work with the injuries he inflicts." He replied to the look, not worried about the guard hurting Adam. If he could take down Alpha Night, the guard would be just a warmup, "You just insulted the one who is the mind behind the well laid out pack compound we visited on the way down." Rufus had got permission to take a quick look at the Wild Valley pack compound on the drive down but was hoping for a much more detailed and extensive tour during the conference and was thinking he would need to visit in a couple years, once everything was settled and they had the bugs worked out.

The guard shook his head and tilted his head back, baring his throat in submission. "I am sorry for the offence, Alpha Adam." He replied, knowing the Alpha could kill him for the offence, since his own Alpha wasn't willing to stand in the way of his disrespectful comment. "I just have been taught Alphas had to be a century old."

Adam had an amused look to his face, "Well, we did plan on following that *custom*," He replied, emphasizing the last word. He had looked it up, and talked with the elders, and there was no law anywhere which said an Alpha had to be a century, it just was the custom, and the belief the Alpha needed experience before taking the power. He shrugged, "But Alpha Night decided he didn't want to live after I defeated him, and what had been his pack declared me theirs."

The guard gulped and turned white, looking like he might want to run, as the reek of fear came off him, not at all wanting to face the one who had taken out the Alpha who had killed several Alphas and many more lesser wolves.

Adam smiled and nodded, letting the issue drop and be mostly forgotten. Leading them to the room and explaining how the cards worked. He let them get settled in, much to the relief of the guard, he got off with just a scare as a warning. But as he calmed down, he started thinking about what he had been taught and how much was custom and how much was the actual laws. He had seen the innovations at the pack house and though maybe they did need a younger wolf in charge to bring much needed changes. As they relaxed, he ended up discussing it with his Alpha, who clearly respected the younger Alpha as a peer, even if they were inexperienced.

It was a busy day as Adam greeted several others arriving. Fabian, the head of the training program, was put in the hands of their former pupils, John and Bri, who were honoured and delighted to give him a tour of their home, even as they did the work as the Alphas for the pack during the conference.

Forest Edge and Longview delegations showed up together with another pack, Wildpaw which was south of Longview, as Forest Edge and Longview had stayed for the night at Wildpaw, as like Mac Tire' Dona, was outside of a good driving range for a day.

"I am glad to meet you," Oscar said as he greeted Adam, "It is good to have some young blood to stir up new ideas! I would like a tour of your new pack compound, when it's finished. I'm curious as to how you make it."

Adam smiled at the greeting, not having known how that Alpha would be, "I would love to. It is likely be next spring at the earliest before it is finished, but I am planning on a daytrip up to show what we have completed so far during the conference."

Oscar nodded, and pulled a she-wolf forward, "This is my mate and pack Luna, Olwen."

"Luna Olwen," he greeted, giving her a good hug and sniff.

Packs will have an Alpha who is the leader and protector of the pack Brook had told him, when he first heard the term *Luna* instead of *Alpha* for the female leader. *In some packs, the male is more of the leader, and the female does the soft skills, and caring for the pack. For us, we do both and do it together. So, for us both,* Alpha *is the title. It's also I prefer the strong title, rather the softer title.* She had added. *But don't get any Luna or female Alpha riled up about pups; you'd rather tangle with a mama bear!* This Luna felt like she gave as much as any Alpha, making him think it was mostly just a personal preference as to the title one claimed.

They had four guards and an assistant. He passed each their guest ID and introduced them to Brook when she came forward.

Adam smiled at Grant and Louise, "It's been a while." He said, as they hugged in greeting.

"Yes, and your sister is a bit put out you haven't come to see her." Louise replied, with a grin, "I did tell her how much work you two are putting in, and have her follow me for a day, so she could see how much work we put in on an *established* pack, let alone what you are doing! All with setting up a brand-new pack, the construction of a new pack house, *and* having the pack split at two sites, several hours run away."

"How'd she do?" Adam asked, almost wished he could bring his sister into his pack but thought it almost better she is in a separate pack. If Tara asked, he would grant it for her and her mate instantly, but it would be wholly her decision. He had dropped hints of it to her and would leave it for a few decades. Likely would say something after she was Turned, and their mother had passed.

Louise grinned, "Fell asleep before dinner, and it was with a nap at lunch!"

Everyone laughed, "Tell her when you get back, I'll call her as soon as I have some time."

Louise nodded. "With us is..." And she introduced their two drivers and assistant.

Adam treated them to a hug and sniff, just like the Alphas. He guided the Alphas with their assistants and guards to the guest wing, then the guards and assistants to their rooms up on the second floor.

Several packs, like Forest Glen, which was north of Forest's Edge, had sent their Next Alpha to the conference, which some might think was a slight, but both Adam and Brook had felt it was respectful enough, as it was more likely the Next Alpha would be more of their peer, and at an event like this, would be authorized to fully represent the pack and for anything they didn't already have the leader's wishes, most would have the authority to make the decisions.

By supper at the end of the next day, everyone who was expected was there. Adam was glad he didn't have to greet Sentinel Star or Feral Star, as it seemed Maria had herself scheduled for when they arrived. He did hear they took it as an insult that a *male* didn't greet them. If he could avoid interacting with them one-on-one, he would be happy. He was glad they weren't aware he was a changed-wolf, and at this point, there was no scent to show he had ever been human. With both MacLaren and Wild Valley, it wasn't a secret; it just wasn't spoken about, as all decided it didn't matter at all. Even the Elders had decided it was the best to keep it as quiet as possible, at least until the session about being turned came up.

Sentinel Star had sent six guards, four drivers, and two assistants with their Alpha, in two vehicles. Feral Star, when Adam heard, he had to shake his head, as they had sent eight guards, six drivers, a valet, two assistants, and had brought three vehicles. Tyler didn't have a mate, as far as anyone knew, and Tom never brought his when he travelled. He almost thought they didn't trust the sanctity of the gathering would be respected, or the hosts would not be able to provide security. Maria had confided to Adam and Brook when he commented on it, in both packs, they expected the females to stay at home, and rumour was Tom's mate rarely had anything to do with her mate, and even refused to mate in her Heats, after she gave him two pups. Either way, they had decided to not acknowledge the insult sending so many could be taken as, since they didn't want to have a major confrontation over something which was minor, with everything else which was happening, and didn't want to have it derail the entire conference, which it could do.

All the other Alphas who he personally didn't know were at most bringing a couple guards who doubled as drivers, and some had a single assistant, often a younger wolf who knew computers and had brought a laptop.

Martin had the guards helping with security around the conference centre on rotation and sharing training tips in a clear area near it – well other than the two "star" packs, who refused to share their training with other packs and refused to do anything but guard the rooms assigned to their pack or follow the Alphas as bodyguards, and often stood against the wall behind their Alphas.

*****

Walking into the first conference room, the first morning of the official conference, with Brook by his side, Adam exchanged greetings with those there, taking their seats near the head of the table. Tom and Tyler were shooting them glares, several had curious looks, and the rest had friendly looks, knowing they couldn't force an Alpha from a pack.

Adam very much liked the suit-like clothes Susanne had made for him. They were not stifling and moved with him nicely, as they had been made with some stretch in them. Susanne had made matching outfits for Brook, and since they were basically the same size, and knowing how they preferred to share clothes, had told them they had been made so they would fit both of them. She even grinned as she had offered up along with the pants, long skirts which matched, and went to about mid calf, and short ones which was a bit above the knee. She had teased him, "There's several of each, so you can decide who's wearing the pants and who the skirt."

He had considered them, as they were much lighter than the pants, but had decided he needed to give a good face to the other Alphas, many of whom were 'old fashioned'. He was representing the pack, and they didn't want to have issues with the others. Maybe in a few decades they would not have an issue.

He greeted Zane, who was sitting at the back, with several other pups, including his own, as observers. Unless they were directly asked, they would be not involved. John and Bri were also there, as time and their duties permitted.

Gareth and Maria walked in, and to the head of the table. As the host Alphas, they were the ones running the main meetings. "This meeting was called for the fact we have a new pack, and they are wanting to sign onto the Inter-Pack Treaty. Other items were added to the agenda you have before you." He also put it up on the screen behind him. Lea had spent a day teaching him how to work the tech, so he didn't need help, and would make him look all that much more the host and up to date.

Gareth gave them some time to review it, "Is there any other last-minute items which need to be added at this point?"

Nobody brought anything up.

"If any do come up during the conference, let me know, and we will try to add them in." He said before starting, "Ok, first item, is the joining of the Inter-Pack Treaty by Wild Valley Pack." Gareth stated. "Are there any concerns?"

"I have a major one." Tom said, standing up, "Neither of them are old enough to be Alpha, thus cannot sign." He pointed at Adam and Brook.

"I second it." Tyler replied.

Zane sent a silent inquiry to his uncle, not sure why they were so upset about his age. They seemed old enough. *They looked to be about twenty*, he thought, forgetting how werewolves aged much slower.

Mike didn't change his expression when he replied, having a seat at the table, being the Pack's ranking representative, but while not a vote for this part, as only packs which were already members of the treaty could vote, he could suggest amendments or ask questions, *As far as Tyler and some of the much older Alphas and some Elders are concerned, you shouldn't function as an Alpha until you are at least a hundred. Some don't think if you're not a century, you can't be in any senior role. Frankly, many of the older less progressive Alphas consider people even my age as barely being more then pups. Our Alpha doesn't but I know of a few. If Josh had to take over his pack now, he would be facing similar reactions though likely not as blatant.*

Zane was more than stumped. It was something he had never come across before in the pack which he could think of, but he hadn't had to deal with many different packs. As he was trying to wrap his mind around Mike being considered barely more than a pup by some, he missed some of the other conversations.

Gareth looked around, "Anyone else?" Waiting for a moment, "OK, we have a concern of them being too young." Tom sat with satisfaction, a smug look on his face.

Opening the binder for the Treaty, he turned to the eligibility section which he had flagged, as he had expected the challenge, and read it out, "All packs which meet the pack minimum pack size are eligible to join and have at least five packs agreeing to their joining." Turning to the addendum, he read out, "For the purpose of the treaty, minimum pack size is an Alpha, an Elder, three Betas, nine Deltas or Gamma-Enforcers, and fifteen Theta. To be counted, they must have an age of at least twenty years and all must be a bonded member of the pack. The Elder must also be at least at four centuries." Turning to Tom, "Where is it stated in the treaty the Alphas have to be a century old, since it's not with the eligibility?" Gareth asked, dropping the four-inch binder down in front of him. It had been printed specifically for this, on some nice paper, with tabs for each section. He was glad it wasn't the old, blurry version, or worse a hand-written version, with multiple amendments written in the margins.

There was a workshop of half a day to merge many of the amendments into one document, to clean it up, and modernize it. It would then have a copy sent to each pack which was a member, where they could then send all their own suggestion of any further changes, or accept the document as provided. At the next conference, they would take it in another workshop, and take all the amendments provided, and merge them into it, and then send it out again. The process could be up to four more cycles, before a final version would be presented. At which point, the packs would sign the new one or decline and leave the treaty without penalty. One change was how the re-write process would be handled, with the draft being sent out before the conference, and a merging of one round of new amendments, and sent out for a review, and then would have only a second round, not up to five rounds. Negotiations of amendments could be made outside of the conference, as well, so they were already agreed to, and could be immediately signed off.

He looked insulted that he would have done the work himself, "I don't know, I never read it. It is what I have always been told." Tom countered, not bothered with looking for it. "I refuse to support any pack where the Alphas are not at least a Century."

"How old are you two, for the record?" Gareth asked the two.

"Thirty-Two," Adam answered.

"Thirty," Brook answered.

Gareth looked at the table, "Alphas, how many support the motion for the fact they are too young?" Gareth took a count of hands, there being several others in addition to Tom and Tyler. "Against?" There was a clear majority there. "Failed. The motion of them being too young while they are over the stated requirement of Twenty is rejected, as there is no proof provided for the statement given for the Treaty requiring them to be a Century, and the eligibility section currently has two decades as the minimum. If you wish to have this changed, you will need to go through the Treaty amendment process." An amendment to change the eligibility requirements would need at least a year after being tabled, for discussion before it could be voted on, so could not be done during the conference. Once it was noted down, Gareth continued, "Next motion?"

Tyler and Tom tried to do them on the pack size requirement, and they both showed they had clearly more than the number by at least double. Triple for some ranks. They even showed the numbers didn't even count those who were currently working towards a higher rank and had been given a tentative promotion while they finished the qualifications but showed only those who were at the official and current ranks, with a section after of those who were tentatively or provisionally promoted, and what was their 'official' rank.

Then they challenged the validity of those who were ranked at each level. The fact they had the records from the trials, which they had not been one of the officials, with enough who had done and passed each rank, including the Thetas, had them growling under their breath as it was certified they had enough. None supported their challenge of the Elders who had written their certification of the ranking tests, with several growling at the implied besmirching of the Elder's word. Two Elders who were watching, glared daggers at the two Alphas, clearly getting more than annoyed. In a couple cases, they almost looked ready to challenge the Alphas themselves.

Several other attempts to block them from joining the Inter-Pack treaty were attempted, with each having only the two Alphas supporting it, as those who had supported the first couple motions saw they were being petty, and not considering the facts. They could see both Adam and Brook working hard to remain calm.

Adam and Brook were getting annoyed when they broke for a lunch break. *Jess, we need a private lunch; to calm down,* He called as they stalked out of the conference area, and up to the pack house. Seeing one of the small board rooms free, he nearly broke the sign as he moved it from *Vacant* to *In Use*. *We are in meeting room three.*

Both just sat there and meditated till Jess arrived with a good selection, "I take it, it's not going good?" Jess asked mildly, as she placed out the spread, heavy on filling meats, and included stuff hopefully to calm them down.

Adam nodded, "Could say that. Tyler and Tom are trying everything they can think of to try to block us from signing the inter-pack treaty. They started with age, then pack make up... we ended up having a lunch break called, and they are probably thinking up more."

*****

An hour before the end of the day, Rufus slammed his hand down on the table, after the latest block was defeated, "Enough!" He yelled, "You two have failed enough times." He said to the two alphas, before turning to Gareth, "I motion to accept Adam and Brook as Alphas of the Wild Valley pack and accept Wild Valley into the Treaty."

"I second that!" both Oscar and Grant said at the same time.

Gareth grinned savagely at the two, "The motion is to end challenges and move to acceptance. Those in favour? Against?" All raised their hands, many with a sigh, when asked those in favour, except for Tyler and Tom.

Brook smiled, as they had been waiting for this part, pulling out a stack of copies, "As you see here, we have already integrated the treaty rules into our Pack Laws, and have had those laws ratified by all pack members. We have highlighted the parts which tie into the inter-pack treaty." She ignored Tyler's tearing of his copy into little pieces, a sheet at a time. Tom was at least pretending to give her courtesy of listening, even though his copy sat unopened. The others were speed reading the rules, as they had highlighted the ones related to the Inter-Pack Treaty.

Grant growled, "Tyler, if you are going to be disrespectful, leave." He challenged, when the sound of the paper tearing had started to get to him, as he started on the fifth sheet.

"Fine!" Tyler yelled, slapping the desk and pushing away, knocking his chair over, as he stalked out the door.

Tom growled, and stalked out in his wake, seeing the others against them and silently protesting the treatment of Tyler.

Grant sighed, and looked to Gareth, "I apologise for my outburst."

Chuckles came from many Gareth included, "That is fine," Gareth replied, "Now, where were we? Right, the laws."

Irwin of Broken Pine Pack nodded, "I see the laws clearly, and see the punishments, which are in line with the treaty. I motion to accept the laws as they are."

"Second!" Called Louise. Each pack only got one vote, so even if both of the leaders were there, they had to decide how to vote.

Gareth or Maria only got to vote if there was a tie. Adam and Brook, as the pack coming in, had no vote, but were at the table, to be available to answer questions.

"Discussion?" Gareth asked.

Everyone was silent, it had all been very clearly laid out what the laws were and the punishments for breaking them were. Many had a list of available punishments. The serious ones had at the severe end being 'Made Omega, Banishment as Lone or Rogue, or Death'. Omega would keep them in the pack, but where they were unlikely to ever get a position better than Theta and would never join the Elders, even if they survived that long, which was very rare. Banishment as Rogue meant the pack considered them totally untrustworthy, to the point they couldn't be trusted to not attack if their back was turned. Some packs had kill-on-sight orders for rogues. Others just would not allow them into their territory, and if they transgressed at all, then would be killed. It was rare for a pack which would allow them to petition for a review of their sentence. MacLaren did do it occasionally but had to clearly prove to him and his mate they deserved a second chance, and that the rogue designation wasn't warranted.

"All in favour of having Wild Valley, under Adam and Brook's leadership join the Inter-Pack Treaty?"

Hands went up.

"Opposed?" Gareth asked. No hands went up. Several Alphas sighed in relief, as all preferred consensus over a split decision.

"It's unanimous." Gareth stated with a smile. "Welcome to our newest members!" With it being unanimous, there was no way they could be challenged for the membership in the future.

Adam smiled, "Brook and I would like to have the actual signing at the Wild Valley, also so we can give a tour, as many of you have requested one, as well.

Many nodded as it sounded like a nice idea. it would give them a break. They had two days of items which impacted several packs, but then could take the Sunday and have the breakout meetings after they returned.

"Now it's scheduled, we don't have enough time to start the next topic, I am adjourning the meeting till nine tomorrow. Any apposed?"

Silence.

"Then what are you all sitting there for?" Gareth said with a smile after a moment, and the Alphas all laughed and headed to the main dining hall, as they were dining with the packs.

Zane was shocked how much jockeying and dissent there were between the packs at the beginning, but once they had the two alphas out of the way, the rest worked together almost as one pack, each listening respectfully, eventually unanimously accepting the new pack. He didn't think he would like to be doing something like that, ever. His wolf snorted in disagreement in the back of his mind but refused to say more.

Arriving as a group, the gathered wolves instantly gave attention and were silent.

"First day was a bit slow, and we only got one thing done." Gareth said, pausing for effect. "Wild Valley was approved and is now a full member of the Inter-Pack Treaty!" He exclaimed. The gathered wolves howled happily for a bit, knowing it was the biggest item on the agenda.

Adam added once everyone calmed down, "The signing will be done at Wild Valley on Sunday in front of all there. We have scheduled to leave here at eight with some buses and do the signing at One. The afternoon will have some tours for the Alphas, and then after dinner, then buses will return." Adam added, letting them know the schedule. "All of Wild Valley I am *recommending, but not ordering* to be there." He knew any who skipped it would be upset once they realised how historical the moment was for the pack.

Once the Alphas stepped down, the wolves were freed to eat, as the servers brought out platters of elk meat. Several times, the wolves had to be separated from fighting over the meat. Usually without either getting any, as a third had come in as they were fighting and took the piece which they had been fighting over.

*****

They had been there several days now, and it had been interesting. Everyone was relaxing after pigging out on the elk meat the night before. For the first few days Zane or one of the other dominant team members had been near Tessa, Oscar, and Olivia. For most of the time Oscar had been staying very close to Olivia though he was trying to keep it from being obvious. He had his reasons, but it hadn't the time to talk about it.

When the pups had gone for runs, Mike or Malcom had been close to her. He hadn't really thought about it, since they were in a strange pack. Zane had been keeping a close eye on his team and who was around them. The team had met several other pups in similar positions, and it had been really nice. For Tessa and Oscar, they had met a few pups with the same dominance level. They did it differently here, but their levels were the same. Some had teams they looked to and others didn't yet, or they simply took care of the pack.

Oscar hadn't realized several of the other pups near his age had found Olivia interesting and didn't care she was human. It had become obvious to him when a boy near his age started talking to Olivia. He had made a few comments of she was really nice and cute. They weren't bad comments, but it looked to Oscar the boy was interested in her. It put his wolf in a hard spot since they really were drawn to her. Though he hadn't mentioned it yet, Oscar had a feeling she was going to be his mate, *"Zane, I need you where I am. I... I... Just come please?"* This was going to be hard to admit. He really hoped it wouldn't upset Zane since he was so protective of her.

At first, most nights he was in his wolf form in Olivia's bed. It had started when he and Tessa had been selected by Zane and Olivia had needed someone there to make sure she didn't need help. Now it was something he didn't even think about; when she went to bed, he did as well. He might change in his and Tessa's room, but he would end up curled next to Olivia. It was much like Zane and Tessa tended to sleep together.

Zane frowned when Oscar contacted him. It didn't feel like something was threatening him, but it was an emotional reaction. He stood and excused himself politely as he left. He didn't realize but his blank neutral look settled down over his face. Even though it had been a year since their parents had died, he was still impacted by their deaths. He had slowly gathered a few more friends but many of the pack and humans were kept at an arms distance.

When he finally found Oscar, he glanced around the room. Oscar was sitting next to Olivia though he was looking distressed. There was a boy or two near their ages who were talking to Olivia. Nothing seemed to be amiss, but Oscar definitely wasn't happy, *What do you need Oscar?* He had been preparing for a fight or something like that.

Oscar looked in Zane's direction when he walked in before looking down. This was going to be horrible hard for him since he was just a junior wolf. He knew what he knew but it was still going to be hard, *Team leader...* He took a deep breath, *My wolf has sensed Olivia is probably going to be our mate when we are old enough. I don't know how to tell the others to keep their distance.*

Zane had to stop and stare when Oscar told him about what he was feeling about his sis, *Um... Wow. Didn't see that at all. Knew you liked her but not... Ah, we will talk about it later. I need to wrap my mind around the idea, but I don't have a problem. You will take good care of her, and I know that. I will deal with this.* Only thing he could think of was to be fairly direct. "Hey sis, need to talk to Jacob for a minute. Jacob, we need to talk. Nothing major, just something came to my attention."

When the boy looked up, he met Zane's eyes before looking slightly away. He was close in dominance to Oscar. He stood and walked over to Zane to see what he had to say, "What do you need to talk about?"

Zane grinned and gave the boy a man hug, "Nothing major, just a team member wanted me to ask about something." He walked him out of the room. Once they were far enough away, he turned to the junior wolf, "Make it known that Olivia is off limits, please. If you want to be friends with her, it is fine. Nothing beyond that though or I will take exception to it. I know she is nice and cute, but she has someone else waiting for her to be old enough to be his girlfriend." Once he was sure the boy understood he wandered off.

The boy sent to his Alpha directly, *Alpha, I was informed by the wolf pup Zane that Olivia is Oscar's future mate. He asked me to let everyone know so nobody tried to see her. Will you please take care of this?* His mental voice was very submissive since he was both a pup and very junior. It was all he could do to contact the Alpha directly and only because the Alpha had stated many times, he was open to being contacted by all and there was no need to have something just go up the chain. There is no way he would just send to the pack in general.

Adam was surprised he had even linked him, as while he had no problem with it, most Thetas couldn't bring themselves to contact him directly, *Sure Jacob.* He commented, knowing Jacob would never think to pass it along to the others directly.

He decided to pass it along to MacLaren, not just Wild Valley as he was still technically ranked as Second and had the authority. He gave a mental cough to catch the attention of both packs, *It has come to my attention: the human she-pup Olivia is known to her mate. Please treat her kindly, but in friendly terms. She is off-limits for even flirting. You don't need to congratulate her, as it is rarely sure till they are of age. Let's make sure these American wolves get a good impression of us Canadians!* He got many wordless responses as everyone went back to what they had been doing.

Zane walked outside and leaned against a distant part of the porch. What Oscar had told him had tossed him for a huge loop. It simply wasn't something he had considered or would have for years. Hell, his uncle was in his 50s, even if he didn't look it and had just found his mate, *Uncle Mike, I need to talk to you for a moment. Oscar just informed me Olivia might be his mate when they are of age.* It never even occurred to him not to talk to his uncle about this.

Mike didn't smile since he had a feeling about the two. Zane might not realize it but many of the junior wolves found their mates earlier than the more dominant. There were lots of ideas why about this. The one he liked was it was simply once you found a mate, you would start having pups. Not many or very close but if a dominant wolf mated early it would make for too many dominant wolves. It wasn't the problem, but it would lead to an imbalance in the ranks of the wolves. The more junior wolves the better a pack was taken care of, *We will talk later and thanks for letting me know.* Another thought was, there were always more work the junior could do, not so much for the more senior. There were also many fewer senior role positions, so with fewer around, there were less who could be your mate in each pack.

Zane ended up looking out over the property and the view was spectacular. The view from their house back at the pack was wonderful as well but this called to his wolf. How he wanted to change and go for a run, but he wasn't sure what would be allowed.

When Alpha Adam came out, Zane was still looking over the view. He felt the dominance of the wolf and turned towards him and met his eyes before submitting, "You have a lovely view of the world from here, sir." He turned and looked over the railing and appreciated the view. Why Adam was there didn't cross his mind since it was his territory, or some of it.

Adam smiled, "I agree, and can't wait for my own pack house to be done. The view there is totally untouched." The view here had a fire access trail which followed a ridge. If you didn't know it was there, most didn't see it, but to his eyes it was a glaring scar across the mountain.

Sitting down on a bench built into the railing, "You probably didn't know this, but I was turned by my mate. I know you were turned by a Rogue. If you need someone to talk to, or help with being turned, just contact me." He pulled out a card, handing it to Zane, he had written his personal direct extension and email on it. Not even most Alphas got it.

Zane took the card and looked at it. It actually surprised him Adam was a turned wolf like him. At least he had a choice in it and hadn't lost his family in the process. As he was looking at the card one hand went to his shoulder where the bite mark was. Most of the rest of the scars from the accident were gone. The bite mark was going to be there forever from what he had understood, "Congrats on finding your mate sir. I was turned by a rogue and lost my family in the process." He shrugged and stopped talking since he didn't want to talk about it much. It was his way of protecting himself from the memories and how he felt about it.

Chapter 20 – Pack Tour

Adam decided if Zane didn't want to talk, but he could find another way to try to get Zane to open up, "I know you and your team have not taken advantage much of the ability to run as wolves. If you wanted, since Brook and I aren't involved in the conference today, we could do a run up and show you the pack house we are building." Adam offered, "It will be about a four-hour run each way." Well, for Brook and him, it would be more of a trot than a run. There was a meditation of an issue between two other packs, which was touchy, but other than the elders and the couple of alphas doing the mediation between the packs, most weren't attending. Some were having private meetings one-on-one, but the three he had offered had declined, as they had seen how he had been respectful, but holding his position and didn't need a private chat.

When Adam offered to take him and his team to the other location he tilted his head, *Uncle Mike, Alpha Adam offered to show me and my team another location. If you don't mind, I would like to. My wolf wants to stretch his legs, and I am sure the others would as well.* Maybe not Oscar since he wasn't going to want to leave Olivia at the moment.

Mike was relaxing with Josh and several of the local senior wolves. They had been swapping stories of some of the rogues they had dealt with. The recent fight was still at the front of their thoughts, and it was obvious Josh was still hurting a bit. Even as a wolf, it was hard to recover from having a lung damn near ripped out of your body. It was only because of the quick actions of others to get him first aid, then to a Healer which had saved his life. *Sounds like a good idea, be good and don't do anything I wouldn't do.* He had to tease the boy some as he knew Zane and Tessa had become active recently; it was nearly impossible to hide from a werewolf's nose.

He had to growl slightly when Mike had replied since he knew he was being teased, *What, you mean like knocking someone up? That won't happen and I am a good wolf, darn it!* When he growled, he winced before looking at Adam, "My uncle was teasing me. He said it would be fine though."

Adam smiled and nodded; teasing families were fun, and he didn't think the growl had been directed at him.

Everyone, Alpha Adam has offered to take us for a long run. Oscar if you wish to remain it is fine. It wasn't his job to tell the team Oscar had identified Olivia as his probable mate. Eventually it would be obvious but for now he was leaving it alone. It was something he was going to have to decide to talk about. The rest of the team would assume he stayed to ensure Olivia was taken care of.

It was a short time later when his team were outside and almost bouncing in excitement. Zane couldn't help but grin at them as he was stripping down. He still wasn't totally used to the nudity, but he was getting used to it. Before he shifted, his hand touched the bite again though he didn't realize it.

When Tessa noticed him touching the bite mark, she touched his hand and leaned against him, "Let it go, Zane. It wasn't the right way to be changed but you are a good wolf." She gave him a light kiss even as he blushed at her leaning against him.

Zane cleared his throat before shifting to his wolf form and gave his body a good shake. It felt so good to be in this form as well. He had long since decided even if he hadn't been changed by a rogue, he would have ended up with a mate and been turned. Being a wolf was simply so comfortable now. At first it had been uncomfortable but now? He loved the feel of his wolf body and the feel of dirt under his paws. It didn't change the dark memories he had.

Adam smiled and collected the clothes into his pack which Brook brought as she and his four—he considered Sam and Lea his, even if they still had parents—joined them, soon after the rest of Zane's team. Slipping it on, he shifted to his wolf and greeted each of the pups, before heading off to the now well scented trail which was one of the main routes to the new pack. To the eyes, there was only the barest trail, and at many times, there were no marks of where it went between bushes and following the easiest climbs for the most part. To a wolf's nose, the trail was clear, as if there were signposts of all those who had gone before and what way they went.

Not sure if it is known down there, Adam said privately to Zane as they ran, *But it is known up here, now that you have the turn complete, once the Rogue is killed, your turn-scar will fade and disappear. Also, I don't talk about it much, but I lost my father before I turned ten. I have an idea of the heartache and know it's worse than mine. Do get to know Toby and Robin. They are birth-cousins, Robin lost his parents in a rockslide, and it took Toby's father as well. Toby's mother had passed me guardianship of them, and she is rarely seen, from missing her mate. I know it's going to be sore, so I'm not going to say anything more about it unless you bring it up.*

Zane nearly stumbled when the Alpha shared the personal fact *he* had lost his own father young. Robin and Toby had shared Adam was basically their father, but not the fact of why. *I'll keep it to myself, sir.* He promised. He remembered some comments from the two.

Adam lightly shoulder checked Zane, *Stop calling me 'Sir', it makes me feel old!* He teased, *Call me Adam or, if you must, Alpha Adam.*

Thankfully being in wolf form kept him from crying. The mention of losing parents was enough to start making memories come back, *Yes sir!* There was a slight teasing tone when he sent to Adam. It was simply how he was raised and tended to speak without thinking, *Habit to call people sir or ma'am. My parents taught me to use those terms.*

He would consider talking to the other pups but at the moment he didn't want to. It was still too fresh in his mind even though it had been over a year since his parents had died. Not knowing how long ago they had lost their parents he didn't want to possibly drag their memories up as well, *I don't know about talking to anyone right now, sir. I mean Alpha. It is too fresh to me. I will consider it. You have my sympathy for losing your father.*

If you don't do it before you leave, make sure to get their contact information, and you can chat. It would be good to have others who are not part of your pack to talk to. I do know they are discrete. Adam replied.

He responded to the bump by eventually bumping Melody off her paws, *Oops, I blame it on the Alpha! He bumped me first.* Zane knew he was going to get jumped by her and even though they were running, his wolf wanted to play.

Melody growled at him as she scrambled to her feet, *Likely story, since it was several minutes ago. You are so going down, you horrible wolf.* She did as he expected and jumped on him which started a play fight. Even Tessa joined in and nipped him several times.

Adam chuckled, watching the pups play, as even his four got in on the play fight, *If you want to make it for lunch, we have to continue the run! Play as you run!* He called out, as he turned and ran a wet tongue across Zane's face playfully before darting off a little

Zane hopped up after being taken out and started running, *Food sounds good.* He sent to Adam, *Catch me if you can you slackers!* He sent to the others. As they were running, they were playing and having a great deal of fun. The trail was clear to his nose, even if it wasn't clear to his eyes.

They stopped for a short time later at a lookout point beside a small waterfall which cascaded off the ridge and down over a hundred meters to the ground below for a short break and a few slurps of water, and for the weaker to catch their breath. It was a nice refreshing green taste, from passing through all the moss.

*****

Reaching the work site, Adam shifted and started pulling the clothes out, bundling it up and tossing to the various wolves. He could tell whose clothes was whose, by the scents. Once all were dressed, he led them to the mess tent, as Joshua met them there. He smiled, as it also would allow them to make sure everything was ready for the signing and the Alphas coming for a tour.

Adam wrapped an arm around Joshua, hugging him to his side and introduced him to the pups, "Everyone, this is Joshua, who I have in charge here for me." He also introduced the visiting pups by name, and Joshua gave them a hug and sniff of the neck before leading them into the tent, which they could smell the food.

Zane still wasn't very comfortable with the casual contact most wolves seemed to have. He let the other give him a hug and sniff but didn't return the hug. He did catch the scent of the young man and gave him a polite nod. Since he was in charge based on what the Alpha said he submitted to him.

After lunch he took them on a tour of the site, which was starting to show the shape of what it would be eventually. The wolves at the site smiled greetings, but all knew they were fighting time to get the outsides done, so they didn't have to work with snow while building. The view of the untouched valleys was one which Adam was proud about. All the buildings were designed to hug the hills and ridges, making them nearly impossible to see from any distance, to not ruin the view, but also so anyone hiking the surrounding mountains wouldn't see them.

*****

Even as Zane and the rest of his team were doing the run to the other site Olivia and Oscar were slowly walking around the area near the house. They had walked out shortly after Zane had talked to Jacob. She was frowning since she had a feeling it had something to do with her, "Oscar, why did Zane talk to Jacob?"

Oscar tensed and then sighed, deciding honesty was the best, "Because I told him I think you might be my mate when we are old enough. I really like you and my wolf does as well. I didn't want to say anything but having another boy paying attention to you really upset me and my wolf." He turned to her and took her hands before giving her a very earnest look as he spoke.

Olivia stopped when he turned and talked to her. When what he said hit, she had to look down and blushed a huge amount. She really did like Oscar and knew he wanted her as a girlfriend, but he hadn't asked of yet. Now she was thirteen and very close to fourteen, she had been hoping he would ask soon. She and Zane were almost exactly two years apart. He was going to be sixteen soon and right after that, she would be fourteen. When school started, she was going to be a Freshman and she was looking forward to it, "Oh..." She didn't know what to say.

Before they could say anything else, Olivia squealed as a cold nose touched an arm. It was so unexpected she jerked away and almost knocked Oscar over. When she turned, she found a huge wolfdog look-ing at her with amusement in its eyes, "Um, hi? You scared me." Since the dog looked upset for having made her scream, she started petting his or her head, "Are you a wolf like Oscar?"

Oscar shook his head, "That's no werewolf. They have a different scent." It was obvious to him the dog did have some wolf blood, but it wasn't something he had scented before. It had made him pause before he realised it wasn't the scent of a werewolf.

"We raise wolfdogs" Alpha Maria commented, walking up, attracted by the scream. "They were exposed to werewolf blood a long time ago, so are very intelligent, and they bond with people. Shelly seems to desire to bond with you. It is up to you if you accept her or not."

Olivia looked up at Maria and then at the dog. The wolf was almost as large as Oscar when he changed which made her look huge, "Oh, what do I need to do? She is lovely and..." She didn't know what to say, "Why is she wanting to bond or what have you with me? I am just a hu-man though Oscar seems to think I might be his mate." That thought was so odd she really wasn't sure what to think. Well, and the wolfdog wanting something from her.

Maria smiled, "Often they bond with the 'just humans' who are involved with the pack, as they give an additional protection, and they will stay with you. Even if you eventually get turned, they will still stay with you. To accept, you just have to touch heads together." Times like this, she could almost see the hand of the Goddess in the offer. It was one which she would help along, and not interfere with it, even if in the case of Amber, it lost them the most striking furred one. She was glad that one was staying with Wild Valley. If Orca's pups also had the same striking black and white fur, she thought to ask to have some come back down.

Olivia looked at the woman before looking at the animal. If she accepted what would the wolf do? How would she deal with not being around her family and friends? She would be leaving everything she knew, "But what about her leaving to come with us? Wouldn't she miss her family?" Even now Olivia thought about animals as having family and missing them, "I would hate to have her miss her brothers and sisters."

She looked at the wolf and then at Maria, "I know what it is like to lose family and..." She couldn't help it, but her eyes started watering, "I miss my parents even though I have Zane and Oscar. I would hate to have her miss her family as well."

Oscar pulled her close and held onto her as she started crying, "Luna, Liv did lose her family and almost her brother. I can understand what she is worried about." It was obvious he was deeply involved with Olivia as he was talking.

Maria sighed and knelt down beside them, even as Shelly was whining and nuzzling Olivia's head in sympathy, "Shelly is trained to work by herself. Often, we have ones who go into human homes without anyone but the one they bond to. She will go with you to a wolf pack. She will make new friends and will basically join your family and will be able to play with the wolves. She is registered as a service animal, so you could even say she is a comfort animal." She pulled both into a hug to offer comfort. "We had the report of his turning, but not your loss, what happened, if you wanted to talk?"

Since Olivia was still crying Oscar answered, "Zane was attacked by a rogue wolf. The only reason he survived was because they were hit by a vehicle. The rogue had pushed them into a street when he attacked. A month or so later when his family was coming to visit him at the hospital their car was struck by another and their parents died in the accident. It caused my team leader a great deal of hurt when he woke to discover it." Since Olivia was in shorts the scars on her leg were obvious.

"Even now, he is hurting from what occurred and so is my mate. She wakes sometimes at night with nightmares of from the result of the accident and what happened to her brother. Or what could have happened..." He rested his head against hers as he was talking. Oscar knew she might have a nightmare this evening since they were talking about this, "It greatly upsets Zane's wolf, and it makes mine whine. We want to protect her but how can we from nightmares?" Even he was trying to resist the urge to cry.

Shelly moved even closer at the emotions of the person she was drawn to. There was a soft whine and a slight nudge of her nose against the girl. She knew she would be a good wolf for her. Even now she could scent the slight pain the girl was in even though she seemed to be moving fairly normally, *Accept me?* It was more an impression than actual words.

Maria nodded, "Shelly might be able to help, since she has had the advanced training for helping with stress. She would probably give her an outlet and some more help." Her wolf wanted to howl out for the pups who had lost so much. She hoped Shelly would go with them, as she had a feeling it would help.

Olivia looked at Shelly and pressed her hands against her cheeks, "Do you really want to leave here and come with me? It is a long way from here, but it is your choice." She leaned forward and pressed her forehead against the wolf's. Listening to Oscar had upset her as well since she knew he did care, and it meant a great deal to her. The whole mate thing was still so new she wasn't sure what to think, "Only if you really want Shelly."

Oscar knew having a 'service dog' would help Olivia since she could carry some of her stuff. Even now, after the surgery, a long day at school made her leg ache. Anything to help his future mate meant so much to him. He met Maria's eyes, and they showed how much he appreciated the wolf-dog's urge to help Olivia.

Shelly wagged her tail as Olivia accepted her, before whining and giving her cheek a quick lick.

Olivia gave the dog a good hug before standing back up. The wolf-dog was huge, to her, and having her in school was going to be interesting, "Thank you Shelly, I will do what I can to ensure you are happy where we live. I am sure Zane will let you run with them. I can't as much as I want to. All of them are so beautiful as wolves." Oscar was smaller than the others much like Tessa, but he was still huge to her.

Oscar gave the wolfdog a good pet, "Thank you for being willing to look after Olivia for me. I will do what I can to take care of you as well. Mind you the cat might decide you are a good sleeping spot. She seems to have decided my shoulder is a good place to relax." His wolf was still amused by the darn thing. Why a cat had decided they were a good sleeping spot he didn't know. Frankly, he was stumped when it came to the cat. It liked him and his sister, tolerated Zane and the team but hated the other wolves.

Maria smiled, "Come you two, we will get her papers, and some gear. I will let your Alpha or Luna know the details and particulars for her." She stood and led them to the kennel office. She included a large pack for Shelly, since she would be able to use it instead of Olivia needing a backpack at school.

Shelly whined in happiness at the pets and leaned into the attention. She walked along with them as they headed over to the building, hidden in the trees at the edge of the clearing.

Maria explained what they needed for them to take Shelly with them.

The attendant smiled as they came up to the counter, and looked at Olivia and Oscar, telling them directly, "It will take a couple days to get all the paperwork for the US registration. I will drop it off when it comes in." The attendant told them, as he printed off the Canadian paperwork and records showing she was up to date on her vaccinations. Then handed over the service dog vest, collar with her tags. The requested large pack also sported the bright labels of Service Animal took a moment longer. He slipped the paperwork in a waterproof pouch, and placed it, the harness and the collar, along with a leash, into the pack and showed how the pack slipped on and fitted. "You don't need them here, but she will need to wear the collar, and either the harness or the pack when you are outside of a pack's territory, so she is marked as a service animal according to the human rules. A copy of the rules are included in the papers. Any questions?"

Even as Oliva leaned over and hugged the dog, Oscar did the same. He could sense the animal had some basic pack bonds, *Thank you. Take care of my mate. She is important to me and even more so her brother and uncle. I will be here with her to help as well.* He stroked the wolf-dog's fur on her head and shoulders.

Olivia listened as best possible. What was being said was hard to listen to since she was so tied up in accepting Shelly as a service animal. It didn't feel right but then again it did. There was something about the wolf which drew her, "Thank you Shelly. Don't know what else to say other than thanks. I hope you, Zane, and my cat get along. She is named Silly since she does get along with some of the wolves like Oscar." She kept petting her even as she looked at the woman who was handing over paperwork.

Oscar realized he needed to talk to Zane and Mike, *A wolfdog chose Olivia as her owner. We are getting what is needed for her to go with us. She is a beautiful animal and is trained as a service dog. I think it will be good for Olivia.* Olivia did have pack bonds since she and Zane had been accepted into the pack, but he blocked her from what he was saying. He took a moment to give both the Luna and the worker a good thankful hug.

*****

Mike had to blink before looking at one of the local wolves, "Wolf-dog? What does that mean? Something about my niece being accepted by one?" It wasn't something they had heard of as of yet.

Martin, who Mike and Josh had been discussing differences in security with, laughed. Once he had calmed down, "We have had some dogs which had been exposed to werewolf blood long ago, as an added defence for the then tiny pack. They gained many werewolf traits, and abilities. It includes a basic pack bond, and a much stronger bond to one they choose. If your niece has been chosen, then congratulations are in order. It is similar to a mate bond, in how personal it is, but it is weaker. The dogs gained a much longer life, are much more intelligent, a werewolf's immunity and healing abilities, and their size increased. Some are about the size of a Theta wolf. They do have basically telepathic bonds but speak in symbols or ideas more than words, generally. They can also take complex commands, and abstract ideas of 'guard from harm' and will protect them, but not from casual or friendly contact."

He had to stop and think for a few before he finally replied to Oscar, *Keep me in the loop. I will take care of what might be needed from an adult view.* He looked at Martin, "Thanks and I hope this isn't a problem with your pack."

Martin shook his head, "No, our wolfdogs are trained to go out in the world. They are trained as service animals, and our smaller 'dumber' ones are sent out to humans as very smart service animals and will be able to stay with her around the clock. They can tell if they are in the pack's territory, and when they are safe, will take themselves for exercise, go out to relieve themselves, or make it known otherwise they need some assistance with something."

*****

Zane was still at the new pack house when Oscar contacted him. He leaned back in the chair he was in and looked out over the woods, *Inter-*

*esting and keep me updated Oscar. By the way: I do think you and Olivia will be good for each other. I had to think about it, but I can see how much you care for her. Give her as much care as you can and I will approve.** What it meant to have a wolfdog choosing his sister, he didn't know but it sounded like a good thing. He was going to have to talk to Adam about it.

Zane had noticed a dog keeping close to Adam but hadn't thought much about it, "Alpha, what does it mean to have a wolf dog choose my sister?" If anyone could answer Adam could, he hoped.

Adam blinked then smiled, "Our Wolfdogs are like Charlie," He pointed at Charlie, who sat beside Adam with intelligent eyes. Describing it for one who had been turned was easy for him, "They are almost werewolves but can't shift. They do have some bonds and can hear your metal commands as well. They are protective of the one they are bonded to and are intelligent enough to follow fairly complicated commands. Take them as a mix of a bodyguard and service animal."

Adam's answer almost made Zane cry again. What the hell was it with coming here? He kept wanting to cry as memories kept coming back. It had been over a year since he had lost his family and almost a year since he had woken. He should be done with all that crap. Zane had to clear his throat, "Good. She keeps a crutch handy to threaten me with when I get too protective. Not sure what she considers too protective, but she has several in the house."

Tessa and the others snickered at his comment. "Zane, I have said it before, it is because you are her older brother. She can take anything you do as being overprotective. I don't blame her for being annoyed since your wolf did chew up part of a crutch..." She had felt him starting to tense up. The last few days his face had been closing up slightly. Because of this she changed the subject for him.

He grumbled at Tessa, "That was my wolf blast it! He was grumpy with her for poking me one time to many. All we did was hand Oscar her backpack." Zane did grin and was glad the subject had changed. His wolf had laid there and chewed the crutch up in front of Olivia even as she was yelling at him. Trying to explain it was his wolf's decision was almost pointless.

Adam could see the hurt in Zane's eyes, *The wolfdogs are also registered as service animals, so they will be going with her, even to school. They are also all trained in guarding, and some can even win against a Delta. It should help your protectiveness and concern for her safety. I think we need to go have a chat away from too-sharp ears.* He made sure it was a request, not an order.

Zane looked away for a moment, *Not now Alpha. Later maybe but not now.* His walls were coming back up and the expression on his face was... Not dead but so very neutral. It wasn't the expression of a year ago when he dealt with the two fuck wads. It was his reaction to people trying to push him too far too fast. He had to take time to think before he reacted.

Adam looked disappointed, but nodded, and didn't push. He would be patient for the right time to have Zane would open up to him. He could see a clear need to talk to someone who understood him, so he could deal with the hidden hurts. And likely needed someone who was strong enough he felt safe to let his walls down but wasn't so close he could be embarrassed about breaking down.

When Adam pointed at Charlie, he gave the dog a good look. At a guess Adam had been bonded with the dog before he had been turned, "Hey boy. If you are even close to Shelly's size my sister is going to feel small." He gave the dog a good pet.

Adam laughed as Charlie leaned into the petting hard. He was as big as a full-grown Beta, "She is bonded to Shelly? She's smaller, but she's the size of Tessa in her wolf shape. Charlie is one of the largest, which for me is perfect. He has already protected my back in two pack fights; not to engage, but to make sure I knew before they attacked or if I was busy, to disrupt their attack. I know Shelly was fully trained for being a guard dog and has been trained for stress support."

When Zane stopped petting him, Charlie head butted him, nearly knocking over the teen. It got a grumble though Zane took the hint and started petting again, "Good. Not everyone at school is the nicest. Olivia is too nice a person sometimes." He gave Adam a toothy grin, "Not all of us are." There had been a few clashes with the remains of David and Leon's flunkies. They had been subtle and kept away from the adults. There was only one attempt against Olivia. They had made it very clear she was to be left alone.

Adam smiled and nodded, knowing he would have protected his sister and friends from bullies. He steered them down a concrete lined tunnel. With a heavy door at the opening, "This will be our gym. The building is done ahead of schedule, so it is just waiting for being outfitted this fall." Using his badge, he unlocked the door and held it for the pups.

They spent the rest of the day walking around the place. Zane kept trying not to drool over all the tech stuff they had in the secure storage area. He had a decent computer and a game console but sheesh. Mindy was definitely looking impressed. There were many racks, high-end commercial switches—he didn't know what they were called, but they were bigger than a PC tower on their side, and some didn't have many ports, they did have some, large servers, and stacks of wires. He told them about the size of their data centre but couldn't show it off.

Adam was proud of his accomplishments and liked to show them off. The pack house was a little too dangerous to go inside, but they could see the sheer size of it. They were starting to get the third floor in position on the two wings, so the shape was showing. The third wing was only on the first floor, with a "temporary" roof right on top of the floor slabs, with "temporary" walls where it would connect to the central area. They currently weren't working on building it, to save the money, as they didn't need the space yet.

Eventually, he showed them into the mess tent for a dinner before running back down to MacLaren.

*****

Oscar was walking around the pack house while Olivia was resting a bit in the afternoon and came across Cody and Amber. He stopped and sniffed the air and turned to the two. She looked maybe eight or nine but had the scent of someone changing to a wolf. There was an additional scent of a male wolf on her though not sexually. He looked at Cody and realised it was his scent, "Mate and changed?" He kept his voice quiet as he talked, since he wasn't sure of what was going on.

Cody looked at the other wolf and pulled Amber closer to him, "Yes." He didn't say anything else about Amber since it was still so very new to them. Amber hadn't been told about being Mates, till her wolf brought it up, and she had then been told the full story, including a brief bit of sexual education. Both her and her wolf had decided they were not ready to do it, and Cody had told her he didn't mind waiting till she was ready.

He moved over and settled down in a chair across from them, "I hope you don't mind my asking." Oscar looked away for a moment since even as a pup Cody was more dominant than he was, "My mate is human also." His eyes met the girl's before meeting Cody's, "I am Oscar and from Oregon in the U.S. My team leader thought it would be a good idea to come up with Beta Mike to meet other pups."

"How long have you known?" Oscar didn't know they had just recently met though there was the scent of a new/changed wolf on her. He hoped the boy would talk since he had been thinking about talking to Beta mike and Zane about maybe changing Olivia. She had been found by one of the wolfdogs, but he still was scared for her. He hadn't been included in the discussion Zane had with some kids at school. He had found out later.

Cody shook his head, "Not long. She had become separated from her mother, and we had been called in to assist in search and rescue. I was on my first assignment as a trainee to a Patrol, and we found her before anyone else. I could smell her but nobody else seemed to be able to track the scent, so they had me lead. When I got close, I could tell she was my mate." He smiled and hugged her, "Shortly after that Alphas Adam and Brook arrived, as they were in the area and were also helping look, and when they realized what she was to me, had them brought here, as it was closer than a human facility. The Alphas and her mother decided it was best to turn her now than wait till we were of age."

Amber pulled a face, "The first part hurt and sucked, but now my wolf is talking to me, I love it! I was told it's still a month or two before I turn." She sighed, "I so want to run as a wolf with my friends."

Oscar looked down slightly, even more than when he had shown the other wolf, he wasn't a challenge, "Until just the other day Liv didn't know what she probably was to me. I hadn't wanted to tell her or talk to her until she was older. I love my team leader and wanted to talk to him first. Jacob forced my hand. I had to mention it and..." He didn't feel bad for admitting Olivia was going to be his mate. He really liked her and knew she liked both him and his wolf. The idea of changing her hadn't really been considered since they were so new. It was also since he hadn't talked to her or anyone about what he had sensed.

When Amber mentioned running as a wolf he gave her a shy smile, "Shaking out your fur and running is enjoyable. Being included with our team's play is very enjoyable. Zane and everyone take care not to be too rough when Tessa and I play with them." He didn't know how they looked at teams here but to him it was now his world, "She was accepted by one of the wolfdogs. Her name is Shelly, and she has been staying very close to Liv."

Amber motioned to the striking black and white one which was dozing near them, "Orca chose me almost as soon as I arrived. It's nice to know they are there for you and will guard your back."

Cody smiled, "It also helps my wolf stay calm, knowing there is one who could take on a Delta and guard her till help arrived."

Olivia walked in and Shelly was following her. She walked over to Oscar and settled down in his lap even as Shelly hopped on the couch next to them, "My shadow is thinking about a run. I wish I could go too but when I thought about riding her, she nipped me." When Shelly grumbled and nipped at her sleeve Olivia snickered.

Amber laughed, "My Orca was not very impressed as well when I thought about it, either. When I am with my Cody, she goes to run herself, when she needs one, as she then knows I am not needing her. She had one this morning, so is tired. A couple of times Cody has let me ride him for a bit."

Oscar looked at Shelly, "So you want a run? Cody, would you come with me? I have been shown around but would like someone who knows where I can run." It would give Olivia and Amber time to talk. He couldn't broach the talk about maybe changing Olivia. It was simply something he couldn't do.

He stood and quickly stripped down and changed. He ignored Olivia's light blush to his nudity and once changed, he nuzzled her before giving Shelly a good nuzzle as well. As of yet the wolfdog hadn't seen his other form, *Run Shelly?*

Shelly wagged her tail and hopped down to sniff the werewolf which was about her size. She knew where the nearest door was and headed out at a trot, pawing it open and taking off running towards one of the wolf-trails which went through the forest, leaving the two werewolves to catch up.

Amber blushed a little, but was trying to get over the body shyness, as it confused her wolf; she understood since they didn't have fur, they wore clothes instead, and needing to take them off to shift was normal, so was confused about being embarrassed over it, when it was normal. As Cody headed out, Orca yawned and shook her fur out, before sitting up, seemingly knowing Amber was staying here while her mate headed out.

Olivia noticed the blush and moved over next to the young girl, "Believe me I know. Watching my brother and some of his team change drove me nuts." Oscar was so damn attractive, "It doesn't help I do find Oscar really... He is so good looking." She could see why Zane was attracted to Tessa since she was as cute as her brother was. When she had originally met Oscar, she had been drawn to him. There was something calling her to him, even if she hadn't realized at the time, he felt she was going to be his mate.

"I am too young to have those kinds of thoughts!" Amber said shyly, "I am trying not to be embarrassed by seeing him without his clothes, as it is normal for wolves to shift." Trying to cool her blushes, "I'm Amber, and this is Orca." Orca had laid her head in Amber's lap, and she was absently stroking her fur. "I only learned werewolves weren't just in stories a few months ago."

Olivia groaned, "Believe me I felt the same way when we arrived at the pack." She rolled her eyes, "My intro to wolves was my brother poking me with his nose after he had changed. Before that, I wasn't sure I really believed, even though I had been told. He has a really cold and wet nose." She leaned over and petted Orca, "She is a pretty dog. I am getting used to having Shelly following me around. It is weird having a dog follow me around, though I do find her comforting." Even as her brother tended to rub the bite marks, she tended to rub her scars from the various surgeries. One hand started rubbing the scars on her right leg as they were talking.

"My intro," Amber replied, "Was Cody coming up in wolf form while I was lost, and me feeling a connection. He made me feel safe and protected. Apparently, they had been asked to help find me by the Mounties. They then had me ride Cody, and they took me by helicopter here."

It sounded like Amber had a better intro than she had, "I didn't know until Zane and I were moved to a hospital near the pack. He had been bitten and I was trying to recover from the accident which killed my parents." Her hand was still stroking the scars, "I won't say anything about getting wolf blood to help my healing." She had to make a face, "Cody is a good-looking wolf. I think Oscar is a really cute wolf as well." Olivia made a face, "Don't tell him that since boys and cute don't get along."

Amber giggled, "They are both cute. Boys are silly they don't like cute. I can't wait till I can shift and go running with them." She added with a sigh.

Olivia groaned and covered her face with a hand, "Oh fudge! What is my cat going to think about my bringing home a wolfdog?" Hopefully Silly—yes that was her name –would treat Shelly like she did Oscar and consider him something to relax on. She was sure her cat would consider the wolfdog an inconvenience and not much else.

"Boys are weird that way. Oscar is really cute though he doesn't make much of a stink about the term. Zane does, so I call his wolf cute occasionally. Not often since I found teeth marks on the chair in my room." She didn't actually know if it was Zane or not, she assumed it was.

They quietly chatted until Oscar, Cody, and Shelly came back. Much like when Zane had first changed, Shelly trotted up behind Olivia and sniffed an ear. When Olivia squeaked, Shelly gave her an amused woof. She was one of the more playful young wolfdogs which tended to irritate the older ones, *Run fun.*

Olivia had to jerk and then glared at Shelly, "Not funny you! I will sic my cat on you when we get home." Shelly didn't seem worried and Olivia had to reach over and scratch her ears, "Why do I have a feeling I am going to have to hide my few remaining crutches from you?" Getting an ear wiggle as she wagged and panted didn't help Olivia, since she was sure Shelly was laughing at her.

Chapter 21 – WereNet Starts to Take Off...

Both Adam and Brook were at the next morning, as it dealt with the Wolfsbane they found. All the Alphas, and all the representatives from the other groups were there. It was a major concern.

Adam stood before them, as he had been the one most involved, other than the actual disposal.

"I am going to give the details, not in the order we found them, but in the chronological order." He said as he started, with his notes on paper instead of on the computer. "We were able to recover the records and notes from Alpha Night, so have a history."

Even Alpha Tyler and Alpha Tom were silent about it, as even they didn't want anyone using Wolfsbane.

"His wolfsbane program was started many decades ago, which when discussing it with the Elders, had even predated the Inter-Pack Treaty itself, they had been doing some secret breeding of some Wolfsbane plants, to make them as lethal as possible, while also producing more. They had started a refinement of it, to reduce it to make it more concentrated as well." He paused, "I am intentionally being vague, as the *how* they produced it is not being shared out, and even I don't have the details, the only two who know more were the two who made the process for the disposal. Even they had been Alpha-Commanded to share the details with others. As soon as the last of it was disposed, the last of the records were also destroyed. All of them had been on original papers, and nothing had ever been on any computer."

Many Alphas relaxed or nodded, as if someone was to want to do it, they would have to start from scratch.

"It seemed initially, the researchers were making it to be used defensively, and from the timing, it seemed that it started about when the Inter-Pack Treaty was started, it started to be more for a desire to dominate the other packs, and they started to target what he perceived as his strongest opponents, namely Arctic Shadow and MacLaren."

Rufus nodded when the others looked to him, as had been quietly told that part when it had been found, but it hadn't surprised him at all. He had opposed the granting them amnesty after the first offer, from how dismissive Alpha Night had been then, and since then, how he had tried to take over other packs, but never enough to get a full attack organized.

"They had to do it in secret, even from their own pack in general, as even their pack laws had it as being an instant death sentence, and several of the then Betas had dealt the blows to the pack members when they were found, even before the Alpha was aware they had been caught. All of those Betas had some sort of severe punishment applied afterwards, with them either being put down, or kicked out as a rogue. Brook and I believe it was for that action, from the Alpha's notes of how upset he was, even if the official records don't have any mention for it." Adam paused for the growls of agreement from the others. "For several decades, it seemed they just were working to make a stockpile of liquid wolfsbane, and there is no mention of active plans to use it."

"About a decade or two ago, it seemed some sort of agreement was made with the Nameless Pack, for them to assist with taking out the packs which were on either side of them." Adam stated, moving onto the next part. "The details of that are not really of any importance, but it was the start of when they started to do more active plans to go against the other packs. Alpha Night seemed to be wanting to have the Nameless Pack be the aggressor, and them just sit back and support from in hiding. While strong, he considered MacLaren to be less of an issue, as they seemed to not attack outside of their territory, except when supporting another pack in their own defence. The plans, in broad strokes, was to disrupt the packs, then while the treaty was trying to respond, to attack others with stealth."

Adam paused, but seemed nobody had any questions for him, "It seemed the plan was disrupted first, by a wolf from Night Depths, instead of taking only a portion of the supply, instead took the entire supply to the Nameless Pack, and then us taking out the Nameless Pack by attacking their initial attack before they could start their attack, and before they could recover the supply. It then had them trying to take it by force while we were dealing with the remnants of the Nameless Pack, then trying their own attack on MacLaren, which resulted in Alpha Night deciding death was preferable to defeat." Adam shook his head, "If he had accepted defeat, I was not ready to take over a pack, so would have left him with his pack, and just an agreement of not attacking."

Oscar leaned forward, "How concentrated was it?" He asked.

Alpha Gareth sighed, "A single drop or two would likely be enough to kill." He told them, "By my estimate, there was enough to kill every single Werewolf, of every pack on the globe, several times over. The barrel was melted down, and the resulting metal was then melted again, before being disposed of with the humans." No Were would want to be connected at all with even using the metal.

There was many shocked comments and many shudders as they imagined what could have happened. There were several comments about it, and several who asked about the records.

"These are the last of the records." Adam said, holding up the papers, "The rest of the papers have already been burned to ash."

At the end of the talk, Adam led the others outside the door, to a prepared fire, where he placed the papers into the fire. "I for one, hope to never have to deal with Wolfsbane again. It is one of the items I kept at an instant death, to be given by any Enforcer, Delta, Beta, Elder, or Alpha, regardless of their rank."

With the papers being ashes, they broke for a lunch break to get over the shocking details.

After lunch, Adam brought forward the network plans, starting with showing the results of the several penetration tests he has commissioned. All but the very first one showed totally secure, and even the first one only got through the first level before it was trapped. It may have got in, but it had also been detected internally.

There were now several packs which had been connected, and Adam was using this as a platform to get the idea out farther. The discussions would be going on beyond the conference, and each pack would need to be arranged separately.

He showed how the basic link had allowed for secure communication with unrelated pack, as soon as he corrected a fault in the settings, even without any further security. Most of the questions were technical, but one really stood out for him:

"How does this affect my pack's independence? Would we be giving control of the connection to anyone?" Irwin asked.

Adam shook his head, "It shouldn't affect it at all." He replied, having expected that sort of question, "Communication to the human networks would not be affected, as it only affects communication to other packs. Each pack, also, will have their own controls to turn it off or on independently. I didn't want any one group to dictate how the network will run, so it is designed to work between equals, not a leader and followers. Also, in no way will this network dictate how you have your internal network configured. There are recommendations, to support all the features and abilities, but if you don't want to have a part, you can skip it."

"Who will support it?" Another asked.

"Your own pack, generally." Adam offered. "I want to have at least two at each pack trained to do the support and will set up a system for the different packs to share the issues with the other techs, for issues they don't know how to fix. For major or complex issues, I am considering support contracts from my pack. But again, this would be voluntary and other packs who wanted could also offer tech support services. Or you could have your own pack trained to support your own equipment."

By the end, several of the packs looked like they were going to jump on, and it would mean more work to get them all going. Each would have to take it back to their pack to decide whether they do so or not. Part of the papers provided in the session included all the details for how to set up their network connection and what needed to be arranged to connect to a hub site. It also had a link for if someone decided they wanted to be a hub site, but the requirements were much greater, and he doubted any here would consider it. Each pack generally would connect to the nearest hub site, but they could connect to one farther away without any issues.

*****

Adam smiled as the buses arrived. Many Alphas had joined Brook and him on the run up, deciding it was preferable to sitting on a bus for several hours. With the powerful wolves being their only companions, they could set the pace much faster, and with only minimal breaks.

Several Alphas were panting heavily and were looking with new respect as Adam and Brook were not looking tired at all, just exercised when they arrived. It demonstrated they clearly had the speed and power, and plenty of endurance, to be their equal. Those weaker Alphas were glad they just clearly wanted to live peacefully with their neighbours, and didn't want to push others around.

Still, the runners had beaten the bus by a good time, and Rufus, Oscar, and Grant had helped Adam set up the table and chairs for the signing. The others wandered, looking at the site, or with a few who just lay there, catching their breath.

*****

The pack let out a very loud howl as Adam signed the first copy of the Inter-Pack Treaty, making it official. Adam and Brook signed off on several copies, as every other Alpha did as well. Tyler and Tom were nowhere to be found, and the rest just shrugged it off, as it seemed they were boycotting the signing, as a way of saying they didn't approve of it. Irwin had been surprised they even bothered to show up to the conference, but thought now, it was just to try to block the joining. They hadn't left with the runners and hadn't been on the buses which came up, so were still down at MacLaren. As was usual, their staff had brought food into their rooms but hadn't seen them come out yet.

After the signing, Adam and Brook took them for a tour around the site, showing off the basic plan for the pack house, which the exterior on the first floor was done, and they were starting on the second. The inside was currently on hold, as they had enough done so the pack could start sheltering there if needed, and wanted the exterior done. Insulation was being installed, but the walls were still open, as the utilities hadn't been run yet.

The alphas were all drooling over the size of the gym which they had, and the fact they had a greenhouse, and space reserved for a garden. Much of the natural forest had been left around, where they could. Joshua talked about where they were going to be planting more trees, to replace those they had to cut down for equipment accessing the various sites, and where they were keeping some meadows. The inner area right beside the house was going to be grassed, and they told everyone how they used it to identify where the young pups were not to pass. If they were caught outside it, they knew they would be punished.

Adam and Brook fielded many questions, the ones about their security setup, they deflected, answered only vaguely, and the rest they refused to discuss. Other packs had no need to know the details, as it was a pack secret. As such, they didn't show them the cave they had set up to hold any captives, or the secured areas for the security office, and server room.

Many of the elders kept asking when they could move in. It was getting close. They were told definitely by fall; they would have it done enough they could move in. The moment the pack house exterior walls were closed up, they were going to start work on the kitchen. The large propane tank was already settled in its enclosure, as Lupita had begged for gas stove and grill in the kitchen, and he had given in, for some more treats. He did have wires run for electricity, but left the spaces with blank faceplates, and no breakers in the panels, just the ends of the wires capped. It meant they didn't have to do major renovations to make the switch.

They did show off the fact every single roof was going to be covered with solar panels or solar heating collectors, and both on some. There were even a few wind turbines which were going to be installed, with a few right on the main lodge, as it was the tallest building there. They did have a power run into the property, and with a couple who were Master Electricians, they had wired up the link from the pole they had set up at the edge of the property, to the power bunker. Right now, the meter was showing negative, as they were generating more power than they needed, even with charging the battery banks.

Several Alphas looked impressed and thoughtful, as it reduced the costs to run the power, from being a major bill to being something which generated credits, at least in summer. Even with the large start-up costs, it worked out in their favour in the long run, if done right.

Eventually, they wrapped up the day, and after a good meal which Lupita made for them, most headed back on the buses. Adam had found his tolerance for vehicles had dwindled and preferred to run instead.

Getting back, they relaxed a bit and talked to some of the pack, but soon headed to bed, after a good shower. Even though a wolf didn't sweat, they did occasionally get dirty, or twigs stuck which they couldn't shake free.

*****

The next morning, the Alphas decided to talk about the pack house, and even Tom and Tyler were there. It seemed they not only wanted the information but were there to heckle and belittle Adam and they ignored Brook, and the other females.

Many of the Alphas were very interested in the ideas of being green, and by reducing the reliance on outside sources, for stuff like power. "I almost think you're a doomsday prepper." Oscar teased, getting much laughter from the others. It seemed he had multiple redundancies for everything.

Adam grinned, "I have to say I did take some of their ideas when designing many of the systems," He agreed, "But I also took ideas from the recommendations to survive forest fires. The exterior, if you noticed is going to be stone, and the roofs steel plates with fireproof insulation. The steel shutters on the windows as well, but they also double for security in case of an attack." It caught many of the Alpha's interest.

Many were very interested in the 'feature', as it would allow the buildings themselves to be secured well, even without anything further to help them. It would make sure there was time for the pack to all get to the safe rooms if the worst happens.

"The buildings are rated for a strong earthquake," Adam continued, "And for withstanding a firestorm, although they would need some work after, as items like the wind and solar would be destroyed." Taking a breath, "The disaster which, to me, is unlikely but could happen is a massive solar flare. I have some procedures which would attempt to save the equipment and systems, along with working on long-term plans if it does happen, as it would damage the ozone layer. Others, I would love to do, but right now are too pricy, but have left provisioning to do them in the future. This building was designed to be easily upgraded as new technology or ideas come out."

The rest of the morning was discussion on how to do various retrofits on pack buildings to make them better. Some were considering the shutters, and they were basically an off the shelf system, with the automation to the controls added.

Many of the packs, as like MacLaren and Wild Valley, were deep in the forest, so there was a need to secure them from forest fires. Lately, the fires had been larger, and more intense. If their building were better secured against it, the more likely they could survive them without losing everything.

"One thing I didn't need to worry as much about," Adam said at the end, going back to the 'preppers' thought, "Was too much about medicine, or food. I did work out plans for those, but if the worst happens, Wild Valley would expand to take over more territory, and would work with other packs as needed to supplement hunting and what the garden and greenhouse would provide." Two different next-alphas there kept quiet but smiled at each other, as they now understood the 'contingency agreement' Wild Valley had done with them, even though they weren't very close, and which in it had them expanding to protect some of the human farms which were on their territory or just outside it; it was to secure the crops. They silently discussed it and would bring it to the Alpha and Elders. Both shared the idea they might expand the security to the farm owners, and even let them into the secrets. Some of their packmates already worked as farm hands, maybe some more could do it?

*****

Alpha Tyler was honestly looking for a fight. That damn pup-Alpha had been ignoring him for the entire since he arrived five days before. Add to the insult he had been given when he had wanted the pup to meet with him months ago, he wanted a fight. Who it was, he didn't care; he just wanted a fight. He didn't bother caring he would be breaking guesting laws, which forbade fights outside of a challenge circle; as far as he was concerned, since he was Alpha and made the laws, they didn't apply to him. He didn't bother heading to the gym where he could just ask for a bout of any there, as that was beneath him; it would show a weakness of needing another.

The meeting had broken for lunch. The details they had shown that morning, which pup had designed for his pack were somewhat interesting, but there was no need to protect the weak; if they didn't heed the warnings to get to the safe room, or were too far from it, it was no loss. The size of the pack he was designing for was obscene; there was no way to control so many! They needed to be watched, or they could rebel, as every wolf wanted to be Alpha, and if they didn't, they were only good to do cleaning. From the way it looked, if he wanted to try to take it over, he'd have to sneak the force inside the house before it was detected; hard but not impossible. You just needed the patience to work out the patrols. The automated sensors he dismissed; those were easy for a wolf to get around, if they were competent.

The afternoon meeting, he was going to skip, as it was on how to better hide the packs from those pesky humans who spread their stench, noise, and filth over the once beautiful planet; he had better things to do. His thought was they should have a fatal accident from an 'animal attack' then be left to be found at the edge of it, as soon as they were found within his territory. He walked outside and almost snarled. There was the scent of one of those pathetic changed-humans. Nothing better than jumped up, oversized dogs. It seemed there were several around, fouling the air of this pack. If he had known there would be many here, he would never have come, as the only good use for them was doing the slop work for the pack; work which was beneath any born-wolf. They weren't even worth taking to bed since their stench was nauseating. Once the scent had crossed his nose, he looked around the people standing around outside.

As his eyes were travelling around his eyes stopped on a couple. It was one of those pansy ass American wolves. They lived in large houses, drove everywhere, and their winters were barely even worth noticing. The pup was there as an acting Alpha for his soft pathetic American pack. The packs also submitted to a *council* which could dictate to the Alpha what they could do, and none of them cared about how an Alpha should be at the top and answer to nobody. He had managed to get some information from the one playing as the Alpha and he was the senior Beta enforcer. Even worse one of the pups he had brought was a changed-human and was dating a low dominance wolf.

It was what he would expect from a changed-human. What he, the boy, thought his dominance was, it was a joke. He would never be as good as a born wolf; they would always think about being human first.

Dating and mating with a low dominance wolf was the best he could do, "Those American wolves are so pathetic. Had to bring pups along with them for some stupid reason. So pathetic to bring a changed-human as well. Not even a mate-changed wolf." He wasn't being loud when he said it, but he wasn't being quiet either. He hadn't taken a close sniff so hadn't noticed the tell-tale scent of being force-changed by a rogue, nor would he care, except as another way to sneer at him.

Zane heard the man and stiffened. After looking at Tyler he knew he was an alpha but for the comment alone, he wasn't worth respecting, "Thank God most of the wolves here are worth respecting. Alpha Adam and his mate are some really good people." He told Tessa making sure to be loud enough to be overheard.

She had heard the other as well and leaned against Zane and shivered. She had seen the wolf, and he made her feel scared. There was just something about him which told her to keep her distance, the pack juniors had warned her as well to stay away from him too, *Don't Zane, please don't make him angry.* She didn't think her team leader could go against him at all.

Tyler knew the comment was directed at him and he snarled at the brat. He was Alpha and it alone demanded respect. He had been an Alpha for over two centuries and deserved the respect of lower dominance wolves, "Brat! You aren't anything, just a crappy changed-human. Don't even have a mate to make it somewhat understandable. Nothing but an oversized dog. Why the she-pup is even interested in you is hard to understand. Can't she do better than you?" He sneered.

When the man insulted Tessa, Zane lost it. This shit head was denigrating his team and his girlfriend, "Lousy excuse for a flea-infested, mange-ridden wolf." He screamed as he launched himself at Tyler; his eyes started to almost glow with his wolf being forward in his mind, a hair short of causing a shift. It was stupid since he wasn't an adult or near Tyler's dominance nor had he had anywhere the amount of training to fight or strength which Tyler had, but this was his team the fucker was disrespecting. When he hit the man, it was anything goes. An elbow strike here, a knee there, a fist somewhere else. Even his wolf was helping provide extra strength and speed as they worked together. This wasn't a weak human who he had to hold back on to keep the police out of it, and from the stuff he had discussed with Alpha Adam, it had brought back all the memories of the bullies from school, who had attacked Tessa at the mall; this one was just another bully who needed a lesson. Here he could let go and not worry about needing to pull the hits to not kill them, as this wolf was acting like a bully, not an Alpha.

Adam had heard the exchange, but was staying just to the side, as he had to clean up the stuff from his presentation in the room. When Alpha Tyler decided to not only insult the visiting pup, but also start in on Tessa, his wolf started to growl. As an Alpha, he felt the need to protect all wolves, and protecting the Theta who rarely fought was doubled, add in it was protecting pups, and even he was aroused and couldn't stand and watch any more. He started to step forward. If he wanted to fight a changed-wolf, he'd learn better, as he would take the fight.

"Shit!" Escaped his mouth as Zane started to move just as he stepped out the door, showing they weren't alone. He dropped everything, not caring about the computer or the mess of papers, *Alert! Alpha Fight!* He called out to Gareth, Maria, Brook, and Martin as he started to move to intervene. He reached them as Tyler was just starting to come out of the stupor with the suddenness of the attack, but not soon enough.

Adam growled, "Stop!" Putting the full force of his alpha powers behind it, as he had never had to do before. He pulled Zane back behind him, as he moved forward, even as his power hit the pup. He felt the other Alphas move in behind him, as he stood in front of the young wolf, blocking the Alpha from reaching the pup. Both the human and wolf were in agreement; they would not allow the Alpha to touch him as long as they were alive.

"What was this fight about? You are both guests here! Alpha Tyler, as an Alpha, you should be above brawling. And with a pup! Does your pack not honour and protect pups?" Adam growled. He spoke loudly, so the others could hear. There was some noise behind him, but he was dealing with this wolf, and didn't dare turn away.

"He attacked me!" Alpha Tyler defended, "It was an unprovoked attack!" He tried to excuse his actions. He really had thought nobody else was around; the Alphas had said they were eating with the pack, and thought they had all left. If he had known any Alpha was there, he would have gone elsewhere.

Zane growled, "He was insulting my team, me, then the choice of Tessa to be with me." Even though Adam had stopped the fight almost as it started, Tyler had still hit him hard several times. It had broken his jaw and speaking was a bitch. The growl was forced out by his wolf as well. They had tried to jump back at the man, but someone had caught him before he could do anything else. Zane was doing everything he could to get free. His wolf was as angry as he was. What made it worse was it was the memories being brought up. It was making him think back to feeling like a monster.

"Was that so?" Adam asked Tyler gently, as if about the weather. Both he and his wolf agreed this Alpha wasn't worthy of his title.

"No, I never said anything like that!" Alpha Tyler lied.

Adam growled, "I happened to hear what was said, as I was around the corner. *And* I can smell it. You just lied."

Alpha Tyler winced before he could smooth his face; he hadn't realized Adam had heard. Others growled behind Adam, also smelling the lie.

"Alphas; should Alpha Tyler have his guest-right revoked?" He called back, not taking his eyes off the wolf—he refused to think of him as an Alpha now, as Alphas were truthful at all times, and *protected* all pups. He was calling him a wolf mostly a courtesy, as he couldn't think of something low enough to attack a pup. Even dung had a purpose, to return unused nutrients to the enviroment, and Tyler seemed to have no purpose except to oppose everything and everyone. He didn't want to have a fight, and chance escalating the issue farther.

"Yes." Stated Alpha Rufus, "Arctic Shadow agrees he broke his guest-bond with a fight outside the ring."

"Yes." Agreed Alpha Oscar, "Forest Edge supports it."

"Yes." Echoed Alpha Grant, "Longview supports it."

"No." Disagreed Alpha Tom, leader of Sentinel Star, "It was just a pup, and a changed-wolf! They shouldn't have attacked an Alpha. He was just applying a punishment." With a changed-wolf, any punishment was allowed, in his view; they needed a much stiffer punishment to have it stick.

"Yes." Josh growled, "As the representative of Fossil Valley, I agree." Alpha Tyler snubbed him every time he could, as not being Canadian, and not actually 'being an Alpha' in such he didn't have a pack, even if he technically had the rank. And he kept demeaning him by calling him a 'pup', even though he hadn't been one for several decades.

"Yes." Agreed Gareth. Since it was his pack doing the hosting, he could revoke the guesting for any. "Alpha Tyler, you and your pack are no longer welcome here. You have one hour to leave."

"This is outrageous! I refuse! I challenge Alpha Adam for the right to stay."

Josh stepped forward, "No! I will accept the challenge, since Mike is a Beta and under my protection. I am an Alpha Heir. I will deal with this since I took them under my protection, since they are junior to me." He hadn't directly but he was senior to them and had arranged for them to come, "Stupid fucking wolf. I will thrash your tail and keep it as a souvenir of being in Canada."

Adam gave Tyler a feral grin, "I will step aside and allow Josh to accept your challenge on my behalf. When do you wish for the fight, as the challenged, Josh?"

"Now works for me, Alpha. I don't see any reason to delay the fight. He insulted a wolf, denigrated his girlfriend, and indicated American wolves are shit. I will deal with him now and give Zane or Mike his tail to take care of the insult. I will thrash him for the insult paid to us." Josh's voice was layered with derision and anger. The other wolf had insulted a pup and his girlfriend. Goddess only knew what he might say about Oscar and Olivia, her being his human mate and female. He was going to frigging destroy this sorry excuse of a wolf and beat his alpha title into the dirt. What might happen with the other's pack or territory didn't cross his mind as angry as he was.

Even as he was talking, he was removing a number of weapons from his body, placing them on a nearby table. Several knives, a pistol (which was a restricted firearm), brass knuckles (which was a prohibited weapon in Canada), and even a shillelagh... That garnered him some attention since why did he have a 4-inch fire hose section with a handle? Josh didn't bother removing the clothing as he called forth his midform, "Shall we dance old man?" The clothing was shredding as he was changing.

Behind him, Zane jerked since he hadn't seen this form before. He knew of it, but it was something he couldn't do yet and hadn't seen as of yet either. Their pack didn't use it much, as they were close to humans, so had more chance of being seen; a wolf was easier to excuse away. When Josh had finished changing, he was beyond massive in the boy's eyes. No wonder this place had high ceilings! Not only was he much taller, but he was also clearly more than just fit. The muscles were clear, even under the fur coating them, and the claws were long and looked sharp.

"Not in the hall!" Gareth barked. "Outside there is a challenge ring. You will fight there!"

Josh nodded, as he stalked out of the house and to the ring. When he reached it, he turned and bellowed out a howl at the other, "Will go down!" Since his wolf was with him, he wasn't the most coherent. Even his wolf was showing the derision for the other. He was nothing more than slime and maybe a runny dog turd, "Come fight, back down and I take yours!" He was alpha and he knew what fighting the other could mean. Even being from a different country, he knew what taking an Alpha down meant. If he won, the pack and territory would be his to do with as he wished.

The two burliest Alphas had to nearly drag Tyler out to the challenge circle, since he was refusing to go without help, as he tried to get out of the fight. Alpha to Alpha challenges, even when dealing with one who was the Next Alpha, could not be rescinded once accepted. Alpha Tyler had to fight. If he lost, he could lose his pack, lose the territory but keep the wolves of his pack, or the winner could decide to not touch the pack. Since Josh was not the Alpha in charge of a pack, his pack was safe and untouchable.

Molly stood next to Josh, and she was growling as well even as she was holding Zane back from doing something stupid. She could tell he was hurt and looked at Brook, "Medic! He is hurt and needs to be seen immediately."

Brook growled as she took her eyes off Tyler and realised the extent of what had happened, *Healer McCoy to the challenge circle, STAT. Injured pup.* She moved to look at him, *Broken Jaw, I can see. Has other injuries.* She nodded, "Healer is on the way, and will be right here." She put her hand on his shoulder, "Stand down pup, this is for the Alphas to deal with." Her growl turned to a snarl. "If *he* survives, I challenge him for the attack!" She advised the gathered pack. There was never a reason to break bones of a pup. Broken bones during a training session, especially those who were training to be enforcers, could have accidents, but never for a punishment.

Many of the other alphas echoed the growl in agreement. To deliberately cause enough harm to a pup, let alone a guest, to need medical attention was unthinkable. Many were out for his blood now. If Tyler beat one wolf, he would have another take their place before he could leave the circle.

It was all Zane could do not to keep growling even louder. The fucker had insulted his team and his girlfriend. The hit to his jaw *hurt* but damn it: they were his to protect, "Mine! My team, mine to take care of. I will fucking kill you!" He was in agony from the hit as he started to feel it, but this was his people; he had taken responsibility for them and that meant protecting them to his last breath and then lamenting he didn't have any more. His wolf was forward, and it showed in his eyes, even as his wolf helped to supress the pain. This was no human he had to allow to live or could cause major issues with their pack, this was another wolf, who had attacked his team, then his girlfriend and junior wolf. He *would* protect them with his life.

Mike came over and carefully placed his hands on Zane's face, "Zane look at me." When he spoke his dominance showed, "Stop. Get healed, we will deal with this, as we did with David and his friend. Love you and take care of you. Let the medic deal with your jaw. Let Tessa comfort you. This is an order from your uncle and a more dominant wolf."

Zane wanted to keep fighting but with the order he couldn't. He finally lowered his eyes, "Yes Beta, we will do as you command." His voice was low yet still angry with a growl. Even as he was struggling to deal with what his uncle had ordered his team surrounded him having felt the anger and the injury and wanting to help and comfort him.

Melody wrapped an arm around the two of them, "We are here for you Zane. Tessa is as well." Even as she was talking Olivia worked her way into the hug.

Brook waved the healer over as he came with a couple of burly attendants, and a huge medical bag.

Putting his hand on Zane's shoulder, "Broken Jaw, three cracked ribs, hairline fracture in his arm. Who's the wolf who attacked the pup!" The last was a growl which boded bad for the one who caused it. When Zane tried to talk, "Later; let me heal you first." He ordered as he turned back to the pup. Turning to Brook for a moment, "Hold him." He ordered.

Once Brook held Zane around the forehead, the healer moved, "This will hurt for a minute, but try not to move." He quickly re-aligned the broken pieces of his jaw and held them in place as he applied his special power which made him a healer, fusing them into the correct positions. Moving to his ribs, he made sure they were still in position, then added some healing. His arm didn't need anything, as it would be healed by morning as if nothing happened. "There. How's the jaw?

Zane did his best to not move even though he couldn't due to Brook's strength. When the man adjusted the broken jaw, he had to scream. It hurt like... He couldn't come up with the term needed. It bloody frigging hurt to high heaven; it hurt more than when he was hit! Didn't they believe in painkillers? Once it had been set, he almost collapsed in Brook's and Molly's arms as the pain mostly stopped, going from a sharp pain which shot through his chest with every breath, to a dull ache. As he was struggling to breathe as his ribs were healed, having Tessa hold him helped a great deal, "Man that friggin' sucked." His jaw was clenched, and his voice was strained as he spoke.

Mike looked at the healer, "Tyler was the one who did this. He insulted my pup, his team, and..." He had started out talking normally but ended up with a mean and nasty growl. If Josh hadn't offered to deal with the wolf, Mike would have. It might have ended up ugly for him, but he had to take care of his family. It was all he could do to keep from changing and doing something stupid. Even with ordering Zane to not do anything, he was struggling not to himself.

The healer nodded, and scanned Zane again with his power, "Take it easy for a couple days, and be light with that arm till morning, or the fracture can turn into a break. Chew gently when you eat tonight. Shifting will help speed the healing. If the pain gets worse in any way, come see me."

Even with Tessa and his team comforting him he was snarling and growling, "Will do healer." God, he needed something to do to release the anger.

*****

Josh heard Molly call for a medic and his anger grew even more, even if he didn't take his eyes off Tyler. One didn't hurt a pup for any reason. Discipline was one thing but to actually hurt one enough to need to call for a medic? It was a totally different issue. He could feel his wolf drawing strength from their pack. Once the challenge was over, he was going to need to call his father but at the moment the challenge was going to happen. Even as the other was almost tossed into the circle, Josh leapt towards him.

The fight was brutal, and he received a great deal of damage. The other was an alpha and older but when all was said and done Josh was the one standing. The other was laying there half unconscious and was barely moving. Josh had broken his hand punching the bastard in the face to knock him out, "Damn it! No wonder he is still around, his head has to be made of granite." He said as he tried not to shake the broken hand, as it would hurt it more, "Challenge accepted, dealt with, and I am the winner." His wolf howled their satisfaction of winning even as they were trying to heal from the wounds.

Not including his broken hand, Josh was bloody, had broken ribs, a broken arm, a possible fracture of a leg, and probably internal injuries from being punctured by claws. He thought he might have re-injured his lung as he was having a tough time catching his breath. The other was looking as bad or worse since there were a number of puncture wounds, claw marks, and other injuries.

The Healer was waiting as Josh stepped out of the circle. Touching him to diagnose, "Don't shift, and come with us. I need you to come to medical." He ordered, ignoring the fact he was ordering an Alpha. In MacLaren, even the Alphas respected the Healers in matters of medical, as otherwise how to get an Alpha dealt with?

Josh snarled even as he held his paw out to Malcom, "Phone, need to call dad." The moment the phone was in his paw, he made the call, having to use his claws, "Dad, Alpha challenge, will call later. Healer glaring at me." He handed the phone back before almost groaning and ended up collapsing in Malcom's arms. Josh hadn't completely healed from the injury to his chest. If he had been human, he would have been dead shortly after the impact, let alone made it back to their pack house. If he had by some miracle, made it back, would have been in a hospital bed for weeks, with a cast wrapping around his body.

Molly released Zane and moved over to help with Josh, "Stupid male wolves! Still not healed and you pull this crap? I am going to tie you to the bed until you are healed." She looked at the Healer, "Still regrowing his lung after dealing with the rogues. Too stupid for his own good." For good measure she did give him a good kiss, "And too honourable for his own good as well." She said quietly, with a fondness which the others could hear. He still was refusing to notice the mate-bond.

Healer McCoy nodded, "I can sense that. I have healing talent. It's part of the reason I am having him come to medical. I am going to do a full physical and make sure he hasn't re-injured his lung while I deal with the rest of his injuries." As he said it, a were-sized gurney with large air-filled cart tires to handle the rough ground was pushed up. Glaring at Josh, he pointed at it, "Lay down. You don't want to piss me off too."

Molly growled at Josh, "He won't give you any problems or else... I will deal with him if he does." She and Malcom helped get him on the gurney, "Be a good wolf or else!" She was glaring at him even as they were moving him into the house.

Josh was avoiding her eyes as she was growling at him. The fight had been needed but damn it, he was hurting. Even as he was laying down, he could feel the lung aching, "Yes ma'am. I will listen to an irritated she-wolf." He closed his eyes and started taking some slow deep breaths to control the pain.

Another gurney was wheeled up and Alpha Tyler was loaded without much care. Word of the Alpha who had caused injury to a visitor, and a pup, had already reached them. Most were not going to stand for it. He was strapped down tightly to the gurney, ignoring his injuries.

"Take Tyler to the secured room. We Alphas will have to decide his fate once Josh is released." Gareth ordered. The medics paled but nodded, the room was mostly used for rogues who they were providing medical care, hopefully to bring their sanity back, but was designed to handle an Alpha as well, if needed. Usually if an Alpha was put in a se-cured room after a fight, it was for them to decide further punishment, and when it involved a pup, their choices were very limited, and the time was more spent on what to do with the body and any other fallout from their removal.

*****

Zane was still growling even as they took the other away. It was hurting but his wolf couldn't help it. They were still bloody furious, and it showed. Below the anger, what had been said was gaining even more foot hold as it seemed to be stuck on a repeat in his head. Even his uncle was being held back by several of the local pack as he growled and snarled. He was swearing and cursing as well even though Josh had taken care of the issue.

Zane was struggling to keep his human shape since his wolf wanted out as well. If Mike hadn't commanded them to behave, he would have lost it already, "Damn it! Uncle, help? Going to lose it!" He staggered away from everyone, and it was obvious he was having trouble remaining human. All the others growling around him wasn't helping either.

Chapter 22 – Adam Talks

Adam stepped forward, "I'll take it from here," He reassured Mike, seeing Mike having his own issues. "Zane, shift and follow." He ordered, as he pulled his clothes off, and headed off at a hard pace for Zane. His wolf needed to be tired out, as he was still worked up. For a wolf, a hard run was a good way to relax or calm down; hopefully, it would be enough for Zane.

Zane was already mid shift when Adam told him to follow. Even with the injuries he ran his ass off. He and his wolf needed the run, and they knew nobody from his team would follow. The pain from the change was bad as his body focused on speeding the healing of the wounds. Once changed he did his best to run his anger and fears out.

They ran in a roundabout route, but climbed up into the ridge, eventually getting to the hidden hot spring. Adam was panting a little; Zane was fast! He had to work hard to wear out the younger wolf, but it worked.

Shifting to human, Adam slipped into the hot water. "Come, relax here." he asked. "It is nice and hot, so should relax you, and will keep you from cramping up. Knowing he was still a little body-shy, he turned to look out over the ridge, showing a nice valley.

When they reached the hot spring, his wolf jumped in before they shifted. "Darn wolf! Now it is going to take forever for the fur to dry out. I am going to make you sleep on the floor tonight." He was grumbling to his wolf, even as he started to relax. Damn it, why did that idiot have to pull this shit? He had started being comfortable being a wolf. Hearing the bastard's comments brought back memories of thinking he was a monster, like the rogue. His team, family, and Luna had worked hard to help him, and the bastard had brought it all back.

Adam smiled and joked, "Didn't you know our fur was shake and wear? We won't get sick from it."

"How do you deal with being a wolf, Alpha? I am still trying to deal with this and that bastard... Damn it to hell!" He hated swearing but right now he needed advice and to talk to someone. Mike was his guardian and, in a way, his superior. Adam wasn't. He was a changed wolf as well. Even if he had been changed by his mate, he was somewhat like Zane was, as he wasn't born with his wolf, and could relate better or so he hoped. He felt somewhat comfortable talking to him. It was almost like a Luna, but also the rock-solid protection of Zane's own Alpha.

Adam gave Zane a sad look, "Part of what being wolf is... is thinking of the pack instead of yourself. Once I stopped looking at myself being 'me-first' and being 'us-together', many of the differences between wolf and humans made sense. In a wolf pack, it is Pack-togetherness which makes wolves strong. Individually, we are not very strong. Look at the way your team helps support you when you are down. I am sure if you asked, your wolf would think of them as part of you."

Zane simply couldn't look at Adam. When he finally spoke his voice was tense, "Do you have any idea how hard it was to let anyone other than Uncle Mike and Olivia close? It took me breaking down in the Luna's arms before I could really start to deal with it. Even knowing I took responsibility for Tessa and Oscar as my junior wolves was so damn difficult." His hands were making fists as he was talking.

Sitting back, "When I lost my father, I was angry and upset for years. I didn't feel I had much support and was angry for him abandoning me. He had broken promises to me. If you let them, you have a pack which will surround you to help. Your team will be the first there for you." After stopping to let it sink in, he shared part of his own story, "Partly, when I was turned, I was looking for a change in my life, and the fact I could completely change my life was one way. I accepted I wasn't human any longer. I didn't try to cling to my human beliefs or ideas and embraced the pack's way. I *did* question those beliefs, and a couple have changed already, to the better of all. Others, once they were explained to me better, I accepted them. Your turn is totally different. The fact you were under for most of it didn't let you grow into it, and it wasn't your choice and something you wanted to happen, makes it harder to deal with. I do understand how hard it is to let others get close, as you then can be hurt. But turn it around, if you do let them get close, you then have many you can lean on for help. I am very sure they are just waiting to help you any way they can, and from what I can see, they are not going to wait for you to ask for it."

"I didn't even know beings like us existed. I woke up with a wolf in my mind. I felt I was a monster like the one who raped me." To him being force-changed was much like being raped. It wasn't with his choice though he had never said it before; he had never been willing to even think of it that way. It wasn't a sexual rape, but it was a very physical and mental rape, "It almost killed me knowing my family was dead. If it hadn't been for Liv and Mike, I don't know what I would have done. I don't know where I would be now." Zane had to cover his eyes as he started crying. It had been so hard to admit it was what it felt like.

Adam moved over and pulled the pup into his lap, giving him a shoulder to cry on. "I too didn't know they existed, although I did think there were way too many stories of them for werewolves to not exist. I learned they exist when the wolf I rescued from the rocks shifted into a woman while I was trying to figure out what to do with it. But it is a story for another time." Thinking for a moment, he agreed the forced turning by the rogue was like a rape: it totally changed his outlook to life and caused an irreparable change to him. He'd never be the same as before it happened, nor was he given a choice; it was forced onto him.

Adam decided for the bare truth, and not to beat around the bush with it; Zane felt to him like he wanted the full truth, and he would share it as he had been taught by the elders. "Without your sister and uncle, and the support of your pack, you probably would have gone insane, gone rogue, yourself. Then if the pack which found you couldn't get through to you at all, you would have been put down as gently as they could." He said bleakly, speaking the bare truth. "If they got to you before you went insane, they would have given you counselling, and a private secure area to come to terms to your new life, and you would be kept there until you went totally insane or till you recovered."

Adam sighed, "Those who survive, like you did, from rogues are very rare. Gareth said you are currently one of four rogue-turned wolves alive on the continent. Most don't survive the turning, and those who do, often the rogue kills them himself, either because the new wolf tries to take them down or from a second encounter, or they go totally insane and get put down. None have survived outside of a pack. The bonds of being in a pack help ground and centre you, to keep you functional enough to heal."

All Zane could do was cry. He had finally admitted he felt like he had been raped by that frigging bastard. Even leaning against a male didn't distract him from what he was thinking. The tears hurt as he was crying since they felt like they were being ripped from his deepest soul. Even as he was leaning into the hug he was curling up in a small ball and crying his heart out. Being held by an Alpha allowed him to relax, as he knew deep down this Alpha cared and would give his life to protect him. He also understood him in ways nobody raised in a pack could. He had also lost someone close to him as a human, so could understand the loss in a way another could never do so, without the loss. The loss to those in the pack, they had much more support, so it wasn't the same.

What he hadn't realized was Tessa had followed them though it took her far longer to reach them. She moved forward and looked at Adam. She was obviously concerned about Zane, *Help my Team Leader, Alpha.* She begged before she changed form and settled down on the other side of Zane though he didn't seem to notice at the moment.

From what she could tell the tears were from his deepest heart and they were hurting him and her as well.

Adam nodded at the plea, *I'm trying. He is hurt soul-deep, and it is going to take decades to totally heal. The rogue stole his very identity when he changed him. He no longer could call himself a human. That his family was torn apart is a total separate wound on top of it and is hard to separate the two wounds to his mind and soul.* He replied sadly. His own wolf was pressed forward, wanting to help the pup, but knowing it would take a long time to heal. Some of it had festered and would take many tears to bleed the poisons so he could recover. "Zane, you are a good wolf, you are very much a leader, and I will share what help I can, whenever you need it." *If he wants to join my pack, I will do whatever is needed to be done* Adam promised himself and would only remember years later.

Tessa had heard much of what Zane had said before she entered the clearing. It tore her heart out that Zane was still this angry and upset over what had happened. She had seen him break down with the Luna, she had seen him try and deal with his emotions. He was still healing, and it hurt her badly since she was so close to him, "Thank you Alpha. I think this is the first he has really talked to anyone about this outside the family. He is my team leader, and I do love him. He protected me from some bullies, and I can't explain just what it means to me." She pressed her face against his back as she was sending, *Love you Zane, my boyfriend and my team leader. Let him help.*

Right now, Zane wasn't in a place to really listen to Adam talk since he was crying his heart out. It was the first time, even considering the Luna, he had admitted what it felt like to have been changed without his consent. As a male, he had been struggling with the idea of what being changed had felt like; he had not been able to find the right words to give voice to it. He still had times he felt like a monster such as the one which changed him. Even knowing his team and family loved him unconditionally, it was a very hard admission.

Adam just leaned back and kept his arms around Zane, letting him cry himself out. He was a safe male, one who wasn't close enough it would embarrass him but was one he was willing to trust while he was at his most vulnerable. Even his wolf felt protected, allowing them to show their hurts.

Tessa sat on the other side of Zane and simply held on. She was going to do what she could to help. What Zane had told Adam she didn't know but it was obviously very deep and hurt. She had spent enough time with him to know there was something still bothering him. It had something to do with his being turned but he had refused to speak about it.

We might be out here for a while; Zane is fairly broken up right now. He let Brook know. *Let Mike know I have Zane and Tessa here with me.* He let his concern show but made sure none of what he had been told passed on.

Will do. The Alphas are wondering how he's doing... Well, other than Tom, who is complaining about Josh beating Tyler. Mike let them know Zane was the rogue-turned. They want his input on what he wants to happen to Tyler. Brook replied, showing her disgust with Tom and Tyler.

Eventually Zane calmed down. Adam sighed, thinking it would take more work and likely he'd break down again, "Tyler is not worthy of being Alpha in my mind. He was taunting you hard, clearly wanting a fight. I noticed he was very surprised with your sudden attack. I know *I* was. I was also impressed on the skills you have already. Don't look at me for how fast wolves get skills; I have a secret I cannot share which helped me advance fast." He let out a growl, "The fact he attacked to hurt you broke several convents: first you are a guest, second he is a guest in another pack, and this was not a challenge, third you are an under-age wolf—not going to call you a pup, as I have seen you don't like the term." He took a breath, "Brook says that once Josh is finished in Medical, they will be sitting down. The laws would allow Josh to take the pack and territory, and even make Tyler a Lone wolf. The attack on you adds making him a Rogue as an option. Our local treaty would allow him to be sentenced to death for the attack as well. Did you want me to pass anything on to her, so they know your wishes, Zane?" Brook already had his thoughts on the matter. If he had the room, he'd want to take in the members of the Feral Star who were willing to abide by his rules, but even taking in the fifty which the pack was said to have was not possible till the new pack house was ready.

*****

When Brook had told him Zane was talking to Adam, Mike almost collapsed against a tree in relief. The healers had been worried since Zane was still hiding or resisting talking about something. What it was they weren't sure but had sensed it was something to do with an emotional issue. As of now all the injuries caused by the rogue and getting hit had healed. All that was left was the bite mark which Zane worked hard not to pay attention to, and it would not start to fade from a fresh-looking red scar as long as the rogue lived. "Thank the Goddess. Keep me updated but what he tells the Alpha is between them." He was torn between offering to give Tyler a silver nitrate suppository or hoping even though it had been hard on the boy, he would finish talking about it.

*****

Zane leaned against the Alpha, his wolf felt very safe and comforted between him and Tessa, "I don't care Alpha. I don't want to deal with it anymore. I think I am going to go back to the room and relax." Even if it was just for a short time, he knew his team would find him. This was something he could never speak about again.

Adam nodded and slid out of the water when Zane did, "You are welcome to come here, or even bring your team. I don't think many have found this spot. Just try not to damage it, so keep any playing away from here." He shifted to lead the two pups back the shorter way, instead of the long roundabout way.

Thank you, Alpha. After changing he shook his still wet fur out and was poked by Tessa since he had splashed her. Once she changed, he rested his chin on her shoulder and sent her his thanks for coming to check on him. He turned and followed him back towards the pack house.

*****

Once the healer was done, Josh took his phone from Malcom and made another call to his father, "Dad, had an Alpha fight due to Beta Mike's nephew being insulted and injured by one. Not sure what is happening in concern about this. I will call you back as soon as I have more information." How this was going to work out he didn't know. They weren't directly under his protection, but they had come with him, and his wolf had taken exception to the other.

Andrew leaned back in his chair and shook his head, "I want a full report once you are done with the punishment. Keep me updated on the Zane-issue. Your mother is not very happy since she knows you were hurt again. Might want to apply for asylum for a few weeks." He had ended up forcing her to change and go for a run to work her fear and anger out.

Josh walked into the meeting room gingerly, still in some pain, but he was breathing fine, thanks to the healer. Since it wasn't they were needing to spread out across many, he had used more of his power, and mostly just had tenderness in the bones which would fade in a day or two. Their meeting was hastily convened to deal with the issue. Everything else was on hold till it was dealt with. He gingerly sat down at the spot left open, "The healer has told me to take it easy for a week, but I will be fine to attend the meetings." He shuddered, "Never piss off a Healer; Tyler was screaming from the care he was getting as I left, and I could hear it from outside the soundproofed room." They were missing Tom from those he expected. "Tom not coming?"

Gareth grinned, "He walked out when we refused to let Tyler go free and to punish the pup for the attack. We can decide what to do better without him anyways." One more outburst from Tom, and he planned on revoking his welcome as well. It seemed he thought Tyler couldn't do any wrong, and any punishment was wrong. Everyone else agreed to not assign any punishment would undermine their laws, and even the Inter-Pack Treaty as a whole, badly. The attack of a pup, who was a guest, while the attacker was another guest... it just was too many of their core laws and traditions being broken to be overlooked had been agreed by the other leaders.

"I call this meeting to order." Elder James called out. The Elders mediated the meeting, so there was no opportunity for even the appearance of bias. "We are here to discuss the fate of Tyler. The fact he lost the challenge, the order for eviction from this pack and revoking his Guest status for him and his pack is confirmed." Looking around at the gathered Alphas, all were in agreement. He played the short video of the verbal attacks and how the pup resisted attacking back, even if he responded verbally back, and how Tyler had escalated his attack intentionally. Many of the Alphas growled at the attacks Tyler had done to the pup, as they were clearly disrespectful and intentionally trying to get a rise out of the pup.

"Alpha Adam had shared the memories he had of the events leading up to it, and it matched with the feed from the camera, so we will take the camera as correct and full. Next, there has been evidence put forward clearly shows the verbal attack towards the Pup Zane as the start, and how when it didn't work, Tyler escalated several times. As the pup withheld himself enough while he was verbally attacked personally, and then when his pack and team were denigrated, and only attacked when his girlfriend and a Theta under his protection was attacked directly, was totally understandable and showed a remarkable level of restraint and maturity. The fact it was not the first time she was attacked by another is interesting and shows how protective he is. The Alpha then attacked the pup physically and caused injuries requiring immediate healer attention." He pulled out the note from the healer, "Shattered Jaw. Two cracked ribs, two others had hairline factures. Another hairline fracture in his arm, and a sprained wrist. Multiple soft tissue injuries, which without taking him to Medical he didn't individually identify, and didn't feel it would be good to take him there." It actually shocked him the pup was ignoring his injuries and kept trying to continue.

The gathered Alphas were nearly vibrating with anger. Most were growling under their breath, trying to stay calm. The described level of injuries all thought went way beyond a punishment in this case.

"Thanks to Alpha Adam, it didn't go farther." Someone commented out loud, to which all the alphas nodded in agreement.

"I am assigning several charges," Gareth started, "Breaking Guest Laws to attack without a challenge. Unprovoked attack of a Guest. *And* attacking a Pup." The three charges were considered by all there as serious offences, and very much so as an Alpha, who were the Law-Makers and Law-Enforcers. Again, the Alphas were in agreement.

As they were part of the Inter-Pack Treaty, and the attack was at MacLaren, with him being a visitor, was how they would sit in judgment. Older traditions allowed for the host Alpha to deal with Guesting Law breaches directly and immediately without any need for consultation of anyone else. If those were to be applied, death was the only acceptable answer, as they broke their word, and only rogues did that, and only rogues attacked pups, meaning they needed to take out the rogue.

Guests could be challenged, but the fights were in the challenge circles, where the 'no fighting' part of Guesting Laws was suspended. Pups were the future, so were sacrosanct and could not be attacked and like Elders, could not be challenged to a fight but could make the challenge to an adult, even when they attacked, as to an adult, even Zane's attack would not have hurt him seriously. The laws considered words could be the first volley in an attack, so were taken as such. It didn't mean they couldn't be disciplined, and with wolves, physical discipline was still used. But breaking or fracturing bones was not allowed and was considered an attack.

"Any challenge the fact the attacks happened, or need further proof of Tyler's actions?" The elder stated formally. What happened was clear, and with an Alpha if not an eyewitness, was an ear-witness of the verbal, and several of the Alphas were there to see the result. There was also the surveillance system, which even had audio, which made it even easier to see *and hear* what happened. None of the Alphas said anything and just the slight growls of many were heard, as they tried and failed to completely suppress them. "Then we are done. We will move to assigning punishment."

The elder pulled out his notes, as he had discussed it with Gareth already so had worked with the other Elders as to what options they had, "For the laws he has disregarded, with him being an Alpha, we cannot turn the punishment over to the pack, as we could for any other wolf. With it being serious enough to rule out no punishment and none were willing to accept him into their pack, it limits us to what we can do here as the leaders: being made a Lone or Rogue Wolf, or death." One who attacked a pup with violence once would have no problem to do it again, so they would permit the permanent solution, as with their lifespans, and how an incarcerated wolf would go insane, a prison term was not feasible. "For the challenge, his pack and/or territory is up for transfer." If the Alpha was kicked out or killed, if the pack didn't have someone able to take over, and the winner didn't want to take the pack, they would cease to exist as a pack, and all would become pack-less Lone Wolves. The actions of the Alpha would not be held against them by almost all packs, so could fairly easily find a new one.

The elder turned to Josh, "As the combatant, what sort of punishment are you looking for?"

"Before you answer," Brook interrupted, "Wild Valley is currently only has about one hundred members. Adam agrees, and once our pack house is complete in about a year, we would be willing to absorb all those willing to follow our rules and join our pack. Until then, they would need to be put up by another or maintained where they are." They had the territory and would have the pack house space for a permanent pack of four times of what they currently had.

Elder James smiled, "That is mighty kind of you, Brook."

Brook smiled, "Adam passed along Zane's... desire is to not be further involved. There are reasons for this, and they are between my mate and Zane." They would have to ask Zane directly to talk about it, or for any further details, but the Alphas had already decided if the pup didn't want to be involved, they would handle it for him and let him recover.

Josh looked at the Elder and frowned. Technically he could take over the pack, but he had a feeling it wouldn't work. He was angry enough by the actions of the other, it was very possible he might end up taking it out on the pack, "I talked to Mike and..." He made a face since the deep application of silver nitrate suppositories wasn't something to mention. He understood but it wasn't going to get mentioned, "The best way to put it, is he wants him strung out and slowly roasted over low coals. I am not saying that is what should be done but he is still dealing with the loss of his brother and sister-in-law. He almost lost Zane to being a lone wolf as a pup, or worse. My recommendation would be death, but he is a part of your country."

Elder James nodded slowly, "One call for death. Do we know the state of the pack?" He had expected that, from the way he treated his peers, the other Alphas.

Gareth nodded before glancing at his papers, "They are about fifty according to last *official* records. Tyler rules using fear-respect. He has no Next Alpha, nor a mate, and no Second, according to records. His Betas, when I was there a decade ago, weren't even close to the ability to challenge him. There is nobody there to lead them, even in the short term, with the support of one of us. As Brook stated, we do not have room here to house them. Nor do either of the packs we took down recently have facilities fit for them to live in. Adam and Brook are already stretched with having to go between the two pack sites, and they are a reasonable run. Where Feral Star is located is not feasible to leave them there while they build their pack house."

The elder nodded sagely, "We will need to deal with them first, to not bias the decisions." He turned to Brook, "Am I correct in that you have reported you have the Gym building done?" He asked, having an idea for housing them.

"Yes," She replied, "But right now it is mostly just a concrete shell. And it will be till the fall, when the supplies to outfit it are here..." She trailed off. "I see where you're going!" she exclaimed. "That would give shelter till we can have the pack house done enough for them to move in there. One moment," She asked as she relayed to Adam what had been said. She blinked, "He likes the idea. Although we would require assistance for food supplies, as we do not have the storage for it, and won't till the kitchen is outfitted, and isn't till the fall either."

"I will supply weekly food runs." Rufus offered, "Either from my stock, or purchased from the nearest humans."

Josh wished he could do something for the pack, but they were from a different country, "I will speak to my father later and see if we can send some sort of financial support. It isn't the pack's fault from the sounds of it. It might not be a great deal, but we will do some. If you can get a list of things like clothing and toiletries needed, I can personally help there." He had money he could access.

The Alphas looked relieved; the pack was not going to be abandoned by the other Alphas, even if they were by their own Alpha, by his own actions.

"That settles the side topic. I now need your votes." The Elder said, "The options on the table are Release with other actions to be determined." He didn't bother debating them, as with already one death vote, it only took one more to remove that option. "Eject as a Lone Wolf and made to work his way from the lowest up, with us setting the maximum." That one was very unlikely. "Eject as a Rogue, to live alone, without a pack for the rest of his life." That one was unlikely, even with Rogues not having a long live expectancy. "One of us taking him in as an Omega, to be watched." From the shakes of the heads, none were willing to have a former Alpha in their pack, even as an Omega. "Or death." It seemed there was only one viable option for the Alpha.

"Death," Gareth said reluctantly, as much as he didn't like pronouncing death on a peer, it was all they had; he couldn't be taken into a pack, nor could they release him, as he'd probably seek vengeance. "I see no other viable option."

"Death." Came reply from each, as the Elder looked at them, confirming Gareth's thought. Many also added they concurred there was no other option they could live with.

Nodding, the Elder wrote it down, noting the date and time, "Alpha Tyler has been stripped of his rank and pack by the Alphas of at least six Packs, as required by the Inter-pack laws." The record would be sent out to all the members of the Inter-Pack Treaty, with the additional report of the pack's break up, and with how much was being absorbed into Wild Valley. "Now, method of death? And does he deserve a burial or burned?"

They discussed it late into the night, with Bri personally bringing them the trays for dinner, then later snacks, so there wasn't a lower ranking dealing with the Alphas, as all were worked up. Eventually they came to a consensus of a quick death, unless he demanded a Trial by Tooth-and-Claw. If he beat the first Alpha, many felt that they personally would continue the fight, not letting him have only one but all the Alphas to deal with. Brook was also in contact with Adam as he ran back with Zane and Tessa, and shared his views, even though each pack got only one vote. The agreement on what happened to his body they decided would be up to the pack he abandoned. The pack's elders were already preparing the pack, as they had been told, as soon as Tyler had been placed in the cell, as the elders had expected the call for his death.

Calling it a night; they would pronounce the sentence to the packs in the morning, and the Elder would contact the elders in the pack to discuss its fate, now that it had been decided.

*****

Even as the Alphas were meeting, Zane, followed by Tessa, avoided the crowd at the back of the house. He slipped into a side door which led to the guest quarters. He settled down on a pad and curled up in a small miserable ball of fur, flipping his tail over his eyes, in clear Wolf that he didn't want to be disturbed. When Tessa settled down with him, she settled as close as possible, curling her body around him and putting her head on his neck. Since he had remained in his wolf form, she had also stayed wolf.

As she was comforting him the rest of his team came in as well as Olivia and Shelly. They all settled around him with Olivia by his head. She had seen the entire thing and felt even worse than he did in her mind. Even as he almost lost her, she almost lost him, and she could see how badly he had been hurt. Shelly had helped comfort her a great deal and maybe she could help Zane, "You okay Zane? It looked like you had been really badly hurt."

Melody looked at Olivia, "He won't speak about it right now. What was said brought back his memories. He is trying to deal with those right now." She made sure to meet Olivia's eyes and gave her a firm look. Zane needed the comfort of the pack and not to be asked about what happened, "His *physical* wounds are already healing or healed. By to-morrow he will be mostly healed."

Adam knocked on the door, *I have some food for you, so you don't have to leave.* He called to them. The walls were soundproofed to were-ratings, so other than the specific knock spot, someone could scream in the room with the door closed, and they wouldn't hear it right outside the door.

Oscar stood and opened the door, "Thank you Alpha. I don't think any of us feel like going anywhere. I have informed Beta Mike where we are. He is dealing with his anger right now but will be here once he is calmed down." *I don't know if Zane would talk to a Luna but the presence of one would probably help.*

Adam wheeled the cart with covered trays of food into the room, "When I talked to Ben, the head Chef here, he whipped up some food which should help you, Zane. There is even some cake for all of you." Seeing Zane clearly not wanting to be disturbed, and Tessa curled up with him, he told Oscar privately, *We don't have a Luna here. Brook and I are both the leader and the comforter for our pack. I have already helped a bit, but I will see if one who is visiting would be willing.*

He had Charlie slip in and snuggle down against Zane too. With his size, he easily cuddled up to Zane and Tessa, hopefully to give him some solid comfort. "If you need me at all tonight, I'm having Charlie stay here. Ask him to call me, and I'll come. Or come find me, I'll probably be in my room for the evening."

Oscar took the heavy tray from the cart and set it on the table. He didn't know when Zane would be able to or willing to eat. Oscar could serve the others starting with Olivia and Tessa. They were going to need it the most, *Thank you Alpha. I just know he responded to the Luna of our pack when Olivia was in the hospital for a final repair on her leg.* He wasn't going to say anything else about that time. He had a feeling it was due to the female presence. It was the mother figure over a father figure.

Melody watched Charlie settle down next to Zane and Tessa, shocked at how big Charlie was; he was almost bigger than Zane, *Thank you Alpha. If we need you, we will call you.* She leaned over and petted Charlie before going to refill a dish of water for the two dogs and Zane if he didn't change back soon. If he didn't, she was going to see about getting some raw meat for Zane, not having noticed there was some on the tray.

Molly poked her head into the room, "Josh asked me to come and check. He is in a meeting and Mike is busy right now." She gave Adam a slightly angry look. It wasn't for him but that someone could even consider doing something like this to a pup. She moved over and settled down near the group of children and started to relax.

Adam slipped out silently, closing the door and putting a do not disturb sign on it. *Let the pups know when you feel it's right,* He passed to Molly, *Tyler has been sentenced to death. The method and what happens to the body hasn't been decided, yet.*

Molly's eyes flashed ice blue for a moment as her wolf felt satisfaction, *I have a feeling it would be better to just leave it for the moment. If you are going to decide to do a public execution, I will talk with Mike and have them taken for a run. I know they will eventually find out, but I *don't think it would help for any of them to see it.** Since Mindy was close to her, she reached over and stroked her hair to help comfort her.

Zane's wolf could feel the agony of his other half. For the moment they needed food, so he 'encouraged' Zane to go to sleep. Once the other half was asleep, he sat up and nudged Tessa before looking at Oscar. He asked for some food so they could keep healing. Eventually the two of them would both be asleep. Having the adult she-wolf would help, and he might just settle down next to her and try and sleep. He knew the Alpha would understand what he was doing.

*****

Adam growled as he went to his room. He hoped that rogue who harmed that pup so badly when he was turned, would make it up here, and he would be the one to take it out, so he could ask if Zane wanted a rug or a coat, or just the head mounted on the wall. He was also nearly in tears from the agony he could feel from Zane over the loss of his family.

His own pups were there waiting for him, and he pulled them into his arms for a cuddle. Brook was still in the meeting where they were deciding the details of *how* the sentence was being carried out, and he wasn't in the right frame of mind to help with the discussion. He wanted to challenge and tear Tyler apart, and his wolf was wondering how small to shred him, for hurting Zane so much and bringing up the issues from his past. He couldn't bring back Zane's parents, or undo Olivia's injury, and couldn't protect him from his mental hurts.

"Let's watch a movie." He told them and moved over to queue up a movie from the network. It was easier to have the movies stored on a network space, and have them stream from there, instead of worrying about the actual DVDs and Blu-Rays they were from. Those were stored in a locked cabinet in the library; to prove they had a legal copy.

Relaxing with his family allowed his own emotions to recover. He would talk to Mike about having the pups back up next summer, when the pack house would be nearly done, and it would be quieter. His pups couldn't do the exchange, well, not for how long Mike had discussed, due to their specialized training and duties they had. He had some others who might be better for the exchange. Or may just have them up for a relaxing break and some time where they could have fun.

*****

The next morning when Zane finally woke, he found he was back in human form. Thankfully, he had shorts on, even if he didn't remember pulling them on, and the girls had short shirts and shorts on. Everyone was piled around him on the floor including Mike. As expected, Olivia, Oscar, and Shelly were in one of the beds. There was no reason for Olivia to try and sleep on the floor. Even being a wolf, Zane felt rather stiff at the moment. Thanks to the change, most of his injuries were just minor aches now, although his jaw ached, and his arm and chest were twinging. He knew it was just from the bones being tender after the healing.

He carefully extricated himself from the pile of bodies and slipped into the shower. After all the fun last night he was sure he had a funk going. When he smelled Melody climb into the shower, he decided to ignore her for the moment and settled for letting the water flow down. It felt good, but he wasn't going to take very long due to the sheer number of people at the pack house at the moment.

Melody started working some soft soap into his back, "Tessa is still sleeping. You had a number of nightmares last night and between her, Molly, and Mike, they kept you asleep." She gave his shoulders a good squeeze before finishing his back, "Don't you dare feel bad either, or we are going to be wolf piling you for the next month. What the monster said to you, and yes, *he* is a monster, had to have hurt. Thank you for trying to defend not just Tessa but all of us."

"Thanks for letting me know. Right now, I need to think about it and maybe see if I can contact the Luna." He wasn't sure what range they had but he was sure she would help comfort him if he could reach her. He quickly finished showering off and stepped out even as Rico and Mindy entered, "I am going to check on everyone and we will go to breakfast together." He needed his team around him even if he wasn't going to admit it here.

When he walked out Mike gave him a good hug, "We will talk later. Need to figure out what to do about Olivia's new companion and a few other things." He gave Zane one more squeeze, "I am very proud of you for protecting your wolves. Your parents would have been as well." He headed off to his room for a shower.

Tessa was obviously still deeply asleep when Zane knelt down next to her and touched her face, "I am sorry Tessa." He scooped her up and settled her on the bed next to Shelly. It looked like she had moved so there was room between her and Olivia, "Thanks Shelly." He tucked her in between and gave Shelly a quick pet, "Let me know when she wakes, and I will come get her."

The rest of the team was up and dressed. Zane gave them a hard look, "We are going to act normal, like nothing happened since it wasn't this pack's fault. If anyone asks, tell them you have been told not to talk about it. If needed, I will talk to Mike to make it an order."

Melody snorted, "Zane, I hate to break it to you, but you just made it an order. We weren't planning on it, now I am hungry. Once we eat, we can bring a tray of food up for everyone else." As she was talking, Simone was making sure there was plenty of water in the bowl for Shelly.

"You know what is almost depressing Zane? Olivia's new friend is as big or bigger than either Oscar or Olivia. She even makes *me* feel almost small. Charlie is just huge!" The over-sized canine seemed to understand as he panted gently and let his tongue drape out of his mouth. When Zane grinned slightly Simone was pleased, "Now as your illustrious assistant said: I am hungry." They all trooped out of the room and Charlie went to find Adam.

During breakfast, several wolves came over to give Zane a companionable pat. After the third one to him complimented him, he was about ready to scream. Instead, he took a deep breath, "Can you please pass it around I don't wish to talk about it? Thank you for saying it but

I am still too angry about what happened." Angry and scared by giving out one tiny bit of information he had even hid from himself.

They nodded, and could smell the mixed emotions from Zane, "Will do." They said, before heading off to their own seat.

Zane stood up a short time later, "I am taking food to the others." He didn't bother telling his team to do what they wanted since they would end up there eventually. He collected food for Shelly and the other three. Once he was done, he left the room. His blank, emotionless expression was almost settled down on his face again, even as he tried to not have it. Those in the know would understand what it indicated.

By the time he was at the room, Mindy and Rico were there as well. Mindy had grabbed some drinks, and Rico was opening the door. Zane set the tray on the table and placed a bowl of food for Shelly next to the water. When she hopped down, he briefly stroked her head before going and sitting down next to Tessa.

The movement started them waking, "Morning, food is on the table. I brought food for Shelly as well." He stroked Tessa's face before giving her a kiss and looking at Olivia.

Tessa sat up and stretched before moving so Olivia could get to Zane. When she did, she was almost crying due to his expression. About the only thing which stopped her was the darn tie-dyed shirt he had on, "Must have been Mike who put it in your bags." She wrapped her arms around him and held on, "You ever scare me like that again, Uncle Mike wouldn't be able to afford the number of crutches I am going to need."

Zane had to shudder, "I hope not, I was terrified, even as I reacted. Nobody insults my team and gets away with it." After a good hug he rolled off the bed, "Food is on the table, and I think Shelly wants out." He said as he watched the dog head to the door, but before he could move, she reared up pawed the lever handle, opened the door, and padded off. The bowl was licked clean already and there had been a good portion of the water slurped up.

Olivia didn't know what else to say so she watched the dog give the bowl one last lick before leaving, "Yup, she will be back soon. Thanks."

She slipped off the bed and gave Oscar a good hug before hurrying over to the table and grabbing the plate obviously for her.

*****

Adam smiled as he woke in the morning. Brook was curled up on one side, and the pups were all around him. He realized he had fallen asleep halfway through the movie, and apparently had barely moved all night. His stomach was complaining about being very empty.

Adam stretching woke Brook up, "Morning!" She commented, "I didn't want to disturb you. It was decided Tyler is going to be given death, then a pyre. If he demands it, he will be allowed another Trial by Tooth-and-Claw this morning."

Chapter 23 – The Fight

*H*ate to disturb you two,* Gareth sent almost as if he was reading their minds, *But Tyler is demanding a Trial by Tooth-and-Claw with Adam.*

Brook growled, for a moment before swallowing it as she looked at the sleeping pups and stalking out the door. Adam stroked Willow's fur for a moment till her wolf woke up and nodded. She yawned, stretched, and put her head back down, as he too headed out, as she now knew she was on watch and would make sure she only slept lightly.

We got it. Brook is upset, even though we sort of expected it. After breakfast, I assume? Adam asked. He had expected it. At the affirmation, *Let Mike and Josh know. I don't think the pups need to be involved, especially Zane. Maybe have them sent with mine to town and do some sightseeing?* Even if they went into all the stores, it still would only be a couple hours, as it wasn't a large town, and they didn't have many tourists who weren't just passing through to the back country areas. They did have a store with clothing for the mountains, and one for gear; hiking, climbing, and camping in summer, and cross-country and back-country skiing, snowshoeing, ice climbing, and some camping gear in winter. There were a couple of restaurants, a general hardware store, and a supermarket. A few other stores came and went.

Following his nose, he found Brook in a small meeting room snarling, "Come here," Adam coaxed, pulling her head down, so her nose was against his neck.

They relaxed together for a bit, just standing and clinging to each other till they both calmed down before heading to breakfast.
*****

Adam was waiting for the prisoner—no longer an Alpha—to arrive wearing just some light bike shorts he didn't care about, as he expected to not have them get out of the circle intact. All the other Alphas and guests were there, as was a bunch from the pack.

There were several Enforcers and Alphas around Tom, to make sure he didn't interfere.

Tyler stalked into the circle, as if he was still an Alpha. Many of the pack had decided, since he had already been sentenced, to not bother show up, showing the outcome of the fight was of no concern to them; it would be considered a grave insult for an Alpha like Tyler. Nor did they have any doubt about who would win, so there was no interest in seeing the challenge.

"Tyler, you have been sentenced to death for an unprovoked attack of a wolf, attacking a pup with the intent to harm, and worst: breaking the Guesting Laws while doing both. You were found guilty by a tribunal of Alphas, as required by the Inter-Pack Treaty. You have requested a Trial by Tooth-and-Claw, as is your right. If you win, you will be released as a Rogue." Gareth stated. He knew there was a list of Alphas who had stated to him, and would challenge the release, and would step in to fight, if Adam didn't win. Few in the pack had any doubt, and the few who were there to bet, were only betting on how many hits Adam would take, how long the fight would last, and what would be the final blow.

Josh was sitting up straight in the chair he was in. Molly had arranged the seat for him, and ordered him into it, stating he was still healing, so would sit. Her hand was on his shoulder, and he had no real interest in removing it, even if it meant she could keep him in the seat. He waited patiently as Tyler was being presented with the charges and sentence, *Alpha Adam, when appropriate I have a personal question for Tyler.* He didn't bother with his former title since he no longer deserved it. He had lost it when Josh had beat his ass into the ground and would have to try and fight to get it back. It was if anyone was willing to allow him to try.

Adam shared a savage pleasure, *Did you want to do it now, before I start, or when I beat him? Although if there is any cheating, he'll just be dead,* He had never liked Tyler; from his first letter of demands to his trespass and demands at Wild Valley, to the attempted blocks to joining the Treaty, to now with his refusal to accept the consequences of his actions. If he had paid at least lip-service to the treaty laws, he would have left him alone. But the disregarding of them, he would make time to deal with this rogue.

He stood at rest, staring at Tyler, waiting for him to start. Tyler started to hurl insults, but both Adam and his wolf let them run over them like fog. They ignored the taunts about his age, and how he wouldn't have had a pack when he was finished, and how Tyler was going to take over his pack. To the last insult, Adam's wolf snorted, as from the previous fights, they were much stronger, and he didn't have a chance, even if in human form Tyler was a foot taller than they were. The fact Zane, a pup with very little training, had got in some good shots which connected showed how weak this... creature who pretended to be an Alpha was; he also kept his pack under control by removing any who neared his power! There was none in the pack with the strength to take it over showed it. Not having any who could put up a challenging fight meant he had an overestimation on his skills to defeat others.

Josh gave Tyler a cool look, "I have one question for you Tyler, how did it feel to be beat by a pup who still isn't recovered from a rogue attack?" His voice was as cool as his expression was. It was obvious he had enjoyed asking the question to anyone who listened. Many looked to Josh in shock. He had beat the Alpha while still recovering?

Zane twitched since he hadn't beat him, *Uncle Mike, what did he mean? I didn't beat him; at best I gave him some bruises and a bloody nose.* There was something he was missing in the question.

Mike didn't look away from the fight when he replied, *He was talking about himself, not you. Remember Tom and Tyler's first objection to the signing.*

Zane was still more than stumped; he would have to discuss it with his uncle at some point. It had been agreed by his uncle he needed to be here today. One of Alpha Gareth's she-wolves had taken the rest of his team to town for shopping. This was going to bother him, but Tyler had caused his break down and he wanted—no it was more than wanted; *needed*—to see the punishment being carried out. Adam had tried to half-heartedly to talk him out of it, but accepted Zane's choice to be there, as was his right as the offended party.

Tyler gave a loud snarl and threw himself at Adam, shifting to his Were in the air. Just before he hit, Adam ducked and rolled, bouncing to his feet, and shifting, shredding his shorts as there was no time out to let him strip them off.

Adam tapped Tyler on his shoulder as he was looking for the other wolf, and when he turned, got a fist to the eye for his trouble.

Come on, Gramps, do you want to play or fight! Adam taunted, getting laughter from several wolves watching.

Again, Tyler tried to pounce, but Adam was much nimbler, and again he caught nothing. Adam tore a strip down Tyler's side with his claws, which were sharper than a razor, leaving four red lines which started bleeding only after he moved back.

Tyler roared and tried to attack again and again, with most not landing. The few which landed were glancing hits, which wouldn't even leave a bruise with the fur padding them. A couple groaned, as they had bet Adam would have no hits land.

Several Alphas were shaking their heads, "Adam's just toying with him. Tyler is totally just rage-fighting." One commented, and none could refute it. All were embarrassed, as an Alpha should know not to let their emotions dictate their fighting, as it would cause them to not be able to fight well. Martin shook his head too, as if this was a fight by any Enforcer of his, even in a casual bout, they would have been suspended from doing patrols and sent for further training, and likely lose any seniority they had. Their standards even to qualify to patrol, which Cody had to meet as a pup-trainee, was higher than what was being shown.

Adam decided he needed to reproduce Zane's injuries on the Alpha. Starting with the arm, he broke it, then the ribs. His jaw he broke with a good swat of his paw, and Tyler started whimpering, seeming not able to stand the pain.

Zane watched the fight and was starting to feel faintly nauseated when he realized what Adam was doing, *Alpha Adam please don't. Just deal with him. I don't want to see him pummelled to a pulp before whatever else. I just want him dealt with so I know my team is safe.* He hoped Adam would receive it and it wouldn't distract him.

Adam nodded mentally at Zane as he could feel he just wanted it to end, and turned to Tyler, who seemed to not be thinking any more. Reaching over, through Tyler's non-existing guard, he gave a hard twist to his neck, and let the body fall to the ground.

Shifting back to human, he stood before the gathered wolves, nobody caring he wasn't wearing anything, "Justice has been served, and the sentence has been carried out." He stated clearly. Inside, he was again in turmoil, as again he had to take a life. At least this one was in the challenge circle, and for a good reason which even he agreed needed to be done, but still... killing bothered him. It was a waste to him, even if his wolf was satisfied the threat was dealt with.

Gareth nodded, and addressed the gathered masses, "Tyler disgraced his name. He will be burned, but there will be no pack ceremony. Feral Star Pack died with him, as there is no Next-Alpha, Second, or even a strong enough Beta to hold the pack together." The Alphas clearly turned their backs on the fallen and headed off together. His pack seemed to have already turned away from him, as they didn't want Tyler back in any form, not even his ashes. He died in disgrace and alone from disrespecting the pack which he was representing. It had shocked the Alphas when the Elder returned the decision from the pack. None of those from his pack had watched his defeat either, having agreed with the pack's decision.

Zane finally stood and slowly left the area and after grabbing something to drink headed to one side of the house. He knew wolves had a rather short list of major punishments. It was especially true when it came to the crimes such as Tyler had been accused of, and for his rank. He had been studying the laws in his enforcer training as well. This was the first time he had actually seen someone killed. It was something he was going to have to really think about. Thankfully where he was at there was a small nook where he could relax while he thought. His wolf just felt satisfied the threat to those in his care was gone.

Josh was feeling vastly differently since he had killed before. The wolf had already started to stink of being a rogue and he was better dead than alive. Even though the wolf hadn't answered his question he had received his answer. It had incensed the other and it showed. With a pleased look he turned to Adam to see if there was anything else needed. If not, he was going to get something to drink. In his case it was going to be something alcoholic and strong.

Adam shook his head as he and Brook headed into the forest, since their room was full of pups, swiftly shifting to their wolves, and heading up to the hot spring. Brook had Adam stand, so she could check him over for damage when they arrived and shifted back.

"See, just bruises, most were just from quickly killing him, when Zane asked. Mark, in Longview, was a harder fight than that." Adam replied, scornful, "It seemed he had no self-control, and the taunt Josh said really hit home. He was mostly flailing about. I considered taunting him myself with the fact of being a changed-wolf too but didn't see a point worth it to lower myself to his level."

Slipping down into the hot water with a sigh, he laid his head back, "Still, it was a good workout." He commented, as Brook settled against his side.

They didn't have to be back till morning, as everything had been postponed to the next day, due to the seriousness of the issues at hand.

*****

Maria found Zane sitting at the hidden nook, which looked out with a clear view of a mountain valley. "Zane, isn't it? Mind if I join you?" She thought she should go see how the pup was doing, knowing Brook and Adam would need some alone time.

Zane heard the woman coming and could sense her status. He gave her a slight grin when he replied, "Well it is your pack territory ma'am." He remembered saying much the same to Esther that first run he had gone on, "Yah, it is Zane and good afternoon, Luna—I mean Alpha." It still sounded weird to call a female Alpha, but it was how they did it up here, "You do have some lovely territory." He wasn't sure why she was there, but he had a feeling someone was keeping an eye on him.

Maria smiled, sitting beside him, "I prefer to co-alpha with my mate, rather than limit myself to just doing the soft side, as a Luna. Many packs up here do it, but there are still some have Lunas, too. Where pups are concerned, us females are very savage. I talked to Brook, and she wanted to tear him apart alive, till he was in bits, while Adam was more judicial, and was trying to show Tom the errors of his ways by destroying the pack which was an offshoot of his." Even though they had separated before he had become Alpha, there was still kinship acknowledged by both.

Taking a breath, "Just so you know, Adam and Brook are in discussions to take in those wolves of the pack who are willing to join them and agree to follow their rules. If we were at their pack, Tyler would just have been killed when Adam reached you, after he attacked; no discussion, no trial, no appeal, just dead." It was a comment he had passed on, about his feelings. Any who attacked a pup didn't deserve to live and needed to be dealt with immediately.

Zane actually choked when Maria said she preferred to be a co-leader and not just the soft side. He started laughing at the comment and it took several minutes to recover, "Sorry ma'am, if you met Esther, you would know better than to call her soft. You should have seen her when two brats at school attacked Tessa. She was more furious than anyone but Tessa's mom. And you really don't want to end up on her bad side. She has disciplined me once or twice... I really hate scrapping cow crap off concrete floors. She has used it against me several times." He leaned against her as he wiped laughter tears off his face.

When she talked about what could have happened or what Brook would have done, he shook his head, "I asked Alpha Adam not to tear him apart. I have never seen anyone killed before, but I just wanted him gone so he wasn't a threat to my team. I came up looking really forward to it. After *it* insulted Tessa... It really hurt and brought back memories of waking up after being turned." He took a shuddering breath. He still hadn't talked to Mike about what he had told Adam, and he wasn't sure if he could. Chances were good he would end up talking to Esther first and go from there.

Maria nodded, "I understand. I have talked to Esther while we were arranging for details for Shelly to go with you, and she is a strong one. You are lucky to have her. It sounds like you want to talk to her. Brook let me know she and Adam are relaxing out in the hot spring Adam took you to before, if you wanted to talk to them. Or I could arrange a private video conference with Esther, if you wish." She could smell his confusion and hurt, and it called to the mother inside her, not just the leader, to help the pup.

He considered the offer and finally shook his head, "It would be better to talk to her in person. There is a comfort she projects which helps. It is somewhat like what you and Adam exude. I am doing okay if nothing else happens. I have enjoyed seeing your territory. Getting to know some of the pups has been enjoyable as well." Zane gave her a tired smile, "Esther is a good Luna. It was hard at first to let her help. Once she did it helped me to start to deal with my loss." His memories wandered back to the break down when he had seen Olivia after surgery.

"It has really helped, having my wolf decide to protect Tessa and Oscar. If anyone helped me, they did. Liv would allow Oscar to help her where I made her want to break out a crutch. Tessa spent many nights curled up in her wolf form to help me with my nightmares. The rest of my team... Such pushy wolves. Wouldn't leave me alone even when I was being a grumpy wolf with a sore tooth." He had to laugh as he remembered; Melody hadn't really given him much of choice and hovered until he gave up.

Maria laughed at the last part as well, "We are all like that; we see a wolf feeling down, we will worm our way close and won't take no for an answer. Curling up together is one way we strengthen our bonds. If one is willing to trust you not to harm them while sleeping near you, it shows they care. If it gets bad, come to any of the Alphas," She replied before pausing, "Well, other than Tom. I recommend staying clear of him. Tyler was a cousin of his, and the pack which now no longer exists, was an offshoot of his."

Zane grumbled at her, "I was human, darn it. Do you have any idea how weird it was to wake up in the hospital with a voice in my mind? I questioned my sanity until Kadrian helped me change the first time. Some days I still wonder." His wolf snorted at him, "Even worse was waking up with a girl in my bed. I know it is a wolfy thing, but Tessa is cute and..." He turned about as pink as possible, "I will try ma'am. It is hard because I am still having trouble... Letting people close. Waking up with mom and dad dead hurt bad. The idea of letting someone else close is a horrible struggle." She was coming across like Esther did which helped him talk.

Maria nodded, "I don't know what I'd do if I woke up in a strange place to find out my parents were dead and had a voice in my mind when society considered it to be a sign of insanity. I do know those of us who grow up as a wolf learn to lean on not only our wolves but also our packs early on. From almost every turned human I have ever encountered, they all say one thing, which having a wolf is having a constant companion who knows your thoughts and will always be there for you. I'd say trust your wolf; and when needed, lean on his strength, if you are unwilling to lean on anyone else." She ignored his waking up with another in his bed; it was something all turned-wolves had to learn to get used to, some took little time, and some took several decades.

"If it had just been my waking up, it would have been one thing. Seeing Liv struggling to move with crutches freaked me out." He sighed before closing his eyes and relaxing. Before he realized it, he had fallen asleep leaning against Maria. He hadn't slept much since Tyler did his thing and she was warm and comfortable. The warm sun didn't help keep him awake either. His sleeping was shown when he started snoring quietly.

Maria chuckled silently and leaned back against the back of the seat, settling Zane a little more comfortably against her, with an arm wrapped around him holding him close.

Mike came out shortly after Zane had fallen asleep. He leaned over and touched his nephew's head and looked at Maria, "If you don't mind let him sleep and give him comfort. I have talked to Esther, and she is going to talk to him when we go back. Damn that fucking bastard." Mike gave his body a good shake before finally standing and leaving. He was still worked up and probably would be until he was back with Annie.

Maria nodded, but stayed silent, having woken as Mike came close, *I'll wake him when it's time for lunch.* She sent; by then she would be hungry too, and it would break what little trust he had to just leave him alone. Relaxing, she closed her eyes and dozed as well in the warm sun once Mike left. Being werewolves, they didn't need to worry about sunburn and knew her wolf was on guard for the pup who was in pain.

Mike gave her a nod before he left since he needed to work off his anger. Since they had been shown the gym, he headed there and started working out. Once he had worked out, he was going to do some weapons training. For that he would work with staffs. Here they used quarter staffs, he preferred half-staff's and had two of them. It was different enough to shock some; he had several rogues who had submitted just being confronted by it.

Martin came in and nodded, "Want to do a bout or two?" he asked. He had known Mike was the head enforcer and getting time to bout with those of his skill level was hard, as they rarely had downtime at another pack.

He paused and looked at Martin, "I will warn you I am doing this to work my anger off. I am seriously ticked off and not sure if I would be good sparing material right now." He lowered the half staffs though his hands were tight as he was grasping them.

Martin grinned, "Even better, I need a good workout. The Alphas are the only ones who can do it for me, and they are too busy right now. If it gets too much, I'll call a stop. I can tell you need to burn off some steam too." He pulled off a staff from the rack and moved to the practice ring.

Mike moved into the training ring and took a slow deep breath. He was trying to calm down and centre before the sparing. Once he was as calm as he could get, he lifted the half-staffs, "Shall we dance?" He had a rather eager grin on his face.

Martin gave a matching grin, "Yes, lets." He answered.
*****

Martin shook the sweat from his eyes as he came out of his near trance and looked around. There were quite a few wolves who were there watching them. He grinned at Mike, "I guess we put on a show!" he said as he nodded at the spectators. Nether had been counting hits, not that they had many connect, and those where only ever glancing. It was almost meditative.

Mike was feeling much better now. As he looked around the training area, he also noticed the crowd, "I guess, you are pretty darn good." He tucked one staff under an arm as he checked a bruise forming on one hip. Nothing was broken but he knew both had several bruises from the sparing. To humans it would look like they were all out fighting. As wolves they could take blows which would hurt or even kill a human, "Thanks, I feel better." He stepped out of the ring and checked his half-staffs and wiped them down.

Martin smiled, "Any time. If you want another round, just come to the security office, and they will know where I am. That was quite enjoyable."

He stretched before he slugged down a good portion of water from a bottle someone handed him, "Sounds good to me. As I am sure you know we came up not just for the meeting but also to let my pups get to know some of yours." He gave the other Beta a good nod and walked off. Now he needed a shower badly. He needed to check on Zane as well to ensure he was doing okay after this morning.

*****

Maria had woken Zane, and he twitched upright before yawning. He considered apologizing, but he had needed the comfort, and he wasn't stupid enough to deny it. Zane might not admit it to anyone, but he wasn't going to deny it to himself, "Thanks Ma'am, being held helped a great deal." He stood and stretched before yawning, "Going to lunch? I am sure my team members will end up eating in town." He would have liked to go with them, but he had needed to be here and watch the punishment.

Maria nodded, "You needed the rest, and for a wolf, there is no safer place than in the arms of an Alpha, or Luna. I assume they will be back some point this afternoon, as there isn't too much in town. I hope you had a good rest." Standing up, she led him to the dining room.

He gave her a wry grin, "I know that now, but you should have seen me after I woke up. Even with my wolf whining at me, I couldn't go to our Luna." Zane commented as he gave her a slight shrug. Once she stood, he walked quietly with her as they headed towards the dining area. The food here was as good as back at his new home. It was a little different but darn good for the most part.

When they reached the dining area, he found his uncle there and he moved over next to him, "Hey Unc, smells good doesn't it?" His nose was sniffing at the massive piles of food on the trays, and everything looked good. Well other than a massive pile of stuffed green peppers. Those things nauseated him. After loading a plate full of the food, he followed Mike to a table and quickly dug in.

Mike grinned, "Hey, free food always smells good..." He frowned, "Well, most of the time. Here it is true. The food is excellent. I almost wish I had brought Annie." He simply couldn't have, and they all understood. Once they had their plates filled Mike headed towards a table with younger wolves. It would allow him to get a sense of how they were treated and Zane someone even near his age to talk to.

Toby and Robin sat down on the other side of Zane, and exchanged greetings with the few already there, "We heard you stayed for the punishment this morning, how's it going?" Toby asked; Adam had asked his pups to stay away, as he didn't think they were ready for it, and didn't think they needed to see an execution, and they hadn't felt a need to be there, so they followed their father's wishes. Toby liked what he could see with Zane caring for his Team. He nodded a greeting as Willow sat down on the other side of the table and was helping several younger pups with their lunch. "Adam and Brook tore out of here this morning, and I wonder when they will be back."

Zane mumbled at them around a mouthful of steak. He finally cleared his mouth, "Can we not talk about it? Not something to talk about over lunch." He took another bite of food and with a roll of his eyes helped a younger pup cut up some meat, "It is good, isn't it?" Once the meat was cut up for the young boy he went back to eating. The boy made him think of the little pup who even now tended to find Olivia and cuddle with her.

"I hope they get back soon; I want to cuddle with Tessa. She always managed to help me relax and deal with issues." He took a bite and looked into the distance, "Best choice I ever made was taking them into my team." It was obvious he cared for both Tessa and Oscar.

Willow smiled and thanked Zane, knowing he was off-limits. "Well, if you need a girl to cuddle until she gets back..." she teased, knowing he'd not be interested. "How do you like it here, so far?"

Zane snorted, "I might kidnap a little girl and cuddle until they get back." He grinned at a girl who had come and said hello the other day. She was sitting across the table from him. She giggled before growling at him even as she was eating, "It is a really nice territory. I have been on a few runs, and it is so clean and vast." He wasn't going near the fiasco with Tyler, "I am glad Shelly chose my sis. She is a really good dog."

*****

Even as Zane was talking, Shelly was walking with Olivia. Her bright brown eyes were looking at each person nearby to see if they were a danger. Every now and then she would glance at Oscar and was pleased. It was obvious the wolf cared a great deal for her human and it was good. What she couldn't do for her person, he could.

Olivia was relaxing against Oscar since he had an arm around her shoulder. Even knowing what had been said she knew he wouldn't do anything until she was old enough. It made her feel somewhat funny since knowing a wolf was almost hers sounded so odd. Her uncle just found his mate but why had Oscar decided he was hers? Having met Cody and Amber made her think as well. Why had he found his mate who was a kid several years younger than him?

Oscar could smell Olivia thinking and it didn't really bother him. If he was right, she would be his eventually and he could wait. When Shelly glanced at him, he met her eyes and smiled. Even if the main bonds were with Olivia, he could feel them as well, *I will take care of your person.* He followed her into a small shop and grinned. It was a clothing store but not the normal type. When she started looking at some of the clothing, he paid attention. If he could, he would pick something up for her from this place.

Melody watched the two and she had to smile. Now it was obvious Oscar felt Olivia was going to be his mate. It felt right since even as outgoing as Olivia was, she was actually rather quiet, much like the twins, "Oh man, this shirt is really hot!" It was something she would wear.

Rico groaned, "Not another clothing store. Can we do something manish? You know a sports store, game store, something like that?" He glowered at the other females, "Might need to talk to Zane about getting more males on the team." Mindy and Simone laughed at him, and he growled at them.

Erin laughed, "Eventually you will be happy there are females on your team. Maybe not as mates or girlfriends but as a balance to having just males." She had seen him eyeballing a few of the girls from the pack. He was of age to see one of them and nobody would say anything. "After this, how about some lunch? Then I can take you to the small store which passes for the sport store." She was known to all the shop owners, as was most of MacLaren. There was a raised eyebrow as Shelly came in off-leash, with it tucked up under a loop on her *Service Animal* pack, but they knew the service animals they had were very well trained, as several of the townsfolk had been gifted with the animals as well.

There were several of the shopkeepers who knew what they were, but it was something which wasn't spoken about, as the town would be a quarter the size, with nowhere near the number of stores. The pack was very good for the town, as much of the clothing the pack got was passed through the town, same with food. Even though it was more expensive, most packs preferred to help the local economy.

Simone leaned against the she-wolf and grinned, "Food good, feed inner wolf." The woman was comfortable, and she appreciated her having come with, "Lots of beef and fries sound good. Sweet potato fries, chili fries, cheesy fries..." She had to lick her lips at the idea of some of the fries which might be available.

Rico poked her and then grinned, "Oh my yes, one massive slab of some sort of meat which is just off the hoof sounds good." Fries were good, but he didn't care for sweet potato fries. Now cheesy fries and such were the bomb.

Erin laughed as she led the young wolves to the restaurant...

Chapter 24 – Wolf Lunch

Erin smiled as she led the young wolves to the restaurant which was run by one of the pack and hired a mix of wolves and humans. They were quickly seated in a section all to themselves, as it was used mostly for wolves. It was off to the side, and not visible to the main part of the restaurant, with a separate door into the kitchen, so the wolf-sized portions were not seen. As an appetizer, she ordered them a large tray of poutine to share.

A large tray of fries which then had fresh cheese curds on top, then hot gravy liberally poured across it, melting the cheese to the fries was quickly delivered.

"Dig in," Erin told them, "It's a Canadian dish which is only starting to be found south of the border. The potatoes are from local farms, and the cheese is from milk not too far either and the cheese plant is not too far either."

As they looked at the menu, she made a few suggestions. All the meat was from local farmers and was dealt with in the slaughterhouse in town. With the amount of meat the wolves went through, it made it easier to have the industry close, so they didn't have to have massive freezers to keep a large stock but could have daily deliveries. It also meant more jobs for the local town, and a place outside the pack which the wolves could work at.

The kids looked at the appetizer and for a moment it was obvious they were resisting eating. It wasn't because the food didn't look good but because they were trying to be good. It didn't last long and though they were tidy it was almost a massacre of the fries. When all was said and done the plates were almost licked clean. Mindy glowered at the plate nearest her and wanted to growl since it was empty of anything, "That was... I am not going to swear, it was really good and more or the table is going to be in trouble."

Rico was also glowering though for him it was because Simone had gotten the last few fries, "Blast you, I am going to steal some food off your plate when it arrives." Before he could cover it, a massive belch erupted and he was almost appalled, "Really good but pardon me." He leaned back and hoped his wolf would have some patience for the rest of the food to arrive.

Melody was feeling rather pleased since the fries had been darn good, and she knew it. Olivia had mentioned having something like this in New York and it had sounded good. If only there had been more. In the gravy was what she assumed was burger of some sort. It had been seasoned just right as well, "That was really good and thanks Erin."

Erin laughed at how fast it went, and caught their server's eye, who happened to be a Theta in MacLaren and nodded at the empty tray. They grinned and nodded back before heading into the kitchen. "I'm glad I had them start working on a second one." As she spoke it arrived, and Erin lifted the empty tray out of the way so the full one could be placed.

"You are some hungry pups but save some room for the entrée!" The server mentioned, amused. "You are welcome to come back another day." Pulling a small plate out of his apron, he pulled some off, and placed it on the floor beside Shelly, who was too well behaved to beg for some. "If you share some of your food, Shelly will love you more." He stage-whispered to Olivia, grinning as Shelly gobbled up the treat, tail wagging.

Olivia had to blink and petted Shelly, "Sorry girl, still learning what you want and need." Just for good measure she added some more fries from her plate, "Enjoy and can you bring her a nice rare or raw steak?

She just recently adopted me, and I am still learning what she needs or wants." A good hug later and she settled back to nibbling on some of the fries. Watching the others devour the food she had to giggle. There was also wonder what it would be like to be able to eat like that and not worry about gaining weight. Just looking at the tray of food made her feel heavier!

Oscar and Tessa didn't eat as much as the others, but they still ate far more than she could. If she ate like them, she would have gained several pounds by now. Once she had finished what she wanted she leaned against Oscar and enjoyed the contact, "So you going to ask me to be your girlfriend soon? I won't say no, just so you know." Knowing how much he cared for her really did help. If she did end up as his mate it didn't matter. She had felt so cared for by him since the day her brother had protected them.

Oscar flushed at her question, "We can talk about it later, Liv. Now isn't the time." He wanted to but she was only thirteen and he wasn't sure if it was right or not. He also needed to talk to Zane and Beta Mike about considering changing her to a wolf soon. Based on what Cody and Amber had done it would be a fairly gentle change unlike Zane's Turn.

The server nodded, "One blue-rare steak for Shelly and some more water for her too, one for yourself? Anyone else?" he asked, looking at the wolves, now the edge was taken off their hunger, "The cattle are grown about an hour south of here, and are butchered right in town. They are grown free-range without any hormones or any other chemicals, as it makes them less tasty to us wolves." Usually, the wolves who came went for the steaks, but others came for something else which wasn't often on the menu in the dining hall.

Olivia shook her head, "Human, and medium rare please. Sorry but I am not into my food mooing at me." She wrinkled her face at the idea of stabbing her steak and having it either moo or bleed, "Lots of butter with the baked potato as well as chives, sour cream, and cheese. Can I get some more iced tea?" She had been thirsty, and the tea had been really good.

He nodded, "And I'll make sure the cut is human-sized, not wolf-sized for you." He reassured her, noting it down on a pad.

Melody gave the man a toothy grin, "Cool, our beef tends to come from our ranch though the bacon comes from a local pig farmer. For some reason, the smell of pigs doesn't agree with many of us." The team had been forced to go to a pig farm and it was even worse than the cow barns. It had made their wolves nauseated and whine for some time.

He laughed, "MacLaren doesn't have a space for them, nor is the territory really conducive for them, as it is south; our winters here have way too much snow and ice. There is a tiny herd of bison in the territory. The pack has arrangements with the farmers, and we even send some help if they ask for it. It isn't technically inside our territory, but it is not inside any other pack's."

Mindy groaned, "Tell me about it but I still love bacon and pork. Good eating for much of it." She gave the waiter a shy grin since he was cute. Chances were he was an adult, but he was close to their age, and she wouldn't mind relaxing with him.

"Did you want some slow roasted ham? I do know they just had a roast which came out of the oven." He offered, seeing her face at the thought.

She paused and then a hungry look crossed her face, "Please, that sounds really good and thanks for the suggestion. I love beef but ham rocks as well." She couldn't resist, "Do you live at the pack or in town? If in town what would be some fun things to do?" He was cute and spending time wouldn't be a bad thing.

Erin bit back a laugh, as their server was not much older than Mindy.

"I live with the pack, and run down to the warehouse, where they have a room to shift in." he commented, "I'm going to be back up there for supper, did you want me to find you then?" He smiled, and knew she wasn't his mate, but thought she was cute enough to spend some time with.

"If you have time, I would like to talk with you. It is interesting being here, but I want to talk with a wolf who is similar to my level. The food here and at the house is really good, thanks." She hoped her blush didn't show, unlike Simone she was white, and she looked down at her drink.

Simone grinned at her and gently elbowed her, "Actually the ham sounds really good as well. A nice big slice along with a spud like Liv mentioned. A salad would be nice with a blue cheese dressing and a refill on my soda."

Rico leaned back and sipped down the last of his ice water and was feeling relaxed. The appetizer had been really good, and he had enough time to wait for the rest of the food. He had ordered a bison burger with fried onions, local cheese, and some sauce he wasn't sure what it was made from. It had a local bread as the bun but based on the menu it wasn't a bun sort of bun, "Thanks and those darn things were so good I might just drag our team leader here.

Tessa leaned against Rico and sighed, "I wish Zane could have been here since he would have enjoyed the food." She didn't want to send to him since he had asked them not to. She was going to cuddle the daylights out of him when they eventually made it back. As they had been shopping, she had picked up a few things for him as well.

Their server smiled, "I'm sure any of the local wolves would show you the run down to town. We do often get a larger rush for dinner and breakfast here of wolves, as it's different than what is offered at the pack house, but lunches tend to be quiet." He said as he collected the empty dishes. "It's about a half hour as a wolf to run through the forest. It beats having to warm up a vehicle and drive on icy roads in winter." Pausing for a moment, "Alpha Gareth called, and is getting the tab, so you can head out when you wish. I hope your visit to Canada goes well."

Tessa gave him a shy smile, "I will have to ask, if you have some time maybe you could show us? Zane needs some time to relax and do touristy stuff. I have a feeling he would also devour the fries even as we did." She was looking at the final devastation of the fries and once the food was done, she had a feeling she was going to be needing a nap. It was good and with Zane not sleeping well she hadn't either.

Melody almost frowned but decided not to even protest the Alpha getting the bill, even though they had brought money with them and hadn't expected it, "Um, thanks and we will still get the tip. Four paw drive wins over four wheel drive many times unless you are talking a long distance." She didn't comment on the visit since so far for Zane it hadn't been the best. For Olivia and Oscar, it had been good but for the moment she was focused on Zane and what he was feeling.

Erin nodded and sort of expected it to happen as he had asked if they planned to take a meal in town before they left. He usually did it for delegations from other packs who eat out, as a good host. She really didn't want to see the bill, with how the price for meat had been going lately.

He smiled at Tessa, "I work late on the weekend, maybe I can show you some stuff on a morning before work, then?" He nodded at Melody's compromise, "If you wish, although tips are not expected, as we are paid a living wage here. Alpha Gareth is like that when visiting wolves come here, he often quietly pays the tab, as a courtesy, since he is the host. Do let other wolves know, as Gareth does consider this as neutral territory, and wolves don't need to check in just to have a meal before continuing on, so we do get a fair amount of traffic." He laughed at the joke, "Around here, with all the mountains, and how you have to go around them to go anywhere, often paws are faster than wheels going to neighboring packs, other than for the weakest and the oldest."

Tessa gave him a pleased look, "Thanks and when you get to the house let me know, I will introduce you to Zane if you haven't met him. I think he would have a good time in town, I had a bit of the maple syrup candy, and I think he would love it." Even though she knew she would eventually find her mate, Zane would always mean a great deal to her. She knew it was the same for Oscar since they were twins. Even if Olivia was going to be his mate it didn't mean they didn't care for Zane for his taking charge of them. She knew their parents loved Beta Mike as well and it was what she would feel for Zane.

Rico gave her a good hug before looking at their server, "Thanks Liam, it is nice to meet new wolves, and I am sure Zane will appreciate your helping us." He gave the teen a toothy grin, "Now food! I's hungry and the table isn't looking that edible." He started laughing at his own joke.

Melody snorted, "I will deal with Rico for you but so far, the food has been darn good and thanks for the service. I can't help but wonder what the main food is going to be like." Several of the others growled at the thought.

Liam smiled, "I'll see you again. If not here, up at the pack house." Taking the last of the dirty dishes away from the appetizer, he headed to see if their food was done. Many were nearly licked clean, as happened with many wolves. Their chef called it 'good to the last lick' and took it as a complement to his work.

He was quickly back with the main dishes, passing each theirs, and even treating Shelly as an equal, where her plate was same as normal. Shelly and the other wolves got steaks which were nearly twice the size of Olivia's. He also placed a tray of toppings for the potatoes, so each could top them as they wanted, then topped off everyone's drinks and water glasses, including refilling Shelly's water bowl from the same pitcher.

They had the wolfdogs in enough they were prepared for them and had no issues. Some of the trainers brought them down when they were pups, just so they could get the exposure. It was also to train them to not beg for food and how to handle all the scents without being distracted.

Olivia looked down at the plate Shelly had and just had to grin, "Even your plate is larger than what I normally eat. I hope Uncle Mike can afford your food." She jerked when Shelly whipped her tongue across her ankle, "Darn it! It is bad enough when Zane or the others do it. From you Shelly that is wrong." She shuddered before starting to eat the food. The steak was darn good, and the potato was baked just right. With the addition of butter, and the other toppings she was going to be stuffed, "Oscar, you might need to carry me out of here." If they had something like 'death by chocolate' she was going to be in a food coma soon.

Erin snickered, "I know Alpha Maria called down and talked to your Luna, and they worked something out for her large appetite. We normally offer a food stipend and coverage of the medical bills. Some humans are just given a bank card, and just submit the receipts." For the most part, if the bill was for the dog, they would just accept it. If there was an accidental bill not accepted, often they just gave out warnings. It was only if it was clearly being abused, did they do any sort of action. Only once was she aware of did they have to cancel the card and give refunds after they submitted receipts. She only knew of a couple other of their dogs which were with someone supported by another pack; in both of those cases, they just gave a flat amount to the pack for the food and paid any medical bills they sent. Their pack dealt with getting the money or supplies to the person.

Olivia snickered at the comment, "Not really worried since I have seen the bacon bill for the team and our house. If we can afford it, Shelly isn't going to be much of a problem." When Oscar snorted, she leaned over and gave his cheek a kiss, "You showed it to me, you know. I made the mistake and asked. I was horrified by what it costs to feed my brother not to mention everyone else."

They chatted with Liam as time permitted for him before they finally left. Erin had been notified and knew the wolf was dealt with, "Time to go back. There will be a fire this evening. Shall we?" She knew they had fires occasionally but when she wasn't sure when or how often.

Liam took away the dishes from the warm chocolate brownies which the manager had given on the house for them. "Did you have a vehicle or need me to call for one?" He asked, having seen Olivia moving with some pain. Word of her injuries had made the rounds of the pack already, especially the lower ranks, who kept an eye out for seeing if she needed help, but so far hadn't needed anything extra.

It had been a long morning for her, but Olivia was doing okay. With Oscar's help she would do fine. Well unless she decided to pass out at the table they were at. By now she was stuffed and really wanting a nap.

Even as she was contemplating the table as a good place for a nap Erin shook her head, "No, our vehicle is close by, and Olivia will be fine. Thanks for asking." Even as she was talking, they were starting to stand up.

Melody had contemplated the tip and tossed some of the funny Canadian money on the table—it was all different colours, and the smallest bill was $5; they only had coins for the one and two, "Thanks Liam and later." The entire team wanted to get back to Zane. They knew today was going to be hard on him, but he had ordered them to go to town for the day. She understood why but would have liked to be there for him.

They trooped out of the place and moved towards the SUV. Oscar and Tessa were making sure Olivia had as few problems as possible. She had taken one of her pills after eating. It was a *NSAID* (Nonsteroidal anti-inflammatory drug), so it wouldn't knock her out, but it would help with the pain.

Once they were in the SUV, Oscar held her close, and she was quickly asleep as they were driving. Once at the garage he woke her up. Erin would be able to drive the eight-wheel thing for Olivia since she had driven it to the garage. Once she was awake, he helped Olivia out of the SUV, "We can relax shortly and talk if you want." He gave her a good hug and moved towards the all-terrain vehicle.

Erin smiled and hopped into the driver's seat of the Argo, as Tessa and Oscar climbed in as well. Shelly hopped into the back, still in her pack, carrying many of the purchases. The rest stripped and passed the clothes and bags of their purchases before shifting to run as wolves. They headed out on the last leg, quickly arriving at the back door of the pack house.

Erin waved as they got everything out and took the Argo to the building they had as a garage for them hidden in the trees. From the large meal, she suspected them all to just go have a good nap.
*****

Zane was relaxing with several of the pups in what he had come to consider the pups living area. There were several TVs, game stations and piles of games stacked neatly on the shelves. There was a Halo game on one and Final Fantasy on another. Based on what he had heard, until Adam had come into the pack, they hadn't had the network connection for some of the games. Several of the pups were eating the games and high-speed connection up. It sounded so weird to him since he had grown up with broadband. Even though his game console had been an old one he still had the connection for it. Some of the pups had commented that even with their faster reaction time, on the old system, due to the lag from the connection, their human opponents had an advantage.

When the rest of his team came in, he stood and after giving his sister a good hug, he petted Shelly. He turned to Tessa and gave her a good hug and kiss as well, "Hope you had fun. I want to go there another day so I can see what it is like." When Melody settled down next to one of the pups he had to grin since she was sitting rather close to him, *Like someone? Good for you.* Zane liked Melody but not as a potential girlfriend. She was his counterpart and was how he treated her. She was female and was good looking, but he didn't have any interest in her as he did Tessa. He settled down with Tessa and relaxed to watch the games going.

Melody mentally stuck her tongue at him before she started cheering. Based on the mood in the room the morning must have been hard for them. Chances were good they were doing this to work off some emotions. She didn't blame them at all. She wished Zane hadn't had to deal with the punishment, but they were wolves and enforcers. It was something they were going to have to deal with.
*****

Adam and Brook arrived back after dinner, having done their own hunt, as both needed to work out some frustrations. Adam, over having to take out yet another pack. Brook over her mate having to fight *another* Alpha in a fight where the other wolf would have been trying to kill him. He knew it would increase his reputation for taking out other packs, especially of those who were farther away.

Looking in on the gaming room, which the pups seemed to congregate in when they were in their down time, he smiled, as they had set up three TVs, in among the games. It seems there was quite a few gaming systems which had been set up. He had provided the TVs when asked along with a wired network connection, but the gaming systems the pups—or their families—had provided. He didn't want to get into a system war or have to get all of them; they could decide for themselves. All he provided was the ability for them to play the more advanced ones which needed the faster connection.

Watching the pups dominate in the games had him snickering. Now they had the connection on the network speed, and all had done the basic 'internet competency' training to be allowed, their faster reactions than the human players were showing through. He had to leave before he laughed at some of the comments he heard. He had a smile as the antics of the pups had finally broken his gloom from the morning. To even it out, some had joined on both sides.

Zane felt Adam's presence and glanced over at the door he was standing in. When he caught his eyes, he grinned before looking back at one of the games going. He was ignoring Melody who was now sitting in the wolf's lap and relaxing with him. He wouldn't get involved unless needed or asked. His team's personal lives weren't any of his business as long as it didn't impact on the team. He was glad she was relaxing with one of the pups. Rico was cheerfully chatting with a she-pup as well. Olivia was relaxing on Oscar's lap, and they were chatting with several other junior pups. Mindy and Simone were calling out both compliments and groans as people did well or bombed.

His eyes caught Adam's again, *My team seems to be happy; I am glad for them.* He kissed Tessa and shifted slightly so he was more comfortable before calling out a jeer as well. Someone had just biffed big time, and their character had gone up in a whoosh of flame.

Adam nodded, having stopped when Zane contacted him, *I'm glad they are, too.* Trying to not bring up the morning any more than he had to, *Have a good nap before lunch with Alpha Maria?* She had told him what happened, as she knew Adam was keeping a close eye on Zane. *We're heading out to the firepit, if you are interested in joining the gathering.* He offered, as he wasn't sure if Zane knew where it was. *I started an idea where at the firepit, all leave their ranks and seniority behind, and just gather for fellowship and community, and enjoy being together regardless of ranks. All are still expected to be courteous and respectful, or they will be asked to leave.*

Zane gave Adam a pleased smile when he asked about the nap, *I did, I felt somewhat bad for making her sit there but it really did help. She felt much like Esther does and it allowed both me and my wolf to sleep without nightmares.* He was going to have to give her a good hug later just because. Talking to Adam had helped but he had really needed the maternal touch as well.

Firepit? It sounded interesting and leaving ranks behind was also an interesting concept. He wasn't sure how it would really work since it was almost ingrained to check others for their levels. Chances were Adam was talking about leaving the 'luggage' behind and simply be family for a while, *That sounds interesting, and I think I will drag my team to it.* He replied, before addressing his team, "Everyone, Alpha Adam is going to show us to where there is going to be a bonfire. I am going and if you want to follow us." It was aimed at his team, and they knew it. Chances were good all the other pups knew of the fire and where it was.

He helped Tessa up and twitched when he was nosed by Shelly, "Girl, that is my side you just poked. Be good or I will talk to your person." He gave her a good pet even as Olivia was standing up. He flashed a frown at her, "Control your wolfdog sis or else. You might lose another crutch."

She snickered at him, "Maybe I told her to do it? Now I can get you back for all the pokes and licks you have done to me. I know you won't do anything to her, so I can have her pick on you all she wants." Oscar was struggling to keep his face clear of any expression. Olivia noticed it and gave him a kiss, "He is my brother, and I can tease him if I want."

Zane growled at her before mock stalking out of the room, "Little sisters are such a pain in the butt." Several boys laughed while several of the girls growled at him. Most of the pups started turning things off and starting to follow as well. A couple made quiet comments on how they lost track of time.

Adam draped an arm over Zane's shoulders, "I know what you mean! I have a younger sister, too. I love her to bits, but they are almost there to be annoying to us big brothers!"

He had to ignore his sister kissing Oscar. She was only two years younger but damn it, she felt too young to be kissing a boy. He still thought of her as a little kid even though he knew better. She had gained several inches over the last year or two and had started getting the 'womanly' curves. It bothered him since his wolf had noticed other boys noticing her. It made both of them want to go and bite them to keep them away, *And she is growing which doesn't help. My wolf wants to go and chew on some of the boys who have eyeballed her. Not he-wolves but human boys. Oscar has made his feelings obvious, so few he-pups have flirted with her. Damn it! I am just a pup, I no wanna be grumpy and growly over my sister growing up!* He lightly elbowed Adam as he was grumbling, since he had a feeling he had felt similar a time or two.

Tell me about it! My sister is four and a half years younger! I really felt it. At least now she is safely mated to a wolf in Longview Pack who I approve of. Like your sister, she's still human, and has a wolfdog to watch her back. Sadly, we were born into being grumps over our sisters growing up! Adam replied, smiling inwardly as Zane elbowed him, glad he was comfortable enough to do it, as he let him go.

Chapter 25 - Firepit

Guiding the pups out, Adam took them on the short walk to the firepit, where the fire was already going well. Even though he had eaten, the thought of a fire-roasted hot dog made his stomach twinge with hunger.

"If you want, there is hot dogs and sausages, and sometimes other meats you can roast, along with stuff to make smores. The urn has a non-alcoholic apple cider." He told the pups, "Help yourself." Before pulling a hot dog roasting stick off the rack and slipping one on it. Moving to the fire, he smiled greetings at those there, as he started to roast the meat over a part which had been left low just for that purpose. Once the fire had a bunch of coals, they would rake out a portion for cooking on.

"What? No alcohol for the kids? I am horrified and shocked." Mike had noticed them coming out and grinned at Zane when he made a face, "Nice idea, though I have a feeling it wouldn't work as well at our pack. We are more widespread than you are and not all live in the subdivision we 'own'." The food sounded good.

Adam laughed and smiled in greeting, "Well, you could do it monthly, and just invite all the members over. We have it at MacLaren on Monday nights, and I've started Fridays up at Wild Valley. There is no expectation or requirement to come, but it is a good way to gather as a family."

Mike scratched his chin as he tossed the idea around in his mind. It was a good one and would be good for pack bonding. Even with all the shit which happened in the last day or two he was gaining some good ideas, "Maybe on the moon nights or just before. I will have to think about it. Thanks."

Adam nodded, "Or have it on the new moon, so it is opposite?"

Josh had to contemplate the idea as well and it was a good one. They normally had a pack meal the night of the moon and a breakfast the morning after. It was a good idea to consider something happening which wasn't related to the moon since emotions tended to run high then, "I am going to have to bring this up to dad as well."

Adam smiles, "You're welcome to it. I like happy wolves, even when not in my pack, so feel free to copy ideas, and if you have any suggestions, let me know." He turned cuddle a wolf who seemed be having a bad day and slumped down beside him.

Zane grabbed a bratwurst for him and Tessa before settling down near a pile of coals which had already been started. When Jacob came over, he gave the junior wolf a light bump, "How goes it? Have a seat and relax. Thanks for taking care of the issue." The boy had been really helpful with letting everyone know Olivia was off limits, not realising he had just had the Alpha pass it on.

Tessa grinned at Jacob, "Town was fun, not a great deal of touristy stuff but we did some shopping. Even picked up some more tie-dyed shirts for Zane." She giggled at Zane's expression though it had been Olivia who had picked them up. There were only a couple, but it had been too funny.

He grumbled at her but kept cooking the brats and chatting with others who had come over. Even as he was getting a sense for them, they were doing the same. What was amusing was all knew what they were doing for the most part. For the most junior wolves they didn't care since their job was taking care of the pack.

Even as Zane was talking to Jacob and some of the others the rest of his team was doing much the same. Melody was relaxing with the he-pup she had been flirting with. Rico was settled next to a she-pup and talking. For the moment everyone was relaxed. Zane still had to deal with the whole mess but for tonight he was going to let it go.

Once he had finished cooking, Adam moved off to where Brook was sitting and smiled, chatting with the other wolves around him. Several came to him for the usual cuddle, before moving on, to let another.

Zane talked for a while before finally deciding it was time for bed. Even though it hadn't been a horribly long day he was tired and still somewhat emotional. After standing he let everyone know he was going to the room and would talk to them later. There wasn't any reason for them to leave the fire early. As he had expected, Tessa came with him and once they reached the room, they quickly changed clothes and fell asleep on one of the mattresses.

Adam wished Zane a good night at what he considered an early night, as he was going to be up for a while more. He put the pup out of his mind and continued to have fun with the others still there. Mike had some funny stories, and not being from the pack all were new, so many enjoyed the new content as the fellowship was across packs. Several of the others from the other packs had come as well.

Mike was telling a story and in the midst of it he stood and pointed his hot dog fork towards the sky, "And after I stabbed him, I held my knife up..., wait, sorry my wiener is getting cold." He sat back down and stuck the hot dog back over the coals. When the muffled laughter started, he smirked, "Not asking to warm it, my mate might object." Josh was almost collapsed on Molly as he was trying not to bellow out his laughter.

Adam was yawning, and it was dark, showing it was almost midnight by the time he and Brook headed to bed. The two of them stripped down to just some light shorts and snuggled up in their bed. Charlie had abandoned them at the fire a couple hours before and was on the pad, snuggled up with the pups who were there; it seemed some of the MacLaren ones had come and joined the puppy-pile as well, which they didn't mind. They were asleep almost as soon as their heads hit the pillow.

*****

Even though Zane was tired he woke in the middle of the night. Like other nights he woke and wasn't in a good mood, he decided to shift and go for a run. He wasn't going to go very far but he needed the time to think. After silently leaving the room, he went out back and shifted. He looked up at the moon and enjoyed the feel of the light on his face and fur. The light felt much brighter, as the area was much darker, it was away from the city lights, even though it was just a crescent.

After silently saying hello to the moon, he set out at a decent pace though he wasn't struggling. The hot spring was too far, though the thought sounded nice. The hot pool in the greenhouse was too enclosed for him as well. Instead, he settled for making a looping trail near the pack house. It was several miles long and was what he needed. He ran for several hours before he finally was calm enough to settle down and relax.

When he did, he found a circular clearing which felt similar to the one he was occasionally drawn to back home. Zane settled down and closed his eyes to think, feeling the comfort it seemed to have. Before he realized it, he had relaxed and fallen asleep, and morning had arrived. With a woof of annoyance, he stretched and headed back to the pack house feeling refreshed.

*****

The next morning, as had already become routine, Adam and Brook quietly pulled clothes on and headed off for breakfast; the conference was resuming today. Adam nodded to Zane, as he padded in from outside in his wolf form, heading for his room, in greeting, as they headed to breakfast. He didn't think about how Zane was returning, or if he had been out most of the night, as was common for the older pups and adults at times spent the night as a wolf out in the forest; sometimes it was even their wolf who took over and had gone outside. Flopping down at their normal table, for once they were one of the first ones there, and it was quiet, and the few who were there mostly were still working on waking up. It did mean they got piping hot food to eat, and they were all very fresh.

Fabian walked up to the table Adam and Brook were at and sat across from them, "I haven't had a chance to speak to you, but I'm glad to see your pack's compound first."

Adam and Brook smiled in greeting, "Welcome. I hope you are finding the time... productive." Adam replied. Meetings tend to be boring, so 'fun' or 'entertaining' were out.

Fabian nodded, "I am wondering if you would be open to the idea of having the Academy hosted at your pack?"

"Yes!" Brook replied, before Adam could even think about it. *It is the most prestigious training school which exists for any Were! You would be an idiot to not want it!* She told her mate astonished and giddy with excitement, *It is a great honour for any pack to be asked to have it, let alone a pack just starting. We will have not only wolves but other Weres wanting to join our pack, just to get close to it.*

Adam smiled, "My mate took the decision from me, but I do agree. Would there be a chance we could attend?" *I agree but let's be calm about it.* He told her, even though he was as excited as her.

Fabian nodded with a smile, "We definitely could arrange something. I have seen what your pups and the two younger ones, their girlfriends can do, and all six would also be candidates. It seems to be getting harder and harder to find new locations to host it, ones which aren't overrun with humans, but you have plenty of room, and even the buffers are totally natural." He sighed, "When I started, three hundred years ago, as an intern after my own training, we could go almost anywhere, now the humans are nearly everywhere, and with the satellites, even harder to hide." Back then, they didn't do any breaks, as travel was much too slow for anyone to go home. Some they have doing a semester or even a year, then having a longer break, and having another there in the seat, and then returning for a later semester. It had been a headache to keep track of everyone and was glad on how he no long had to do it, except in exceptional circumstances. Now, it would be easier too. They had a database of those who were training, with a table of mandatory courses, and any of the electives, they could make an entry for them, and it would show what courses they still had to pass to graduate. It also made it much easier to schedule the classes to not be too large as well.

Both nodded in understanding.

Fabian gave a shake, seeming to pull himself from the past, "You would be hosting it for a decade, with the possibility of extending it up to three decades. We would need to work with you to use your pack house for dorms—" he grinned, "—which from what you have said, half is going to be vacant. And for access to your gym facility."

Adam and Brook nodded, "That's reasonable. As a pack, is there anything we get?"

Fabian smiled, "Ten million US dollars per year for the hosting, and you get to recommend ten wolves. If we renew, in a decade, you'd get to recommend ten more. We would spread them out, but they would be trained at your site, unless it's arranged for the future. Also, the trainees would assist with your patrols and maintenance duties, as you wish. They could also help in the kitchen, or with other cleaning, if you wished."

Adam blinked at the money it would come with; it alone would pay for the outgoing money to build and maintain the pack. *I'm sold!* He told his mate, awed alone on the money it would make for the pack. *It would mean the pack would never, ever want for anything. I could build the entire local network for the pack with that money. Heck, we could build the Medical with the latest gear to rival a major human hospital!*

"We're interested; it would be a great way to get our name as a pack out there." Adam replied. The money would go a long way to finance the pack, too.

Fabian grinned and passed over a folder, "The details of our requirements are in there, along with the details on what training is there." Opening the folder, there was a note sheet attached, "I talked to Gareth when I got here, and it seems half the skills you have enough you could *teach* the course and will be excused; we will just need you to do the final exam, but we can do it before the start."

Both grinned and nodded, "Maybe, if needed and we have the time, we could help be an instructor." Brook offered, "I always loved teaching, but I've been too busy since meeting my mate to be a primary instructor." By the time they arrived, she hoped their work had settled down a bit or they had a Second who could help out.

Fabian smiled back in agreement, "I understand; you have got seven to excel in under a season enough to qualify for ranks they never dreamed they could ever obtain," Nodding at Adam, "Even while working to qualify yourself, and learning to *be* a wolf. Several of the Alphas have already come forward and been wanting you trained, to make sure your ethics are good; they're concerned you are wanting to expand and take over packs." He totally understood, as it was now three packs they had been involved in taking out.

Adam was surprised he knew he had just been turned. His wolf snorted at the idea of taking over peaceful neighbours; those were not a threat and would help with others. Ones which attacked their pack or those under their protection were a different story.

Fabian grinned, "It's no secret; from talking to your wolves, you are a Turned wolf, with less than a year being a wolf, and you have beaten multiple Alphas, and to a Were who doesn't know, they would think you were born among us." He shook his head, "It took me a day to get over my shock you could do it. I have never seen someone who was turned less than a century before able to react like you do! Usually, I see those who have been Turned take years to even decades to stop reacting like a human..." He trailed off, hoping they would share a reason, if they had one.

Adam and Brook grinned back, before Brook stated, "Now *that* is a secret, which we don't want out," Brook said, "It shocked the elders when they were told, but it is all you are going to get to know. We do not wish to have any more knowing the secret." At his nod of agreement she continued, "Just treat us as you would if he had been born wolf, and we will be fine."

Fabian smiled, "In that case," he took a pen from a pocket and noted on a few more courses, "I don't think you would need to take those ones, as they are for dealing with being turned."

Adam grinned, tapping the electronics and math courses "I took ones like those a bit over a decade ago at a technical college."

Fabian laughed, "It is just a sample idea, we would want a list of what training and certifications you hold, so we can get a plan worked out. As you both have different skills, you would be in different classes, and we would make sure to work around your Alpha duties."

Adam looked at the dates when they would be coming in: the spring just under two years from now. "One thing," he started, tapping on the date, "We hold a Spring Trials in May. It starts on the first and goes till everyone has done all they wanted."

Fabian nodded, "I am aware, and it is why I'm having them come middle of April. They would have two weeks for orientation for the staff and the few students, then we would have them join in with the trials. It would give us a baseline for everyone, and let your pack see how they stack up with them. Our instructors and support staff would provide additional staff to run it."

"That's reasonable." Brook replied, "We should have the pack house totally finished by next spring, even though we are gearing for moving them into it within a month on cots in the main floor, till we finish the interior."

Fabian smiled, "Having your pack work at making their home?"

Adam nodded, "It gives them a sense of ownership and pride with them helping to make it. It's also 'many hands make light work'; and it keeps them all busy without us needing to keep a close eye on them."

Several others had come to sit and listen in. Elders Elise and James were among them. Elise had shocked pleasure showing on her face. The pack had just been formed, and they were already getting the nod from a training school which every wolf who knew of it wanted to be in.

The exposure usually had several from the host pack being offered spots, from all ranks who showed potential; she had missed how they had several seats they got to nominate someone for.

Adam was reviewing the requirements and passed the sheet to Healer McCoy which had the medical ones, as he had joined them as well.

"We have almost everything, but a couple of the pieces of equipment we don't have on order are expensive—" he started.

"Order them." Adam said decisively. "If you have anything which is not on the list but want or items which are approved you would like to upgrade, give me a list, and include what it is and how it would help." He had already pocketed the money order for the first year which had been in the folder; they should have the money to do almost anything. They would have to get into the bank to have it placed in their accounts as soon as they could. This amount would require Brook or himself in person to go. *We just got paid a large check for the first year.* He told their head healer silently.

The healer nodded, looking pleased. He had tried to be frugal, but now he could see about upgrading some of the orders from base models to the higher versions, which could diagnose more, or do the treatment easier.

Gareth walked by, "Conference," He mentioned. They looked startled and looked at the time. They had ten minutes till the next item was starting.

Jess gathered the two Alphas, and Fabian's dishes, "Just go, I can deal with the dishes today." She ordered with a smile.

Adam kissed her head, "Thanks," before heading off for the conference.

*****

"This item is on hiding us from the humans who don't know of us." Gareth started, as the last sat down. "For this, we have a rogue-changed wolf," He motioned to Zane, "Zane. Who has an uncle who is wolf-born but had been unaware of us till after his turning. We also have a mate-turned wolf," he motioned to Adam, "Adam, who is among us."

Mike had reminded Zane about it that morning at breakfast, so he grumbled at him, but knew they were going to have him speak, so for today he was sat at the table beside his uncle, instead of with the observers. He hadn't realised it until he sat down, Alpha Gareth was on the other side of him!

Tom exclaimed, interrupting Gareth, "How is Adam among us then? How can a changed-wolf become an Alpha?" He hadn't known Adam had been born human, as he appeared totally wolf, more so than any he had ever known in his over three centuries of life. He would have known, if he had looked at the session's description, which had been part of the papers at the start of the conference.

Adam shrugged, "Because I have the skills?" He replied, deciding to ignore the implied insult, as he saw no need to challenge over it, he didn't need to defeat *another* Alpha and possibly take on *even more* pack members. "I would have been satisfied being a Beta of Tech within MacLaren. I never tried to become the Alpha, but the more I became in tune with my wolf, the more he pushed me to excel and learn skills which I never dreamed I'd have. I never even thought about becoming a Second, but when it was offered, it felt right to help the pack, and started to learn those skills." He shrugged, as he didn't bother saying anything about how he had taken on Alpha Night and after defeating him, the Alpha had taken his own life. Looking back, he likely would have just held him until they had some sort of binding agreement to stay within his current territory and left him with his pack, but the Alpha had other thoughts, and the pack had declared him their Alpha for beating their Alpha.

Elder James cleared his throat from the seats of those observing. Gareth nodded, for him to have a voice. He stood, "I am the Lead Elder of MacLaren." He said in introduction, even though most knew who he was, "I can say with full certainty *Alpha* Adam has earned his rank. He passed all the trials, including the runs. The fights: he took out Mitch at

The Nameless Pack, when he tried to take control of those left behind when the Alpha attacked MacLaren. Next, he defeated the insurrection of those securing the facility who went rogue afterwards, and finally, he defeated the so-called Alpha Night. Not to mention, he defeated Tyler in front of us all." He looked at every Alpha in the eyes, "Do any of you dispute it? Do any need further details of his abilities?"

There were shakes of heads. Tom just sat there stunned; he had thought Gareth had fought Alpha Night then assigned his Seconds as Alphas. He had fought Alpha Night and barely escaped with his life, due to some very loyal wolves who protected him, with one losing his life as he gave rear-guard. Even he could learn new things. Turning to Adam and Brook, "I am sorry I doubted you." He apologised, "I seem to have been taught some things which are not true and will have to discuss with the Elders of not only my pack, but others, to find out what is true." He bowed his head, before turning away. If they had been able to defeat Alpha Night, he wasn't going to be happy till he was back in his territory, and safe with his wolves. Tom knew he was very close to annoying Adam enough he would challenge him, and if he did, he now knew he would fail, and from what Adam and Brook have done, they might leave him without a pack, if they left him alive at all. Just look what he did to Tyler!

He wanted to make it to his next century, and retire from being Alpha, and let his grandson inherit the Alpha-ship and be an Elder and not need to do the day-to-day annoying duties of being the leader. If he continued to follow his older cousin Tyler's lead, it looked to him he would not make it, not thinking about how it would also mean his grandson would have to pick up the pieces, instead of an orderly transition.

Of the seventeen who Tyler had brought, all eight of the guards, both assistants, two of the drivers, and the valet had petitioned to move to his pack, not even waiting to see about Wild Valley's laws. He had accepted them but had sent them back with two of the vehicles they had brought, along with one of his own vehicles, four of his own guards and two drivers, as he didn't need them here. He realised Tyler had decided to bend the truth to him and biased him against the new Alphas before he had a chance to meet them. He had heard a story of how Tyler had gone to their pack and demanded a meeting, when they had refused one. Tyler had always expected others to deal with his whims. Being rebuffed and made to leave immediately would not have sat well.

The remaining four drivers Tyler had brought didn't have ties to his pack and were considering Wild Valley. As such, they had been provided with a copy of the laws they were to agree to before joining. He knew more had been sent to what had been Feral Star Pack, to see how many would be interested in relocating. Tom had also sent an offer to absorb any who wanted. A few had already accepted, even though it hadn't even been a day. They were packing and would be at Sentinel Star Pack before he got back.

Adam and Brook looked satisfied with his apology, thankfully.

"If we can go back to the topic," Gareth replied, having expected the outburst, "Now the side note was dealt with. Since we have the two changed wolves, basically from the opposite ends of the spectrum, their entry to our world was totally different, but both had not known about us before they started getting involved." He told the gathered wolves.

Placing a hand on Zane's back, "I'm going to have Zane tell us his introduction to the werewolves, which is s worst-case scenario." Gareth said. *Feel free to skirt, or not mention anything you feel is too personal; we just need an overview.* He told Zane privately.

Zane took a slow breath and called on his wolf for strength before he started speaking. He knew of this section, and he would be asked to share part of his introduction, he had worked out what he would share and at his uncle's suggestion, had some notes in front of him. "Alpha's, Beta's, and others. I was turned by a rogue somewhat over a year ago. I was out running, sensed something following me and ran faster. The only thing which saved my life was getting hit by a car. It hit the rogue as well and chased him away. Some aspects of my change I will not talk about. Beta Mike and Alpha Adam know of some of them." He paused to gather his thoughts before he continued, "I woke in the hospital after being in a coma for three months. When I woke, I discovered my family had been almost destroyed. My parents killed and my younger sister badly injured in a vehicle crash coming to visit me. Because of the rogue, I lost everything I knew. I woke in a different state, with a voice in my mind, and after being released from the hospital, a wolf form."

He took a sip of some coffee before he could continue. His voice was showing his loss even though he was trying to keep it as neutral as he could. Chances were everyone in the room could sense his distress as he was speaking as well, even Tom didn't interrupt, "I discovered I was a monster like the thing which did this to me. That was how it felt to me: I was now a monster. The rogue took everything I had ever known and tore it apart. Different state, had to join a pack, from what I understand I was close to becoming a lone wolf." He didn't mention that several times, he had been told if he went Lone-Wolf, they doubted he would do well, and would likely go Rogue, and need to be put down. "After what happened to me, I found it virtually impossible to let anyone close to me other than family. The idea of having a bunch of monsters talking to me in my mind scared the crap out of me. To know I had the ability to change someone like what happened to me gave me more than a few nightmares. I still have nightmares about what happened, and my girlfriend and junior wolf Tessa can attest to that." He cleared his throat and looked at Gareth since he wasn't sure what else to say.

Gareth nodded sadly, "I'm going to add, the rogue is still at large, and there is a global watch out for them, as they have been rated Class One."

Grant leaned forward, "Do you think there would be any way we could have had your introduction smoother, any way which could have helped." He asked gently. He knew if he went Lone Wolf, it was unlikely he would have survived the decade. "To me it is beyond worst-case. Adding the trauma of losing your parents on top of having your identity ripped from you."

Zane tried not to give the alpha a pitying look. The only way it could have been better was to not have happened, "How could it get better, Alpha? I was attacked by a monster I didn't even know existed or believed in. It wasn't willing, I didn't ask for it, and it took almost everything from me. I guess I would have to say there isn't anything which could have been done differently. The one thing which probably saved me from losing it was Olivia going into the hospital for a surgical repair." He met the wolf's eyes though it wasn't a challenge. He was making a statement, and it was showing, "I walked into her hospital room after she came out of surgery and fell apart. I lost it, since all I could see was her after the accident with nobody around to be with her. I could see my parents laying in the vehicle with their dead eyes staring at nothing and Olivia dying before help came. Uncle Mike and part of my team took me home and handed me over to the Luna. Before that, I simply couldn't go to anyone and talk. Between her and knowing I had to remain for my sister was about the only thing which saved me."

He had to close his eyes and struggle to force the memory of the breakdown away. As he had said, he still had nightmares at times and Tessa was about the only one who could calm him. It did help if one of his other team was there but just because what Tessa was forced his wolf to calm to keep from hurting her. Zane was finally able to open his eyes again though they were very bleak and hard.

Adam placed a calm hand on Zane's shoulder, having walked around the table to help him, "I think in this case, there was nothing which could have been done." Seeing the bleakness, "I am going to ask for a half hour recess."

There were several seconds to the motion, "Granted." Gareth said, as the others vacated the room, to let Zane calm down and recover. Luna Olwen came over, and sat on Zane's other side, and tried to project comfort and peace to him.

"I'm thinking we have enough of your tale." Adam said sadly, knowing it would be hard on the pup but though he should be given the choice to stay and help or to leave, "Would you be able to stay or need to leave? I think your insight would be valuable on updating the procedures, for those in better shape than your introduction. Not much could have been done in your case, unfortunately."

Zane lightly leaned against the Luna; he just couldn't think of them differently though he did know better. Part of it was because she was female and easier to accept comfort from her. After Adam asked if he could stay, he was torn. Even as he was thinking Tessa slipped into the room and settled down on the other side of Zane, pushing between Mike and Zane's chairs and leaned against him. It really did help since he knew she wouldn't make fun of him for being this emotional. He and his wolf felt utterly safe next to her and had the utmost trust she would help as much as possible, "I think I could if my junior wolf can sit with me. I do get strength from all my team, but Tessa helps in ways the others can't." He was still trying to figure out why it was that way, but he was still learning about wolves and being one.

Mike had slipped out, but he came back quickly with a large mug of hot chocolate and handed it to Zane, "Thank you Zane. I know it was hard, but they needed to hear it. The more humans there are, the more likely this sort of thing will happen. Not just rogue turnings but finding mates. We don't like the idea, but chances are good we aren't going to be able to remain hidden for too many more years." Sections of the government knew about them, and it was almost more than acceptable. Anytime someone had come even close to revealing their secret, the person would vanish, but even that was getting harder to have happen, with all the forensics, cameras, and various ways of tracking someone's movements. It kept most of them relatively honest.

Adam nodded, "I have no issues with you having Tessa stay with you." Sliding Mike's chair over a bit more, he pulled another in for Tessa to sit in. "I agree with Mike, partly it is the prevalence of all the cameras and instant communication. With the changes to our ways to try to fit in, I think we might be able to make it fifty to a hundred years, but no more. Due to that, we need to start planning how we could come out to the public, while minimizing deaths. With how nosy the governments are getting; it may be less."

Luna Olwen sighed, "We only have these conferences, at most, once a decade, due to the fact if we are caught, it compromises not just one pack but many. Due to advances in the human sciences, we can't just have the human who discovers us disappear. Sometimes they join us, which has greatly increased the number of turned-wolves, we have two in progress, which before the beginning of the century would have been unheard of. Now, it's common to have several in the pack who are turning at once."

"I have two turning right now, and myself who's finished, in my pack." Adam added, "Gareth has a human member, and three human-mates and another three who were born human and were turned. Longview has my sister; also a human, along with several who had been born human. What the elders tell me, it seems this century has doubled the number of human-mates alone."

When Zane asked if she could remain Tessa almost gulped. She hardly ever dealt with the Alpha and Luna of their own pack, let alone an entire room full of them. When Zane was having such a hard time dealing with Olivia and her with the bullies was the most exposure she had ever had. She had known Beta Mike, but he was different since her parents were on his team. Just knowing there were so many Alphas in the room scared her slightly.

Zane took her hand and held it before giving it a light squeeze, *Thank you Tessa, I can feel your concerns, but you will be fine. Alpha Adam, Beta Josh, Uncle Mike and others are here. They will protect us. If it bothers you too much you don't have to stay.* If she didn't stay, he wasn't sure if he could. He hated leaning on her like this, but her and her wolf were so comforting. They gave him strength as well.

She gave his hand a squeeze, *I will stay for you Zane.* She leaned against him and relaxed; as her presence would help him, having his scent around her would help her. The Luna had explained why he received so much comfort from her and Oscar. When someone brought her a cup of hot chocolate as well, she thanked them and decided to relax and do her best not to listen.

When the Alphas returned, a few smiled at Tessa, but none said anything. All understood what she was doing there and since she really looked overwhelmed by all the senior wolves, they were not going to say a thing. Her presence did help their wolves stay calm, as getting upset would scare her, and for most Alphas, they didn't want to scare the Thetas who were the pack's foundation.

"I'm thinking in Zane's case," Adam said, picking up the thread from where he called for the break, "There was almost nothing which could have been done, as the additional shock of losing his family would be rare."

Tessa quietly addressed the room, "Alphas, it wasn't just losing his family. It was waking to find his entire world destroyed. He started in one world, the human world, and woke in the supernatural world. He woke with the voice already there, his parents killed, and little sister badly hurt. Being in a different state, his uncle not there because of work, and his aunt unavailable." She fell silent again, Zane had asked her to mention it.

Chapter 26 – Changing Rules

Adam smiled at the Theta, "Thank you Tessa. I'm going to make the suggestion, where unless absolutely necessary, to not move the wolf being turned in until they are aware, to allow for them to be better grounded by being in a place which they know."

Many agreed with nods, thinking if Zane and Olivia had found themselves kidnapped by aliens and Zane found he was one, it would have been somewhat similar reaction.

"If he had not lost his parents, it would have been quite a bit different, and his parents and sister would have known then what he had become." Adam suggested, thinking hypothetically.

Many nodded sadly. The multiple hits of both being turned, losing the foundation of his parents, and the not even knowing where he was had been what threw him for a loop.

"Currently, only direct family are normally told, but sometimes one a little more distant is told," He looked at Mike, as he had discussed a little about Zane's case, and knew his aunt had been told before they went on the trip to New York, as he was going to need to interact with the pack which was located there.

Zane noticed the look Mike and Adam exchanged and almost smiled. He knew they were talking about Aunt Joli. She had kept insisting he and Olivia spend a good portion of the year with her when she wasn't on trips. There had even been a suggestion of them coming along on a trip or two. She hadn't understood why they were saying no un-til Zane showed her. He had finally gotten tired of the arguing, stood, and stripped before changing in front of her. When he changed back, he pulled his clothing on and said, 'that's why!'.

"I'm thinking we could relax the rules on who is told," Adam con-tinued, "But leave it up to the one turned, in consultation with their Al-phas and Elders to others in their family, or very close friends, as to what they are now."

Tom leaned back in his seat, as he could live with this change, since then he could veto any human being told, and as long as the turned-wolf was in his pack, they would have to listen to the order. He didn't even like their families knowing, but the rule was even older than he was, and he had been taught to respect the elders. It was one he was going to chal-lenge when he *became* an Elder.

Adam turned to Zane, "Do you think it would be better for others turned in the future?"

"I'm not sure what you are asking Alpha, if you are talking about not being moved, I don't think it would have mattered. Either way I would have woken to pretty much the same and then being told I had to move. For me I think it was better than I was never asked about being moved. I woke, it was done, and it removed one thing for me to worry about. If you are talking about letting others know? I really don't know enough to say. All my friends were back home. I had to meet new ones, and they were all wolves in the beginning." He took another sip of the hot drink since the sugar was helping.

Adam shook his head, "I was more thinking hypothetically, where someone was turned, right now the rules, at least in this area, are only immediate family is supposed to be told. I am thinking, opening it up would give more security, as there would be more humans who if some-one noticed them doing something strange, they would understand and be able to deflect the problem. Or not comment about it to others."

Zane had to give an almost helpless shrug, "I don't know how to an-swer that. I was just going into high school when I was turned. I can't think of many kids I would have trusted to know. For an adult? I really don't know." If someone did let the cat out of the bag an enforcer would be sent to deal with them. He didn't feel like he was in a position to really say anything useful.

Adam nodded, "In that case, do you think we should keep the general restriction to adults being turned, for the most part?" Most of the Alphas agreed, having two very different points of view was better. They had argued on the run back, and Adam had refused to have Amber or Olivia being involved, saying they were too young. He hadn't even wanted to have Zane this much involved, but had to compromise, with the agreement he do most of the speaking. He was wishing Chris wasn't so busy with all the security sensors up in Wild Valley, as he would have been a totally different view. None of the others in MacLaren were at all willing to be involved when they were asked.

Tessa and Zane discussed it over the bonds before she spoke again, "It is a two-sided question, Alpha. I talked briefly to my brother and his gut reaction was yes. Knowing how close he came to losing his mate in the accident scared him badly. He would feel safer if she was a wolf than as a human. For Zane, his response was almost the exact opposite. Nobody should be turned with out them knowing everything about it. As far as underage, his reaction is coloured by what happened to him. He knows about Amber and Cody and why, but his reaction is still no unless there is a very good reason, a life and death reason." She gave Zane's hand a light squeeze. For this answer, both felt having Oscar's opinion would be good as well.

Adam nodded, turning to the others, "My case was totally different. From what Brook told me, she smelled me on the wind while out on a run and was just wanting to get close enough to know who I was and was going to shadow me in the trees. The rockslide and the fact I had seen her and felt compelled to help, then having her shift before me, had me knowing about werewolves. I was not very surprised, as I had already decided there was way too many legends and stories about werewolves existing for there not to be some truth behind it and had decided if I ever found out they were real, I would accept it. After a discussion, and the fact I was already feeling the mating bond, we mated that weekend." The details were private and didn't need to be share, but Grant and Louise had a slight smile when he looked at them, "And I started learning about what I needed before being turned, which at which point was a decision I couldn't make till after the mating changes completed."

Taking a sip of his own drink, "I have to agree, we need a protocol for turning those under-age." He gave a brief overview of what happened with Cody and Amber meeting, and what he had been told about her turning young, and of what actually was happening. "I consider Amber's turning one-off, as she and Cody felt the mate-bond much earlier than is normal, and to have it nearly impossible to have the two any distance from each other, her mother, Gareth, myself, both our mates, the Elders of both packs, and the attending Healer decided it was best to allow the turn early, which would settle the mate-bond till they were ready, and if not of age, nearly there, and should actually mate."

Mike had to growl briefly, "And now knowing Oscar is feeling the bond with Olivia we are going to have to decide how to handle the same issue. She is a different case since she is now a teen." He knew Tessa and Zane had become active, but it was too soon for Olivia even though she was close to fourteen, "With her, I have a feeling the bonds started forming after she was given the werewolf blood to help her heal. It wasn't enough to change her, since it normally requires a bite. I think what it did was to start activating her dormant wolf genes."

Zane almost groaned as Mike was talking. His sister was too young to him to even have a boyfriend. It was silly since he had a girlfriend, but this was his little sister they were talking about now. He completely trusted Oscar but still! Next to him he could almost feel Tessa mentally snickering at him and his thoughts.

Many alphas looked thoughtful. Adam nodded, "I am thinking setting the youngest to generally consider for turning being sixteen, in most cases. I will get the records we have, or make them, for tomorrow morning, of the steps we did with Amber and Cody, so you have them.

It was mostly just a turning, and it formed only a weak temporary mating bond, which will suffice until they are of-age. The steps didn't have them being intimate, as I would have not permitted it, as I feel she's too young for that. For Amber, both her and her mother have joined the pack, and are living here." He took a breath and looked at the other leaders, "It was decided, turning her now would allow her to grow up as a wolf, and not have to learn the whole new ways when she becomes an adult, and grown up here, being a part of from many events and activities, instead of being forced to be excluded because of not being able to shift. Part of why we permitted it, was she and her mother have joined the pack, and they are living at the pack house." He didn't bother adding about Amber also being required to show the same self-control and ability to not shift under stress as anyone else before being allowed out of the pack's territory.

Zane had listened very carefully to what was being said and the point Adam made was a valid one. Having Amber slowly grow into her wolf and grow up in the pack would make a hell of a difference. If he had been changed that way, he wouldn't have the problems he had now. Though he didn't use the term anymore, there were times he still felt like a monster. If Oscar did ask to see about changing Olivia, Zane honestly didn't know what he would say. He didn't want his sister to be a monster like he was but if she wasn't changed, Oscar would lose her sooner than later because she was human.

Taking a breath, Adam added, "If I had to do it again, I would have wanted to have prepared Amber better, with more knowledge being shared before, and her knowing more about us first." Turning to Mike, "Olivia has been living among us for over a year, so would know some. Maybe having her know more of the pack ways and laws before she makes the decision to turn or not?"

Mike couldn't help but grin, "Olivia has been going to all the general training classes for junior wolves. Since she is human, she wouldn't show a dominance as we do. Those classes include the by-laws, Council laws, mates, customs, and more. Zane has been getting the full Enforcer selection of classes, since he is going to be an Enforcer. He has the dominance and talent for it. I would have to go over the section on changing again but Olivia has been educated on it."

Zane almost made a face at the mention of his extra classes. Some days he wondered how he had enough time for everything. School in the morning and then afternoon followed by Enforcer training. Go home, do homework, do Enforcer and pack homework, pass out, repeat. Saturday morning more Enforcer training and review of the homework he had been given. He had started shadowing some of the patrols on the weekends as well.

Adam nodded, "I do know both Olivia and Amber have been hanging out together lots, which I do approve of, since it will also give both a friend they can relate to. I did set Amber up with a pack account and e-mail, so she could decide if she wanted to arrange with her to communicate."

Mike had noticed it as well and especially after she found out what Oscar had said. Once she found out she was going to be his mate, she had gone looking for the girl. Even though they were about five years apart, she had been talking with her and Cody. He had a feeling it was also because they had those oversized wolfdogs following them around, "I will mention it to Olivia in case Amber doesn't mention it. She has a pack account as well but tends to use her Gmail most of the time."

Adam grumbled mentally and made a mental note to have a chat with Mike and Olivia about how insecure the human email services were. Many of the "free" email services had horrible security and mined the communication for ways to make the company money. He didn't want her and Amber using it to communicate, when they had the secure e-mail to use instead. Any incoming message from one of those services had a big red bar at the top warning about it being an un-secured service, and not to say anything about the Were-Secrets. Or seeing if he could do a talk for all those there, as he doubted many realised how much one of those services was a security risk. He ended up doing both.

Josh cleared his throat to address the others, "With her mother do you have plans to offer to change her? I am assuming she either doesn't have a mate or hasn't found one yet. We have a young woman who was forced to carry a rogue's child. She is human, the baby isn't. She doesn't have a mate yet though she is seeing one of the pack. With her being human but her child a wolf, would you extend her the option to be changed?" He was curious to see what their thoughts might be. Not all wolves would find their mate. Josh had a feeling with Kylie, she would be one so she could be there for Ash.

Adam nodded, "She has been informed being turned is an option, and has been provided all the pack notes, so she can make the *informed* decision. No pressure is being given either way, so she can decide for herself. Her questions are being answered as fully as we can, as well. For the most part, the humans who are part of the pack have that option. We have one who decided to not follow a warning when he joined the pack, about the headache, and as such, will have to wait about being turned." They weren't going to say who it was, nor what exactly had happened, but the Alphas would know it was taking a human drug for the bond headache, which caused the bonds to be brittle and needing a decade or two to heal.

Josh stood and walked over to the credenza and refreshed his cup. When he came back, he had brought the thermal pot and offered it to who might want to warm their coffee. At the mention of a human ending up with a headache, he had to wonder why. They still used the blood ceremony in his pack and many of the others. With that way, the bonds were formed immediately and permanently. He might have to ask how they did it up here out of curiosity, "Much as you mentioned, she is being schooled on the pack laws. As of now she hasn't asked about it and we haven't brought the suggestion up. If the wolf she is seeing decides to ask her to be her mate, it will change obviously. Even if she did ask, she would need to wait until her son is a year old." Other wolves could nurse the boy but if his mother started going through the change when he was too young, it could cause problems.

Mike mentally flipped through what they had been talking about. He couldn't see Zane needing to be there much longer. "Unless you have more questions for Zane, I think he could use a break." He was doing better than Mike had expected but there wasn't any reason to keep him there. *Olivia and Oscar are going to the hot springs if you want to go and join them.* He told his nephew privately.

Adam nodded in agreement, and silently suggested the same place to relax, not knowing Mike had just done so when the Alphas were silent and didn't have any more questions for Zane.

Zane stood and helped Tessa out of the chair. He met the eyes of the dominant wolves before submitting and quietly leaving. Once they were out of the room he stretched, "Man that really sucked. A good soak is just what my wolf and I want."

Tessa was still holding his hand and gave it a good squeeze, "The rest of the team is going to head that way as well. They are done with the chores they were asked to help with." With all the people here, they had cheerfully pitched in and helped. It also taught them more about this pack and how they did things.

*****

Adam waited for the door to close behind Zane and Tessa, "I am open to any other questions which you were holding back while the pups were here."

They continued to discuss the topic for another couple hours but ran out of topics to discuss a bit early.

"Well, since we have also discussed the topic for this afternoon, we will re-convene to discuss the issues of rogues tomorrow morning." Gareth said, "Enjoy your free afternoon. You are welcome to run, but please take a local wolf with you, or stay on the marked wolf-trails, as there are areas of humans around." Many laughed, as they broke up.

Mike walked out next to Adam, "Adam, I am going to talk to Martin since Zane was wondering about going on a patrol or two. They are talking with Amber as I am sure you know and was wondering if he could go with Cody. Also, he was wondering what hunting might be allowed.

His wolf would like to bring Tessa a bunny or something similar. Back home we keep rabbits and other small prey animals for hunting. Especially for hunt training for the young wolves. I didn't know if you had anything like that here."

Adam laughed, "Yes, if he wants to shadow a patrol, talk to Martin, he arranges them. Normally we wouldn't put more than one pup on a single patrol, as it can be dangerous, as you would know. As for hunting, there is enough bunnies around they are welcome to hunt them. They are all wild, so they can be vexing." He remembered his own learning to hunt. "There are also some game birds here, including some wild turkey which you don't need permission. Deer and larger; you would need to speak to Gareth or Maria to get permission." It had been noted as part of all the rules, as often hunts had to be individually requested, but Gareth and Maria had given blanket permission to all for the smaller animals, as there was currently enough to handle it.

He got a contemplative look on his face at the mention of a turkey. It had been ages since he had hunted one, "I will let them know and I think he is just feeling the need for some fresh warm blood. It has been stressful on him, and it would make him, and his wolf feel good bringing one to Tessa." His team would take care of Oscar as well if Zane didn't, "Thanks and I will let them know." He sent to Zane and gave him the limits.

"I understand what you are saying about the patrol. I think it is a case Zane knows Olivia likes Amber and he is doing his best to get to know Cody. I will see about having Martin set something up. Maybe tomorrow or the next day." He nodded and left Adam to go and find Malcom and see about a hunt.

"I have homework," Adam said to Brook in mock-annoyance, as they headed to lunch. He already had the Elders extracting the information they had, so it would be fine for a while. "You want to do something for a bit?" he asked her.

*****

Olivia set out to find Amber since she hoped she would talk to her. She had seen how much Zane had been hurt by that asshole who insulted him, his team, and Tessa. She assumed the man would have indicated she and Oscar would be even lower than Zane and Tessa. She was glad he was no longer a problem, but she wasn't sure death was the right thing, but Mike had explained why they had to respond that way, but she still wasn't sure it was right, but it also was her human upbringing.

When she finally found Amber, she was with some pups about her age. Olivia walked over and settled down next to her and rubbed her hip, "This is a really lovely place but darn it, the walking is too much. I mean, does it have to be so darn large?" Frankly by the time she left, she was either going to need to be carried around or she was going to be stronger and in better shape.

Amber giggled as did some of the other kids she was getting to know, "Sorry you were hurt, Kacy, could you get her a drink if she wants?" Even though she hadn't changed yet, her senses were getting better. Olivia smelled like there was a bit of pain, "Whatcha doing?" When Shelly gave Orca a lick, she petted her head for a moment, "Hi girl."

"A Sprite please, if you have one. If not, some iced tea would be nice." When Kacy came back over with the pop Olivia had to grin. Zane had never been able to get back into them. Flavoured water was one thing, but pop made him gag, "Actually if you don't mind, I'd like to talk to you about your being changed." She made a slight face, "I have a feeling Oscar is going to talk to me about it, once we get home."

"Not sure what I can really say about it which I haven't mentioned." They had talked but not a huge amount, "Couldn't your brother answer the questions?" Olivia had mentioned he was a changed wolf.

Olivia made a slight face, "I am not going to ask him. His change wasn't nearly as nice as yours." Her expression hardened, "I don't want to talk about it, but he woke to being a wolf and finding me hurt. If I asked him, it would bring bad memories back."

"What do you want to know?" Depending on what she might talk about it and other things not. Some of it she was really getting used to.

As young as she was the entire 'mate' thing sounded so weird. Amber really enjoyed being around Cody and curling up and being with him. Beyond that, she didn't know what to think.

"Mostly I want to know what the change was like and what you have been feeling." She had seen how hard it had been for Zane, but it was something done to him. If Oscar did talk to her, it would be something she was choosing. She wanted to know what it was like from that aspect. Adam wouldn't work, since he was an adult and definitely not Brook; she was a born wolf.

"The bite was painful," Amber said, "Then I passed out, and Cody said I was in and out for about four days. During that and for a while after, I couldn't leave the room, not that I had the energy even to get to the bathroom—Cody had to help me—*and* all my food and water had to be specially made. I'm told it's because basically my immune system had to be remade. I felt like I had a very bad flu." She sighed, "That is the worst part. Then it was about a month before my wolf started talking in my head, which is the best part." There were tears of joy in her eyes, "It alone makes the pain all worth it. You never know how *alone* you are, till you feel your wolf in your mind."

The idea of being stuck in a room again for that long made her groan. When she did, Shelly stuck her head in Olivia's lap and whined a bit, "Nothing to worry about girl. I have grown to hate hospitals as much as my brother. The first time I was hurt I was in the ortho ward for just over a month. When they went back and fixed my leg, I was in the hospital for about two weeks and then in the pack clinic for another two weeks. The idea of being confined..." She made a revolted face. She looked down at her leg, at least the scars would fade. Thankfully, nobody had really asked much about them.

Amber smiled, "I've still not shifted, so not too sure on that part, yet. So, I can't tell you about it." Remembering one thing, "It is really rare to turn kids, as usually they wait till you are an adult. My mom, the pack elders, *and* the Alphas had to agree to do it, and then medical had to say I was healthy enough for it. Before they even told me about what it was and then asked me if I wanted it. They said if we waited for me to be mated, when I become an adult, it would be less time and would turn sooner, but it is *years* away, and I will be turning in *months*."

"What's it like having the voice? I know Zane complained about it occasionally. Something about his wolf giving him weird looks and commenting about human's being weird." It wasn't nearly as bad now as far as she could tell. There were still times he would get a strange look on his face and shake his head but not nearly like at first.

"It was strange at first, as the first thing we are told is to share all our thoughts with them, so they can understand us, and to not hold back anything. It was a bit embarrassing, but when you feel the love from them, no matter what you have done, it feels good." Amber said, a bit of a blush on her face. "After that, it is like having a friend who is always at your shoulder, and you can chat with, without anyone else knowing. They also do make suggestions and comments or get bored and want to do something else."

Olivia was listening before a sudden realization hit, "Oh god! When Oscar and I mate I will probably end up part of Zane's team. That is so wrong. It's bad enough he is my older brother and overprotective. It would just give him one more reason to be even more overprotective." She dropped her head to Shelly's and groaned again before sitting up, "I think it answers most of my questions and thanks Amber." She pulled a dog snack out of Shelly's pack and offered one to both dogs.

Amber snickered a little at her expression, "I think if you were a wolf, and could defend yourself, he would be able to cut back it a little." She smiled and hugged the older girl, "Adam has already set me up an e-mail address, although—" she made a face, "—Both him and my mom can see it till I'm sixteen!" She pulled out a piece of paper from Orca's pack, and quickly wrote it down and gave it to her new friend. "From what I have overheard, they have a business-IM software which can even do video chats, but not allowed to do it alone." She knew a few reasons, but felt they were over-reacting.

She had to roll her eyes, "You haven't seen him when he is being over-protective. At least with Oscar helping me, he doesn't hover as much." She took the piece of paper and pulled a small notebook out and tucked it inside. She jotted hers down as well before tearing the piece off and handing it over, "Don't have that problem thankfully. Well, the e-mail being looked at. It isn't like I am going to be flirting with any other boys now." She wasn't sure about any video software. It wasn't something she had bothered with, "Not sure about the video stuff. I'll have to ask Uncle Mike about it." She tucked the notebook back in the bag.

Since Cody wasn't around, she assumed he was on patrol, "Hey, wanna go and hit the hot springs? I could use a good soak, either that or if you know where a hot tub is? It usually helps my hip relax when it starts aching." Mike had one installed at their new, new house. They had been forced to move one more time after they found Annie was pregnant. The second one they had moved into was large enough for them but not for the baby.

"The hot tub *is* the hot spring, in the greenhouse," Amber replied with a slight giggle, "The pack made it when they built the building and have a pipe which captures the hot water. I would love a soak!" Standing up, she offered a hand to help Olivia up.

Olivia paused, "Um, I am going to guess it is clothing free? I am still getting used to that." *Oscar Amber and I are going to soak in the springs in the greenhouse. My hip is bothering me from all the walking. If you want to join us, it should be fine.* "Would you mind if Oscar joined us?" She looked down at Shelly and grinned, "Let me get the pack off before you decide to join us."

Amber shrugged, "If you want to wear a swimsuit, you can, but everyone else won't." She added, "He'd be welcome. Cody had to get back into being on the patrols, or he was going to be dropped from it for a year. He is very proud to be helping the pack, and being taught to patrol, even before he comes of age." Her voice showed how proud she was of her mate, "He won't be back till around dinner, at the earliest." She missed him and was planning on joining him on the patrols as soon as they would let her. Her teachers had already made sure she was in the right classes to be able to have the skills, but the classes weren't starting until after the Alphas all left.

She had been expecting it was clothing-free, "No, I will survive. Good, he was helping do some laundry for the team. He is pretty much done, and it can be folded later." Since Amber had offered her a hand getting up, she had taken her hand and Shelly's harness to stand. Once she was up, she kept holding onto the harness for a bit of extra support. Shelly was learning what Olivia needed when it came to her leg and had braced herself so she could pull on her, "Shall we?" She tossed the pop bottle into the recycling as they passed it and headed out.

Orca had got up and shook to settle her pack before racing ahead a bit before coming back and nudging Amber's hand with her head, wanting pets, and walking at their pace. Amber stroked her head absently.

Oscar caught up to them just before they reached the greenhouse. He wrapped an arm around Olivia and gave her a light squeeze, "Thanks for letting me know. I think the rest of the team is going to be there as well." He gave Amber a light hug as well, "Thanks for keeping Liv company. She wanted to help with the laundry, but everyone seems to believe in wolf weight bags of linens."

Amber smiled, "Well, it is a wolf pack!" she said, playing it from the other side, "I have been doing some light cleaning for Jess, but it is doing bathrooms!" She said making a face. "Luckily, it is in the Senior Beta and Elder wing, as those seem to be better at not making a mess than others I have heard of. They save those for people on punishment duties." She didn't mind doing it for the Elders, as often they would chat with her, and share stories of them when they were younger. They would also answer any of her questions she had and didn't want to bring to anyone else. Eldest Elise always was asking her how her day was going and had told her she could come to her at any time with questions, or even if she just wanted a hug.

Olivia grinned at Amber, "Oscar lets me do a bit of light cleaning every now and then. I finally broke him of taking care of everything in my room. Sorry but I like to put my own laundry away. That way I know it is where I want it." She gave Oscar a knowing grin. Once she was well enough, she put her underthings away. He might be a junior wolf, but he was still a boy.

When they walked in Oscar helped removed Shelly's pack, "Do you want to keep your folding cane handy Olivia?" She had one which could be shortened, and it fit well on the pack. Since Zane was coming, he figured she would get a giggle out of it. Before she bothered answering he put the cane down near where she had sat before. Even as he was doing that, she was stripping so he kept his eyes away.

When Oscar pulled the cane out, she did giggle before turning away slightly and stripping. Once she was undressed, she neatly folded the clothes and put them on the pack. Shelly was standing on the edge in case she needed help getting into the water. As she was moving forward Oscar gently grasped her arm while Shelly was on the other side, "Thanks both of you." She settled down in the water and winced as the heat hit the scars. It would take a few minutes, but soon they would feel better.

Every time he saw the scars he wanted to scream. Once he realized she was his future mate, his wolf started to become angry when he saw them, "You are welcome, Liv." He grabbed some bottles of water since the others would be there soon. As he was doing it, he politely nodded at some of the other wolves in there. Once he had everything, he settled down next to Olivia but not too close. He didn't want to make her uncomfortable.

It wasn't but a few minutes later before Zane and the others arrived. Everyone quickly stripped and slipped into the water. Zane looked at Shelly and shook his head, "I am glad you will be sleeping next to Liv. Not sure about having a wet dog curled up next to me." He gave her a quick pet before he leaned back and relaxed, "How long until Cody is back? We will keep you company if you would like, Amber."

She smiled, "Thanks, it would be nice. He's out on Patrol, so suppertime-ish, as long as they don't find a problem. If they do, then it is, 'whenever they are finished.'" She watched as Orca moved behind Zane and licked an ear before darting back and padding over to lay on the edge, with her muzzle on Amber's shoulder, looking innocent. *You're getting some bad habits from Shelly,* She mock-scolded, thinking Zane needed some teasing.

"Cool, I am going to talk to Uncle Mike about maybe doing a few patrols while I am here. I figured I could talk to Cody to see what they have him doing for the patrols." He was about ready to say something when a wet tongue nailed his ear and he growled, "Orca, I know it was you. I might talk to your person about a bowl of hard brown chunks for dinner." He started laughing as the others did as well. He did pause to glower at Olivia, "Don't even think about the cane or my wolf will chew on it again. Either that or hide it from you."

Melody poked him in the side, "Think about it and you will have tie-dyed pajama bottoms, underwear, and shirts to wear for the next week. They won't match either." She settled for leaning against his other side and watched Shelly paddling around in the massive springs. Considering the size of the pack, the springs were huge and had several different pools. Shelly was hopping in and out of the pools though she checked on Olivia frequently. Most had shallow parts which a wolf could lay on and have their head above the water.

Amber smiled, "Cody says talk to Martin. He's the head of security here and would be the one to see if you could go with a patrol. Mostly he is just shadowing the actual patrol and learning what they do."

Zane contacted Mike and asked him to investigate it. Depending on the next patrol Cody was on he would like to go with him, if it was permitted, "Thanks and pack bonds are very handy, aren't they? Oh, can you contact someone about seeing what hunting we could do? I would love to catch a bunny or two for Tessa." He kept his face completely straight when he next spoke, "I am sure Oscar would like to bring Olivia one as well."

Amber nodded, "It's better than having a cellphone! No need to worry about batteries or charging it. Nobody can take it from you! Best of all, it works in the middle of the forest if you're lost." Quickly asking Cody about it, she laughed, "The bunnies here breed like bunnies, so you are free to hunt them all you desire. If you want deer, you will have to talk to the Alphas Gareth or Maria for permission on their territory, as they work with the humans to manage the herds. He said there is even wild turkeys in the area which you could go after."

Olivia turned and glared at Zane before she grabbed the cane and poked him with it, "I darn near lost it when you dropped the kitten in my lap, and I thought it was a bunny. If anyone drops a bunny in any state other than alive and healthy in my lap, I will thump you with this." Even as she was glaring at him Melody dunked him in the water even as Tessa helped her.

Melody gave Amber a resigned look, "Shortly after Zane woke from being turned someone said something about bunnies being good eats. His uncle told him no bringing a bunny to his sister and dropping it in her lap." She waited until Zane was almost on the edge of the seat and pushed him off again for good measure.

Rico looked really interested, "Oh good, maybe later we can go. My wolf went 'yum' as well." He might see if the girl he had been flirting with might like to go with them. He was sure Melody would consider inviting the wolf she was getting cuddly with as well.

Amber looked wistful as the wolves thought about going out hunting. Her own wolf was thinking it would be tasty, but till they turned, it wasn't possible for her to join in.

Zane started to give Amber a knowing look before he was poked again by Melody, "No offering to bring her a rabbit. Her mate might object, and she couldn't eat it yet like we do. I am so going to mutter at Beta Mike for that darn comment."

With a slight grin Zane nodded towards Oscar to see if he wanted. If not, Zane would bring him a rabbit or two. As he expected he remained with the girls, "We will bring you some rabbits Oscar and you can eat them later. Take care of everyone please." They left the hot spring. Instead of bothering with their clothing they neatly stacked it next to Shelly's pack and shifted before heading out.

Chapter 27 – Rogue Issues

The next morning, many of the Alphas had papers and documents with them, as many had Rogue issues they wanted to bring up. Adam had asked Zane to not come, as he knew it would be hard for him to discuss with the issues he had with the rogues. Some of the details would be bloody and didn't want to give the pups more nightmares, or any other issues, than they already had.

"OK," Gareth said when the last had their seat, "I'm going to have Josh go first, as he had a large problem recently with Rogues, and was the cause of his health issues, as he had been personally involved."

Josh had his tablet out already, "Regrowing a lung sucks, in case any-one wanted to know." He took a sip of some tea his mother had sent with him. It was supposed to help with the healing, "Starting off with we had several rogue issues. Mike and his team helped with the major in-cursion while the other is related to the female I was talking about. The rogue pack, and I do mean pack, it wasn't just wolves. There were several other were-creatures mixed in. How it happened we haven't been able to find out since the pack was destroyed. We discovered them…" He went over the portions of the report which weren't classified for the others. The parts withheld were their strategies and how they ran the patrols, neither of which really mattered to what they were discussing.

He spoke for a while before finishing, "It was later confirmed the rogue who attacked me was the alpha of the pack. I can attest to it since only someone near alpha status could have done as much damage to me.

In total we removed..." Josh talked about the number of rogues killed as well as pack members killed. Once he was done, he glanced at Mike to see what he might want to add.

Mike didn't bother flipping through the papers before speaking, "As Josh said, Mac Tire' Dona pack was involved as well as several others. We guarded the southern aspect of the neutral area as well as sending in kill squads." In the process he talked about what they had done, killed, or had killed. He touched on the various lone wolves captured as well. Once he was done, he glanced up at Gareth after a final look at the last page of his report.

Gareth nodded, "It is concerning. Rogue Alphas are not something I would want to ever encounter." Many nodded or shuddered.

Josh waggled his hand, "I don't know if he had an Alpha level dominance but at least he would be a high-ranking Beta. Based on the fight, he was very close to my level. If it wasn't for my Henry .45-70, I am not sure I would be here now." The rifle had to be sent back to the factory for repairs.

The other Alphas asked questions, but the report had been detailed. The discussion was more on how if it was found to happen again, how they could have done it better in the future, and prevented the attack on Josh.

Most agreed having an unknown Alpha go rogue was difficult. With them almost releasing Tyler as a Lone or Rogue, they unanimously decided releasing him was not going to be an option. Together, they started the amendment process for the Inter-Pack Laws where Alphas could not be released as a Rogue or Lone wolf, which would limit them to leaving them in charge of their pack, another pack accepting them as an Omega, or death, which were the ways it usually happened anyways. If an alpha was kicked out of his pack by other packs, most agreed they would either try to get the pack back or go for revenge against the others involved. They also agreed an Alpha needed a pack to remain stable. A pack-less Alpha as a lone wolf, would go insane and become a rogue, and none wanted to have that outside their pack; they would be something no human would stand a chance against, and even most werewolves.

"Now you said you had another rogue which related to the human pregnant with a pup?" Gareth asked, a bit intrigued. Hints had been given about it, but nothing substantial had been said.

Josh couldn't help the rather evil smile which crossed his face, "I did. He is several hundred miles away, so it isn't practical for us to try and go after him. He has been reported to the Council and his DNA added to the databank. He has been around for a long time and there are other hits on his DNA. After a great deal of discussion with my father, we decided the best way to deal with him was a contract. I contacted Snarl about considering the contract. She accepted but with one stipulation, she wanted to meet the mother and child to get the scent of the rogue." He wasn't going to mention the payment since they had sworn not to. "As a side note, this particular rogue and Snarl have history, he was involved in the death of her son. I don't have any idea how long this might take but I am pretty sure he is going to be otherwise occupied." His wolf let out a very satisfied growl at the end.

Molly was in there, working as his assistant, "Alpha Adam, the young woman in question is known to Ethan. She was one who spoke for him after he was captured. She allowed him to spend time around her child and potential mate who is a junior wolf and is working for the pack in the kitchen." She wanted to make sure Adam knew she appreciated Ashleigh's willingness to allow Ethan to help with Charles, "He was one rogue which had been recently captured by the Alpha. As soon as he was captured, he surrendered. He was from the Night Shade, excuse me, Night's Depths pack and reported as a rogue though he wasn't."

Adam took up the thread, "As I have informed you all, Alpha Night was very liberal in ejecting wolves as Rogues for reasons which were fake or mostly fake. In Ethan's case, he asked for elaborations on his orders, and was reported to the Alpha as insubordination, and refusing to do the work. He had been kicked out without anything but the clothes on his back. He was lucky to survive the several years alone."

Adam was unable to hold in a growl and paused before continuing, "I have a list which I e-mailed to all the Alphas I could get, and about three quarters have been accounted for. Happily, about half of them are happily in new packs, and I have passed on contact information of relatives or friends I have in my pack who wanted to reconnect. I don't know in most cases if they got a response, but it is private between those people." He may have provided, with their permission, the contact details of his members who wanted to reconnect to whoever told him they were now in their pack, but beyond that he wasn't involved. A couple had let him know what happened, but he didn't expect to be know.

Now he had the bad news, "A quarter of them have been identified as deceased. Several had been buried, but after the change in status, have been removed and cremated. The other quarter, either are in hiding, changed their names, or are some of the unidentified rogues which had been reported back to me." He passed out a list of the names which were outstanding, along with descriptions, and in a couple of cases, photos.

Taking a drink, "For Ethan, he has joined Wild Valley and is a very hard worker. He has been ranked as Delta for now, but I think he could eventually be ranked as a Beta, if he wanted to work at it. He's helping with the pack house construction. Once it's done, he's been approved to start training as an Enforcer." He would not be surprised in the least if he became a Patrol Leader for the Enforcers once he had enough experience to handle the job.

Molly looked really pleased, "Thank you Alpha and I will let Ash and Kylie know. They have been worried about him and wanted to know how he was doing." She went back to taking notes as they were talking. As she was taking notes something occurred to her, "Ah, one more thing, Alpha Gareth, I am a wildlife specialist. My training in it is what helped identify there were different Weres working together. If you find a pattern of kills which don't make sense it could be a possible reason. I will talk to Josh this evening and see about making my report available to you."

Adam smiled and took a piece of paper and scribbled the e-mail they had made for Ethan, and handed it to Molly, "They can contact him there. If he wants to visit, I see no problems, although we would want to get him a human passport. The same with if they want to visit, after we have Wild Valley built."

Grant was more interested in the other comment, "Molly, what other kinds of Weres did you find and what sort of work did you do to identify them, as long as it's not a secret." He asked; he had several who worked in forestry or with animals, so probably had the same skills. He had never thought of looking for that sort of information to track rogues. He made a mental note to get them involved the next time they had to do a rogue hunt.

Molly took the paper even as she was getting ready to reply to Alpha Grant, "Starting with how my training helped, as a wildlife specialist I am learning how animals think. Wolves have this type of territory, they do this type of thing to protect it, if they are forced to move how would they do it. The same goes for other predators such as the various types of Cats, and others. It was a combination of Josh's training as an Enforcer and Security Specialists and what I am learning in college. He was looking at it from the Enforcer view which told him he was missing something. If the pack had been all one type of animal, then it would have been fairly easy for him to figure out. With the mixture of different types of supernatural it threw it off." She had to take a sip of water.

"I looked at it as a wildlife specialist and it had looked like there were possible kill sites missing. As far as identifying the range it was a lot of time in the pack library researching the similarities and differences between normal animals and Weres. As far as the types of other Weres most were ones we are familiar with. There were obviously wolves, a few felines, a dingo..." She had to scratch her hair, "And for some reason a were-badger. Some were hard to identify since they had been in human form. Others we recovered their bodies in their other forms. There was one we couldn't identify since there wasn't any similar record in the DNA database." She looked to see if he had any other questions.

All the alphas sat forward, "That is very interesting." Gareth said, "I think many of us have wolves trained in some sort of wildlife studies," He said with most nodding, "And we will be using them to try to predict the movements. I think I know the books you used; they were..." he went on to list several which were known to Weres, but humans hadn't had them in print for centuries. Back then, humans knew much less than Weres on the movement of animals, other than the "foresters" which were often, but not always, Weres.

Molly couldn't help but sigh at the mention of the books, "Those and..." She mentioned several others she had used, "There were a few times I thought I was going to have to beat my head on the desk to wake up."

Josh looked very pleased with Molly as she was talking. She was being respectful but wasn't letting her being female stop her from showing her intelligence. If Tyler was still there, chances were good there would be a fight over slights to Molly. Tom was so quiet; he had almost forgotten he was there. Even if he was there, not contributing anything, but did have one wolf who was taking notes. "What we are trying to identify is where the rogues came from and how the pack formed. We have sent out the information on all the Weres found and some information we have but not enough. It looks like some of the rogues started out as several small groups. Not packs but just a group of rogues. Somewhere about five years ago it looks like something impacted on them and they started to merge. It is a guess but based on what our elders and elders from other packs think it is a good guess."

Adam replied, "Could it be then that the 'Alpha' was the one who brought the packs together at that point?"

Josh again waggled his hand, "It is the view we are leaning towards. Until we know for a fact, we are trying to keep an open mind. One thing Molly mentioned was something felt off with the patterns. We don't know if it is because the rogue was insane, crazy smart, or what. I do agree something just felt off even once we decided there were various types of Weres involved. I will say I am positive the rogue I killed was the most dominant." He did give them a slightly wry smile, "We did gain some pack from the whole thing. Some of the loners asked to join."

Mike grinned at Josh since the family had asked to join as well. Their children were casual friends with Zane, Olivia, and the team, "We gained a few as well. Several loners decided it would be better to join a pack or pride for protection." It had been a very messy fight, and a few loners had been killed in the process, when they refused to submit to the Enforcers. They had been given last rites after being identified as just being loners who mistrusted packs for one reason or another.

Adam wondered, since he hadn't been passed any names or descriptions, "Could any have been former Night Depths?" He still had ten unaccounted for wolves. His wolf wanted to growl; they were all lost members until they had been confirmed as rogue or in another pack. If they could get closure, it would be best.

"The loners? I suppose it is possible. I will contact my father later and have him ask around. Two groups were families. One joined our pack and one Kadrian's pack. Those two groups I know are American for a fact. We have their records and everything. As far as the others they are still being integrated. As I am sure you know many loners tend to be very secretive." He watched Molly make a note to check, "Do you have a bio, DNA, or any identifying information on the missing? If so, let me have it and it will help a great deal."

Molly was already creating a message to the packs involved requesting information. Even now many packs tended to keep the list of their wolves classified. The less other packs knew the safer it was. It was especially true when it came to rogues finding out. With the loners it was a different case.

Adam tapped the sheets he had passed out earlier, "That is all we have on the ten whose status is unaccounted for. If you want, I can e-mail you a copy, and you can forward it to others. A simple 'deceased', or 'now in the pack' is enough for me; my wolf just considers them potential pack and wants to know. Several have family, and all had friends who would like at least closure."

Mike and Josh hadn't looked at that part of the packet. Even though it had been mentioned it didn't directly apply to them, "Do that please, Alpha. Even as Josh send it out to his contacts, I will send it out to mine. We are at almost opposite ends of Oregon. We will both have similar contacts and different ones. We will do what we can to get any information on the missing wolves."

Adam nodded, and quickly pulled it up on the laptop in front of him and forwarded the copy to the two of them with his e-mail he sent out related to it. "Have your contacts forward it as well. The information is 'were-only' but not secret."

Josh met Adam's eyes, "Do we have permission to give a status on both packs removed? If the loners and others know the packs are no longer and there is a newer, more progressive Alpha it might help. Not saying give all the details but enough to assure them it is true? If so send us something we can forward to the packs we trust. We can also forward it to the local Council of wolves."

Adam nodded, "I trust your judgment. Give them your observations. As far as the packs up here are concerned, that pack never existed officially, and Night Depths ceased to exist at the death of 'Alpha Night'." He sighed, "The Nameless Pack just killed any wolf who didn't follow, and only four ever escaped the punishment, the rest the pack captured and killed. Two who escaped are safe in MacLaren. The others are a pair of Lone wolves under MacLaren protection. In both cases, their names don't need to be known generally."

The three foreign wolf's eyes almost instantly turned the colour of their wolves. There was a low angry growl before they managed to pull their wolves back. It was obvious what had been said infuriated their wolves. Once they were calm enough Josh spoke, "Pardon, what fucking crap..." Even now his voice was deep with the rumbles of his wolf, "Maybe a break for a few."

"Agreed." Gareth said, looking at the time, it was less than an hour to lunch, "We will continue after lunch, at One-thirty."

They stood and left the room. As they did Mike growled, "Martin might get the rematch he was asking about." Later but for now they needed to eat and finish the meeting.

Martin caught them as they headed to the dining hall, "Gareth said you might be needing to hunt. If you wanted, we could go for a couple deer for lunch." Gareth had mentioned taking them for a hunt and had given approval for it.

The three of them didn't even need to think about it, "It would be greatly appreciated. If there is any cost related to it, we will take care of it." It was going back to paying for a cow if you wanted to hunt one. To Mike and his wolf, the idea of fresh hot meat had them starting to drool.

Molly growled, "Deer tartar coming up please. I might even let Josh share my deer." She gave him a knowing look which made him blush slightly. Chances where she was also considering something else if they had time.

Martin nodded, and led them to a door, and stepping onto the deck outside the door, stripped, stuffing his clothes into a cubie which was there for that purpose and shifted. He waited as the others did so as well. He knew it was cheating but had used the sensors to find out where a reasonable herd of young bucks and led the way to them. They didn't have the hours to spend to track them down normally.

When they came back, the three were feeling far better. They were still angry, but the savage anger was mostly gone. Thankfully, all in the room would understand their reactions. You took care of pack; it included not killing pack without a very good reason and members can decide to leave a pack without issue. Once they were back, they shifted and headed towards the room they had been using.

Martin limped back into the security office, having pulled a muscle during the hunt. His wolf was well satisfied for the time, having got to share a fresh kill with Mike. He grinned; he was one tough Beta. They didn't charge for the meat, as it didn't cost them anything; the forest service actually paid them for the work in maintaining the population! It helped a were had gotten pretty high up in the forest service, and had got that arranged, instead of paying human hunters who took what they wanted: the ones best to pass on their genes to the next generation. Those they left, as they took the slow, weak, and sick.

Mike had run his ass off even though Josh and Molly had worked to run his ass off even more. By the time they were back they were ready for the meeting. He had one or two minor bruises from the run. Hitting trees or boulders at a high speed was annoying. He was moving somewhat slower than normal.

The afternoon several other packs detailed other rogue encounters, but they were nothing like what they had south of the border. Mostly were fairly small. Many had brought some alarming statistics, which showed there was starting to become many more rogue encounters on all the packs.

"They seem to run as soon as they are detected," Rufus told the gathered Alpha, "Some patrollers swear they have had the same wolf multiple times, too."

They discussed ways to try to reduce the attacks, as the tactics of the actual fights was pack secrets.

Josh frowned slightly. When he spoke, it was related to the security systems. It was vague to an extent, but it should make a point, "This is why a number of packs in our area have contracted with our pack tech company. We provide the sensors, repairs, networking, and such. Each pack has its own sensors and servers which handle them. When support is needed, my pack takes care of it much like in the human world. Each pack has an IT specialist who normally manages the system. Beta Mike is an example. He and his team manage and monitors their sensors. When needed, he contacts our pack, and we provide support. When we had the rogue attack where I was hurt, we activated our own, although much more limited in scope, inter-pack treaty. Even as each pack monitored the sensors they were also being fed to our pack. It allowed us to provide real time information on where people were. Our people, rogues, humans, possible loners, and others. If it hadn't been for this the fall out would have been far worse."

He glanced at Adam before handing over a thumb drive, "This has a training scenario which gives an example of how this works. It is all CGI but is a valid training scenario." With the sensors they used they had found they had been able to identify wolves and others who used the neutral area based on heat signatures, sonic sensors, and others. With enough data they could identify the wolves as they passed through. It wasn't mentioned but it was part of their systems.

As Adam took the drive and plugged it in to his laptop and got it ready, Gareth sighed, "Now you've done it. Adam has had a similar network here and has been building it out to the acquired territory, prepare for a headache! It really reduced the number of wolves we lost in the first attack, but the second, they seemed to know about it and was a fluke change in wind direction which gave them away, so it doesn't replace the need to maintain a good set of physical patrols."

Josh had to grin at Gareth, "Sorry, Dad purchased a failing tech company back around two-K and handed it over to me. I had two choices: fail, and show I wasn't alpha material or run with it and make it work. I ran with it, and I now have a small call centre on the property, two regional offices, and several packs we do tech support for. It isn't including the various human companies we are contracted with. Short term it was a major pain in my rear. Long term it allowed us to start to coordinate our defences and security. Look at the video and it will give you an idea of what we can do. I won't say how many packs, prides, or other supernatural have treaties with us. I will say it has helped us reduce rogues to an extent. The recent issue was minimized by what we did together."

"Has expanded," Adam corrected, "They're done expanding the sensor net on the territories as of this morning." Adam commented, correcting Gareth's comment about expanding to their other territories. They hadn't been scheduled to be done for another week, but Steve had notified him as they broke for lunch the last sensors were now online; it seemed all the off-duty enforcers, the techs, and many others had done some work to help get it all done early.

"Both territories have had sensors and even cameras scattered and in such a way we can move them at will." He grinned, "Many paws and an incentive of time off if they finish quickly but do the job well had them working double shifts without being even asked. They now have free time for a couple weeks. Once Wild Valley's security office is operational in about a month or two, they will be taking control of monitoring the territories, but I have—With Gareth's permission—left the link, so both our security offices will back each other up, and if we put something out in the other territory, it would provide a third control room which could be used. The system we are using here is similar to Josh's, but each can do the controlling, not just one way." Each of the territories they were also secretly making a backup security centre, which would house the actual controls for the sensors for each site, but normally right now, was going to be unmanned, and just relay out to Wild Valley. Adam planned to have a secure bunker which had a backup security office, for if the pack house had to be evacuated for some reason, and the transfer was not possible, there would be a hardened secure control area. Only Gareth and Maria knew about the plan outside of him and his mate. Once their pack house had free workers, their security managers would work with an engineer to design it.

Hitting Play as it was ready, he sat back and watched the video along with the other Alphas. The video was one of the many examples of what could be done with the systems. It started with a small incursion of 'rogues' into a pack property. It was followed by another to a different property. As the multiple threats were identified all the systems came online and meshed. The central location was sending information to the other packs. Not orders but passed on potential threats. By the time the simulation was done there had been four attacks on three packs and the results showed. Most of the rogues had been taken out with a minimal loss of life.

Josh had to speak, "Keep in mind we do have better access to rifles and pistols than you do. It was accounted for in the sim on both sides. Personally, I carry a .45-70 lever action Henry. You get hit by that and you know I love you. I also have two Grizzly .500 magnum pistols as well. What you might have up here I don't know. Different countries and different rules." He scratched his chin, "I will deny Little Dove carries a grenade launcher. Don't need silver for that."

Adam was grinning like it was going out of style, "I have configured a very similar interface system, but was also able to get my hands on some holographic equipment and have a table in the security offices which under normal conditions displays the territory in 3D and where the patrols are in real-time. If there is a single alert, it automatically zooms in to the area and provides more detail. If there is a second incursion, it goes to full overview and highlights the attacks. It also alerts all other offices there is a multi-hit attack. On the interface, it can be noted what the attackers are using and can prioritize the different attacks, due to an input threat number." The interface for configuring the threat details was complex, and one he thought Steve, Chris,—and maybe Martin now,—knew how to use. He wasn't bothering learning it, as he would never need to know it. He knew Toby and Sam had some work on it, and eventually would be maintaining the Wild Valley one. Once they were old enough, they would be sent for a full vendor training course.

"I want in!" Grant said, looking envious, "Right now, we just have patrols, and if they don't give good information, we can't decide well." Sometimes the patrols were just too busy trying to stay alive to pass on details.

"As do I," Rufus agreed.

Josh looked at Grant, "Keep in mind the equipment is expensive. Not sure about Silver Orca which Adam uses but Silver Fox Industries does specialized equipment for us. It is more expensive than normal sensors. This is due to the needs to pick up non-humans. To do the original sensors for the pack back in the early two-K's it was a good three million just for the sensors. Toss in the servers, networking, and related software it added about five million. Mind you once we started contracting with other packs it paid the outlay back, but it isn't cheap. We also run a school to train techs for the other packs, prides, and others. Mike is one who attended, and I have a feeling Zane and his team will be as well." He took a drink before leaning back in the chair.

Molly snorted, "He is even putting me through it since I am 'just a user' and need to learn more. Can you say school while at college and when I am on break?" She leaned against him and stroked his arm, "Then again it is to protect and take care of pack."

Adam smiled, *One million, not including the table, and installed. That was for the MacLaren Pack, and the standard sensors.* He told Josh privately, not wanting to openly brag in front of the other Alphas.

"I'm not going to say how much we spent, just it was less." Adam told the others, "Right now, I have not finalised the two other territories but went with all the bells and whistles for Wild Valley—Silver Orca carries the supernatural sensors standard; it seems they have more demand for them—to have it set up. I have Chris, and MacLaren has Steve; they joined us, and were certified installers for Silver Orca and Silver Fox. Both have advanced vendor training and have been helping to train others. Chris still has contacts within 'Orca, and with us setting up two additional territories, they were willing to cut us a deal for them. I have all the hardware and software licenses to build the third security office in storage, as well. And for all three sites, I have spare parts for all the essential components." Which was including automated failover to backups not only in the main datacentres, but also backups in each secondary data centre, for if a server glitched. He considered the security systems 'life-critical, so had at minimum 100% failover for everything, meaning for each and every part there was at least one other part which would take up the work instantly.

Nodding at the two Alphas, "We will need to discuss it privately with each of you, as the systems are fairly complex, and needs to be configured for your specific territory. Linking the various centres together will require a specific agreement between the packs and would run over the WereNet, so would require it to be operational first." He had talked with Brook and the pack's Elders, and they had decided they were not going to give it as an option to run it over the unsecured human Internet; they would require the secure connection the WereNet offered.

Both nodded but looked pleased.

Tom shook his head, "Too much tech. I prefer in person stuff. Too easy for wolves to become complacent."

Irwin nodded, "I agree, I prefer traditional methods for security; they have worked for centuries, why change now?"

Josh leaned forward and looked at both Tom and Irwin, "What is more important? Protecting the pack or trying to ignore what can protect the pack? Don't give me the complacent crap. I damn near died and it wasn't due to sitting on my ass in some security room. I was going after the alphas. You do remember my fight with Tyler? Kicked his ass with a lung still regrowing? We have patrols, we have ongoing training with a wide variety of weapons, and hand to hand. Our training includes ambushing patrols and that occasionally includes some injuries."

Mike leaned forward as Josh finished, "If you want to know the training my pack goes through go ask Zane. He attacked Tyler for insulting his team, him, and his girlfriend. He did damn good for a pup of his age since I know Tyler had some injuries from him. Don't try and tell me our sensors make us weak, pathetic, or complacent. I am the Beta Enforcer for my pack, and I would be more than happy to meet anyone in the gym in a sparing match." He leaned back and waited for anyone to say anything.

Gareth shook his head, as it looked like wolves were getting a bit grouchy, even if he agreed with them, "Seeing it is almost dinner time, I am going to end the session for the day. Tomorrow I am going to call a rest day, and if there is any new business, see me by the beginning of session the next day to have it added to the agenda."

*****

Adam smiled, turned to Josh, motioning him to stay while the others filed out. "I have approval from Gareth to show you the security office, if you are interested?" He really wanted to show off his 'toys' to the other wolf.

Josh gave Adam a toothy grin, "Cool and I have permission to show you some of the schematics and diagrams for our offices. I know Alphas rarely leave their pack but if you decide to come down, I will show you my setup." They walked out of the room together.

Adam led him to the high security office, and through the double secured doors. Several wolves were waiting, with the screens blanked, "Gareth authorized this tour." Adam reassured them, as Martin came forward, and waved them back to their desk, where they unlocked the red button, re-enabling all the screens of cameras.

"This part is where they monitor the cameras of the pack and territory." Martin said, as Adam deferred to his friend, this was his domain.

Leading him back farther past an open blast door, "Welcome to the brain." Martin said, "This room is reinforced to survive a bomb in the outer office and has its own isolated environmental and power systems. There are several independent shielded network connections, and wireless backups." There were four monitors on one wall which blinked through the cameras showing on the screens in the outer office, with one moving through cameras of the entryway and the outer office. There was fold down bunks lining one wall, with a door marked 'Kitchen' and another 'Bathroom', there were several workstations, each with four monitors, and a webcam. The lights were set low, but the wolves could see fine.

There was a big set of monitors, which were currently off, "I can feed any camera I want to the screens, or if I'm bored, can watch a movie from the network." He joked.

Centre of the room was a large bowl which currently showed MacLaren and Wild Valley packs in 3D. It showed a flag with names for each of the patrol leader around on the territory, with blue dots for the individual members. There were two yellow virtual pins on the map moving towards a patrol.

Josh looked around the room and gave a low whistle. The security office in their pack was nice but this was obviously all new equipment and could still smell the off-gassing from the new parts, "Nice setup you have Adam. Ours is similar though not all the tech is this new. A 1080 monitor works as well as a 4K monitor." The same went for servers and other hardware. The hardware they tended to keep upgraded was the remote sensors. They already had fibre, gigabit ethernet, and heavily secured wireless APs scattered around. It allowed them to move sensors occasionally.

"Since my office works as the secondary security office, I have several smart boards and a smart table. It gives us a very good view of what is going on. Anything entered there is shown in the central security office." The other office was in the safety bunker and getting in there would be an ugly mess. If someone managed it, the pack would have been lost so it was a moot point. Some of the ideas Adam had brought up were valid and he was going to talk to his father. They didn't have to worry about fires nearly as much, but the security windows would be a good addition. Worst-case scenario would give the pack more time to get to the secure locations under an attack.

"Perfect!" Martin said and tapped on the virtual map where the pins were. The big screens turned on and showed Bri and John stalking a patrol who didn't know they were behind them. The view of them moving off jumped ahead as the two moved forward. "It will track the points automatically, unless you tell it to hold a view, and you can control what cameras, or even adjust the cameras which move, with this controls," He motioned to the centre station, which had a control panel with a joystick and lots of buttons in front of it.

They watched as Bri and John moved and took out half the patrol with paintballs, before the two who dodged regrouped, and took out Bri before John could get them too.

Martin noted down and shook his head at the two who failed on an electronic document, then the other two in a separate note. "That is one way which we keep the patrols on their toes. If they fail badly enough, there is formal punishment given." He pointed to a copy of the picture of pups pouncing on sleeping wolves, and the one below of the shock on the pounced. "That was one of the worst! Taken out by pups, when they were technically to start a section of a patrol after a break, but within the start window allowed to help randomize the patrol rates. Nobody was on watch and were out hard enough the pups could get close enough to pounce, *while* Adam was taking pictures!"

When they indicated the patrol and the two were going to ambush him, he watched the action. After Martin pulled the feed up on the screen he had to grin. The paintball guns were a good idea also. It would teach wolves to pay more attention and if you used a variety of colours, it would be even better, "I can already feel a set of paintball guns appearing in my near future." When he glanced at the picture Martin pointed at, he gave a grunting laugh. He hoped the patrol had received sufficient punishment.

Tapping in a few commands, Adam enabled the view of the network to support the sensors, showing the extensive net of connections covering their entire territory, with the wireless, ethernet, and fibre in separate colours. "I have not only fibre-optic feeding many areas, but there is also covered with a mesh wireless network. Each access point connects to at least three others. They all are hardened as well. If one of them goes down, it sets off an alarm, the Fibre is used for better bandwidth but isn't required."

Tapping another, he had the current sensor layout, colour coded by the type of sensor. "Chris is working on redoing the sensor network here. The sensors automatically triangulate due to signal strength from at least three APs. We have already mined the territory between the two packs, as well." He added, as he pointed to the area between the two packs.

He had to laugh, "I have a feeling saying mining territory means something different to both of us... I will deny having remote controlled mines in our territory." They didn't, but they had the capability if needed. Josh was somewhat startled at the information Adam was showing him not to mention how their tech was being used.

Adam grinned, "We have pepper-spray and flash-bangs set up. Incapacitate but where we can capture them. After the Nameless Pack attacked with wolfsbane bullets, we wanted a way to remotely take them out."

That comment received a growl from Josh. Wolfsbane was a certified death sentence for anyone using it. It didn't matter why you were using it you would die, "I can tell we have different views of some things. I guess you could say ya'll are nicer than we are." He gave Adam a toothy smile, "Then again we do prefer to hide over having to use violence."

Adam nodded, "We use less-lethal, so we can capture and do an interrogation before they are executed, so we can decide if they deserve a fire, dropped in a ravine, or left in the forest for the wild animals. It also lets us feel better, that they deserved their punishment."

Josh had to admit it was a good way of looking at it. They did try and capture the rogues and talk to the lone wolves. They knew it was the better way to do it but sometimes it was easier to kill and be done with it, "We have a really deep cave we use. It isn't on the maps and was a mine which was tapped out decades ago. We let those who deserve it rot in hell before they are returned to the pack in the sky or the world." He didn't know what the beliefs of Adam was. He wasn't going to ask either, frankly it didn't matter and wasn't any of his business.

Hearing some rumbling stomachs, "I have another thing to show you, after we have some food. I think you will be surprised at these..." Adam told him as he grinned at Josh.

He sighed, "Surprises might not be a good idea right now. I am still pissed at the fight and how the pup was impacted. It looks like he is still having some problems which has Molly and I worked up." Wolves protected pups and Zane had been badly hurt. Even with the healing he had been hurt and it had showed.

Adam growled, "I am glad Zane had me stop, as I was planning on breaking each limb, and have him beg for death. For him, I just simply killed the *alpha* who was whimpering for the injuries which Zane had and was still wanting to fight!" Shaking his body like a wolf, "I know Cody and Amber are relaxing with Zane and his team, and Zane asked to go on a patrol tomorrow, so don't think they will be doing much this evening. You'll like these surprises..." He said slyly, leading him for a quick dinner.

Josh had talked with Mike to an extent, "Glad you didn't. It wouldn't have been right for Zane. I have seen a few hurt pups, and it wouldn't be what he needed." He had wanted much the same after he had found out the injuries the pup had been given. "Good for Zane, I don't know everything, but he needs something to keep his spirits up."

Adam nodded, "Or at least to distract him from his problems."

Chapter 28—Pups Relax

Cody flopped at the table with the pups and shook his head at Zane, as he gave Amber a hug, thanking her as she had already made him a plate of food, having felt him return and just need to check in, "I don't know why you would want to go on a patrol; it is the most boring thing to do! Yes, it's needed, but mostly it is just boring and keeping a watch on everything." He had noticed she was getting very mature and disciplined for her age. She was also very smart, and with the encouragement, was doing much better with their education than she had been in the public system, before joining the pack. His parents had also commented it could also be from there being fewer in the class, so she got more help from the teacher too.

Zane gave him a tight look. When he spoke, his voice was low and dark, "Because I was turned by a rogue and it destroyed my life. If I can learn enough to protect my pack, my team, and my sister I will do anything I can." He pulled the collar of his shirt to the side, "I bear these as a reminder of what happened to me. I don't know when the cause will be dealt with but sooner than later hopefully." He held Cody's eyes for a moment before glancing at his sister, "You have seen her scars as well. The rogue might not have caused them directly, but he is at fault."

Cody looked shocked, at Zane's reply, "It is a very good reason," He said quietly, "I didn't realise you had dealt with that side." He smiled, "Martin told me to have you report after breakfast, if you wanted to go for a patrol. He did say it would be all day and would be back late afternoon to dinner-ish. Lunch would be 'fast food' while you are out there."

Tessa ran a hand up and down his back and he took a slow breath, "Sorry Cody, bad memories have been brought up recently. Besides, it is nice to get to see new territory. What I might learn I can take back and teach to our Enforcers to protect our pack." He gave his body a light shake, "Thanks and I will ensure my pack is ready this evening."

Rico did roll his eyes, "I must admit the patrols can be boring but needed. We had the fun of helping to rescue a human who was a total novice at kayaking. He chose the wrong place to practice the skills he didn't have..." It had been such a pain in the ass as they carried him out of the ravine, they had found him in.

Zane snorted, "I still want to do some gardening..." He grinned at the evil grins his team gave him, well other than Tessa and Oscar. When Amber and Cody looked rather confused, he explained, "Some bullies at school decided to try and pick on Tessa and Oscar. We visited one house and pretty much chewed up anything not nailed down. We were going to come back for the mother's 'flower' garden but were ordered not to."

Olivia made a face, "You forgot to mention the piles of poop you left behind. I heard about it at school and just ick!" She shuddered and went back to eating.

Zane did want to comment about how they were just marking their territory, as that was what his wolf was feeling about it, or commenting about just needing to go, but he decided to just not say anything about it in the end. Officially, it had never happened, and they preferred to keep it that way.

Cody and Amber stared for a moment before laughing, "Oh, that sounds like nice revenge." Cody said, "Out here, we are schooled by the Elders, as we are too far, and they wanted to give us classes for the wolves. We have a gearing towards what we need, but also schooling which meets the human requirements. We have been told it is much less biased than what they get and covers more history of this continent." Their classes included what was actually in the treaties which the natives signed, and went to what they actually had been given, and what the Europeans who had made them were trying to do and some conjecture on the reasons why they felt entitled to do so.

Others laughed as well since they had deserved it, "We have the fun of going to human school during the week with wolf stuff in the afternoon and part of the weekend." Rico was sounding disgruntled, "I thought it was bad before Zane added us to his team... Now? Not sure how we are surviving. Enforcer training, pack training, school homework, occasional patrols not to mention quarterly testing to see how we are doing as wolves."

Zane sighed, "At least we aren't working with the beef on the hoof, bunnies in the cages, and all the other lovely stuff." He gave Cody a warped grin, "Be glad you aren't dealing with humans nearly as much. All the lovely scents at school are enough to make our wolves cry." He didn't mention it was who was doing who, the drugs, alcohol, pain of abuse, and even *that* time of the month. Just thinking about it made him wince and his wolf whine.

Olivia made a face, "Maybe I don't wanna be a wolf? I have listened to you and your team talking about it. It is enough to make me feel queasy." By now most of the food was done and they were mostly relaxing.

Cody shuddered, "We had to go into the public schools for the semester end exams... I had trouble getting my wolf to quiet down enough to concentrate to pass! Too much noise and scents, as you said." He shuddered, "I am glad we aren't there! Even though having more friends my own age would be nice."

Simone had to poke fun at Zane, "At least we don't have to ride the public buses now. I remember you and your wolf reacting to it." She had gotten her drivers license not long ago and when they needed, she could drive them.

Zane gagged slightly, "Thanks for reminding me about that memory. I thought the school bus was bad but that? I try to not remember it."

He shuddered even as his wolf whined in the back of his mind at the memory.

Cody shook his head, "The town is too small for it, and we generally just run down to the warehouse and shift there and walk into town. I have never been to a larger city. In Night Depths, pups were not even allowed to be out of the territory, period."

The last comment got everyone's attention and all they could do was stare. It was Oscar who finally broke the silence, "What? That..." Even as a junior wolf he had the freedom to go to town for the most part. There were times he couldn't, and all the pups had a curfew of some sort but to not leave the property ever was just wrong.

Zane gave Cody a sly look, "Maybe we can invite you down at some point, introduce you to the joys of public transportation, movie theatres, and greasy pizza." Even the movie theatres smelled bad to an extent. That and they had to use ear plugs to keep the noise down.

Cody smiled, "The pack maintains a warehouse, and they have a room just for wolves to come and go, and you just leave the front door as humans, and can spend time in town. We must get permission to go, but as long as you have been good, it is usually not a problem." He shuddered at the mention of a theatre, "There is one in town, but I prefer to do it here. Alpha Adam is having our own theatre room made in the basement of our pack house and promised we wouldn't need earplugs!" He didn't want to comment how it was rare any Theta ever had permission to leave the territory as adults, and then usually were on an errand for the Alpha, not for pleasure. Other than the 'favourites' of Alpha Night, it was very rare for any pack member to get permission for a pleasure trip out of the territory.

He had to make a face even as the rest of his team did as well, "Due to a couple of human boys, we were restricted to the property unless we were with an adult. I think they were concerned about the bodies of the boys vanishing and not being found." He turned and wrapped his arms around Tessa, "They attacked one of my junior wolves. They were the ones who tried to bully my junior wolves and got worse when I told them to stop." He gave her a gentle kiss as he was holding her.

Cody growled, "If anyone attacked..." He took a deep breath, "I am surprised they survived the first encounter!"

Melody leaned against Zane since she was sitting next to him, "We were in the mall. We couldn't do that." She gave Zane a very pleased smile, "He scared the crap out of the two and offered to 'not' kill them. He promised nothing else other than he just wouldn't kill them. It was when I knew he was the right team leader for us. He had problems due to his being changed but he cared. He took Tessa and Oscar under his protection, added us, and let everyone know. From what I have heard, dickhead one is still having nightmares of the threat." Her wolf gave an appreciative rumble for Zane and what he had done.

He leaned against Melody for a moment, "I will blame two certain non-pushy people and one annoying slightly less dominant wolf for bullying me into trying to care again." He gave her temple a peck before he looked at Cody, "Don't know how you do it here or what dominance you might end up at but if you end up with a team, be very selective as you pick them. Oscar and Tessa are..." He gave both of them a very tender look, "They helped keep me from losing it." He reached over and gave Oscar's shoulder a light, for a wolf, squeeze.

Cody nodded, "MacLaren tries to show less preferential treatment and doesn't have teams, but we get taught about teams here. I am already qualified as a Junior-Delta, which was something new this year; any wolf over fifteen, with their parent's consent, could try most of the adult tests, and if they passed, they get duties and responsibilities, but also more privileges." They also got paid for their time working or training, he had happily found out.

Amber reached into his shirt and pulled out the medallion, "And they get this!" She was very proud of her Cody.

Zane and the others looked impressed, "We can't get our first rank until we are eighteen. It is being in a human school and all that. We know what ranks we will start as but with everything else going on we tend to get assigned to a section of the pack which should fit us." He had to frown at the term preferential, "Not sure I like the way you describe your views on teams. To us it isn't preferential so much as creating core groups to help protect and take care of the packs. If a wolf needs our help, we give it to him or her. It doesn't matter if they are on my team. Tessa and Oscar help keep us comfortable and centred. Melody will end up being my assistant, Rico one of my senior enforcers, and Simone an enforcer as well. Mindy will end up being my computer expert. When I step into my position as one of the junior enforcers, they will help me take care of those assigned to me." He wasn't sounding angry since he was simply explaining how they looked at it to Cody.

Cody listened, "I guess it isn't preferential. I never really got teams too much. Mostly, since we live all together, it is encouraged we just look out for one another and work all together. I do see how it would work better. Amber said you live in houses, instead of a large pack house. Right now, members are in a bit of a flux, as some of MacLaren is becoming Wild Valley, and Adam had mentioned they may even get some more from another pack... can't remember the name."

Melody spoke since she had grown up there, "Yes and no. We do have a pack house, and it is a decent size, but it was decided years ago to make it look like some sort of fancy subdivision. America, several parts, are far more populous than here. If you had two hundred people living in one massive house, it would look weird. Due to it, we do have a number of houses. Beta Mike has Zane, Olivia, Tess, Oscar, his mate, and pup in one house. It is almost like a mini pack house since there is a living area for Zane's team. Several Mike's team have mates, so they live in either houses or some of the suites in the pack house."

Zane knew the name of the pack which was just disbanded—partly from his actions—but he wasn't going to mention it, "So it seems. It is confusing having all the people coming and going. Catch one set of scents and not much later there is another set." He finally stood. "I am going to check my pack. If you and Amber would like to come and visit it would be fine."

Cody nodded and swung Amber around, so she could ride his back. She clung giggling, as he started to grab their dishes to put them in the bins beside the kitchen door, before Oscar grabbed them, and smiled in thanks before grabbing his pack. It wasn't the first time he had done it for her.

"Adam said it was easier to make one building and control the members, than to have a subdivision. There are people who try to force their way into private communities here, so by making it seem almost a 'cult' to the uninformed, it allows us to live in peace."

Rico didn't manage to control a lip twitch, "The last person who tried it with us needed a new car. They didn't realize the gates were reinforced steel... Well, either that or they were drunk and stupid..." It had been several years since parts of the town knew what they were.

Cody smiled, "Both pack areas here are 'private property' so they can't enter without permission. Here, the nearest road is thirty minutes, and the access road has a crash barrier designed to arrest a semi. Wild Valley has a full security shack, fence, and crash barrier so would be able to prevent it.

When Cody started to pick the dishes up Oscar took them from him without thinking. He and Tessa gathered up all the plates and stuff and took them to the bins just outside the door to the kitchen and put them in the proper places. Once done they headed towards the rooms.

Zane watched what they were doing and gave Cody a wry smile, "I had to speaketh firmly to them before I could occasionally do the cooking. They take the idea of taking care of the team very seriously. It allows us to focus on taking care of the pack." He left the room and headed towards the guest quarters. When they walked in, he pulled his pack out and pulled everything out to make sure he had what might be needed.

There was a reasonably short though wide sword. Much like his uncle he used the half-staff's, and he checked them before putting them and the sword back into their places. It was followed by a small medical kit, spare clothing, food, and even some water. There was more but it was simply checked and tucked back into the pack, "Well everything I should need is here." He set it off to one side and leaned back against the wall near where Cody had dropped his. Once he was comfortable, he pulled Tessa into his arms since she had been as upset as he was earlier. Mentioning David and Leon had brought back memories, and he started to comfort her.

Cody relaxed and shook his head at Zane's pack, "You have a kitchen sink in there?"

Zane snickered at the question, "No, or I have found it as of yet. I honestly think Mike and his trainers like tossing things in just for giggles. I will say running out of TP wasn't fun. It was on a weekend excursion recently. Leaves don't cut it..." When Olivia groaned, he laughed, "I have seen your pack has similar types of packs. I think the biggest difference is we use carbon fibre, Kevlar, and nylon instead of leather."

Cody smiled, "We use aluminum frames, as carbon fibre is brittle in the cold, and the leather covers the Kevlar lining to protect it as replacing the leather is easier and cheaper for the trainee packs, and the vests of the adult ones have an option for ceramic bullet plates." Realising he told a secret, "Don't tell anyone; I shouldn't have talked about the plates... I'm not even supposed to know, yet." He had seen Adam and Brook's after one fight, and them working to replace the protective plates.

He considered what Cody was saying and started to pluck his lip, "From what I understand it isn't a problem for us, the carbon and cold. As far as the plates won't say anything. I don't have an adult pack since, well, I ain't adult yet. Not sure what all they have but I like what I have as of now. The frame is titanium and something else. For my wolf it is light and other than ruffling his fur, isn't a problem." He pulled it on and settled it. Before anything else he quickly snapped out the sword and then slapped it back in. Next came the half-staff's and they were quickly put back in as well, "It is very comfortable though and easy access to my weapons."

Cody nodded, "It is how we have ours too. I think they intentionally make the pup ones heavier, so we can learn better. I'd better tell you this now, keep a watch out. There are four paintball guns, with *pink* paint-balls around. The two Next Alphas, Bri and John, and Alphas Adam and Brook have them. They stalk the patrols, and test to see how well they respond to various attacks."

He stared at Cody before his lips started twitching. He was thinking back at some of the threats Olivia had about a pink collar for his wolf. It hadn't gone down well and the idea of being nailed by pink paintballs didn't either. Pink was okay but not a colour he cared for, "Ah... Um..., Oh man so wrong." He chose not to mention female wolves being okay with the colour since he would probably be chewed to death by some of his team.

"One patrol," Cody said, "Happened to be napping hard, and Adam and Brook brought in four pups who were on hunt training, which were able to pounce them, and while Adam was snapping pictures." He shook his head, "They got de-ranked, two months' house arrest, then a year of garbage and the worst bathrooms to clean, then two more years doing other Theta jobs. *Plus,* the pictures of them being pounced up on the wall in the main pack area." Not mentioning there was a copy in the security office of what *not* to allow happen with a list of their punishments, and at the bottom of them needing to reapply and requalify as Enforcers, if they wished to return.

When Cody talked about the patrol ambushed by pups Zane's jaw dropped. His wasn't the only one in the room and they stared at him. Melody finally tried to say something productive, "Um, crap, it must have been, um, I can't even think of how to describe how the patrol must have felt." The punishment was acceptable and reasonable since it endangered the pack. Having the pictures on the wall had to be even worse, as it would be a reminder.

Zane finally took a slow deep breath before sitting down with Tessa on one side and Olivia on the other, "Enough of that stuff, sit, relax, and talk. Need an evening of teen sort of talk." He needed a bit of space for a few hours since he hadn't been sleeping well.

Cody pulled Amber into his lap as he flopped in a chair, "Want to watch a movie?"

Before any of the girls could speak Rico growled at them, "No rom-com's, gooey kissy stuff, or feel-good movies. Blood, guts, gore, type movies!" He knew one of them was going to mention that type of movie just to annoy him and Zane. He gave Cody a slightly annoyed look, "It can be annoying having more females than males on the team."

Zane laughed at Rico, "Sure, whatever with in limits. No werewolf movies though. Can't do them anymore." Even the old Teen Wolf movies bothered him.

Cody grinned and tapped the TV onto the network store, and pulled up the main list of movies, handing the remote to Zane, "You pick. The movies are all on the network here. Last time I looked, there was about ten Terabytes of them."

Zane flipped through the categories and finally settled on a movie most of them could enjoy. Since Amber was still a kid, he made sure it was kid rated as well. Once it started, he settled back in the chair and relaxed with Tessa. When he noticed Olivia was now sitting on Oscar's lap, he frowned at her just to annoy her, *It's okay Oscar, I am just annoying my little sister.* He wanted to make sure Oscar knew he wasn't upset by him.

Olivia stuck her tongue at Zane and just for good measure gave Oscar a peck on the cheek. Now that she knew he was supposed to be her mate, the faintest of warm and tingles could be felt. It was something she had noticed before but had assumed it was simply in her mind. Now it made sense from what she had learned in the wolf class.

Cody smiled and enjoyed the movie. Amber was almost asleep in his arms by the end of the movie, so he just slid the chair back farther, and rested, the companionable time with the pups was nice. If he fell asleep, they were in a safe place.

Oscar gave Cody a slight smile since Olivia was almost asleep in his arms as well. She had been forced to take one of her pain pills. They had been walking around so much it was starting to hurt her. He knew it was good for her but knowing she was in pain upset him, "Bed soon." When he spoke, he was fairly quiet to keep from disturbing her.

Tessa looked at Zane and he was asleep as well. She shifted slightly so she was more comfortable and carefully leaned the chair back. It was a Lay-Z-Boy and once she had lowered it back, she curled up closer, closed her eyes, and started relaxing. If they slept there, she didn't care as long as Zane actually slept without a nightmare.

None moved as those awake covered the sleepers up. Cody and Zane had a busy day of patrols coming up.

She looked at the one covering her and Zane up, "Thank you." She relaxed into his arms and let her wolf take over. Her wolf would watch while Tessa slept. Zane needed this and it showed to her. With a slight murmur of comfort, she slipped off to sleep.

Rico looked at Cody and then Amber, "Do you need help standing? If you do, we can pick her up so you can stand." He didn't bother worrying about Cody stressing over the offer to help him and his mate. It was assumed in their pack they wouldn't do anything to interfere.

Cody just yawned and leaned back farther, "If you don't mind, we'll just sleep here." Looking over, Orca and Shelly were curled up together too, on one of the mattresses, he said accepting a blanket to cover him and his young mate, as he knew she was already asleep in his arms, as she cuddled into his chest. He was glad her mother didn't have an issue with them sleeping together, as his wolf would have taken over every night to find her. He was already very protective of her.

Olivia settled down on the bed and curled up next to Oscar. She had gone and changed into shorts and a night shirt earlier. The other kids had as well and quickly the room was filled with the sound of sleeping pups.

*****

After dinner, Adam led Josh out the door and down a trail which was barely there, warning Josh to stay on the trail. Eventually they reached a mostly hidden bunker, with a vehicle trail leading from one side. Tapping in a code, and providing a handprint, he opened the door, and motioned Josh in.

Josh was still feeling a bit irritated with the idea of having to wait for the surprise. When they walked into the hidden garage he had to laugh, his annoyance forgotten, "Nice! We have a few armoured vehicles but not like this. Mind you one of our old wolves has a thing for antique military vehicles. He is working on restoring a M4 Sherman Tank. He has a few other vehicles from W-W-Two." He moved over and touched one of the LAV's. They didn't have weapons currently, but it didn't mean much.

Adam grinned as Josh looked over the armoured vehicles, securing the door, "So, do you guys have anything like these?" He said with a chuckle, "I'm still working on getting some for my pack, they are hard to get!" With the Academy payment, he could just order them new to his specs.

He had to shake his head, "Not like this, our armoured vehicles are aftermarket. They look like normal SUV's or cars and upgraded. It tends to get you looked at weird when you are driving around in tanks and such." One could purchase them, but you couldn't use them very often.

"Up here, these are street legal, but till the RCMP got used to them, I heard they kept getting pulled over thinking they were armed. Luckily, they didn't even have guns in them and showed the officers the fact. They work great with eight-wheel drive on the snow, and we have even made tracks for slipping over the wheels. We had found the wolfsbane it was discussed and had to take it out under fire; these worked well, as the attacker's bullets just bounced off it." Other than a couple of lucky hits, they barely scratched the paint.

Adam grinned, "MacLaren has a tank too, and it just has a welded barrel. Didn't get to see it in action, but Gareth said on one occasion, an attack was aborted, and they gave up, just by it turning and pointing at them."

"It is legal down there if they are demilled. If not, then you can't drive or own them. We just find it easier to use an armoured SUV than some sort of APC. Draws less attention. I will give the off-road ability of the LAV's though. They are designed for it. Taking an upgraded SUV off road is a bit harder. We do have a couple Humvee's which have been upgraded and military quality." Just because he tapped the side of the LAV with a knuckle and smiled at the dull thump he got back.

Adam grinned, "Well worth the wait for the surprise?"

Josh grinned, "Still hate surprises but nice. Wish you could come down and visit. I would love to show you our setup as well." He had been very impressed with the tech install done. From what he understood it had only been done recently but it was very professional, and it was all top of the line.

"Maybe after Brook and I get passports, and our pack is settled in the pack house, we will."

*****

As they headed back to the pack house, "So, interested in stalking some patrols tomorrow?" he said with a smirk. He had borrowed John's paintball gun just for this.

Josh grinned, "Sounds like a deal to me. Ambushing patrols can be a great deal of fun." He was rubbing his chin contemplatively as he was thinking.

Adam grinned in reply, "Be up and have an early breakfast. We need to be out before the morning patrols. I think the one with the two pups—Cody and Zane—will need a wake up a half hour into the run. I did mention to Cody we would be out, and to make sure Zane knew, to level the playing field."

*****

Both Cody and Zane reported fifteen minutes early to the hall outside the security office, where the patrols met up. Martin was there and quickly checked over Zane's gear and smiled, "You have everything you need."

Zane gave him a pleased smile though he did glance at Cody, "I left the kitchen sink back in the room, Enforcer." He wasn't sure of the rank of the other, but he was more dominant than he was, so he used a rank he felt comfortable with, "Beta Mike and his senior enforcers are teaching me and my team what to pack and how. It is all standardized and in the same place. It makes it easier to find things if someone else needs something from your pack."

"Normally we run with four," Martin advised, "But it was requested for both you to stay together, so I am having six plus you two." He held up a hand as Cody opened his mouth, "I know we are going unusual, but Zane is a guest, and you are still underage, Cody. While we have the Alphas gathered here, we are running at heightened security level." He also had two of a patrol where the other two had needed a shift off, so was working out well.

Seeing the others for the patrol were there, he introduced them to the Enforcers, and the other two, "You eight are doing an eastern edge run up to Wild Valley and back. Should take you four to five hours each way. You are to report back here within fourteen hours." If they didn't arrive back or have a report of the delay with the updated ETA, another patrol would be dispatched to investigate and had better have a good reason for being overdue without notice. He did a three-strike rule; if they had three times where they didn't report they were going to be over their window without notice, they had major issues. The first time was a warning, second time, the team was broken up and they had to redo the training about patrol windows and the need to report in, and if any of those in had a third within a decade... so far, he hadn't had any, but he had said it would be severe. Any major issue, which being overdue without a report was one, and they lost the credit for they year's experience was how he dealt with the issues. It affected promotions, seniority, and pay increases. If they thought they might be getting close to the end time, he had no issues of them reporting being delayed, where they were, and revising the arrival time. It was normal to do that.

"Yes!" Cody said. Martin just smiled indulgently. *We will be up to the cousin-wolf pack Adam put under his protection,* Cody told Zane, excited. Even the adults looked pleased, as the patrol was a choice one, even if there were a few harder sections of steep climbs. The disgruntled look had faded from two, for having been saddled with pups, when they heard they were given a choice patrol.

Zane cocked his head. Taking an actual wolf pack under a pack's protection had never occurred to him. It sounded interesting and he wondered if they would see them, *Interesting. Never considered it but we don't have wolves like that where we live. Most of the other predators are coyotes and a few cats.* Or rogues, which didn't count as far as he was concerned.

"Well, why are you still here?" Martin said, when they didn't have a question. They quickly pulled their clothes off and packed them before shifting to their wolves. Evan quickly took the lead, with his mate, Kuri, taking tail while the rest moved out between them, with the two pups in the protected centre. Both decided they were going to use part of the time, and simulate an escort role, towards mid-morning. They didn't often get to train on those formations, so would use it to get some checks on the advanced skills.

Zane was stripping even as the others were. When he changed, he nosed Cody lightly before greeting the other wolves as well. As he changed the pack had adjusted as well. After a quick shake to ensure it was settled, he followed the others out of the section they were in. It felt good to do a patrol even if nothing was likely to happen. As with the others he was moving as silently as possible. Hopefully, there wouldn't be any problems but if so, they would deal with it.

Chapter 29 – Patrols

The silence was split with the pop of a paintball gun, and the yelp of a wolf, *Again? You get my ear again?* Complained the wolf, as there were more paintballs flying around, tagging the wolves. Even the pups weren't immune to the attack, but the adults were trying to guard them as if it was an actual attack. Evan had called out the attack as he heard the first pop, as that was what they were trying to get all the enforcers to do; call the alert, then if nothing, it can be stood down. Martin had reassured everyone that calling it in for something which turned out to be nothing wasn't going to be punished. Even the Alphas would prefer them to call it in instantly to having them think about it, and possibly have an ambush preventing the alert.

Zane almost ended up sitting down when a paintball barely missed his nose. It was quick enough he barely even saw it as it went past. When it did, he jumped to the side over a bush for some protection. He listened and focused on where the paintballs seemed to be coming from. Once he had that in mind, he shot off into the forest to see if he could loop around and ambush them. What the others were doing he wasn't sure since he wasn't part of the pack.

Josh had to wince when one wolf appeared to get a paintball almost in his ear canal. It had to have stung big time. He tried to shoot at Zane, but it looked like he missed by a whisker as the boy skidded to a stop and almost landed on his butt. When he jumped over a bush to get away Josh turned to one of the others and started shooting.

Adam kept an ear out behind them, and a slight breeze brought the scent of a wolf to him, and he turned just in time the dodge Cody's pounce and tag him on the side with a paintball at nearly point-blank range as Cody landed. "Have to watch the wind; it is treacherous.

Josh was listening as well but didn't move in time when Zane jumped out and hit him. It was only a glancing blow, but the pup had gotten him. He did get a shot in before he went down with a grunt, "Good job Zane, I will have to talk to Mike about this."

Zane had looped around, and he had a feeling the only reason he had managed to even get close to Josh was thanks to Cody distracting him. He was going to have to thank him later. When he was shot with the paintball he jerked since it was on one hip and the darn thing stung. Before he realized it, he was licking where he had been tagged and had to make a face since the paint tasted nasty, almost like cough syrup.

I thought you might, when you mentioned it to me yesterday... Cody said, slyly.

"Alright," Adam said with a smile, "If the pups had just taken off for safety," He glared at the two, "They would have gotten away safe and sound. Although the four of you took hits, you did get the alert called in. You passed." He said as he passed out elk jerky to them, and to the pups.

Zane moved over to Adam and leaned against his side, *How could I have just left? If you were actual rogues and I left if someone had been killed, I would have felt horrible. This is why I have chosen to be an Enforcer. It is to protect others from the monster which turned me.* He rubbed his head against Adam's chest before taking the Jerky.

Adam nodded, petting Zane's head, "That is for when you are of age, while you are underage, everyone would mourn you. The Alphas and the wolves who put you out with the patrols would be devastated; pups are to be protected." He sighed, "I do understand the drive, just be careful, and *please* don't be hurt."

He understood but what else could he say? This wasn't just about him, it was about his sister and his junior wolves as well, *I know that *but if I protected the twins and my sister... It would be worth it. I do try to not to be hurt and we have similar rules when we pups are on patrol. This is why I am going to be an enforcer. I will protect my family, team, and sister against the monsters.* * He managed not to say monsters like him. It was still there deep in how he felt but it was slowly getting better.

Adam did grin, "Protecting a weaker or younger pup is good. Right now, those are yours to protect, especially your team and sister. It is why I made the Junior ranks; to formalise and recognise officially the strongest, trustworthy pups, so they know we trust them to protect the younger pups." It also showed the younger pups who were the good role models, and to reward them ones with extra privileges and pay for their hard work. He would rather dangle a steak to get the pack to follow, instead of just trying to herd them with teeth and claws when they did something wrong.

Zane moved away from Adam and after a quick bump of shoulders with Josh he headed to the patrol. They needed to move along to finish the route. He trotted along side Cody since they were again in the centre of the older wolves as they headed out.

Seeing the end of them, Adam smiled, "So want to do some more? I know general patrol routes, but they are instructed to take random paths and random breaks, so there is no way to time each patrol. Only Martin would know where exactly the patrol is, and it would be cheating to have him tell us." Brook had decided that morning to sleep in, and Charlie stayed with her as he shared the thought of sleeping in, so it was just the two of them.

Josh grinned at Adam, "Hell yes, that was more fun than I have had for some time." He had to grimace, "Maybe a bit slower on the run, my chest is hurting some. If I come back hurting too much Molly might sit on me." She had pinned him down a few times and kept him in bed when he pushed too hard.

Adam laughed, "OK, I'll let you set the pace; head off that way." He pointed in a direction which another patrol was. "Remember, if they find us first, they may turn the tables and start stalking us, so keep alert. If they get one, they get a week off with pay, and both for a month!"

He stretched before he headed off, he could see the patrols wanting the paid time off, but it also made it more realistic in where the patrols would want to take out the attackers. When they went back, he was going to be beat, but this was worth it. Not only did it help the pack here, but it was also fun.

*****

That evening Zane was relaxing in one of the lounges with his team. Cody and Amber were there as well as some of the other pups. He had discovered this was a lounge where the kids tended to gather, "Meeting the wolf pack was really cool. It felt odd since the largest wolf was smaller than either Tessa or Oscar. Even Cody and I were heads and shoulders over them in size." Neither had reached their full growth even though they were mid teens.

Olivia wished she could have seen them but from what she had found it was a long run to reach there. For her to see them she would have to have someone drive her in an Argo or ATV to get there. She wasn't going to even consider asking anyone about it, "I am so jealous Zane. I would have loved to have seen them."

She looked at Amber, "I am almost jealous of you since you will have a wolf soon. If I had one, I would want to go and see them and say hi." When Shelly nudged her Olivia grinned, "Yes girl, you are probably bigger than they are but still. Real wolves and not humans in wolf skin suits."

Cody had to grin as well, "Best part is we can understand them to an extent, sort of like Orca and Shelly. Not as well but similar. Also, they were not afraid of us." He gave Orca a good pet even as he gave Amber a good hug. He was glad Amber had her, as it allowed his wolf to not stress about protecting her as her turn progressed. Sniffing her hair, he was starting to detect the fur-under-skin scent of a Were, and he thought it was getting stronger.

Zane had to agree, "Yup, something like that. Think something like a little pup, you can understand them if you listen well enough." He grinned when the little pup in Olivia's lap growled at him. For some reason she seemed to attract the toddlers and little pups.

Cody laughed and patted the little pup. "Come up another time, when we have Wild Valley done, and I will personally show them to you. Remember, they are a wild pack, so don't get too close to humans."
*****

Adam had commandeered one of the other lounges which just had couches, no electronic entertainment, just a nice view west, as they watched the evening age, and the start of sunset.

Mike, Josh, Martin, and a few other senior members from MacLaren and Wild Valley had joined Adam and Brook. Charlie was dozing, being a footrest for him, and Brook was snuggled up to his side. As with the pups, they were re-hashing their day to the others who hadn't been there.

They had got back mid afternoon, as Adam didn't want to tax Josh's healing body. They spent a relaxing couple of hours soaking in the hot spring, enjoying the remainder of the day off.

Josh and Mike were relaxing while they were talking. They had hot tubs back at their packs but not in the middle of a green house. Their wolves were greatly enjoying the smell of the plants around them. He decided for the evening he was going to settle for light chatter about what they had done with the ambushes.

"Both pups were able to dodge the paintballs, and would have gotten away clean, if they hadn't tried to come after us!" Adam said with a smile; he was impressed. "The six actual patrollers tried to take the hits to protect them, but we made it nearly impossible to protect them, and still the closest was one which just missed Zane's nose!"

Martin laughed, "I watched you two all day have fun; those camera systems are better than any movie, especially the patrol testing. I never knew what was going to happen!" It also meant he didn't need to pass on the alert, as he knew it was a test before it happened. The patrollers were never told, and with those with the paintball guns randomly going out, it meant they didn't know when there would be a chance either.

Mike had to laugh, "He and Cody were talking about it when they came back. Zane was complaining his tongue still tasted like the paintball stuff." He was going to have to have a conversation with Zane about running if there was an actual attack while on patrol, unless a weaker pup was in danger; he was still a pup and needed to be protected or escape, even as he learned to protect.

Josh returned the laugh, "I was pleased he even got close enough to even bump me. Still got him though. I must admit his reaction to the paintball going past his nose was good." He had been one very startled wolf.

"Don't pass it around, till it's announced, but we have been asked to host The Academy, starting in a couple years."

Jaws universally dropped as Adam and Brook grinned.

"Wow... Just wow!" Martin responded, stunned. "MacLaren has never gotten it!" He knew the head of the Academy had come to the conference, but not why he was there. It now made sense; he was there to see how Adam and Brook handled everything.

Grant shook his head, "No pack in this area has had it. It has not been on this continent in the last century." He was awed they were picked, and was a bit envious, but knew he didn't have the room to host the Academy. From the tour, he could see Wild Valley had the facilities which could easily be adjusted to handle having them there.

Josh and Mike knew what they were talking about. They had a school for the same thing which travelled around America as well, but was not as well respected internationally, and outside of the US it wasn't well known, and few were accepted internationally. It tended to be held in very rural locations to keep humans away, "Good for you. It will be a nice income for you and your pack." Mike was pleased for Adam and Brook.

Josh was pleased for them as well. It was considered a great honour to have a pack chosen. Even with it being moved frequently it was rare for a pack to be selected. It was getting harder to hide the training schools. He wondered if they were going to be the cause of the Weres being outed to the humans in general.

Adam smiled at Mike, "We get to sponsor some wolves. I would like to sponsor Zane to go."

When Adam told him he wanted to invite Zane back Mike was very pleased. The offer of a sponsored seat was shocking, and something he couldn't decide right away, "Thank you, I will have to talk to Kadrian and Esther. Don't mention it to him yet, Alpha. He has enough he is dealing with currently."

Adam nodded, "I wasn't planning on it; I knew you would have to think about it, even if it would have to go to your Alphas first. I didn't want to presume. This Academy is moving here from Siberia in about two years, so it is about a year before confirmation would be needed. If you need to have details on the school itself, Fabian is the current head of it. I'll have him pass the official offer for Zane to your Alphas to accept or decline."

"Just the thought of going to do training in Siberia is enough to make even my wolf shiver. We get enough snow in the mountains, and I have seen pictures of the snow out there." Mike shuddered at the thought.

Adam snickered, "Even here gets really cold. There were times we were snowed in with a blizzard; I never felt the cold much once I shifted, as our wolves grow thick winter coats. It is why there is tunnels to all the outbuildings."

"It'll give you time to get the facilities completed and setup. Bring in new wolves and hopefully some new mates." Josh would let his father know as well. There were usually applications for the school submitted several years in advance. Back when Josh was younger it had taken almost five years before he went to the American one. Some packs simply didn't bother to apply, even with the prestige of having a wolf or two having gone there, due to the high fees charged to the students.

He grinned and nodded, "Yup; Fabian has already given us what requirements they have, and most are already done. Medical needed some stuff, but our Healer is already on it. Turning the Loft into rooms for them is easy, since it had barely been done, and just needed a slight change, but was well within the designed upgrades to the structure, and with not being completed, even cheaper to do. Funding it was easy, as they already paid us the first year." They also had their workers removing the temporary parts for the third wing, and they had the parts on order for it, so would be done before they finished the roof on the other two wings.

"I wonder how much they are going to be charging per application this time?" Josh wondered. The school was expensive, and it cost the packs a pretty penny for each student. It was another reason some packs chose not to send or apply. There were other training centres, but this was the best and thus the most prestigious available. He would have to look into it and maybe seen about getting another person up here. Maxom would be a good choice. He would talk to his father once back home. Josh would definitely have to talk to him about it.

Adam shrugged, "Not sure how much they are going to charge for a student. I do know any I sponsor are given a full scholarship, and don't have to pay any." He replied, with a glance at Mike. He had also looked more at the details, and since they planned on just including them with the meals, they could charge a flat 'per head' fee for the food and bill them monthly.

Mike scratched his chin in thought, "When you get the training setup let me know. There are several packs who would be interested in sending people. Is it going to be limited to just wolves or open too other supernatural or types of Weres?" Some packs would limit it to just one type or a certain range of types. Personally, he thought it would be a stupid idea in the current environment.

"From what I have been told, it is open to any Were." Adam answered Mike. "The training is more of moving the instructors and students here. From the numbers they gave me, they have a maximum of

150 students at any time. We will have the facilities built, probably by spring. One thing I am already getting done now is some upgrades to the access road to being year-round. Talk to Fabian if you are interested."

I have one last sponsor spot, if you have one you think would be good? He asked Josh silently, not wanting it bandied about, but was willing to share it around. There were others he planned on but would be if they renewed for the next two decades. He had already checked with Fabian, and trading the seats was permitted, without restriction.

Adam or Brook would just need to pass on who the spot was going to, and if it was just being traded to a pack, Fabian would just contact the Alpha for the name and details from them. If, like the one for Zane, he was offering it to someone specific, they would send the forms of the pre-approved application to the Alpha, for them to accept or reject the seat. Fabian had told them he was always shocked when a pack turned down a seat offered, and if it was due to financial issues getting to the location, they had funding to help, usually with splitting the costs with the offering pack. If it was due to an issue with the host pack, usually they would accept it, if they postponed it to another pack.

"Good, I have heard of a few 'issues' related inter-were disagreements." There had been one issue while he was going through training. It had been hushed up and those involved quietly removed. Personally, it should have been made known and dealt with, but he hadn't had any say in it. Having met Adam and some of the others he had a feeling it would be well run, and they would not allow an issue like that to be hidden.

At the mention of road improvements Josh started grinning, "Why am I having flashbacks to some of the Batman shows and movies? Bushes which move, fences which vanish, massive use of camo nets and sculpted trees to hide the road." He started laughing at the thought since it was just too funny.

*I will talk to Andrew and let you know. There are several and not just from my pack either. One of our neighbouring packs has a were-cat.

His mate is in the pack, so he joined. He is a bit rough around the edges but damn good Beta. He had to admit he was heavily tempted to stick Maxon's name out, but he was better than that.

Adam laughed, "I have considered it, but too much work. I do have a good gatehouse and boulders to prevent those from going around at the edge of the property, and with signs saying it is a private road and no trespassing. There are crash barricades for the gates as well, and other defences deeper in." He shook his head, "We've already had to remove one hunter off the property. Not sure what he was hunting, but he was belligerent till he realised he was caught on camera."

"Ah, not something we normally have to worry about much," Mike said, "We do have a large territory but most of it is non-hunting. We have to worry more about hikers and campers. There are a large number of hiking trails which is another reason hunting is limited." With all the sensors they could track many of the people as well. Guns were allowed but hunting was not.

Josh repeated much the same though there were seasons when hunting was allowed. Their territory was marked private, and no hunting allowed. Most packs/prides tended to do much the same. If someone shot a Were all hell would break loose. They also tended to ensure their territory was kept clean as well. If they found a camp site which had been left a mess it was usually fairly easy to chase the people down. Being wolves, they could track the people as easy as any trained police dog.

"Both packs here are surrounded by public land, so we have issues with hunters. One somehow had missed all the signs, and when confronted apologised and asked politely to be pointed out and left without issue." Adam replied, "Usually, we will not even bother with hikers, as long as they are considerate and leave nothing but footprints. I'm following Gareth's policy for campers; they are discouraged by having a patrol or two serenade them all night if they are in too far. If they leave a mess, we get them for vandalism and littering, then they are slapped with a trespassing to have them prevented from returning."

"We don't bother with the howling as long as they are being good. Oregon has started getting a recovered wolf presence and we don't want to cause any problems for them." He took a drink from his beer, "We capture evidence as well and turn them over to the police. If we end up having to clean it up, we send the bill to those responsible. They tend to choke at the cost which is nice. Rarely do we ever have a repeat. Getting the trash down from some spots took time even for wolves. When you charge a hundred dollars an hour per wolf and then the disposal fee, it adds up pretty quickly."

Mike rolled his eyes at Josh, "I have seen some of those bills. I think you are charging extra just because you can." He had to flash a grin at Adam and Martin, "The biggest problem we have are with ATVs. There is a section of land which separates two sections of public lands. Normally it isn't a problem but when it rains? It can seriously damage the land."

Martin nodded, "If they are just on the edge, or are practising minimal-impact, I haven't done anything but watch. For ATVs, we have issues with them up here too. But we also have to deal with 4x4s tearing up the creeks too." He had to let out a growl, as they took a long time for the scars to erode away. "I always have those charged with whatever we can get them with. If they enter the property, we then confiscate the vehicle too, and since there is no roads to get it out without harming anything, it stays till they pay for it to be airlifted, or the ground is hard enough to not damage it."

Malcom had come in about then and started laughing, "If not then you get a new vehicle? Not sure about here but in some places in the states if the storage fees get too large the vehicle can be sold. We have picked up some decent vehicles." He settled down and grinned at Mike, "The pups are telling stories about the ambush. Zane was saying his wolf is still feeling faintly cross-eyed from trying to see the paintball which almost nailed his nose."

Martin grinned, "If they don't make arrangements after thirty days, we can consider it abandoned and can start to have the title moved."

*****

The rest of the conference went without issue and hearing back, about half the Feral Star was wanting to join Wild Valley; most of the lower ranked wolves, but there were a few of the high ones. The rest had ties with Sentinel Star, and Tom had already left to accept them into his pack.

The four drivers had already joined Wild Valley. As they felt their pack bonds faded, they had gone and asked to join. As with most wolves, the loss of the sense of pack was a much worse feeling than death and didn't even like the fading of the bonds.

Adam and Brook sent the drivers with two buses and a moving truck to go and pick up the rest of those who were joining Wild Valley. Due to the way the roads ran around the mountains, he would meet with them tomorrow evening. Jess would be running up with them, and her and Joshua would be helping them while they swore and bonded the wolves in.

He had offered Chris a sponsored position to the Academy, to help him get going with being a wolf, but he had found a nice she-wolf who while not his mate, was interested in him. She was mentoring him on being a wolf, and he didn't feel he was up to the demands that sort of program would place on him, so declined.

Next, he had offered Ethan it; if he could handle being labelled a Rogue for several years, he could definitely handle the work. He too turned it down, not feeling it was right to go. He had haunted eyes when he said it, so he dropped the idea, and would have to think on some for the last few spots he had of sponsorship; it was a minor thing, and it wasn't like they expired. Fabian had told of one pack who had hosted before even his time, which still had a few seats; they used it to send the Next-Alphas before they could be confirmed into the position. If their mate was found after they took over, they would also be sent. It worked out well, as the costs of the seats were spread out over time, instead of being all at once.

Fabian had left a large stack of notes, and Adam was digitising it, as he preferred not to deal too much with paper, as it was easier to deal with digital forms. Fabian had left that morning, with a smile on his face, and a good hug for the four host alphas.

Adam sighed as they saw the last of their Canadian visitors off. Tomorrow morning their American ones would be leaving. He flopped down out on the couch, "I hope the trip back goes well," he said to Josh and Mike, who were relaxing in the room. "I do hope you will come visit again, but we will keep the other Alphas away." Neither had given him firm if they were interested in the Academy sponsorships he had offered, but he didn't expect them to decide for at least a month or two. He did expect that Zane would go, and if not Josh himself, another who deserved the chance. He had provided them copies of details he had got from Fabian. He was surprised to learn they could bring a companion Theta with them and would be included in some of the training. They even had Junior or Theta wolf training program for them, and a few select positions for others. Mostly, they were for those who while still ranked lower, would be in a somewhat leadership role, or would have special duties to do outside of the usual and typical duties.

Mike made a slight face, "It is going to be a quick drive back. Zane needs to get to the Luna. If it hadn't been for his team here with him, I have a feeling I would have been forced to fly him back already. Chances are it would have been with a healer in attendance to keep him asleep." He was so very glad they had managed to avoid it, "I am going to talk to everyone when I get back. It wasn't your fault, and I am sure both my pack and Josh's understands but I don't want this to cause a rift. As his guardian I am satisfied with the way it was handled." Tyler had his tail kicked and was dealt with, and his pack was no longer. It was the worst you could do to an Alpha; make it so history would remember them for causing their pack to end, and the scattering of the members.

"As far as other Alphas around as long as Twit, Tic—damn it I am bad with names! Oh yah, Tom—isn't around, I wouldn't worry. Zane has a great deal of respect for most. Definitely you, Gareth, and one or two others." He had to make a slight face, "I have a feeling he is going to keep thinking of the female Alphas as Lunas. Not in a disrespectful way but because of how much Esther has helped. He will always think of the female Alpha as a Luna because it is a Luna who started helping him."

Adam laughed at the name, "Tom alone isn't too bad. Tyler was his older cousin, and both had been raised fairly 'traditionally.'" He shook his head, "Brook was a bit annoyed, but it's close enough she didn't bother correcting him. Maria is just amused."

Mike had to take a breath, "He supported Tyler against a pup. By his actions he was agreeing with what Tyler said. I don't think my wolf, or I, will be able to forgive him." He gave a slight shrug since there wasn't anything else which could be done.

"Nor can I or Brook." Adam agreed. "That action alone has very much isolated him from the other Alphas. I would deal with him if I must, but he will not be welcome at my pack as a Guest, ever. Brook wants to castrate him, but as he already has grandchildren, it would be a moot point." He shrugged, "It just means it is likely they will be left in the past, and we can hope for a change of leadership soon withing their pack."

Speaking quietly, Adam replied to an earlier comment, "When Zane called for help and needed to shift, if he hadn't accepted any help, I was going to run him some more till he passed out then have him med-evac'd out and back to your pack." Adam advised; he had been very concerned for the pup. "If he asks to speak to me, have him do so. He has my direct number. I may not have been changed by a Rogue, but he has confided a few things to me which have me concerned." He would not break the confidence with him, as it would break the trust they had formed this far, and he wanted to continue helping him. "Since he has been open to his Luna, he *needs*—" He made extra emphasis to the word, "—To speak to her as soon as possible."

Mike nodded at the other wolf, "Thank you. I—no we—knew there was something he still wouldn't or couldn't talk about. He has been doing better and his team has helped him a great deal. I have a feeling when we get home, he is going to head straight to the Luna and talk to her. I will make sure to have him call and say hi occasionally. Even if he doesn't want to talk to some of the rest of us, he will want to talk to you." Mike yawned, "It is getting late, and we are getting up early for the drive. Thanks for the invite and ignoring a few incidents, I enjoyed the visit."

Adam yawned in reply, "I agree. I checked with Josh, and all communications are totally secure, so even e-mailing would be fine. Check in with the kitchen before you leave, as I had them arrange to pack you all a lunch, so you wouldn't need to stop, if you didn't want to. Have a good night." The costs for the coolers were minor, and if it would help a pup get the help he needed, they would count it money well spent. He had taken the time to talk to Mike and Olivia about how she should be using the pack's e-mail and not using her personal email for chatting with the other pups. He educated, but wasn't the one to enforce it, especially since she wasn't one of his pack, so had no actual authority over them.
****

Zane was sitting in the back of one of the SUV's holding Tessa's hand. Even though he was holding her hand he was looking out the window at the passing scenery. The last few days at the meeting had been better than the first week. He had spent a fair amount of time running on the property, getting to know the other pups, and trying to relax. His team knew better since he was still pretty torn up about what had happened. Cody had taken him on a couple of training runs, and had sparred with him, for some training.

Tyler had ripped the partially healed scabs off his feelings and thoughts. Talking to Adam had helped and even relaxing with Luna Maria had helped put a bandage on it, but he needed to talk to Esther. She was 'his' Luna for lack of a better way of putting it. He hated the idea of talking to her about what had come up talking to Adam, but she had to know. It had come close to forcing Mike to take him back to the pack. Zane hadn't realized it, and chances were good if he hadn't had his team with him to support and care for him, they would have.

What bothered him about it, was it could raise the spectre of a pack war with what was left of Tyler's pack. It would have been due to his injuries, being assaulted by an Alpha, and his probably coming back knocked out and chained to keep him from going rogue. Even now he hoped they would simply let it go. The alpha was no longer, the pack was no longer, who was there to punish? Trying to punish either Adam or Gareth would be wrong since they hadn't condoned what had happened at all. As soon as they saw what was happening, they stepped in and took care of the issue.

He didn't realise the Alphas had thought of the issue and had immediately contacted his Alpha since he had a right to know, and had kept him updated about the issue, and especially what the result was, with the Alpha being taken out, and with nobody to lead the pack, it was then broken up. Kadrian and Esther both had thought it was more than enough punishment for the attack, and considered the case closed.

As he was thinking Tessa was holding his hand and leaning against him. She didn't say anything since she didn't want to disturb him. She did know her wolf was very quietly comforting his wolf. It should help Zane as well.

Simone was in the vehicle as well and she was in turn comforting Tessa. Other than Zane and Adam, nobody knew what they had talked about. Tessa might know some, but she wouldn't tell unless ordered by the Alpha or Luna. Even then she might not be able to tell. She was thankful the others were in the other SUV with Olivia and Shelly. Simone had to smile at the thought of the dog. She was huge for a dog and the pack was going to be staring at her for weeks. School would be fun as well since she made the one other service animal look small.

This year would hopefully be better than last year. Even by the end of the year they were still dealing with the last few of David's pack. This year? There were still bullies, cliques, and stuff but for the moment many were being rather quiet. Hopefully, the drive back wouldn't be too long or boring. They were going to stop at Fossil Valley for the night and then head back early the next day.

In the other car Melody was also looking out a window. Even with the crap which had happened there was a fair number of good things. Olivia had Shelly, and Oscar had admitted Olivia was to be his mate when they were of age. They had met Cody and Amber and Olivia had struck up a friendship with the girl. Having Orca hanging around helped with it as well. Olivia had learned about the 'normal' commands for Shelly and Amber had helped. Most of those were for when in public places. Everyone figured if Shelly just started doing things without being told, people would wonder.

Olivia was relaxing against Oscar even though she was giving her dog funny looks. It was warm enough for the windows to be down and Shelly had her face in the wind, "Oscar, that bothers me. I know she is part dog but..."

He laughed at her and gave her a hug before reaching over and petting Shelly, "She is just catching all the new scents. Let her be silly for the moment. Just think, when you are eventually changed you can do it too."

Malcom snorted at both kids even as he glanced in the mirror, "I have even seen wolves do it before. Something about hunting things, though. Sometimes we do it just to make others think we are dogs even if oversized." He laughed, "Knew one guy who had a VW Bug and was pulled over. The officer wanted to ensure he could see around the 'horse' as he put, it in the passenger's side."

It was received with a number of laughs before they kept talking as they were heading home. Stop late tonight, up early, be home before suppertime.

The stop at the Fossil Valley pack was nice but fairly quiet since they had gotten in late. Food was provided even as Josh, Molly, and Mike had been called into a meeting. Zane didn't know what it was about and was tired enough not to care. They all settled into a single room and piled up in their wolf forms. When they left the next morning, it was again quiet since it was early.

As they were getting closer to home, Zane had to admit it was now home to him, he felt the bonds getting stronger. When they were close enough, he sent to the Luna, *Ma'am, if you have time after we arrive, I need to talk to you. I am sure you know about what happened up there. I need to talk to you about some memories and stuff which came up.*

Both she and Kadrian had been kept up to date on what had been going on. It wasn't just the fights but the meeting as well. It had for the most part worked out quite well from most aspects, *I will be in my office with a mug of coco for you. Come right in and I have as much time as needed. There will be food waiting as well.* She sent a warm thought to him before letting go. Alpha Adam had called them directly after they had left and had told them Zane would need to talk to her, even if he didn't tell her details, just the fact he called specifically and personally about him and was concerned about the pup was enough to show how seriously he considered the need. For this, they had kept their evening clear.

Uncle Mike can you drop me off at the main pack house? I am going to talk to the Luna. Food will be there, and she'll let you know how long it might take. The closer they got the more scared he became. To tell Adam was one thing but someone inside the pack? Far, far scarier since it was part of the pack, *Tessa I am going to talk to the Luna, help the others get our stuff inside. I will be fine, and we can talk later.*

Mike had a feeling it was going to happen, *No problem and take what time you need.* He would ensure everyone else left him alone for a while.

Tessa settled for relaxing with him and gave his cheek a light peck when they reached the house. Once they had dropped Zane off, they headed to Mike's place. From there the others could come back the next morning to start getting laundry. Most of it had been done but there was always something needing doing.

When Zane walked into the house Damien was waiting, *Mom asked me to bring you to her office. Keep the others away and all that.* He grinned as they turned to go up, "Tomorrow you will have to have

Olivia bring her new friend over. Mom and Dad have seen the pictures but aren't sure they believe it." He didn't bother inviting Oscar over since his parents needed to talk to him as well. They didn't say why but it must be important.

Thank you, Damien, it would have made it harder if I had to stop and say hello. He was trying hard not to let the mask slip back down but at the moment he needed a bit of distance, "Believe it. Oscar and Tessa are about her size, Simone, and Mindy are not much larger. Alpha Adam has one named Charlie, and *he's* almost as big as me!" He had been quite shocked to realize just how big the dog was.

The rest of the walk was in silence. Before Zane walked into the office Damien gave him a good hug before walking away. Some of what had happened he knew about but obviously not everything. Zane walked into the office after returning the hug. After closing the door, he walked straight up to Esther and wrapped his arms around her before he started crying.

She hadn't expected that, but she could feel his fear of something. Esther hoped it wouldn't take too long for him to admit to what he had been hiding. It had been long enough for him to deal with it and once admitted they could help him come to terms with it. When he finally spoke, she was shocked and horrified.

"Luna when that monster attacked me, I realized he raped me. He took everything, most of my family, my life, who I am. He took it with pleasure and..." It was all he could say as she held onto him as he cried even more.

She moved over to a chair and started applying hints of her powers. It was going to be so hard on him. It didn't help this was a subject which werewolves rarely dealt with. The more she thought about it the angrier she was. Esther was calling on the Goddess to help keep her calm as well, "We will deal with this Zane, we are here for you..."

Zane's story continues from here in Why Us 2 by Brian Clark... to be published in 2025/2026

Chapter 30 – Recovery

Adam sighed as the convoy of vehicles left for the US, "It's already seeming very quiet here." He commented to Brook. They had driven the Argo with their stuff down to where they had them parked, and to see them off.

Brook chuckled, "Well, there are much fewer wolves here now. I like it. We can have our room to ourselves now."

Adam smiled and nodded, "Although my wolf liked having all the pups close by." They had let Joshua know there was going to be more for the fire, and they planned on starting the bonds the next day. From what he had learned, the packs really liked the weekly fires and enjoyed the gatherings.

Brook agreed, "It has been a long three weeks. I hope the next conference is elsewhere." She replied as they headed off to meet with Gareth and his two pups. She had asked why Maria rarely attended, and she said she had better things to do than sit in an office, when Gareth knew what she wanted, or could at least relay it.

It had been announced just before the conference broke up that Wild Valley was the next host of the Academy. Many of the Alphas were happy for them, and the few who weren't had only grumbled among themselves, mostly over the fact a new pack got it, instead of them, if they were looking for a pack in this area. Many of those didn't think about all the stuff needed for it, or how it meant opening the pack to many guests, with many of them future Alphas, for at least a decade.

Many of the packs around them were excited, as they tended to get some spinoffs of it, with contact requests or contacts with those in the program, or wolves deciding to move to their packs. Also, they tended to get a better look at for any applications and the fact if they were accepted, there was minimal travel costs.

They headed in for the meeting which had been put off during the conference. There were enough private meetings to have covered nearly a week, even if Tom hadn't bothered staying for most, he had left on civil terms. Having his cousin die showed his own mortality, and Adam thought he might be able to deal with his pack in the future. After all, they had helped get Ethan back over the border easily.

"So, it's all done." Gareth said, relieved. "I talked to the Alphas, and none want another conference for another couple decades, as this was longer than the last two *and* an Alpha had to be removed. They hope by the time the next one rolls around Tom will stop complaining about you two." Or is no longer the Alpha, he didn't add. They were glad the Alphas had a maximum time of three weeks they would have for a conference, as they were three days away from hitting it. There had been other minor squabbles, with most just taking it to the challenge circle to have it fought out as equals. The healers were annoyed at the work to put them back together, but mostly they had taken it out on their patients by making the healing bite and growling at them. It was why most Alphas, and all other Weres, had a healthy respect for the healers; those who knew how a body was put together knew how to take it apart, as the saying went.

Adam nodded a greeting as John and Bri joined them. "Yea, I agree. It will be at least that long before I recover from that stint." John said, lots of respect for his father, "I had no idea it was so much work! I am no where near ready to take over." He shuddered at the thought. "Those werewolf stories where the parents toss the Alpha to their child as soon as they come of age and disappear? Then the now-alpha seemed to just care about himself and his cronies, with snubbing others... I would be surprised if the pack doesn't dissolve within the week! It is a lot of work.

If I hadn't had the training, I wouldn't have been able to do it! Yet, for some reason, they often describe that pack as 'the largest' around... as if they could just take over suddenly, with no experience!"

Bri nodded and gave Adam and Brook a hug, "I am sorry you had to do it so young." She said with sympathy. "And without the training we got!"

Adam smiled, "Key word: delegate." He advised. Gareth laughed, as Bri and John looked confused. "Surround yourself with a team of wolves who will deal with the day-to-day work, so minor decisions can be dealt with without involving you at all. Make sure they have the experience, or they have mentors who are those who have lots of experience in the role. *Trust* them to make the decisions which follow the plan and outlines you give them, and not only give them the plan, but also share the vision and goals, so they can help towards the long term-goals, and the authority to change the short-term plan items to meet the long-term goals. *Trust* your pack to deal with it, and don't hover on them."

Brook nodded, "By having those there, you are free to do the larger decisions, or to deal with the problems they bring to you. It allows you to keep an idea of what is going on, or so you can work on changes or ideas you can't have another work on." She didn't add but had agreed, when they brought problems or asked for a decision, let them implement it, as usually they were happy to do it, they just didn't want to have to make the decision.

Bri still looked confused, but John started to get it and nodded.

"We'll talk later," Brook told Bri, as it was a tough concept to work out.

"I agree with the other Alphas," Adam said, going back to before they got sidetracked, "I don't want that many meetings for a while!" Gareth nodded, "And someone else can host!"

"When are you taking in the others?" Gareth asked.

"This evening." Brook replied, "They are coming in time for the fire pit gathering, and then starting the swearing in tomorrow."

"We're also going to be checking out the first floor and lower levels, as we actually have a wolf who is a building inspector who has joined us." Adam replied, "So she knows what to look for and what problems could be there."

It had surprised them on one of the visits they did to the pack. Annie had come for a random inspection, and everyone—including her—had been very surprised; she had known about the old pack, but had tried to stay away, and had been too out of the loop to know the pack no longer existed. Joshua had given her the total tour of the place, including some parts which according to the human records didn't exist. She had turned around and asked to join without knowing the rules, just from how happy the wolves were, and could see how hard they were working. Joshua had provided the information they had sent to the others joining but had agreed to let her stick around as Guest and to oversee the work being done as an inspector.

When she had met Adam and Brook, she nearly begged to join, having read all the details, and realising they would be a pack which cared for all. Adam and Brook didn't need to discuss it, since she had been helping with the building supervision and had already corrected a couple of issues which were minor, since the walls hadn't been closed up, but once they were... would have been a major headache.

So far, she hadn't given her life story, as she had asked for a fresh start. There was a record of a female who had been kicked out of Night Depths at sixteen, when she refused to drop out of school, the few details they had gotten out of her matched with that female. She was listed as a 'dangerous rogue who attempts to subvert others to her ways of ignoring good discipline in the pack.' And she had been kicked out for 'refusing orders of the Alpha' which they both had suspected was the only thing correct on that report, in she refused to drop out as soon as the human education system allowed, and seemed he took her refusal of his order as trying to subvert others. They would wait for her to decide to tell them her past, once she was more comfortable, and they would give her the fresh start she wanted, as they had done with most of the members.

A few other Lone wolves had also approached and been accepted. It seemed many were scared to approach an established pack, for the thought they may be mostly kept on the edge. Many saw Wild Valley as a way to get in before groups formed.

"If the first floor checks out, we'll be closing up the walls and ceilings and start moving them in." Brook stated, "We are very impressed our wolves are basically doing double shifts, so they can move in, along with what had been the Feral Star. This was offered by the members, not requested."

Adam replied, "We will have thirty-one who are coming from Feral Star. It will give us a total of 159 wolves in our pack." He was astonished they already had so many who wanted to deal with them as Alpha. "Only Forty-Five have transferred from MacLaren."

Gareth smiled, "I do know of quite a few who are waiting to transfer till the pack house is ready." He waited with a grin on his face.

"How many?" Adam asked thinking he was being set up.

"About thirty," Gareth replied, before breaking out laughing at their face. It took a while to stop laughing. "I have also had comments from about ten more who are considering it."

Brook recovered first, "If they all go, you will be down about a third here."

John and Bri sat there blinking, still stunned at the numbers.

Gareth nodded, "If they do, we can consider the split a success. We will still need to follow the Pack-Laws and keep it open for the requisite five years, but I think we would have few who move when we let them know we are at good numbers."

Adam nodded, "Add in the population which will be there for the Academy, and it will fairly full. We would have room for maximum a hundred more. At the rate we are attracting Lone wolves, I think we should be able to handle them. We may want to see if some want to join MacLaren pack as well."

Gareth shook his head, "I still have no idea how you were able to wrangle *that*. Mostly, The Academy has been done in northeastern Europe or Northern Asia but has been down in South America and even in Africa. It has only had a single decade in the last century on this continent. I am definitely envious." Even before then, it had only two other packs in the east who had hosted it.

Adam laughed. "I think Fabian was drooling over our facilities. The gym and outdoor running trails alone, let alone our look at being good to the environment."

Brook nodded, "I think what sold it was our treatment of the two Alphas who came. We treated them with the correct respect but didn't let them push us around."

Gareth nodded, "It could also have been the endorsements from the other Alphas helped, since you now have a pack, so would not be able to travel to attend. I had sent one in as soon as you became Seconds, as you seemed to be the sort of wolves who would go there."

He turned to Brook, "I can tell you now, I had sent one in for you when Bri recommended it, when they started, two years ago."

He smiled at her slack-jaw; she seemed stunned.

"So, how many changes, other than the rooms did you have to do?" Gareth asked, curious.

"Medical, we have one instrument which Healer McCoy had not bother asking for, as he thought it was out of the budget. Plus a few with the extra cash, we have upgraded the models we are getting. A few other ideas I had for eventual upgrades we are now looking at pushing forward, including paving the access road. With current exchange rates, we got a very nice price when we cashed the draft." It had added almost another half to the value. "The third wing, which had not been scheduled to be built for a while is already started, and the temporary walls and roof have already been removed." Adam added, "The fourth floor is going to be a full floor, not just hidden under the roof, and the inner walls for rooms are going to be done. They also were putting in some more solar hot water tanks in the attic, so they had more hot water before the on-demand system would kick in.

Gareth grinned, "Now, any problems you know of popped up?" He asked, coming to the official meeting. They discussed the few minor issues they found. Bri and John had the most, with the fact they were not involved in the conference. Most were minor issues and were dealt with already.

"Once we have the first floor done," Adam said at the end of the short meeting, "We will mostly be staying there, and won't be down much, as we will be moving the Elders and the Pups at that point and those who stayed to support them."

Gareth nodded, "I did expect that. You need to show the separation on the pack, and you are there more. I have already been leaving you free and will be officially releasing you from being acting-seconds for MacLaren at the next Howl. I didn't want to do it with any visitors here, as it could have been taken as a demotion, and where I no longer have trust in you."

Brook nodded, "What rank will we have?" She was an Alpha, but they were still under Gareth and MacLaren. Breaking the bond between the two packs, she knew was going to really hurt.

"Officially, you will be rank-less, but unofficially, you will rank as Alpha and be answerable only to Maria and myself." Gareth replied. "I am thinking we can leave the bond between the packs till John takes over the other area, in a century." He nodded at the relief on Brook's face. "At that point, some may want to move to there instead."

Adam nodded, "By then we would have room to take more as well. Let's put that plan aside, as it won't be for a long time. Who knows, maybe the humans will know of us, and we will be at peace."

Gareth nodded, "Or at war, or in hiding with a much-reduced population."

"Or I could have become Alpha for another pack which my Mate has, and not be interested." John added and got the laugh he wanted from everyone.

"So, what's your plan for the week?" Gareth asked Adam and Brook.

"Heading for an early lunch, then up to our pack," Adam said, "We have the former Feral Star coming in just before supper. We will have a formal welcoming and then the pack fire. In the morning, we will start taking oaths and doing the bonds."

Gareth nodded, "In that case, don't bother with a Monday meeting. I think we can move it to the first Monday of the month, as there doesn't seem to be enough to discuss."

Brook grinned, "And once we have our Elders moved up, we would have only that meeting to keep us here."

Gareth smiled, "That too. I do know many will still like you for the fire."

Adam and Brook nodded, "Then we will be down Monday for supper. After the meeting, we are going to take Jess up, so will need to find a replacement."

"Mikan has already got one ready to go, who has been working to take over from Jess. I'll let them know the official swap-over is Tuesday morning." Gareth said, making a note. "I assume you're going to be starting to pull your people out?"

Adam nodded again, "Robin and Lea headed up with Chris and a few others this morning. They are starting to work on getting the network ready, as the basement is done, and the servers are starting to arrive. I had saved the commands and will be fairly simple to spin them up. The fibre just needs to be connected and tested, so barring any issues, the primary feed is done." He paused, "With your permission, I would like to make the two networks 'trusted' which would allow the other to use their logons and would allow for sharing network resources."

Gareth was confused, "You can do that?" he asked.

Adam smiled, "Yes, and it is fairly easy to set up too."

Gareth shook his head, "Go ahead, just don't give me a headache."

The four younger ones grinned and laughed, "OK." Adam replied. He would work out the plan and steps, and once they had the domain controllers up, he would work with Erin and Aurora to have it done at this end. It was ten or eleven steps when he looked it up.

He already had the reservation of IP addresses they needed from their ISP, and the details for the configurations. Mostly, it was step by step directions which would be set up. Robin and Lea were going to work with Chris and a few others to get the server hardware installed, and get the switches all wired up, so they could start getting the software set up.

They had purchased some land which was at the edge of the town, but there were several mountain ridges between them, so until a trail was found between them, it wouldn't work. They did plan on doing it when possible, but was way down on the priority, so until then, they had to show up in vehicles. The warehouse was similar to the one MacLaren used but was much bigger. They had built it with a refrigerated area, so any refrigerated deliveries could be kept cold. They had a connection there, too, for the network, and would allow for a secure link. Part of it, they had also made a secure parking lot for their vehicles.

"Begone!" Gareth said with a smile, dismissing them, when none had anything to add. Adam and Brook laughed as they headed off for an early lunch.

*****

There had been several packs which had stepped forward with toiletries and various personal care items to help the new members. Most had very little, or from the reports of the few who went to pick them up, were nearly falling apart. They would be handed out when they went to bed, as needed. Both were touched how the supplies just showed up without request, including a couple who just dropped them at the gate and left without a word. Most of the Alphas who were at the Conference had sent supplies or cash to help them take in the wolves.

Adam and Brook were on-hand as the bewildered wolves arrived, a little frightened. "Welcome!" he called out, once they were off the buses. The gathered wolves looked startled, "You all had time to review and decide you wanted to come here. As you can see, we are still building our new home. You will be able to help us get it done. Right now, the only shelter we have is the gym, but I'm estimating we'll be able to move you into the main floor of the pack house within a week or two."

Motioning to stop the murmurs, "I am Adam, and this is my mate, Brook. We will be your new Alphas. The formal oaths and bonds will start tomorrow. Tonight, we have a dinner then a pack gathering around the fire."

"How can you be Alphas? You are too young!" Called one wolf.

Adam jumped off the stack of construction material he was using as a stage and walked up to the wolf, "Name?"

"Rudy," was the short reply.

"Well Rudy, there is no law about being Alpha, as long as you are of age, and that is at twenty. I am thirty-two, and Brook is only a couple years younger." Adam replied lightly. "Would you like to see a demonstration of my strength?"

Rudy nodded, as Adam directed him to the area which had been kept clear with a challenge circle. Both stepped in. "Since this is just to demonstrate how strong I am, and not an actual challenge, I will go easy on you, and it's till submission or first blood."

Rudy quickly agreed, and they started, without waiting for a referee. Adam quickly had him down on the dirt, seemingly without any effort, and Rudy quickly yielded, knowing he was greatly out matched.

Rudy shook his head, "I take my objection back. I was one of the strongest and you are much stronger." He turned his head, exposing his neck in submission to Adam. This close, he could feel the strength from his new Alpha, and while he would have a few bruises, he knew the other hadn't used his full power, which made him respect him even more. While he was showing he was stronger, he did it in a way which didn't humiliate him.

Adam smiled, "Anyone else? While you sat on the bus, we did a four-hour run from MacLaren."

Nobody said anything. Some of those watched chuckled, since it wasn't the first time, he dealt with it. He had noticed that most werewolves preferred actions to words.

Adam smiled, "Then I don't want to hear any other complaints about not being permitted just because my *age*. As you can see, I can easily take one down. I have been involved in several major fights, and have personally taken out both Alpha Tyler, and Alpha Night—" That got a swift intake of breath from many, "—Showing you I have the strength so I *can* lead you and provide protection to you." He bent to pick up a little girl who had her hands out for it, and turned to her mother for permission, who nodded looking surprised at his looking for permission. Picking her up, he continued as she cuddled into him, "I do not want to rule you by strength of arms but be there to lead you because you want to be here." He took a breath to let it sink in. "If any of you don't wish to be here, Brook and I will help to find you another place. I would prefer it before we do the oaths and form the bonds, but I will not force anyone to stay who doesn't wish to be here and changes their mind. Just be honest and open to us, and we will with you. You will be permitted to leave the pack, at any time, if you decide it is your wish, and nobody would stop you." He smiled, "We may ask you to reconsider, or find out why, but just as joining is at your wish and desire, the leaving is too."

He saw tentative smiles on many faces. They could feel the honesty. Their old alpha would have ignored the pup, not picked her up and let her cuddle, nor would she even have come up to him at all. The simple act of caring alone showed they were at a better place.

"To dinner! Pups, and those who are caring for one have priority, and can head straight to the front of the line. Rank is not to determine how fast you are served. Don't worry, there is plenty of food and seconds, even thirds are permitted." He called out, standing beside the start of the buffet table. When her mother came, he handed the little girl back with a smile and moved to the end of the line, showing clearly even the Alphas ate the same food as them and had to follow the rules, to the surprise of the newcomers.

Brook came and stood beside her mate, as they exchanged personal greetings, a few touches, and the rare hug with those who were becoming theirs. They were the last to eat, showing they cared for their wolves enough to let everyone go first. The two elders were in tears of joy and thanked them. He quickly directed them to a seat. They looked like the other elders had when they first took them in; much older than they should.

Joshua, are there any rooms which are ready? he asked. If not, they would need to figure something out for them.

There's a few which are mostly ready. Was the reply after a minute, *Why?*

The two elders need something more than a pad on cold concrete.

I'll task some to put a couple beds in. They will have at least a bed to sleep in before it's time to turn in. Joshua promised.

Getting their food, they sat across from the elders. "I have arranged for you to have beds at least. You wouldn't be able to sleep on a concrete floor. Joshua is arranging it after dinner."

"Thank you." One replied, relieved. The other just looked relieved. "Since Tyler had taken over, he ruled with an iron fist, and refuses to listen to advice, and especially of females." Adam nodded in understanding before they continued, "His father was one who thought of females should never be out of the house and never should be in power."

Brook growled, "Cave wolf," she muttered with disgust.

Both elders smiled, "Exactly. When he retired and became an elder and over the next decade, all those older than him seemed to die quickly, till he controlled the Elders. Then the laws protecting females were removed, and even the Beta females were made lower than all the males."

Brook snarled, "That is why there was quite a few females in happy tears." She commented, after getting herself back under control.

"Yes. It shows in the laws you sent, where the pack has a say in any of the changes." The elder smiled, "So the Alpha can't force a change like that."

Adam nodded, "I follow the saying of 'Power tends to corrupt and absolute power corrupts absolutely'. I don't want to become corrupt, so I made sure there was checks on even an Alpha's powers."

Brook smiled, "And equal power for me. We can be each other's balance. And we will consult with all elders weekly, when possible. You are a treasure. You have lived and survived. We should use your knowledge so we can learn and grow. We want to be able to look back and not make the mistakes of others because we didn't think it could happen to us."

The elders had tears in their eyes, "That is a good vision." They were so happy they now had Alphas who were there to support the pack, something none of them expected to live to see happen.

Rudy stood beside the table, "Alphas," He greeted respectfully.

Brook smiled, "Rudy, come have a seat. We are not talking anything more than our vision for the pack." The disagreement had been dealt with, and it was no reason to have any issue.

Rudy sat gingerly, "I overheard what you said, and it is a nice vision. I would like to know how it's going to happen." He cringed inside; Tyler would berate any who asked. He hoped the new alphas would be more open.

Adam nodded, "It is a valid question. First, is by listening to the pack, and letting them have input." He said to the surprise of the others at the table, not just the elders. "We are working to have a good place for all here. As such we are basing ranks on individual merit than who their parents are and what their rank is. In the spring, we will be having Trials, which are used to adjust rankings. They are not only based on strength in fighting, but also knowledge and leadership skills."

"That's three seasons away!" Complained one wolf who had discretely been listening in, and realised the new Alphas would take input without issue.

Adam nodded, "We have considered a mini-trial, once the pack is together, if the snow hasn't already come. Once all the bonds are done, we will have a pack meeting."

Most of the wolves were satisfied. Looking around Adam noticed most were finishing desert or were done and chatting. Standing on his chair, he gave a short howl, to gather the attention of all there, "The fire pit has some unofficial rules, first: leave your grievances behind. You are there to have an enjoyable time with everyone else. If you don't like someone, just stay away from them. Two: ranks mean nothing there. We are Pack, it is for all to enjoy equally. Even Brook and I won't claim special privileges. We will offer hugs and cuddles to those who want them. It is a time to bond and allows everyone to relax with others. Three: the fire pit gathering is not mandatory, so if you don't wish to go, you don't have to, or you can come for a short time then leave. Four: if you come and cause problems, you will be asked to leave for the night. If you repeatedly cause issues... well, a punishment will be assigned." Some looked skeptical. "Come, let us enjoy each other's company."

Stepping down, he led the way from the tables under the stars, off to the forest a bit, following a trail. Reaching the fire, which Joshua had just kindled and was starting to catch the larger pieces. Jess passed a mug of a hot drink and started passing them to the others as well.

Adam sat down on a reasonable bench, but not the best. Those who had been to a fire before helped those new ones learn how it was and to fit in.

*****

The next morning, the older of the two elders let the alphas into the half-finished lounge room, where they had placed beds for the Elders. "How did you sleep?" Brook asked as they sat for a moment.

The elder grinned, looking younger already, "Better than I have in decades! That was a very nice bed."

Brook smiled, "I'm glad. Any questions?"

She shook her head, "None right now."

"Do you wish to join the Wild Valley Pack?" Brook said, starting the long day for them. By supper time, they had dealt with fourteen of them, all the singles who had been in Feral Star. The next days would be families.

*****

Adam and Brook took a final look around on the first floor of the pack house Monday mid morning, having finished with the bonding. With the extra hands, they had finished it the day before, and now the paint was curing, and Lupita was directing the fitting of the appliances in the kitchen, with the massive walk-in fridge and freezer had been turned on and were cooling, as was the larger freezer in the basement. It would be a day or two before they were settled at temperature. There was lots of noise from the second floor, as they had started working on it. A temporary roof over the opening in the main area had been installed, mostly just some plywood with 2x6 framing to support it, and a tarp over it. It was there until they finished installing the upper floors and the roof, so they could use the main floor.

Lupita was sending a truck for food supplies in the morning and would be having the first meals when they got back. Adam and Brook were heading back down to MacLaren to finish off that chapter of their lives and get going for the next. Everyone who was left had been told to pack up, and they would be leaving in the morning.

Jess had packed up their room; he was going to miss it, but the new Alpha Suite was better. He knew how much of his stuff was still in the storage, and would have to be moved, once their construction stuff was out of their storage area. He planned on doing a good purge of papers and other stuff too. He hadn't bothered worrying about his tools and other stuff he had already donated to MacLaren, and instead had helped gear the pack with a selection of new ones.

The buses had been sent down with drivers already for the vehicles which were now theirs. Lunch was a quiet affair, with many wishing them a good journey and to hurry back.

Chapter 31 – Start of the Next Chapter of Life

Arriving just before dinner, they dropped their bags in their room, for the last time.

"I'm going to miss this room." Adam said, after shifting, as he pulled on some clothes. "We made many memories here."

Brook sighed, "I know, and I am going to miss this pack, too." It was really hitting her hard, she was a member of this pack in name alone.

Adam pulled her in his arms before they both started to cry, "So, we are starting a new pack. What better legacy, than to be considered the founders? Even after we eventually die, we will have left a mark on it."

Brook smiled sadly and nodded, "Still going to miss MacLaren."

Adam nodded, "And you will; it will fade as we make new memories."

A knock on the door startled them from their kiss, "I thought I sensed you arrive," Gareth said as he poked his head in the door. "It's time."

Nodding they moved to walk with Alpha Gareth and nodded a greeting as Maria joined them as they reached the dining hall. Moving forward, a few noticed them, but there wasn't a noticeable change in sound.

Stepping up on the stage for the announcements, more noticed and there started to be a slight quieting. Gareth had to howl to gather the pack's attention.

"As it has been rumoured, Wild Valley is complete enough for them to move the pups, elders, and the others who until now have stayed with us." Gareth said. A sad howl of goodbye was given from the wolves. Many had friends who were now going to be at a distance.

Adam smiled, "We have discussed it," He told the wolves, "And we are going to keep an open-door policy between our two packs. What it means, is basically a member of one doesn't need to request permission to come visit friends at the other."

Many wolves had smiles on their faces.

"We would just request," Brook said, taking up the thread from her mate, "Wait to come visit till we have the pack house done, and everyone settled in, unless you want to be put to work helping finish the house." She got the laugh she was looking for, even if it was true. Some looked thoughtful and might just come up to lend a paw to getting their home done a little sooner.

Gareth smiled, "With the changes, Adam and Brook are no longer Acting Seconds, but officially have no rank in MacLaren. But..." he paused eyes scanning, "As they do have the rank of Alphas, you will still give them the courtesy and respect to one being an alpha. If you don't, they will let me know." There were few he would think would challenge the rule and decisions.

"With that, lets eat!" Gareth called out.

A large howl erupted, as all wolves loved food.

Sitting down at their usual table, Martin smiled as he passed them updated IDs, showing *Alpha, Wild Valley Pack*, and only place it referenced MacLaren was on the back it listed their main access levels *Wild Valley Pack: Alpha Clearance* and *MacLaren Pack: Alpha Clearance*. Pulling out a stamp, he marked both of their old ones as *Void* before handing them back, "I thought you might want to keep them." Turning to Adam, "Your security office isn't quite ready, so everything is still here. Chris is working on commissioning and testing the servers; by Friday that part should be done. The screens within a week."

Erin and Aurora smiled, "I hope you aren't hanging us out to dry," Aurora said, "We still need to pick your brain from time to time." They told Adam.

Adam laughed, "Definitely will be available for help. I have approval, so I am working to get my end set up for sharing authentications. Once we have it configured, cross network sharing will work."

They discussed what they would mean; basically, both pack's computers would run as if they were at their pack house, no matter which one they were at.

Many more of those who were staying commiserated as they ate the delicious meal, which had a huge cake which had several sentiments from the kitchen staff written on it *So long, You will be missed, Make sure to visit,* and other sentiments they shared out.

*****

Most of the pack followed the Alphas out to the campfire, where most of the wolves stayed up late, including many of the pups. Many wolves cried as they said goodbye to the two Alphas, along with many others. There was plenty of singing and stories which they tried to keep upbeat.

One topic of discussion was the speed the construction was going; they were almost a month ahead of schedule on the pack house, the plants in the greenhouse were starting to grow, although other buildings were behind schedule, being they had been able to get supplies for the pack house faster than expected, so had less down time for them, most were closed up enough to not have to worry about weather.

Adam and Brook didn't get to bed till the early morning hours. The sky was starting to lighten in the north-east, showing how late (or early) it was.

Yawning, he set the alarm so they wouldn't miss the breakfast, as a last meal before heading out.

*****

Beep, Beep, Beep! The alarm went the next morning. Both Adam and Brook thrashed under the covers, before falling on the floor with a thud, and slapping the clock to shut it up.

"I hate alarms," Brook growled, "I'm glad you turned it off, or I would have broken it. Why do we need to be up?"

Adam smiled sweetly, "We have a breakfast to go to, then we are leading the pack to our territory." It was broken by a yawn, *We can sleep while Jess drives. She and Willow wouldn't tell if we did.* The four of them were taking his vehicle up, although it was now more of the family vehicle, as he much preferred to go running, but they needed to move it.

Both pulled on some light bike shorts and tanks tops, since they would be stuck in the vehicle for several hours; the rest of their clothes had already been packed up. Adam looked around; the room was very bare: everything had been moved or was in one of the trucks moving with them. Jess had packed his computer, and the camera gear which he didn't have in his pack already, in his SUV.

They met the stream of sleepy wolves heading to the dining room. The few who were fully awake were those tasked with driving and had gone to bed earlier than the rest.

The wolves chatted, commiserated, and laughed over the breakfast. There was fresh food brought out for them all, helping them get everything going.

Maria howled getting attention, "This is not goodbye, as Wild Valley is always welcome to come for a visit. Adam and Brook have already said MacLaren is welcome to come visit as well."

Brook stood beside Maria, "To help those travelling between the packs, we are going to make and mark a patrolled corridor which will be monitored, to provide a safe route for all wolves to travel. It is a long run, and as such rooms to rest have been arranged at both packs for visitors."

Many nodded and smiled, even if they would usually curl up with the friend they were visiting.

Maria started singing a song of leave-taking, which they had brought over from their parent pack in Scotland and had been sung for them as they split then. Most of the wolves knew it and sung along.

Most of the Wild Valley stood up after the song, and many grabbed travel mugs of a drink as they headed down the trail to the road. Adam and Brook led the way down the trail smiling.

The drivers checked off the names against those they were taking, as many tossed small bags in the back of a truck or his SUV of the last of their stuff or kept them with themselves for anything they wanted during the drive.

Checking off they hadn't missed anyone, they headed out.

Adam placed the keys in Jess' hand, "You're driving."

"Yes!" She said, scampering to the driver's seat.

Turning to Willow, "You are navigating, and making sure we don't lose anyone."

Willow nodded and moved off, having expected he would task her with it.

Taking his mate by the hand he led her to the back door, "And we are going to take a nap" he said, as he motioned for Charlie to jump in, so he could go lay on the folded down seat, which they had put a thick pad on for him.

Brook sat in the middle, and Adam pulled the door closed. After buckling in, Adam and Brook cuddled together, *Let Willow know if you are falling behind, and is everyone ready?* Adam called the drivers. When he got affirmatives back, "Head out, Jess. Go slow, to let the rest get started, then you can pick up speed. Remember, we want to get there safe and sound."

Jess nodded, "Yes Dad!" she replied, as she headed out. Adam smiled, realising Brook was already asleep against him. Closing his eyes, he drifted off to sleep as well as Charlie pawed the window control and stuck his head out the window.

*****

They were awoken as there was a siren, and they started to slow down. Jess noticed they were awake, "Not sure why, but we're being pulled over. We're about halfway there." She advised.

Adam sighed and pulled his wallet from his pack, pulling the Registration and insurance from it, and handing them to Jess. "Just be respectful" he said, as both rolled down their windows.

Adam laughed as the officer walked up, "Hello Officer Smith." He said, "I'm wondering what we were pulled over for."

The officer looked relieved, "When I saw you pass where I was doing a traffic stop, you and Brook looked really out of it, and wanted to know why."

Let everyone know this is a minor stop, and not to worry Brook passed to the other drivers, so they didn't become concerned.

Adam yawned then grinned at the RCMP officer, "We had a moving party, and were up nearly to dawn. We're catching up on our sleep, while letting Jess drive."

"Moving party?" He asked, a little confused.

"We have the new building done enough to move in. So, we are moving the children and Elders now." Adam elaborated, "We had a party to say goodbye to the friends who were staying at MacLaren."

Officer Smith looked at the stream of vehicles which had pulled over with them. "Interested in a police escort?"

Adam shook his head, "Naw, we'll be fine. Thanks for the offer." He wasn't sure how far he wanted to trust the officer yet, and frankly, they would prefer to not have an escort.

Officer Smith looked vaguely disappointed, "Well I guess you can be on your way."

They laughed as the officer moved his vehicle out of the way of the other vehicles, and waved them on, "I guess he really cares." Adam said, still confused a bit on to why they were stopped.

Since they were feeling rested, and not sleeping, they chatted with the others, pulling out their laptops to get on their never-ending stream of paperwork.

Hitting the security gate, the wolf manning it quickly opened it and motioned them in. The rest of the convoy followed.

They went up the now freshly paved road, to the circle they had set up as a loading area in front of the pack house, parking at the far end so the other vehicles could park too. The work to get it done while still doing the rest of the construction was a pain, but they did build it to handle heavy traffic, using a newer technology in the asphalt which was designed to help with preventing cracks and heaving from frost, and had made the roadbed as well as they could. They still were in negotiations on arranging upgrades to the access road to their territory from the highway. Until it was done, they would need to take the time and effort to maintain it more than the regional road works did. They had an interim agreement with permission for them to do the work.

Almost immediately, they were swarmed by the pack, who opened the doors, to help move stuff as well. Joshua gave his sister a good hug, before moving to Adam and Brook. "Welcome home!" he said, giving Charlie a pet as well.

Adam and Brook gave a good stretch, "I much prefer running," he complained. You get to see much more, and can stop and smell the flowers or chase a bunny...

Many other wolves came forward and started to help move the items from the truck. Adam and Brook carried his computer system, putting it inside the door to their suite, and went back to help the rest of the pack get their stuff from the vehicles, working alongside the rest of the pack, which the pack was just getting used to him doing, as their old leaders would just stand back and give orders.

The pack house itself had been built as a "T" if seen from the air, with all three wings being about equal in length. Initially, they had planned on not building one of the wings, just doing a temporary roof over the foundation, to save the cost. With the influx of the funds from The Academy, they had worked to finish it with the rest of the building. They would need the space with additional people for it as well.

The entire first floor was done, so they helped the Elders choose rooms and move in. The Elders and the Visitors shared one wing. Many of the Elders were astonished on what they were getting for space. The rooms were a bedroom and had a private sitting area with a private bathroom. Each room had another room off the side, and those shared a bathroom with another, for their Theta assistant, if they had one, which was expected. The Elders had been assigned a private lounge at the end of the wing, as a sign of respect for them, which had a door out to the covered patio which wrapped around the entire first floor, and in winter had windows and doors to seal it in, as an additional buffer. There was another lounge for the guests, at the inner part of the wing. That room also worked to insulate the visitor wing from the noise of the central hall.

The senior Beta wing was set up basically with Pods, as Adam had found MacLaren was unusual in that they didn't have Teams that created groups within the packs. Each pod had ten bedrooms, a shared bathroom between each pair of rooms, and a common room. Each of the bedrooms were made to fit two, so when they Mated, they could join them. They also had enough space to have a couple chairs and a small table, as a private sitting area. Each room was soundproofed, so when the door was closed, you couldn't hear them. The Team leader and their Second, each had a private bathroom.

The first one in the wing was larger, with larger rooms, as it was reserved for the Pack Second, which they still had to find. Its common room was also larger, with a dining area, and a lounge, and room for a couple desks, and also had a door outside. So far, he didn't have anyone skilled enough who they felt would do well as Second so technically it was vacant, but Adam and Brook had a few ideas but would take years before they could fill them.

Opposite the Seconds' Pod, was the Kitchen Staff Pod, which had a back door that led directly to the kitchen, at Lupita's request, so her and her main helpers could easily reach the kitchen easily. Since there were quite a few thetas who worked in the kitchen, part of her pod had been turned into a bunkroom for them instead of separate rooms, as it was what they preferred. They had a larger bathroom beside the bunkroom, which had several toilets in stalls, and a larger shared showering area, and several sinks. They also had a private dining area, as they ate sometimes at different times than the rest of the pack. It did mean their pod was as big as the Second's, even if it had many more beds.

The Alpha Wing hallway had the large meeting room on one side, with the Alpha Office and a small private meeting room opposite, then the door further on opened up into their private lounge which also had a private dining area, which had several bedrooms with a bathroom shared between two, and the Alpha bedroom itself had its own bathroom. Jess and Joshua finally had their own rooms, with a shared bathroom between them. Toby, Robin, Sam, and Lea liked how they had been before, and when asked, so they got the same again. There were several other rooms, for any additional staff, guests, or pups they had, including an entire second pod setup, for when they had a Next Alpha. The Alpha's pod had a great view, and the Next Alpha had a bit less, but still a nice view. Nestled in behind the Alpha's office, was one of the areas for official records, so they could easily access them but also protect them.

On the second floor above Senior Beta wing, was for other Betas where each room shared a bathroom with one other, with a couple of pods for Teams. The two other wings were for the Deltas, which were double occupancy rooms, with two rooms sharing a bathroom. The third floor was for the Theta wolves and had several shared bathrooms.

The fourth floor was slightly different. Initially, it was designed to fit under the roof for about half, but they had raised the roof line enough for a full story, which they had built in the idea into the structure, but had not done so, to save costs. With the Academy coming, it was set up with bunk rooms: three bunkbeds were in each, and two rooms shared a bathroom, which had a pair of large showers and two stalls with toilets. Each room also had a good-sized storage room/closet. They had been set up for the Academy students. There were a few rooms on each wing which were for the instructors, and they were single bedrooms with a private bathroom. He wasn't sure why, but there were more rooms requested than instructors and staff.

On the main floor, the central area was the open common room, which would double as the dining hall. The kitchen had been placed in the corner between the Elder/Visitor wing, and the Senior Beta wing. Behind it was the garden and the greenhouse, protected from the north wind by the bulk of the wing. With the kitchen needing its own HVAC systems, it had a service area on an extension of the second story, with a door to get to it, and although it was open to the air, it had a sloped roof sheltering it from much snow.

With the hot springs for a soak, most bathrooms didn't have tubs, to save money and space.

Around the edge of the Common Room, there was several lounges. One large one was set up as the library, another for the pups, and a couple for the adults. Each wing on the other three floors had a couple lounges as well.

The basement, they had set up a movie room, the computer lab, the Safe Area, which contained the Medical, Security, Server Rooms, and access to an even more secure bunker under them. Adam chuckled as he remembered Josh drooling over MacLaren's upgraded security office; he'd turn green if he saw the one he was making. It was currently being finished off and tested. It had bleeding edge level of technology, and items he hadn't even know existed. In the case of the Holo-table, it was the latest tech, and Silver Orca Sensors was using them to develop the latest of it. They had offered it at a good discount, but had to give reports of any issues, and how it worked regularly for the first two years.

There was a central main staircase linking each of the levels, along with one in the middle, and at each end of the wings. The middle and end ones were designed not only as fire escapes, as the building code required, but also as Rogue-Resistant, so wolves could use them to get down to the safe area. They had been made to also be used to the other floors in normal conditions, not just as escape routes. Adam had been in several places where the stairs were only for emergency, and it irked him to no end they couldn't be used for normal travel.

Many of the Senior Beta rooms were still empty, as they hadn't been furnished yet, but many were taking in, not only their team, if they had one, but also many friends as well. Mattresses had been provided, as they were easier to get. Furniture requests were being gathered, and once the other floors were done, they would do one bulk order, to save on shipping, and to get a good deal. Those who were in senior positions from MacLaren, seemed to have gathered themselves a team as well, pulling from not just those they grew up with, but the other newcomers too.

The Second's and Next Alpha's pods had been filled with the single wolves, till the higher floors were ready.

Adam checked everyone was settling in, even though the interior was mostly bare of the mouldings or finishing touches to make it look nice. The second floor had the walls open inside the rooms, with bare drywall on the halls. The third and fourth floors were mostly just framing.

Jess, please grab the special box from the vehicle. It contained what they needed to make the first paw prints for the surprise legacy display.

Sure. Where do you want it? She asked.

By the stage at the end of the main room, thanks. He said, hoping their wolves could curb their curiosity for the afternoon...

They spent the afternoon getting everyone settled in, spreading the word to all to be at dinner. Work was stopping to let them have the time to be there as well. They had arranged with Martin to have MacLaren handle the patrols for it as well, as they wanted every single wolf in their pack there.

*****

Walking into the dining hall, it was packed. Adam worked to hide his surprise and walk to the stage. As soon as they walked in, those who noticed them sent up a joyful howl. *I didn't realise we had this many,* He said with awe, knowing a number is different than seeing a room full of wolves who looked to you for leadership. There was still room to put out more tables, which he was glad, even if it was likely they would have to do shifts for meals, eventually.

"Welcome!" Adam called out, "This is the first time the entire Wild Valley Pack has been together. I even had MacLaren do the patrols, so *everyone* could be here."

Another happy howl sounded; many could just feel the difference of the pack. Most wolves were happy, as they could feel the wolves leading them cared for each and every one and would not just care for their favoured few. Some even had tears of joy in their eyes.

Brook had taken some time with the Elders and had found they had an ancient song of welcome. She started singing it, with Adam and their pups coming in on the next line, as she had taught it to them. It was fairly simple, and easy to remember. By the end of the song, basically the entire pack was singing it. Just because they could, they sang it again all together. Many had tears in their eyes for the feeling of welcome and belonging which rolled warmly through the pack bonds.

Adam could feel the bonds tighten, from the shared experience, and it brought his own wolf forward, as he could see with many of the others in the pack, it was doing the same to them.

"I'm going to unveil the 'Pack Legacy' item after dinner, along with some announcements, so please stick around. I don't want the excellent food to go to waste."

Many laughed, as they either headed to the buffet tables, or started eating, if they already had a plate.

Listen to them, Brook said with awe, as they sat down at the table, *They're* happy! *From some comments, many have had very few happy moments in life.* Those who came from Feral Star, the few females were downtrodden, while the males seemed a little content. For Night Depths, all seemed very skittish when they first met them. Having a job to make a new home together worked wonders when they could see the comforts for *them* which were being made.

I think we did it, we made a sanctuary for our wolves where they can feel safe and heal from their old Alpha's neglect. Adam replied. *I *thought it would take decades at least,* He was having to fight back tears of joy.

Maybe just the comfort of having a home where they can live in peace and security is all it took. Brook guessed. *I think we will have very few who will ever leave.*

Adam looked at the room, which was already fairly full, *I wonder how we will fit all of the wolves from the Academy when it arrives!*

Brook just gave a mental shrug, *Probably just have two shifts of dinner times.* She told him, *You noticed how it was rare to not be able to find a seat? MacLaren had it working well.*

*****

Jess and Joshua were the only ones they had told about the surprise; any more and likely it wouldn't have been a surprise. They had decided those who were part of the pack now or those who joined and helped make the pack, would be in Black and be considered the Founding Members, while a dark Grey which would need to look closely to tell the difference would be for those after, but within the next few years, then they were thinking a Red, Blue, Green, Purple, and other colours, with one for each decade. When they ran out of good strong colours, they planned on using different shadings.

Stepping up onto the stage as the last few were finishing, there was instant, respectful silence.

"I know many of you have asked about it, and we have told none." Many nodded, "Well, you don't need to wonder any more. The 'Legacy Item' is we are going to do a pawprint of everyone who is here now." He had to wave to stop the chatter which broke out. "We will be doing them in Black. Those who join in the next decade, will be a dark grey, and then we will use another colour. We then will change every decade."

He had to howl this time, even though he was amused at the enthusiasm, he was annoyed at the interruptions, "Listen now." He demanded, "Those who are pups, we will be doing one now which will be inset into one when they come of age. Any pups who are born into the pack, will have one taken shortly after birth, which as well would be inset in the one when they come of age." The differences in colour would show up nicely.

Looking at Chris, "To honour those who gave up their life as a human, and have been Turned, we will have them do a human handprint when they join and then an imprint of a wolf paw over it when they first Turn." He pulled out one which he had made as a sample of his own, of the untinted resin. For Karen and any future humans, they would have them do just a handprint, and if they decide to be turned, add a layer for the pawprint once they turned, as a respect for them giving up their species.

Behind him, Jess, Joshua, and Brook were preparing the coloured resin. Pulling a small cart around, Adam placed his right hand in the small box of soft resin, imprinting his human hand. Stripping in front of his pack was hard, but he did it, and shifted to his wolf, as Jess added some lightly-tinted resin, so the human hand could be seen, through the wolf paw before moving it to the floor, to make it easier for their wolves.

Brook shifted as well and stepped up to a blank one Joshua had prepared for her. *With this, we do the first imprints of this pack, starting a pack we hope will last for many generations!* Brook called out, as they placed their right paws into the resin at the same time. This time they joined the pack in a howl. A small plaque was laid under the pawprints, which had their names, date of birth, space to add their date of death in the future, and *Founding Alpha* below it, for the rank. The plaque would be adjusted for members, showing their highest rank. Everyone there would have an additional message of *Founding Member* listed.

Shifting back to human, many wolves were grinning. Amber's was going to be tricky; as hers would be *three* layers, as they would do the handprint now, when she shifted, they would add a pawprint, then when she turned twenty, would add an adult pawprint.

"Starting tomorrow, we will be getting everyone's pawprints so we can start mounting them soon." Brook called out when the howls died down.

"A couple announcements, the Security office will be taking over as soon as it's ready, with Toby and Sam being the ones in charge, with a mentor supplied by Martin. I do know they are not of age," He said to forestall complaints, "But they have been working hard, and already have most of the designations and training done already. The Mentor is one of Martin's older Enforcers who has moved to join us and was looking for a job he can slow down before joining the Elders in three decades. Right now, he will be in actual command but will slowly hand over duties to the younger pair. Most of the handover will be after both have graduated from the Academy." They would be both of age by the time that happened.

"Jess and Joshua will be managing the Theta and be responsible for the domestic side of the pack, other than the food, which is the Head Chef, Lupita's domain. She is responsible for the garden, the greenhouse, and the food stores. If you have specific requirements for any food, or want something special, talk to her." He announced.

"The pack will be offering laptops to *all* members, once the place is complete. The entire compound will be set up with Wi-Fi, so will be able to use them anywhere in the vicinity of the pack house. They are pack property, so treat them well." Many were surprised, especially the Thetas who hadn't thought they would get them, if they wanted. "Also, there will be a computer lab, with some higher end computers in it. Lea will be setting up classes, eventually to teach any who need or want to use it." He had agreed with a comment she made, "Before you can use the technology—including the laptops, you will have to be tested and know how to use a computer—not repair problems, just know how to use it. Everyone is expected to have passed within a year. Exceptions will be very rare."

"Robin and Lea will be head of the Tech section." Brook told the gathered pack. "Chris, due to his background, will oversee the technology security, and making sure the security policies are followed, and our network is secure. He will be equal of both the Security and Technology, so he can work with them to keep us safe, electronically." By making him equal of the other two, as leaders, they would be able to enforce the policies they made to protect the pack.

Rachel was doing much better with the changes; it seemed she needed to have a change to be better. "We name Rachel as the Head of Pups, and in charge of their care, when they are away from their parents, as well as coordinating their education." They had talked to her early in the afternoon about it, so she wasn't blindsided for it, and she had agreed after differing she wasn't worthy of it. Having a wolf strong enough to have passed the Beta speeds, just not have the responsibilities to get the rank, and told the elders she would refuse to be elevated. She finally had let them give her the duties. The pups were the future and showed the health of the pack. Brook and Adam both agreed the position was hers. She had the other caregivers and many of the instructors supporting her, but she seemed to have gained more dominance since she started with the pups. It had reached the point the other Betas had come asking why she hadn't been elevated to the rank she deserved. Getting the duties, she had been told she was now a Beta, and both Adam and Brook refused to let her stay a Delta. They did allow her to not have a rank change party, and this was the first time it was announced to the pack. She would also be working with the Elders, who would be assisting with the education, as many were part-time instructors. She also would have a budget for education, with a certain amount given for each pup, including special trips or any special resources. For courses going over, she would have to request it from the Alphas, with a reason. They expected to most of the time approve them.

They told her to come forward when they announced it, and when they had her on the stage, "We are announcing, to go with her new role, Rachel now is Beta ranked, to have the rights and privileges to go with her new responsibilities and duties." Brook called out.

The wolves erupted as they placed a Beta medallion around her neck. They had assigned her the senior Beta pod which was closest to the middle stairs, and several of the instructors and helpers who looked to her had slipped in their possessions into the rooms, having been told to do so.

A few other wolves were honoured with rank changes or were formalized with positions they had been doing the work of, even if they had yet to be recognised and to receive the privileges, and pay, which normally went with the duties and responsibilities.

By the time they were done, many wolves were yawning, and all worked together to clear the tables away so they could lay out the mattresses. After going to change in their room, many came out and joined in the large wolf-pile, since everyone seemed to want to stay together as a pack for their first night all together in their new home.

Epilogue

Waking up the next morning, Adam had Jake asleep in his arms, with Brook curled up behind him, and he could smell the contented pack around him. Snuggling back against his mate, and cuddling the young pup in his arms, he knew he had found a home and was content. It was different than what he had dreamed about as a human, but he just didn't bother dreaming that big. The few times he had daydreamed of finding a werewolf mate, he had only ever expected to become a regular pack member, never an Alpha and having a pack bonded to him and his mate! As a human, he had few friends, and now had over a hundred werewolves looking to him, which was another thing he had never expected. Even Brook had only dreamed of a small pack.

They would have plenty of work ahead. First thing, they would need to find work for many of the wolves, once the pack house was done. The schedule was getting done much faster than he ever expected it to be. Right now, it looks like they would have it all done by spring, not the fall they were expecting. It made him proud of the pack pulling together.

He could hear some wolves starting to stir. Looking over Jake, he could see Amber and Cody right behind him, and other young pups arranged around him and Brook. **Play with the pups?** Adam's wolf begged; he loved spending time with the youngest. Partly, it was because they could then personally ensure they were protected and happy.

Not today; we have much to do. Partly, it was the getting the Legacy prints going, but they still had much other to do. Chris had to sign off on the network before they could use it, so his computer wouldn't be set up till then. If not today, it should be in the next day or two.

Not wanting to move, Adam just dozed and talked with his wolf, silently enjoying the feeling of a content pack in his mind.

*****

Adam was enjoying his new bed a few days later, when he felt a yelp and call for help from Amber. Rolling out of bed, he landed on all four

paws as he shifted for speed. The bed was positioned with the head towards the door, which they had been set to not latch, so he just took off,
head-butting the doors open. Reaching the second door, he slammed
headfirst into it, as someone had 'fixed' the latch! He cracked it, leaving
a head-sized dent in it. Growling, he reared back and pawed the door
open. Reaching the common room where many were still curled up, he
reached the... wolf pup; Amber had shifted.

What happened? Adam asked gently, as Cody swallowed his growl
as he woke up from the mental cry as well. Brook came at a slower pace,
and as human form, having realised what happened from Adam's mind
as she was climbing out of the bed.

*I woke up thirsty, and went to stand up, and when I fell down, unable
to stand and everything seemed funny, I just called out.* She replied, embarrassed now. Trying to stand on all four paws, she wobbled like a new-
born pup taking their first steps. Cody helped support her, with a hand
to her shoulder, letting her get used to four paws instead of two legs.

You were so fast, and right there. Brook replied, amused. She was
still getting out of bed when he arrived at Amber's side. It seemed the
idea for the position of their head was a good one. *You left a sizable dent
in the door; one more hit and I think the door would have split.*

Adam laid down on the edge of Amber's bed, *We can work on your
new shape in the morning* He said, putting his head down on his paws,
to sleep the night through. He ignored the teasing of his mate about the
door, as she lay down on his other side, as he comforted another pup.
Amber curled up against him and used a paw as a pillow as she went to
sleep.

*****

A couple weeks later, Adam and Brook had arranged a puppy play
time, and Amber was in the thick of it. Looking at her, you couldn't tell
she even had been turned, and had only shifted a couple weeks before, as
she had quickly caught up with the pups her age and was as coordinated
and skilled as them. She was fitting in, even though the healer said she
still turning, you wouldn't know it.

Karen was nearly in tears, when she saw her daughter as a wolf that first morning, commenting how beautiful she looked.

Cody bounded up to her, and they started to play fight a little. He was quite a bit bigger than her, as she was still a younger pup, while he was growing to his adult size.

He snorted a laugh as Orca came in and was playing too, as she was full grown, and was actually still slightly larger than Cody.

Amber, sitting against Orca's belly was mostly hidden, as her fur turned out to be mostly a very light grey, with some slight highlights in white, which would break her shape up in the forest. Talking with Cody, Orca seemed to have a bit of a bond with him too, and she listened to him, unless Amber countermanded it.

Cody was a dark brown, one which was almost black. It amused Adam and Brook to no ends that they were nearly opposite colours.

They were keeping an eye on both, as they seemed to show flashes of being senior, but they were waiting till they knew what sort of aptitude they would have before they did anything else. Amber had said she wanted to be an Enforcer with Cody and had let the instructors know about it. With their permission, he had started teaching her some of the skills she needed and could learn now. One was knowing how to identify different tracks.

*****

Fall came early with a heavy, wet snow in early October. They were ready for it and had all the outbuildings closed in, and even the deck was enclosed in time, so it didn't matter too much. The exterior details had been done on the pack house, with them already up on the fourth floor, working on what was going to be spare space till the Academy arrived. Many were counting down the time, it being about a year and a half now.

Many of the wolves took a break to have a snow fight, and even Adam and Brook joined in for a time before Adam grabbed a camera and started taking pictures while dodging snowballs.

After a while, when they were soaked to the skin, they headed into the pack house, and after changing into dry clothes, straight to the main area, where Lupita had put out urns of hot drinks. Hot Chocolate, Coffee, Apple Cider, and one of just water, so they could mix their own tea blend from the selections of loose-leaf materials.

Someone had also lit the large fireplace, which was more of a fire pit, as it was open on all the sides with a suspended lid. Most gathered on the padded benches which ringed it. The floor had even been a bit padded with a fire-proof fabric.

Brook had finally ordered the wolves to slow down and scheduled them time off once they had the building closed in; the speed of their work was making her think of them burning out. Looking at the layout of the paw prints scattered almost randomly along the edge of the railing of the second floor looked nice. The groupings were at the pack's discretion, with some being families, or by friends. They were bolted in place, so they couldn't move.

With all the rooms done, they had arranged for the wolves to move into rooms. Most were happy with what they got, other than a few who hadn't qualified as high as they had before in Night Depths. Most of those were the few "favourites" who had survived. They had been told, "You get the kind of room you qualify for; we don't play favourites." Nor could they complain about being used to anything, as the rooms they were entitled to were nicer than the ones they had moved out of, they just weren't the best.

The vehicles were in a heated and well insulated garage. They had a second one planned for guests, although it would be also for the Academy, as he knew there would be many driving in. Both had been set up so they could install electric car plugins easily. Currently, there wasn't the range on electric vehicles, so they hadn't started switching over to them, but long-term plans had it happening.

The woodshop and metal shop were up and running, as was their vehicle service garage. They had the ability to do most of the repairs here, saving a bundle on time and effort of getting it to another shop.

Susanne's shop was a hit, as there wasn't another in town, nor anywhere within a couple hour drive. It generated so much walk-in traffic she had to bring in a couple other wolves to help her deal with the customers, and looked to almost need to expand, as she was having to use the warehouse to store some of her supplies, and they now also dealt with her shipping and receiving, which had Shana happily busy managing everything. Adam now had some more nice clothes, as did Brook, although she kept threatening him with her dresses. Even though their pack had got used to the fact he liked wearing female clothes, when they were needing to be formal for guests, they would show the respect the pack needed, and even the elders were just amused now.

The shop was also in charge of making the backpacks, which were selling well to other packs, mostly with them being custom designs.

The future awaited them, and they would have a nice long time to explore it. But this afternoon, it was they were sitting around the fire, while looking out and seeing the blowing snow, and those who had gone wolf instead of staying in were romping in the deepening snow, showing a happy pack which was ready for whatever the future would hold.

Adam had also received confirmation of Zane's acceptance for his training, being among the first to train at his pack. He was looking forward to having him back and hoped it would go better for him.

To all my faithful readers, I have had many ups and downs as I have been getting this story ready for publication. I am dealing with trying to get a new job, including working for new training certificates, editing this book, marketing my other two books, and trying to not go insane. I have also worked with Brian's family to have the copyright of some of his stories transferred to me, so I can publish them.

I had started the final editing in March, as I finished getting WT2 for release, as I started to market it well. It is October 20th, 2024, and I have finally finished the editing. Editing the parts in the beginning of this book, and the crossover with one of Brian's books (Wattpad, it's called A Pregnancy Story), with the existing title not being one he liked, but had never thought up a good one to use instead. I will now have to do it myself.

When I first thought about a publication order, I had planned on getting Brian to have Folican Chronicles 1-4 in print first, as he has them only in eBook format currently. The version he had up on Smashwords has disappeared, but the Amazon ones are still around. Also, to have Why Us and 'A Pregnancy Story' released before I released my WT3. Due to delays with getting the rights to them, I have not done the work to get them ready. I am planning on getting Why Us released next, and likely Why Us 2 shortly after it.

Also, several of us are also trying to poke Mark enough to get his Tiger, Tiger published too, which in the timeline is after WT3.

Editing the parts which Brian had helped me write was hard. I was remembering how much it honoured me that he thought my writing was good enough he wanted to also write in it. The later chapters, with Zane and company, was much harder, as I very much liked Why Us as a story, which while he started it before I had started writing WT1, and didn't finish it until I was into WT2. It had taken some work to convince him to agree to have them 'visit' my pack, and initially had thought I would be writing it, but he then told me he would help with those parts.

For those wondering (and haven't read the first draft), Zane and his friends do come back in Wolf Tech 4. Throughout the entire story, it was co-authored by Brian and me. You will have to wait for that story to hear more about it.

I am very grateful for all the support and encouragement from everyone on the Wattpad site, with special thanks to everyone who had helped point out issues with my story. Brian had also made many comments himself in my story file... and they felt like he was encouraging me even today as I read the last ones, even if I had dealt with making the changes years ago.

Even though this started off as a daydream in 2015... the Adam in the story is totally different than I am. I don't have the skills or mindset to lead a pack on even a hunt, let alone fight against another Alpha. While I do keep adding in tidbits of parts (like the cameras) which do reflect who I am, and don't expect to have them lost, the character's interests are very different than my own.

I still miss Brian greatly, not only from his support, but also as someone to bounce other ideas off of, or just as a sounding board. I am hoping many people will raise a frosty mug of root beer in his memory.

I can be reached at books-interact@adamwebster.ca, or on Facebook, if you want to interact with me directly, which I rarely receive anything. I hope everyone enjoyed this edited, and expanded version of the story.

Reviews

Amazon and Good Reads about the ebook version:
#3 of a Great Book Series now on Kindle!
So glad to see one of my favorite book series being brought over onto a kindle.

Congratulations Adam on your accomplishment! I look forward to seeing Brian's stories brought over as well.

From a reader on Inkitt:
An Amazing Author with not your usual Werewolf stories.
This story has heart and heartache, hope and angst and I am not going to give any spoilers. The worlds are amazing and NOT your usual Werewolf tropes.

Been following and reading this series since I found it in 2016 and am so happy to see the author joining the world of self-publishing.

From Goodreads (about first book; but can be taken for all):

If werewolves existed this is what they would be like

If you are tired of the stories where werewolves are either feral monsters or the 18 year old pup suddenly becoming the alpha and best leader in the world: this one is for you!

A story about people who just want to live their lives with lots of well thought realism. If werewolves existed I expected them to be pretty much like they are in this story.

I knew the proto of this story but am so pleased about the additional content and well-thought changes made in the final version.

A definite recommendation for everyone who likes fantasy-stories that are made in a way it could be real.

One of The best werewolf story I have read!

Love how it's so down to earth. How believable and how easy it is to dive into the book. Very hard to put down.